Praise for *She Ca*...

We hope you enjoy this book. Please return or
renew it by the due date.

You can renew it at www.norfolk.gov.uk/libraries or
by using our free library app.

Otherwise you can phone 0344 800 8020 -
please have your library card and PIN ready.

You can sign up for email reminders too.

...and utterly convincing. It's a real gem of a book.

Gill Paul, bestselling author of *The Lost Daughter*

About the Author

Eleni Kyriacou is an award-winning editor and journalist. She has worked in various roles across publishing and her writing has appeared in the *Guardian*, the *Observer*, *Marie Claire*, *Grazia*, *You*, *Stella* and *Red*, among others. Eleni was the Editor of national magazines *New Woman* and *Looks* and has also worked in digital media. She is now freelance.

The daughter of Greek Cypriot immigrant parents, Eleni has never felt completely British nor Cypriot, but has always felt a Londoner. She was born and grew up in Camden, then Elephant & Castle, Finsbury Park, Tottenham and now lives in Ealing. Every year, she has long conversations with friends and family about leaving London but probably never will.

She Came to Stay is her first novel. You can find her on Twitter @elenikwriter.

ELENI KYRIACOU

She Came to Stay

HODDER

First published in Great Britain in 2020 by Hodder & Stoughton
An Hachette UK company

This paperback edition published in 2021

1

A CIP catalogue record for this title is available from the British Library

Paperback ISBN 978 1 529 33769 3
eBook ISBN 978 1 529 33768 6

Typeset in Plantin Light by Hewer Text UK Ltd, Edinburgh
Printed and bound in Great Britain by Clays Ltd, Elcograf S.p.A.

Hodder & Stoughton policy is to use papers that are natural, renewable
and recyclable products and made from wood grown in sustainable
forests. The logging and manufacturing processes are expected to
conform to the environmental regulations of the country of origin.

Hodder & Stoughton Ltd
Carmelite House
50 Victoria Embankment
London EC4Y 0DZ

www.hodder.co.uk

For Andrew, and my parents

And dedicated to the original Bebba, who was nothing like the Bebba in this book but every bit as stylish

The Greek words and phrases used throughout are spelt phonetically and representative of Cypriot Greek and everyday conversation. Accents are included for pronunciation.

PROLOGUE

It's the biting cold she notices first. She's been chilly through-out the journey but now that the train is pulling into Victoria station, she leans out of the window and a gust of wind smacks her face and messes up her hair. She's spent ten minutes trying to get it just so and now it's dishevelled again.

As the wheels screech to a halt she feels the bodies of stran-gers push up behind her, eager to descend. Outside, the world is wrapped in a milky grey shroud that constantly shifts. She's heard about the fog here but imagined something light and playful, not this thick swirling stew. For a moment she pictures the sunshine and fields she's left behind and doesn't feel sorry at all. What is there back home anyway, except faithless men and recriminations?

Despite the cold her hands are clammy as she tugs the carriage handle from the outside, the way she's seen others do at previous stations, and the door swings open. She steps onto the platform and stares up at the vaulted ceiling. Passengers rush past, some knocking into her, all certain of their destinations. She shivers in her red dress and thin buttoned-up jacket and realises she must buy a coat if she's to survive the English winter. In her hand is a small case and inside that everything she owns. She swaps it from one side to the other and flexes her aching fingers; she's been clutching the handle in her fist for the entire journey.

So, this is London? Everyone starts again here, so why not her? She pulls the lapels of her jacket together, so they kiss at the edges, and steps forwards. She considers herself a rational person, so she puts the sudden dread that floods her body down to the strangeness of it all and her utter exhaustion. And she ignores the thought that scratches at the edges of her mind, the voice that whispers that this place will be her undoing.

PART ONE

I

Madame Sylvie stood, arms folded. An oval yellow pendant nestled like a bad egg between her breasts, and with each breath it rose and fell. A slick of sweat adorned her upper lip and if she was French, I was Marlene Dietrich. She was small but stocky and looked like she'd win any fight. She sized up the line of girls and stopped at the end, where I stood.

'*Mademoiselle* – please! Remove that beastly thing. You are dripping all over my floor.'

Had I annoyed her without uttering a word? *Oh, don't let me ruin it.* I was desperate to get this job. How else would we escape the damp and the rats and cramped bedsit?

I slipped out of my rain-soaked mac but there was nowhere to put it. As she turned and walked towards the bank of sewing machines, I rolled it into a damp, brown ball and let it drop to the floor. A cuff brushed the shoe of the girl next to me and she gave it a sharp kick, clearing a space around her dainty doll-feet.

'Now!' Madame S's voice rose above the metal clatter. 'I don't have time to waste so I'll go down the line and whoever proves herself first will get the job, *oui*?'

She had a well-to-do accent but peppered her sentences with French. With a clash of bangles she made a sweeping gesture towards a vacant chair in front of a dusty Singer machine.

'First girl, please.'

The scene around her was captivating. A dozen seamstresses fed tiny pieces of jewel-coloured cloth through their machines as their legs worked the treadles. Olive-skinned brunettes – maybe Maltese or Cypriot – two West Indian ladies who looked like mother and daughter, and a few women with ruddy complexions. Irish perhaps? Sitting in the corner was one woman who stood out. The back of her bottle-blonde hair looked severe, so close was it cut to the nape of her neck. But as she turned, the contrast was startling; a few soft waves had been carefully teased at her temples and across her forehead, framing her heart-shaped face perfectly. With a cherry-red beaded cardigan draped over her shoulders, she resembled a starlet straight out of *Picture Post*. Every now and again she looked up and around, an exotic bird searching the horizon.

'*Mademoiselle?*'

'Go on!' hissed the girl next to me, shoving me with her elbow.

'Yes, you,' said Madame S. '*Vite, vite*, I have three fittings this afternoon.'

'Oh, sorry.'

I straightened up and walked towards her, keeping my weight on the balls of my feet, on account of the blisters. Bloody shoes. Standing in front of her, I wiped my damp hand down my skirt, held it out and smiled.

'How do you do?' I'd seen films. The English loved a touch of formality.

A bubble of laughter burst behind me. Madame S ignored my hand. She peered at the puckered embroidery on my white blouse and my tatty black skirt and pulled a face.

'So you have a job already?' she asked.

'Yes, Madame.' I moved both hands behind my back and glanced down at the insignia on my blouse pocket. 'At the Coffee Corner.'

'Never heard of it.'

'It's a café, on Wardour Street. Quite small.' *And a dump.*
'I'm head waitress.' *And a liar.* I smiled. 'But I can leave at any
time. Sewing's what I love, you see. Back home—'

She put her hand out, like a policeman stopping traffic. 'It's
an evening job, piece work, five nights a week.'

'Oh – but I thought—'

She shook her head. 'Alterations, repairs – whatever's
needed for that night's show. That's all there is now – though,
if you're very good, who knows? *N'est-ce pas*, Billy?'

I turned to see a scrawny, rat-faced man leaning in the
corner.

'That's right.' He slunk over, all hips and shoulders, like a
cowboy who'd just climbed off a horse. God he was ugly.
'There's always room for talent. But look at you, that hair,
those curves . . .'

My earlobes fizzed with heat.

'. . . we could put you upstairs, behind the bar. Remind the
punters what girls looked like before the war. What's that
accent? Italian?'

Did we really all sound the same?

'Greek Cypriot,' I said.

He pursed his mouth, then nodded in approval, as
though somehow I'd had a say in it and had made a wise
choice.

'I've been here for eight months,' I continued. 'I've got my
papers.'

'Why the Pelican?' Madame S asked. Ratface kept his eyes
on me.

'People say it's the best – nightclub, that is. In Soho.'

She raised an eyebrow.

'Perhaps all of London,' I added. 'And the costumes are
beautiful. I was looking at the photographs outside. It's so –
what's the word? – sophisticated.'

Someone behind me gave a loud yawn. *Ignore them,* gori. *You can do this, girl.* Madame S nodded for me to go on.

I didn't mention the fact Colleen had heard it paid four pounds a week. It was much more than I earned at the café; even a few hours would make a difference.

'Of course,' I continued, 'I've never been inside, but it looks so glamorous.'

Not that the room we stood in now was exactly elegant. We hadn't been allowed through the main entrance; instead we'd been shunted along an alley to a back door and down some sticky stairs. My eyes flitted to the tiny window near the ceiling. The fog had seeped through the rotten wooden frame from the street above and left rusted tracks down the walls. You could almost smell the desperation, but everyone had to start somewhere, right?

'Well, the glamour doesn't just happen,' she said. 'We create it in this room.'

She plucked a sunset-pink leotard from a pile. It was sprinkled with tear-shaped gold beads and, as she turned it over, they captured the light from the bare bulb above and threw it back onto her hands.

'Let's see if you meet the Pelican's high standard. Shorten the straps by an inch, then repair this beadwork.' She laid it across her palm to show me how some of it hung loose from the fabric. 'Fast but accurate.' She looked at her watch. 'Come along.'

I sat and quickly rummaged in the box of cotton reels until I found a perfect match. Winding the thread around the empty bobbin, I filled it, slotted it in place, then started the familiar, comforting routine of threading and hooking the cotton through the machine.

As I set to work, Ratface started talking as if I wasn't there.

'Sylvie, her English is good. Don't you think we should put her where the punters can see her? Have her working the bar?'

'Stop it, Billy,' she said, 'the girl's here to sew.'

I measured and remeasured the straps and shortened them, making sure the extra fabric was neatly sewn down. Pulling the costume off the machine, I snipped at the loose cottons, then threaded a needle and started to hand-sew the beads. I thought of the simple work clothes I'd sewn for friends and neighbours back home, when the sun had been too high to work in the fields. I'd never made much money, but I would have done it for free. After a few minutes I gave the leotard a final check, running my hand over the winking beads that now lay firmly in place. It was the loveliest thing I'd ever held.

'Finished,' I said.

She looked at her watch again.

'Well, you're fast.'

Ratface gave a filthy laugh and I felt my cheeks scald.

She ignored him. 'Now, let's see if you're good.'

Madame S laid the costume on the table gently, as if it were liquid gold and might spill onto the floor. Pulling a pair of tortoiseshell cat-eye spectacles from her pocket, she leaned over to examine it.

Please. Say yes.

Peter had lined up the café job for me when I arrived, but just last week he'd suggested I leave and work with him at Mackenzie's. After all, he reasoned, I'd be paid more and that could help towards a bigger flat. And with my love of sewing, what could be better than a job in a garment factory? I loved him, but days on end with my brother breathing down my neck? Frowning if I spoke to a man he didn't know? My chest constricted at the thought. No, I had to find another way.

She turned over the costume in her hands once more and took off her glasses. Her steady gaze glinted brown and hard like broken glass, but then a smile flickered across her lips.

'Well . . . you're . . . very good.'

There was an exasperated sigh from the other side of the room.

'What's your name?' she asked.

'Dina.'

'And how old are you, Tina?'

'Twenty-six.'

'Every evening, as soon as you can after six o'clock – that's when we open. Two shillings for five pieces. Handwork is double. Does that suit?'

I could see the heaps of shiny shillings, turning into pink ten-bob notes, then green pounds. Money that Peter would know nothing about till the time was right. Till it was too late for him to spend it.

'Yes, thank you, Madame,' I said. 'I won't let you down. And by the way, it's Dina – with a D.'

'*Très bien*, Dina.'

And this time she held out her hand, as if bestowing a precious gift.

* * *

Colleen was waiting by the Pelican back door. She took one look at my face and screeched.

'I knew you'd get it! Oh, Dee!'

She snatched me into a tight hug, and we did a little jumping dance, not realising we were blocking the exit.

'Move it,' hissed the coat-kicker, as she elbowed past.

'Moody cow,' muttered Colleen.

I held onto her arm and regained my balance. 'Thank you for making me come,' I said, 'I would never— Oh Lord! That was quick.'

All around us, Soho had been smothered in a suffocating blanket of fog. Settling deep and thick, it snaked around our waists, climbing higher by the second.

'I know,' she said, linking arms. 'Another bloody

pea-souper, and only September. Come on, Harry'll kill us if we're late.'

She pulled her neckerchief up over her nose like a bandit, while I tugged a scarf from my pocket and covered my mouth. When I breathed, the acrid taste still coated my tongue.

'Not too fast, Coll, these shoes are killing me.'

She adjusted her pace to match my hobble and, as we made our slow trek back to the café, I told her everything.

'So you'll stay at the café? Until it's permanent?' she asked.

'Yes, I'll have to. I need all the money I can get.' Then something occurred to me and my stomach fell. 'But how will I get out of lates?'

'Easy,' she said. 'Get Audrey to cover. Remember that girl last year – the one in the family way? She paid Audrey a shilling a day to swap all her shifts.'

There was a low creak of brakes and I could just make out the red of a bus bleeding through the mist. A handful of people pushed forwards to board.

'Do you really think Audrey would do it?' I asked.

'Absolutely. There ain't much that girl won't do for a shilling.'

So, five shillings a week? Well, it would be worth it. I'd still be left with plenty. A stinging pain shot through my heel.

'Ow, these blasted shoes.'

'Come on. Soon you'll be able to buy all the shoes you want.'

The fog had now risen higher and was playing hide-and-seek with the street names and landmarks. For several minutes, I ran my gloved hand along the wall to make sure we didn't get lost. Just days after arriving in London I'd lost my way for hours and even now I felt anxious when I couldn't see far ahead. Finally, after much shuffling, we turned into Wardour Street and stopped just before the steamed-up windows of the Coffee Corner. Colleen pulled down her neckerchief.

'Let's get in,' she said as she stamped her feet. 'I'm freezing.'
Her dark curls trembled around her face.

'Sorry, Coll.'

'What for?'

'For asking, but . . . would you mind not mentioning the job? To Peter.'

'The horses?'

'Horses, dogs, poker – all of it. I want to save up and tell him later . . . once I've found a place and paid the deposit. Otherwise . . .'

'He'll spend it.'

'Him and money – it runs through his fingers like sand. I know you don't see him often, but . . .'

She looked down.

'Won't breathe a word. Anyway, me and Peter? It was over before it started.'

I wanted to say I was sorry, but I wasn't.

'It went nowhere,' she said. 'Story of my life.'

'You're too good for him, you know. And the others.'

She lifted her head and gave a tight grin.

'So half of London tells me. Now let's get in, before Harry blows a gasket.'

2

I'd worked at the Pelican Revue for two weeks before the blonde starlet spoke to me.

I couldn't wait to get there at six every evening, even though I'd already spent hours on my feet serving grease-slicked meals in the café. Audrey was thrilled to slip the extra shillings into her pocket. And Peter? Well, he was blind to it all. When he wasn't on nights at Mackenzie's earning a few extra pounds himself, he was at the *kafenio* downing double Johnnie Walkers and losing it. By the time he stumbled into the flat and kicked off his shoes, I was tucked up in bed like all good Greek girls.

In the chilly workroom, streaks of fog still wept from the walls, but the gloom had somehow lifted. Treadles clattered, sewing machines whirred and there was a constant hum as the twelve of us talked and joked in various languages, all the time expertly feeding the most delicate of fabrics in a kaleidoscope of colours through the metal Singers. As well as creating outfits for the show, the Pelican took in and repaired clothes for other Soho clubs. Everything from the tiniest, rudest see-through leotards to the most sumptuous floor-length satin gowns slipped through our hands. Occasionally someone would jump up, hold a scanty outfit against herself and strike a pose, and the rest of us would dissolve in laughter. But we were careful. When Madame S came downstairs, we lowered our voices, dipped our heads closer to our work and gathered our brows in sudden concentration.

Next to me sat a Maltese woman who spoke no English. Opposite her, an Indian lady whose only full sentence was 'excuse me please, but I am lost'. And yet, with nods and gestures we understood each other as we whirred away the hours. We also understood why each of us was here; we wanted more. More than we were born into, more than the life we'd been assigned. We were here because we'd heard this was the place where family background or land or lack of it didn't count, where we could escape the generations of poverty and make something new. As we worked away, sewing the fantasies of the men who paid to watch women on stage, our dreams lived outside these walls.

The movie star was a 'finisher' – the end of the production line, snipping stray cottons from necklines, flounces and hems. Hers was the lowliest job in the workroom and required the least skill. But you'd never know it from the way she held herself.

Her hands worked with deftness, and she was silent. I doubted it was shyness for she had an aura, a confidence that spun about her head like candy floss, which I could almost taste as I walked past (and I walked past her often, on the pretext of fetching something or other). Occasionally, she'd take her leopard-skin coat from the back of her chair and pull it over her shoulders, like a cloak on a queen. I'd never seen a coat like it, not off the cinema screen.

The night it happened, Madame S caught me just as I'd grabbed my bag.

'Oh Dina – before you go – would you have a look at that cowgirl's fringing? She's made a frightful mess of it.'

'Yes, Madame.' With my coat on I climbed the stairs to the club itself and pushed open the heavy wooden door. A curtain of smoke brushed against my face and the sounds of jazz filled the room.

When I'd started at the Pelican, I'd been nervous walking

through the crowd of men huddled around the bar. But I soon realised that they hardly noticed me, not when there were half-naked burlesque girls on stage. The punters stood, tribies in hand, macs over arms, feigning a readiness to leave, even though they'd most likely be there all night.

As I weaved my way through the crowd, there was a crash of cymbals accompanied by a whoop of delight. I turned to see the Wayward Twins run on stage. They weren't twins – they simply wore the same golden, shoulder-length wigs – but these men weren't about to get fussy. Fresh-faced, twenty if that, the girls wore shiny top hats, tiny black satin shorts and transparent silver chiffon blouses that gave the impression they were swathed in cigarette smoke.

They pointed to the crowd with their canes and made out to reprimand the men for their noisy reception, which got them cheering even more. The music began and as they started their tap routine, I zigzagged through the crowd, happy to be invisible, and nudged my way into the dressing room.

'About bloody time!' said a sulky redhead wearing a cowboy hat. She sat on a dressing table, sucking on a ciggie, and kicked her leg to show me the fringing.

'Come on, you. I'll miss my slot and she won't pay me.'

I took my time getting the drawstring sewing bag from the shelf and threading a needle, then settled near her feet to examine the damage.

'You do speak *Eeeenglish*?' she asked. 'Do you *understand*? In a *hurry*.'

'Yes, I understand.' I'd been surrounded by English voices at the Coffee Corner and, after learning the menu, I'd always repeated orders in English, even to our Greek customers. And when I'd made mistakes, I'd ignored the smirks and would later ask Colleen how to say the words properly. Within a couple of months, I was taking her film magazines home to read once she'd finished with them.

I took hold of the fringe. The gold tassels hung limply where the seam had come undone, but she must have stepped on it too, as it was ripped. We both knew she would pay a double fine for this – a shilling for the damage and another for trying to hide it from Madame S.

'Keep your legs still,' I said, as I set to work.

She smoked throughout, muttering about the injustice of it all. The other girls dodged around us in the cramped dressing room, ignoring her moans as they squeezed into outfits and slicked on lipstick. Within a few minutes I'd stitched the golden fringing in place and mended the rip.

'There.' I had barely cut the thread off before she jumped up and started rummaging in her make-up bag.

'I don't know why it took you so long . . .'

Needle still in hand, I was sorely tempted to shove it in her bottom. But instead I packed away the bag.

'You're welcome,' I called as I left the room. Ungrateful cow.

Outside, I pulled my mac tight around my waist and made for the exit. That's when I saw Ratface. He had his back to me and was leaning into a corner, talking to someone. I noticed a flash of leopard skin poking out from between his legs. He had one hand splayed on the wall next to her head and the other hovered an inch from her face as he bent close and whispered in her ear. They hadn't noticed me. Her jaw was set firm and her eyes were cast down. She turned her head slightly to edge away from his touch. I often wonder how life would have turned out if I hadn't done what I did next.

'There you are!' I barged in and took her hand, making Ratface jump back.

'I've been looking for you everywhere,' I said, pulling her towards me. 'Come on – we'll be late.'

'But—?' Ratface looked bewildered, like a child who'd just dropped his ice cream.

'Goodnight!' I called. And before he could say anything, I pushed her through the exit door.

We stumbled into the alley outside and the cold night air and ran down the road, laughing. It was only once we'd passed the crowds queuing outside that we stopped to catch our breath.

She leaned against a brick wall, pulled a pack of Piccadillys from her bag and slotted one into a black cigarette holder. She delved into her pocket for a box of Vestas and lit up. She inhaled long and deep, then let out a languorous sigh.

'You're a lifesaver, darling!' she said, her voice all dreamy. 'You don't know how grateful I am.'

'You're Greek!' I was shocked and thrilled at the same time. I'd never met a Greek woman who looked or sounded like this.

She nodded and held out her hand.

'Bebba. Guilty as charged.'

'Dina,' I said, shaking her hand.

'Well, Dina. You are truly my guardian angel this evening. Oh sorry – where are my manners. Would you like a ciggie?'

I shook my head.

'I don't smoke.'

'Really?' she frowned, a bemused look on her face. 'You must be the only person in Soho who doesn't.'

I grinned stupidly, not knowing what to say. My mouth felt dry. *Come on Dina, something clever or funny. You've left it too long. Now she'll think you're boring.*

'Are you from Greece?' I asked. 'I mean – your accent . . .' I suddenly felt self-conscious of my peasant-girl dialect.

'From Cyprus,' she said, 'like you.'

'But . . .'

'I know – the accent fools everyone. My father insisted I had a tutor from the mainland.' So, her family had money. She smoothed down her coat, then took a sky-blue chiffon headscarf from her pocket and tied it around her hair. The street light shone down on her head and, with the cloud of her blonde hair shining through, she looked just like summer.

'Shall we walk?' she asked. 'Where are you heading?'

I fell into step next to her. 'Hampstead Road – just off Warren Street.'

'Married?' Cypriots always did that – got the measure of you straight away.

'God, no.'

She laughed. 'A woman after my own heart. Parents?'

Too soon for details, so I just shook my head. 'A brother, Peter. But he may as well be my father the way he behaves.'

'Oh, I know the type,' she said, as she linked her arm through mine.

I felt a little disloyal but since coming here, he'd laid down the law, checking on where I was, who with, what time I'd be home. This strict father figure act didn't sit well with me, and it seemed even he wasn't convinced. The traffic lights changed and we ran across the road.

'How are you liking the Pelican?' she asked.

'Oh, it's lovely. The costumes are so beautiful and I really enjoy sewing. Much better than my other job.'

'Oh yes – at the little café.'

I turned to look at her. 'Coffee Corner. How did you know?'

'You mentioned it the day you came and took the sewing test.' I had no idea she'd even noticed me.

'Have you been there long?' I asked.

'Oh, for ever. Watch out.' There was a ripped-up paving stone on the ground and she let go of my arm, skipped over it, then held out her hand. I copied her and we continued along Tottenham Court Road.

'I love it there – the Pelican,' I said. 'The music, the acts – everything about it just feels exciting.'

She turned to me and gave a little smile and, although she couldn't have been that much older than me, I suddenly felt very young.

'It's fine for now,' she said. 'But I wouldn't want to work there for ever.'

'No, of course not. But those costumes are gorgeous, and some of those fabrics – they're so decadent. I've never seen anything like them before. Imagine being surrounded by them all day, selling them in a shop of your own.'

'*Really?*' she asked. 'You want to own a dress shop?'

I shrugged and felt a bit foolish for blurting it out. 'I haven't thought it through, not seriously. But just think – it wouldn't have to be an ordinary dress shop; it could be a store for special occasions. You could even create costumes, for clubs like the Pelican but classier. It *would* be wonderful, wouldn't it?'

'All that glitz and glamour,' she smiled.

'I forget everything when I'm sewing.'

'Well, there are worse things you could do for money I suppose.'

And then, as if she'd just remembered something, she glanced at her watch. 'I really must go,' and with that she leaned forwards and gave me a peck on each cheek. 'A drink one evening, perhaps? As a proper thank you.'

'Yes.' I nodded. 'I'd like that.'

Outside Goodge Street underground she hopped onto a number 14 and turned to give a little wave. I waved back and watched as she moved along to find a seat before the bus pulled away. Where did she live? Was she here alone? I'd been so keen to impress her that I'd forgotten to ask. I pulled up the collar of my thin raincoat and started to walk home. Perhaps if we became friends some of her style and confidence would rub off on me. Her clothes were certainly beautiful, and I had no idea where she'd got them from. I longed to look as elegant as her, but it wasn't just about her fashion sense. She had an air about her that suggested she knew how to have a good time. And my life could certainly use a lift. She was exactly the sort of friend I needed.

3

By the time I pushed open the door to our bedsit, it was gone half-past ten. Peter could be back any minute or he could be hours yet. I threw down my bag and peeled off my mac. If the room wasn't ready on his return, he'd know something was amiss. Back home, night would fall suddenly over Ardana, thick and solid, except for occasional nights when a smattering of stars lit up the sky. Here in London, two flights up, the noise and light never shrank away completely. I liked the hum of traffic, the shafts of light coming up from the street below and the sound of people moving in the flat next door. It felt less lonely than the village. I was growing to love it here, Soho especially, but when the cold weather swept in it brought with it this dense, filthy fog, full of shadows, and it made me uneasy.

Taking the rag from the back of the chair, I carefully wiped the tongue of soot that had licked through the window frame, making sure not to let it drip onto the floor. In seconds, the cloth was black. I rinsed it, then swabbed and rinsed again, like a nurse mopping up a fever. The room was dying around us but it was all we had. Once the window was as clean as it would ever be, I bent down and did the same with the skirting and finally the fireplace. A year ago, I'd had no idea that fog could leave a dirty trail, but here I was fighting the grime every morning and night, knowing full well it was a battle I couldn't win.

I scrubbed my hands with the yellow bar of Wright's and patted them dry on my skirt.

Now I took the sheet, which I'd folded onto the end of my bed that morning, and let it drop open. I pinned one end on a hook near my pillow and the other near the foot. On the other side was his bed. Slicing the room in half gave us some privacy and, despite the tiny proportions, at least behind this sheet I felt I could breathe. Last week, I'd got so fed up with his nagging about the housework not being done that I'd pretended I had a cold coming on, just so I could have some peace. The window rattled as the front door downstairs slammed.

Quickly, I kicked off my shoes and shed my clothes – skirt, blouse, girdle, brassiere, suspenders, stockings. I took my floral nightdress out from under my pillow and slipped it on. Darting under the covers, I pulled the candlewick bedspread over me. Damn, I'd left the light on.

The door swung open and his shadow was silhouetted against the sheet.

'You still up?'

'What? Oh . . .' I yawned loudly. 'I must have dozed off.'

'Decent?'

'Yes, but I'm tired . . .'

He pulled the sheet to one side and poked his head through.

I gasped. 'My God – your eye!'

The skin under his brow was as shiny and plump as a fresh red tomato and his eye had swollen shut.

I jumped out of bed and tugged him towards the gas lamp. 'What happened?' I asked, turning his face to one side to inspect the damage.

'Oh, it's nothing – just a scratch,' he said, trying to pull away as I prodded him gently.

'Ouch!'

'Come here.' I walked him to the sink and ran the tap. 'Who did this to you?'

'It's nothing. Look, I need to talk to you.'

'How did it happen?'

'Don't fuss, Dina. It doesn't matter. Look there's something—'

'Shut up and let me help you.'

I pulled a white handkerchief from the chest of drawers, the kind he put in his pocket every day, and held it under the cold water.

'Look at you,' I said, dabbing at the swollen skin.

'I'm fine, honest. Will you stop?'

'Not until you tell me. Was it money or a woman?'

He whipped the hanky out of my hand and walked to the mirror above the sink.

He didn't say anything, which was the same as saying everything. He flexed his right hand over the sink, and I noticed that his fist was swollen and the skin on his knuckles was shredded. Gravel was embedded in the wound.

'Well, where did it happen?'

'Blue Posts.'

I took his hand and held it under the running water and even though he flinched he let me keep it there. The dirt and blood swirled around the tiny sink before glugging down the drain.

'Was she worth fighting over?'

He smirked. 'Her husband thought so.'

I found myself scrubbing his knuckles more vigorously than was really necessary.

He jolted. 'Ow! Careful.'

'One day you'll get into something you can't fight your way out of,' I said, 'and then what?'

The window frame rattled as a draught blew through, and I realised how tired I was.

'We need to talk,' he said.

'Really? Can't it wait?'

Shaking my hands dry, I went to my half of the room, threw my coat over the bedspread and snuggled deep under the double layer. By the morning it would feel as cold and damp as a river in here.

'No, it won't take long.'

'Come on then, quickly. I need to sleep.'

I could hear him undressing: the thump, thump as his shoes fell to the floor, then the familiar clink of his belt buckle. I turned towards his side of the room and watched his shadow flit around, like a giant marionette.

He sat on my bed, pinning the sheets tight around me. I wriggled to get some space. His black Brylcreemed hair fell in a cowlick over his forehead and as he sat there with his puffy eye, in his blue-and-white striped pyjamas, he looked like a hoodlum roused from sleep. He was three years older than me and yet there was something quite naive about him, an air of optimism.

'Don't look so worried,' he laughed.

I shuffled up a little, so we were face to face. 'Well?'

'There's a man at work called George . . .' He paused, waiting for my reaction.

'Please Peter, not again.'

'Just meet him – he's a few years older than me, and he comes from a good family. He's always nicely dressed, in charge of all of us pattern-cutters, and he even runs an importing business on the side.'

'I told you – I don't want to get married yet. I know you want to find someone for me, but please—'

'I showed him your photo – you know that one in my wallet, of the two of us at the fair?' He ploughed on before I could interrupt. 'He said you were very pretty – liked your smile. And then I told him how hard you work, and how quickly you'd learned English. He doesn't speak much himself. He said—'

'Peter, please.' I took his hand, careful not to touch his graze, and looked straight into his eyes.

'Come on, Dina. I wouldn't mention it if I thought he wasn't—'

'Peter. *I don't want to marry*. Not yet. Not after what happened . . .'

He let his shoulders slump and pulled away his hand. The gurgle of the pipes could be heard upstairs. Someone was running the water, braving the mean little bathroom on the landing.

'I don't mean never,' I said. 'I just need time. You understand that, don't you?'

'Nobody here knows what happened,' he said. 'We're in London now, and even if they knew it just doesn't matter any more.'

'It matters to me.'

'All I'm suggesting,' he said, 'is *chai*. Nothing more. A nice cup of English tea.' He smiled. We often joked about how much tea the English drank. 'We can even go somewhere special if you like. You can choose where. Just *chai*.'

'We both know it's not just *chai*,' I said, quietly. I picked at the bedspread so I wouldn't have to watch him lie. I didn't want to be treated like a burden he could just shrug off. Anyway, I'd barely started to live my own life – how could I be part of someone else's? 'If I meet him, I'll have to make a decision and I'm not ready yet.'

He reached out to stroke my arm, but I pulled away and rearranged my coat over the bedspread.

'I'm not stupid,' I continued. 'I'm sure he's getting his own factory, or a shop, or has come into some money somehow. Money that would be very useful to you.'

He stood up suddenly.

'What if he does have money? Is that so bad? He has a place on Camden High Street that he's renting out. Trust me, he'll be wealthy in no time. I've seen it happen.' He paused to see how I'd take this, then, 'I worry about you.'

'But don't you see? You don't *need* to worry about me. I'm happy as I am.'

'Don't be ridiculous. And anyway, I promised father that I'd look after you. And after everything that happened . . . well, we should take every opportunity.'

He patted his trousers for cigarettes and remembered he was wearing pyjamas.

'Come on, sit down.' I pulled him back onto my bed. 'Father's gone; you know that. Or as good as. He wouldn't recognise either of us, let alone remember any promises.'

He ran his hand through his hair, but the cowlick fell down again.

'Peter, you found us a place here,' I continued, 'you paid for my ticket. You could have left me in Cyprus, but you didn't. I can't expect more. Father would want us to be happy – not to argue like this. Mother too.'

The truth was I had no idea what she'd have wanted. She'd left this world the day I arrived.

'I'm just trying to do what brothers are supposed to do,' he said. 'Meet him – for me?'

He wasn't giving up. There was only one way to stop his nagging.

'All right, I'll meet him, but that's all – nothing else.'

'*Really?*' Relief flooded his face. It was breathing space and nothing more. He couldn't *make* me marry anyone.

'Well . . . now don't shout at me but . . .'

'What?'

'He said he might pop into the café.'

'What?'

'You know – if he's passing.'

'Peter!'

'Well a man's got to eat, hasn't he? And I told him the food's not too bad.'

I shook my head. 'The food's atrocious and you know it.

Now go back to your side.' I shuffled down into bed. 'I need to sleep.'

He leaned over me. 'It's the right decision. And don't worry about a dowry because nobody here cares about that.'

'Stop,' I said. 'We're both tired.'

And that's when I noticed how exhausted he looked: the grey smudges under his eyes were darker, his cheekbones sharper.

'Are you eating?' I asked. 'At lunchtime?'

'Yes, of course.'

'You're not skipping it to save money?'

'Don't be silly. Things *will* get better for us, Dina.'

Something tugged inside my chest. I knew the pressure he was under to make our lives better. I felt sorry for him and forgave him a little for wanting to see me married. After all, for me London was an escape and an adventure, but for him it was a test. And if he failed, he'd be the man who couldn't succeed in a land where others flourished.

'I know it'll get better,' I said. 'You'll make it all right, I know you will, Peter.'

His face beamed and I berated myself for never having said these words before.

'I will,' he said, with a dash of bravado. 'The Demetriou kids will do just fine.' He leaned over and we kissed on one cheek. '*Kalinihta.*'

'Goodnight,' I said.

Then we kissed on the other. '*Kaliméra,*' I said.

'Good morning,' he replied. A game we played since he'd started working long hours.

He crossed the room and put out the light. I turned onto my side. Somewhere out there, the man I'd marry already existed and *I'd* be the one to find him, not Peter.

I placed my hand against the wall like I did every night. My fingers searched until they found the neat line of drawing pins that I'd stabbed in the wallpaper to keep it from curling. I ran my index finger over them. If I carried on saving, one day we wouldn't have to live in a flat like this, where even the wallpaper didn't want to stick around.

I'd deliberately not mentioned Bebba to Peter. It was such a funny name, Bebba. Short for something, but what? Everyone I knew back home was always shortening names or finding nicknames. I was Christina but nobody called me that. Anyway, Peter didn't need to know about her yet. A Cypriot bottle-blonde who smoked and looked like that was hardly someone he'd consider good company for his little sister. Just for now I'd keep her to myself.

4

The following Friday, I was washing the dishes when Peter arrived home carrying a small parcel wrapped in brown paper. He dropped it on the table.

'For you.'

I looked from him to the bundle and back again, then quickly rubbed my hands down my pinny.

'What is it?'

'Open it and see. Oh – and your usual, madam.' He put his hand in his coat pocket and pulled out a Bounty bar. Every so often he brought me one home, though I didn't ask how he laid his hands on it as chocolate was still scarce.

'Peter, you shouldn't spend your money on me,' I said, placing it next to the parcel.

'It's only a chocolate bar,' he said.

'You know what I mean.' I put my hands on the parcel and gave it a squeeze. It yielded easily. 'What is it?'

'Well you won't find out just standing there,' he laughed. 'Open it.'

I started to rip at the brown paper, first carefully on one corner and then with more gusto. It had been wrapped a few times and I unwound the paper until finally something fell onto the table.

'Oh, it isn't . . .?'

It was the lilac sweater, the one I'd admired on my way to work and had mentioned weeks ago.

'But how can we afford it? It's expensive isn't it? I mean . . .'

He put out his hand to silence my questions.

'I put down a pound a week every week,' he said, taking off his coat. 'Did you know you can do that with anything at Johnson's? And so, well – it's yours now. That is the right one isn't it? In a medium?'

I nodded, holding it up. It was exquisite and the colour instantly reminded me of the solano bush back home with its delicate flowers that could survive anything. I put it against my cheek and felt its softness. I'd have to be careful washing it.

I wrapped my arms around his chest and squeezed tight.

'Thank you. It's beautiful.'

'You need some new clothes,' he said, loosening his tie and unbuttoning his cuffs. He slumped into the armchair and rolled up his sleeves. It was true I'd bought nothing for myself since arriving, just my uniform and mac.

'For when you start going out, you know,' he continued. 'I mean, George is away at the moment but when . . .'

I gave him a slow sidelong glance but couldn't be cross. After all, it was gorgeous and if I got something out of all this, well why not?

'Turn around, I want to try it on.'

He held his open newspaper in front of his face while I slipped off my work blouse and carefully pulled on the sweater. There was a small shaving mirror by the sink, and I picked it up and held it at arm's length to see my reflection. It was as snug as the softest embrace.

'Ready?' he asked.

'Ready.'

He pulled down his *Express*.

'Well!' He stood to see the full effect. 'Is it too tight? The assistant said we could change it for a bigger one if we return it today.'

'No, no. This is how they're wearing them now. Close-fitting. It's the fashion.' I pulled his face down to mine and kissed his cheeks. 'It's gorgeous. You're definitely my favourite brother.'

He laughed.

'Don't get all soppy now. Get changed and eat your Bounty. I might need to double up as a chaperone, what with you looking like that.'

'Oh, I can look after myself. I love it. Thank you.'

'Well, you deserve it. You work hard, we both do.' He hugged me tight. 'I don't think we realised how difficult it would be here.'

'Well I'd rather be waiting tables than working in the fields. We'll be fine.'

My face was pressed against his shirt and I breathed in his familiar smell, the comforting scent of Palmolive soap mixed with a light tang of sweat after a day's work. We might be miles from Ardana, but right here was a spot that would always feel like home.

'Can't imagine not having you,' I said.

'Just as well,' he said with a gentle laugh, 'because I'm not going anywhere.'

5

I was putting on my coat to leave when Bebba waved me over to her corner of the sewing room.

'I'm going in a minute, too,' she said, picking a few stray cottons from her skirt. 'Shall we have a quick drink?' I thought she'd forgotten because it had been over a week and she'd only smiled at me once since then. 'As a thank you?'

'Yes, I'd love to,' I said.

'Let's go upstairs.'

'*Here*? Are we allowed?' I'd only walked through the club en route to the dressing room.

'It's fine.' She laughed. 'It's all money to them, isn't it? And anyway, it's Monday so it won't be busy. Come on.'

I hesitated. The only female customers wore bored smiles and had their wrists where they could see the time. Working girls. What if we were asked to leave?

'Come on, take your coat off,' she said. 'That's a lovely sweater by the way. Is it new?' She didn't wait for a response. 'Your brother won't be home for a while, will he?' she asked.

'No, not for hours.'

'Well then, live a little. I've been up there before, and nobody batted an eye.'

Why was I hesitating? 'Let's do it.'

'Wonderful!' She gathered her things. 'Hold on a minute.'

She walked over to Maria's workstation, the surly Spanish lady on buttons. There was nobody there and I saw her delve into her leather handbag, pluck two ciggies and slip them into her pocket. The door across the room slammed and Maria started walking back from the lavatory.

'Maria,' called Bebba, 'do you have a cigarette?' She mimed smoking, so Maria would understand. '*Por favor?*'

Maria rummaged in her bag and pulled out a box of Piccadillys. She peered in, frowned at how few were left, then offered them to Bebba.

'*Gracias*,' said Bebba, slipping another one into her pocket. '*Muchas gracias*, darling.'

She turned to me and gave me the slightest of winks. I realised my mouth was hanging open and quickly closed it.

'Oh, don't look like that.' She laughed, linking arms with me as we left. 'I'm sure she swiped a whole pack off me the other day.'

We pushed through the door to the Pelican. She was right about it being practically empty. There were just a dozen or so men leaning against the bar, eyes fixed on the stage where a woman wearing a blue-spangled leotard was folding herself in half. Next to her on an easel was a cardboard sign that read: Ramona the Rubber Girl. A pianist was plinking his way through a song that sounded familiar, stopping for a few seconds every now and then while Ramona held a particularly difficult pose and the audience applauded.

I slipped behind a corner table while Bebba went to the bar. The gas lights were turned low, filling the room with a golden warmth. It all looked smaller than I recalled, but I'd never really looked around properly before. Behind the bar a large mirror hung at an angle. The silvering had worn off at the edges and its tilt captured the group of men around the stage who were precariously leaning forwards as if pulled by a magnet. Cigarette smoke laced the air and, despite the signs of wear and neglect, there was something magical about the place. That was the allure of Soho, I supposed, the grit that ran right through the glamour. I'd walked along its streets hundreds of times, never sure what I'd find at each turn, but always prepared to be thrilled, daunted or amused by it all. It felt like a test. Was I smart enough and brave enough to stay here? I hoped so.

'Gin fizz,' said Bebba, placing a frothy concoction in front of me. She glided into her seat and pulled back her shoulders, so she'd sit up straight. I copied her. 'So, what do you think?' she asked.

'It's actually lovely here, isn't it?' I said, looking around. 'I mean it's a bit tatty but there's something about it.'

She nodded. 'It has a charm, doesn't it?' Then she leaned in and pretended to whisper. 'The acts are frankly either awful or outrageous, but that's why it's fun.'

Ramona brought her foot up to touch her head and was rewarded with half-hearted applause.

'See,' said Bebba. 'They're all so preoccupied with the Rubberband they haven't even noticed we're here.'

'Rubber Girl,' I said.

She shrugged. 'She looks fit to snap. Imagine doing that for a living.' She sipped her gin fizz and licked her lips. 'Bending over backwards and letting punters look up your . . . you know.'

'Bebba!'

She smiled and I realised she was trying to shock me.

'So how about you?' she said. 'Is there anyone you've got your eye on? There must be something to tell.'

'Well,' I stroked the sleeve of my sweater, still not quite believing it was mine. 'Peter bought me this – said I needed new clothes . . .'

'Really? What excellent taste.'

'. . . for going out – you know, prospective husbands.'

'Ah!'

'I know.' I rolled my eyes theatrically, and she did the same and smiled. She understood completely.

'He wants to arrange a meeting,' I said. 'There's someone at the factory where he works.'

'A meeting – so romantic!'

'Dreadful, isn't it?' I sipped my drink. 'I went on a few in Cyprus – you turn up, have one of those *glikó* sweets— '

'Those syrupy walnuts are the worst!' she interrupted.

'—and they shove a glass of water under your nose and you try and wash it all down while making chit-chat. By the end of it you're meant to know if you can spend the rest of your lives together.'

She laughed. 'What will you do?'

'I just said yes to get him to leave me alone.'

'Well, you got a lovely sweater, so cheers to Peter!'

We clinked glasses. 'What's he like, your brother?' she asked.

'You know – overly protective, doesn't let me do anything without him.'

'But I bet he comes and goes as he pleases?' she said.

I nodded. 'My friend at the café, Colleen, she's lovely but she doesn't understand. Always saying I should stand up for myself, as if it were that easy.'

Bebba sipped her gin. 'Only other Cypriots can really understand.'

'I know he feels responsible, thinks it's his job to look after me,' I said. 'But sometimes it feels the other way round.'

'Why?'

'Oh, he can't hold on to money. I try to save, and he just spends it.' Saying it out loud was disheartening. 'Let's talk about something else. I want to forget all that right now.'

'All right, well listen to this.' She shifted in her seat, as if settling down for a good tale. 'You know who's doing well for herself – or so I hear?'

I shook my head. 'Who?'

She leaned in close, even though nobody was sitting near us.

'Madame Sylvie.' She paused for impact. 'Well, the rumour is that she's *fabulously* wealthy. They say she's got a small fortune squirreled away.'

'Really?'

'I heard she's setting up a nightclub. Like the Pelican, where they make all the clothes, but posher. That's why she disappears every now and then, sometimes for days on end. Says she's taking a break, but she's sorting supplies.'

'Oh, I hope she doesn't leave,' I said. 'I like her.'

'You like her because she's always nice to you,' said Bebba, lining up her Vesta matches alongside her cigarettes. 'You're the best seamstress she's got, but she can be an absolute dragon when she wants. And guess who's in charge when she's off swanning around?'

I pulled a face. 'Not Billy?'

'Correct. Hands everywhere, that man.' She gave a shudder. 'Can't thank you enough for saving me the way you did.'

Cheers went up as Ramona went off stage. The pianist stood, swapped the card, and shouted 'Yee-hah! Please welcome the one and only Calamity Jane.'

With a hobby horse between her legs, the sulky redhead whose fringing I'd fixed half-heartedly trotted onto the stage, lasso in one hand. Bebba turned to me and pulled a face.

'It's a calamity all right, darling.'

I tried not to laugh as the cowgirl launched into some complicated song that involved lots of repetition. She caught my eye and frowned as if to say, 'what are you doing here?' Some of the audience joined in but it soon became a mess and a few of them started laughing. Calamity didn't look too pleased. The longer the song went on, the more difficult it was for them to keep up and I found myself laughing, too.

'This is the most fun I've had in ages,' I said. 'And to think – it's just upstairs.'

'I told you you'd love it, didn't I? And we didn't even have to pay to get in.'

'Oh – there's an entry fee,' I said. 'I completely forgot. Is it allowed? I mean – should we offer to pay?'

Bebba smoothed down her skirt. 'You really shouldn't worry so much. Rules are so dull.'

I felt my face flush a little. She was right, of course. Why couldn't I just relax? Deep down, I still felt like a guest in London; if I took a wrong step I'd be asked to leave, like an embarrassing acquaintance at a party. Instinctively, I kept my head down and played by the rules. I saw it in the eyes of the other women in the sewing room, too. We all wanted to fit in. Everyone, that was, except her. Everything about her said she wanted to stand out.

I went to the bar, bought two more gin fizzes and placed them on the table.

'Thanks for bringing me here,' I said. 'When I see places like this I realise I've hardly seen anything of London.'

She gave me a puzzled look, then realised I meant it. A smile spread across her lips and she seemed amused, but in a kind way. 'It's a pleasure.' Then after a moment she said, 'but there are far better places than this. There's this wonderful little club where they play *real* jazz. I'm going next week, with a friend. Why don't you come along, too?'

'Really? I'd love to, but . . .' I hesitated.

'We could have a great time – three girls, out in Soho. What do you say? It'll be fun.'

'I could do with some fun, but I'd have to make sure Peter didn't find out.'

'You said he works late, didn't you? We can go on a night he's busy.'

'And, I can't spend much,' I said. I could tell from the way she was dressed she had more money than me. 'But I'd want to pay my own way, so if it's expensive . . .' I was worried she'd think I was scrounging.

'Oh, you don't need lots if you know where to go,' she said. 'Find out his shifts and we'll go next week.'

Just then, the pianist stood and finished the number with a flourish as Calamity Jane threw her hobby horse to one side and looped her lasso into a circle above her head. The men who were at the bar all stood in a line, as if they'd done this a hundred times. She threw the rope out, pulled it back and tried again. On her third attempt she lassoed a small gentleman who'd taken off his spectacles especially. He grinned at the others in triumph and she tugged him towards her, to the very edge of the high stage.

'Watch this,' said Bebba.

She lifted her foot and just as it looked like it might meet his face, he dipped his head and placed a big kiss on her bejewelled slipper.

'Yee-hah!'

6

'Dina, get here now!'

I walked slowly towards Harry. He stood in the middle of the Coffee Corner, hand slipped inside shirt, stroking his grey chest hair like a Napoleon gone to seed.

'Did she pay?' he asked. 'The woman with the hat? Because if not that's the third—'

'She paid, Harry. I took the money myself.' The lie slipped out quickly, but I daren't admit I had let it happen again. 'It's in the till.'

He stared into my face and I sensed a few customers watching.

'Count it up against the slips if you want.' *Shut up, Dina.*

'You don't need to get cheeky, *gori*,' he said, finger pointing. The stripes on his shirt curved over his stomach and I could smell the whisky on his breath.

'Sorry, I'm just saying she paid, that's all.'

His head dipped to my height. 'Watch how you speak to me because there's lots of other girls who'd love this job.'

Colleen gave a startled cough behind me and I pressed my lips together. He shook his head.

'You don't get special treatment here just because you're Greek. Your brother might have got you this job, but you can lose it all by yourself.'

'Oh, I know,' I said. In fact, despite being Cypriot himself he seemed to hate me the most.

'Excuse me!' someone called out in broken English. 'Miss.'

'I have a customer,' I said. 'Can I go, please?'

He grunted and I turned and walked towards the man in the corner.

'Thanks,' I whispered.

'Don't mention it,' he replied in Greek.

'He thoroughly detests me.'

He looked up at me and grinned. 'No, I think you're his favourite. Can't you tell?'

We had an easy banter – he'd just appeared one day, sitting in this same corner, smiling. And now he came in most days, insisting I serve him because of his poor English.

'You learned any more words yet?' I asked, wiping his table although it was perfectly clean.

'Since yesterday?'

I laughed. 'Well, how will you ever improve if you don't try? I've hardly heard you speak two words.'

'Greek is fine. I don't need much English.' He swirled the *kafé skéto* in his cup. 'If I could speak English any waitress could serve me.'

'And . . .?'

'And then what would be the point of coming here?'

I flicked the dishcloth at him, and he winced and grabbed his arm, pretending I'd hurt him. I didn't know why or how I felt at ease with him so quickly – he was a good ten years older – but I felt pulled towards him, and soon I was finding it difficult not to stare at that face. He was movie-star handsome.

'What about work?' I asked. 'All those overseas deals . . . I thought you were a busy man?'

'Well, that's the beauty of being in charge . . . you can take a break whenever you want.'

He ordered another coffee and I returned with it a couple of minutes later.

'You know, I've been thinking,' I said, as I placed it in front of him. 'You remind me of someone.' I rearranged the greasy cruet set in the middle of the table.

'The man of your dreams?'

'Stop it! No – I know! You look like that actor. What's his name? Moustache.'

'That's a funny name.' He smiled, blew on his coffee and downed it in one.

'Clark Gable, that's it. You're practically his double. Do you know who I mean?'

'I don't look anything like him,' he said.

'But you do.'

He shook his head. 'No, he looks like me.'

I laughed at his nerve. His confidence was thrilling. I hadn't met a Greek man so sure of himself.

I reached to pick up the empty cup and he put his hand on my arm.

'So, can I take you out?' he asked. 'During the daytime so you don't need to tell that brother of yours. Just us – no pressure.'

I didn't say anything. His hand felt warm through the fabric of my blouse.

'We can go on your lunch break,' he continued. 'Have some *chai*.'

'Tea? I see enough tea working here.'

'Not like this place. Somewhere nice. With cake. I think you're a girl who appreciates cake.'

'What's that supposed to mean?' I pretended to be affronted.

'Well . . .' His eyes slid along the length of my body and I didn't mind at all. But there was a prickle down the back of my neck. The rules were different here. What would he expect from me?

'Patisserie Valerie is good,' he said. 'Come on, Dina.' He smiled and something pulled tight in my chest. 'I only come to this dump for you, you know. Say yes. How's Friday?'

7

Bebba pushed the heavy wooden door and stepped into The French House. A familiar fug of smoke hit her nostrils, and a galaxy of dust motes glittered in the dying light that fell from the tall windows. As usual it was mostly men (and certainly no other Cypriot women). There were few places in London she could visit alone without someone assuming she was a Fifi drumming up business, but the arty types here didn't care about rules. In one corner the pub dog, an albino runt, was chasing its tail. A small group of lads stood around, laughing and shouting, while a young girl with heavily made-up eyes tried to catch the wretch.

Newspaper under arm, she weaved her way to the bar, paid for her Schweppes and moved towards the snug room. Shoulder against the frosted glass, she pushed the door open. Just a couple of nobodies, half asleep over their drinks. Perfect.

'Hello, love!'

Christ, that made her jump. It was the toothless old biddy who as good as lived here, standing far too close. The stink fizzed off her and she leaned towards Bebba, showing off her gums with a terrible grin.

'Any chance?' She rattled her red tin in Bebba's face. 'Running a bit low.' And she waved her empty glass, implying it was Bebba's job to keep her in stout. 'Anything will do.'

Bebba shook her head.

'Oh, come on love. Please. I wouldn't ask if I wasn't desperate.'

She shoved her hand into her purse, pulled out a few pennies, dropped them into the tin and immediately turned her back. Once, she'd made the mistake of buying the old witch a drink and she'd sat down next to her and wouldn't shut up.

Bebba slid into a seat. A dull ache pinched at the nape of her neck. She really needed a ciggie. Reaching in her bag, she took out her Piccadillys, matches and holder, lit up and inhaled deeply. As the nicotine rushed to her head, she closed her eyes, enjoying the buzz, and thought of Dina and their evening at the Pelican.

She couldn't remember the last time she'd enjoyed herself so much. Of course, she knew lots of people in London, but they weren't the sort you'd want as friends. And anyway, she'd been absolutely fine by herself this past year. But it *had* been lovely with Dina, drinking gin, chatting about Cyprus, laughing at the acts. Such a relief to relax, to be with someone who didn't expect anything in return. One or two of the men she'd met months ago had become tiresome when she refused to see them again. And female friends? Well, she'd never really seen the point. But Dina was different.

She opened her eyes, looked at the newspaper and started methodically reading the headline for each story from back home. It had been just over a year and nothing. She wanted to stop this routine but found she couldn't. She wasn't one for superstitions – found them ridiculous in fact – and yet she double-checked the lock on the door every night and had carried on buying the *Vema* once a week, when the notices were published.

It was apprehension rather than fear, she told herself. A waiting. But as the months rolled on and nothing had happened – no notices in the paper, no flunkies sent by the old man to dole out revenge – her unease had lessened, and she'd felt reassured.

'*Yiasou, Costas! Bos bayees?*'

The boom of the male voice made her neck snap.

Just someone greeting a friend. So many Cypriots in Soho now. The shadow behind the frosted glass was the right height but hatless. He always wore a hat, didn't he? His shape darkened as he pushed towards the door, then stopped, hesitated and laughed at something his friend had said.

The door swung open and her heart clenched. There he stood in the entrance. Towering, grinning, not him. Of course it wasn't him.

'It's like a church in here!' he shouted, then turned and walked out.

She looked down. Damn it. There was ash all over her lap. As she flicked her skirt clean, she told herself to take stock. She took a deep breath, arranged her cigarettes with the matches on top, her glass of tonic next to them and the ashtray next to that. Her hand hovered over everything, checking the alignment was right.

It wasn't him for the simple reason that he was dead. And there was no coming back from that.

8

I woke early and sat up in silence. On the other side of the sheet I could hear Peter's gentle snores. Perfect. I didn't want him seeing because then there'd be all sorts of questions. As far as he was concerned, my day consisted of working in the Coffee Corner and coming straight home. It certainly didn't involve visiting Soho bars and clubs where I'd need some nice new clothes.

I reached under my bed and carefully pulled out the paper bag. Inside was a dress that I'd been working on all week. I'd owned it for years but never had the heart to throw it out because the fabric was actually rather nice – a stiff cotton with a satiny sheen. It had started life as a shapeless black V-neck shift, which could have fit three of me, so I'd unpicked it and created a younger, off-the-shoulder style. By staying for an extra half hour at the Pelican each night, I'd almost finished.

Peter stirred and I looked up at the sheet. I weaved the needle in and out a little faster, leaving a row of tiny, neat stitches.

It was embarrassing wearing the same clothes when I was out with Bebba. I needed something new; this was the next best thing.

'Dina, you decent? Can I come in?'

I dropped the dress onto the bed and threw the covers over it.

'Yes, *Kaliméra.*'

*   *   *

After flirting in the café for weeks, I'd decided that a cup of tea and a piece of cake with him were harmless enough. That's how Patisserie Valerie – or Pat Val's as locals called it – became our place. Every Tuesday and Friday, I'd rush out of the Coffee Corner and meet him there during my break. I didn't say anything to Bebba. I felt strangely shy about it. What if they met and she didn't like him? And I certainly wouldn't be telling Peter; he'd be so thrilled, he'd have the church and priest booked before I could finish speaking.

Colleen, of course, had seen it all play out. Today she'd grabbed my arm as I was walking out.

'Nice lipstick.' She grinned. 'Hope he appreciates it.'

I gave her a quick peck on the cheek, leaving a sticky mark. 'I'm late.'

'Yeuch!' She smudged it off with the heel of her hand as I ran out.

I usually had just enough time but today, thanks to a fussy customer and some cold soup, I was cutting it fine. A snap of October wind flicked my cheeks as I zigzagged through the Wardour Street crowds. There was a mist starting up, slowly rising higher. By the time I got back, the fog would have taken hold. I barely had twenty minutes now but at least I got a break, unlike Peter. If he left the factory at lunchtime, he had to clock out so they could deduct it from his wages. I glanced over my shoulder, half expecting to see him there. How did he do that to me? Even in his absence I felt him breathing down my neck.

A few people had hankies tied across their faces already, but I didn't have time to stop so I just covered my mouth with my hand and took shallow breaths.

Without warning, a man wrapped in a camel coat stepped from a doorway into my path. On his arm was a woman with a dead fox draped around her neck, its tail in its own mouth. She stopped to rummage in her bag and I almost knocked her over.

'Heavens, young lady!' she shouted. 'Watch where you're going!'

'Watch where *you're* going,' I replied. Bloody rich people. Everything done at a leisurely pace. As if the whole world could wait.

'How rude!'

I ignored her. A few more feet and there it was, the brown-and-gold canopy of Patisserie Valerie. Would he be there already? He usually was. I rubbed a small porthole on the steamy glass and peered inside. Dozens of tiny cakes, studded with dried fruit, were lined up on the shelves with the precision of soldiers on parade.

I stepped inside, relieved to be able to take a deep breath. It was a familiar aroma now, a pungent mix of bitter tea, syrupy treats and anticipation. The room hummed with conversation and laughter, and I leaned to one side of the queue, searching for him.

'Sorry!'

An elderly man with a Pekingese under his arm pushed behind me.

'Oi, close the door,' yelled a waitress. 'We don't want that smog in 'ere.'

With his hand on my back he pushed harder, mumbling 'Sorry, sorry,' as he walked past. It seemed you could do anything in England as long as you apologised afterwards.

I couldn't see past the queue that curled around the counter. A terrible thought raced through my head: what if he didn't want to meet today? Had I misjudged the whole thing? Perhaps he didn't know how to let me down. My cheeks flared. He wasn't here. I'd just leave.

'Table for one?'

An aproned young boy stood at the counter, a smudge of chocolate near his mouth. I hesitated and he led me through to a seat in the corner. Pulling off my gloves, I gave the room a casual scan.

'Whatwillitbe?' asked a waitress, saying it all as one word, pencil at the ready.

Strands of dark hair had escaped the bun on the back of her head, and she tapped at her pad. She was the same waitress we'd had every week. He seemed to know her a little.

'Er . . .'

Should I order or wait for him?

'Just a cup of tea, please.' I pulled my arm out of my sleeve and bundled my coat onto the chair back.

'Really?' She raised an eyebrow.

'Sorry . . . I don't understand.'

'Is that it? It's lunchtime, miss.'

'Oh, and some toast.'

A smirk crossed her lips, she scribbled on her pad and walked away. She knew. He wasn't coming and she knew.

I'd been so sure this morning but now, as I looked at the groups of friends squashed elbow-to-elbow, and couples clasping hands, a feather of doubt floated down and settled in my mind. Had he actually said, 'see you Friday?' Licking my lips, I felt a bit sick. Did I even have time for toast? I looked at my watch again. Barely 15 minutes before I had to be back. My coat buckle was digging into my back and I considered leaving it, as a sort of punishment.

Don't be pathetic. I stood, shook it out and draped it around my shoulders, the way Bebba did. Then I sat down slowly, careful not to let it fall, a tight smile on my face like a stupid shy statue.

On the table stood a small menu in a metal holder: *Patisserie Valerie, established 1926.* Twenty-six years old. The same as me.

I stopped looking up every time the door opened and feigned deep interest in the words on the menu. Eventually, the waitress returned and plonked down a pot, a strainer and a cup that contained the tiniest splash of milk.

'Sugar's in the spoon,' she said then, over her shoulder, 'toast on its way.'

The tiniest mound of white grains nestled in the teaspoon, ready to be dissolved. I started pouring the tea. Oh, for heaven's sake, *gori*. I'd forgotten to strain it and the leaves now danced across the tea's surface. To hell with it. Instead of fishing them out, I just carried on.

I glanced at my watch again. Ten minutes, but I needed five to run back. Harry would kill me if I was late. I blew on the tea. I wished the toast would hurry up. Then I could just pay and get out. He wasn't coming.

'Toast!' The waitress slung the plate in my direction. 'And cake.' A small gold box, tied with a brown ribbon, was dropped in front of me.

'Oh, but I—'

'It's from him,' she said, indicating with her head. 'Romeo.'

I turned and gave a little jolt.

'Oh, I didn't see you there!'

He'd been standing right behind me, arms folded, watching. He gave a soft, lazy laugh and a cloud of bees buzzed in my stomach.

'I didn't mean to give you a fright.'

'It's okay,' I blurted, stirring my tea, not really knowing why. 'I mean you did scare me but in a nice way. I mean, well . . .'

He sat down opposite me.

'You're a wreck,' he said. 'A strong sweet tea is in order. But you'd be lucky to get that round here.'

I smiled, then noticed that the waitress was still standing next to us, hand on hip, looking from him to me.

'Thank you, Irene,' he said, in English. 'You go now, yes?'

'Cake,' she laughed. Then she put her hand in his velvet hair and tousled it. 'The way to a woman's heart.'

He extricated himself and asked for the bill. She scribbled on her pad, ripped it off and threw the scrap of paper on the table. As she walked off, he lowered his voice even though he had switched back to Greek.

'Don't mind her,' he said. 'She loves poking her nose in everyone's business. And sorry I'm late – I thought you wouldn't have time so . . .'

'So you bought me a cake to take with me?'

'Yes. Was that wrong?'

'No. It was very right.' I tugged at the ribbon. 'What is it?'

'Your favourite,' he said, smiling.

'But I like them all,' I said, trying to keep everything light. 'Is it one of each?'

He leaned towards me, took my hand and stroked the inside of my wrist with his thumb. A lick of heat whipped my throat.

'Fog's settling in again,' I said.

'I know.'

I sat back a little and pulled my hand away.

'Thanks for the cake, but I have to be back soon.'

'Will you come dancing with me? One day next week?'

'I'd love to, but . . .'

'You could say you were at a girlfriend's house – what about your friend at the café?'

I grinned. 'You've thought of everything haven't you?'

'Yes – well, I have to keep on my toes with you. That would work, wouldn't it? You've used Colleen as an alibi before?'

'Okay, I'll try.'

I pushed up my sleeve to check my watch, but he covered it with his hand.

'Don't worry about the time.'

His skin was so soft. Of course it was.

'But – I – I need to get back soon.'

My voice cracked a little and his glance told me he'd noticed, and was pleased.

I started to feel cross, not just with his teasing but with myself for falling apart so quickly. I took my purse from my coat pocket, but he insisted and threw some coins on the table.

'Harry'll dock my wages if I'm late. He hates me as it is. I'll get into trouble.' *Stop babbling.*

He put his head to one side.

'Oh, come on Dina,' he said. Then he gave me a slow smile and an actual wink, and I wasn't sure if it was meant to be funny or not. 'I'm worth it, aren't I?'

I pressed my lips together and tried not to laugh.

'Hey! I was being romantic!'

'Look,' I was laughing now, 'I *really* have to go.'

'Come on then.' He stood and took the coat from my shoulders, holding it out for me. 'Let's go.'

I slipped my arms through the sleeves and for a moment he lingered, hands on my shoulders. As I turned to look at him, our faces were just a few inches apart. If he'd tipped his head forwards and moved just a little to the left, he could have kissed me.

But he didn't. Instead, he took the cake off the table and held it out to me.

'I'll walk you back,' he said. 'I've only just found you. Don't want to lose you in the fog.'

9

A few days later, Bebba suggested we spend the whole day together. Her friend had come down with flu, so it was just the two of us. I swapped days off with Colleen and said nothing to Peter. He didn't know about the Pelican so how could I tell him about Bebba? Anyway, he had handfuls of secrets; just last week I'd found some ripped-up yellow betting slips stuffed down the side of the armchair. His moods had been erratic lately – when he thumped around the flat, I knew he'd lost on the horses, but today he seemed jovial so maybe he'd been lucky.

'It's gone eight, you know,' he said, pulling on his coat. 'Aren't you going to be late?'

'I'm not in till ten today.' I stirred coffee in the *jisvéh* pot, struck a match for the stove, making sure the heat was very low. My voice was steady. I was getting good at this.

'Bloody Harry, changing your shifts like that. Do you want me to speak to him?'

'No – don't do that. It'll make it worse.'

'I bet he didn't give you any notice either.'

I shrugged. 'You know Harry.'

'Well if he starts taking advantage tell me – if I'd known what he was like I wouldn't have got you a job there.'

I got an espresso cup and saucer from the cupboard and turned back to my coffee, watching as the thick brown *kaimáki* on top started to gently blip round the edges. You had to catch it just in time; if the bubbles boiled over and fell in on themselves, it was ruined.

'So, if you're starting late, you're finishing later, too?' he asked.

Oh, I hadn't thought of that. How lovely. I pulled the pot from the stove just in time.

'Yes, so don't worry if I'm not back when you get in. I've made dinner.'

There was a covered bowl on the table, and he pulled up a corner of the tea towel to peek inside. '*Fasoulia!*' He sniffed the heap of tomatoey beans, then dunked in his pinkie and gave it an exaggerated lick. 'Where did you find these?'

'The Italian grocer has started selling them. Have it all. It'll be too late for me to eat – I'll have something at work.'

'You're too good to me.' He smiled and, with a quick peck on my cheek, he was at the door. 'Don't let that slave driver work you too hard, will you?' He walked out without waiting for a reply.

I pulled back the net curtain and watched him stop on the corner, light a cigarette and look over his shoulder before making his way down Hampstead Road.

The clock chimed on the quarter hour. We weren't meeting till ten thirty (she refused to get up early on her day off, 'even for you, darling'). I couldn't remember the last time I'd had a couple of hours to myself. I placed my cup on the table next to the tatty armchair, grabbed a year-old copy of *Vogue* that she'd given me, and plonked myself down, swinging my legs over the arm. As I sipped the thick, dark coffee I looked at last season's clothes. On page 32 was a model wearing what they described as a short dinner dress. The navy taffeta fabric twisted around her tiny waist and fed into the skirt, where it fell in wide, generous folds, which she held in her white-gloved hands. The neckline was a deep V slit and I marvelled at the cut and the way the fabric lay on her body, looking both formal and relaxed at the same time, like it was part of her. I searched for clues as to where the seams were, how it had been made, what shapes had been cut to create it. If I could hold the dress in my hands, I'd see how to unpick the magic. Perhaps one day I could earn money creating a dress like this. I pulled my notepad from the side of the chair where I always kept it, stuffed next to the cushion, and started sketching something similar, but with a wider neckline and shorter sleeves. I turned down the corner of the magazine page and moved on, poring over outfit after outfit, reimagining them with my pencil and letting my mind wander.

Two hours later, I stood waiting outside the bombed-out John Lewis building. Some of the city had healed fast from the war but occasionally you'd turn a corner and be confronted by gaping wounds. Houses shredded, rubble mounds dotted here and there, children darting in and out of it all like it was the best playground. Most shocking were the large stores, like this, once palaces of joy and splendour, their ripped edges exposed to the sky.

'There you are!' Bebba put her hands on my shoulders and gave me a kiss on each cheek. 'How are you? Ready to have some fun?'

We set off at a fair pace up Oxford Street. Despite the fact she was shorter than me, I had to hurry to keep up.

'So where are we going?' I asked. 'You know I can't really afford to go shopping.'

She turned to look at me but didn't slow down. 'Who said we're buying anything?' She crossed the road.

'Well, we're up West – I just assumed . . .'

'Don't worry. I've got it all planned.'

A wave of relief swept over me. I hated scrabbling around for money, checking prices and adding everything up in my head before buying the smallest thing.

She suddenly stopped, oblivious to the people dodging around her, and pointed up. We were standing right under a gilded angel in blue robes, the figure that guarded the

Selfridges clock. I'd heard of the store but had never been inside.

'Come on,' she said. She tugged at my coat a little, straightening me out and giving me a quick assessment. 'Your headscarf, take it off.'

I hesitated and she pulled it off and scrunched it into her bag. She pushed my hair back a little.

'What are you doing?'

'Don't slouch. Stand up straight and remember. You've just as much right to be here as anyone else.'

She pushed me through the revolving doors into the cavernous lobby where a dozen or so exquisitely dressed women wandered slowly from counter to counter, surveying everything before them. One of them wore a long chestnut fur coat. Another was dressed in a vivid coral dress and matching coat, complete with hat – a colour I'd never seen on the smog-filled London streets. There was an air of absolute calm about the place.

I felt my stomach clench.

'Bebba, I don't want to. Please – let's go.' I turned towards the doors, but she gripped my arm and started in the other direction.

Nobody took any notice, but I felt an intense unease that I recognised from my early days here. A dry-mouthed, heart-thumping discomfort that I'd felt every time I'd tried to ask for items at the grocer's or make myself understood.

Here I was again, several months later and still feeling like an imposter in a place where everyone knew the rules apart from me. We'd be asked to leave, surely? I looked back at the entrance.

'Dina, calm down,' she said. 'We're not doing anything wrong. We're simply customers looking around a shop.'

I lifted my head and gazed at the ornate ceiling.

'It's just a shop,' she said. 'Dress it up all you like but under-neath it's the same as Woolworths.'

I smiled at this. 'Hardly.'

'Well, Woolworths for rich people. I almost forgot, here.' She pulled a large pair of beautiful cat-eye sunglasses from her bag. 'Put them on.'

'Whatever for?'

'Come on, play along. It'll be worth it – promise.'

I hesitated.

'For me? Trust me.'

She was impossible to refuse. I sighed a little and, feeling daft, put them on. She steered me to a mirror.

'There,' she said.

The person looking back at me was cold, aloof and looked like she belonged here.

'Now keep them on. People see what they want to,' she said. 'Come on.'

She pulled me towards the lift, and we got in.

'Where to, Madam?' asked the young uniformed attendant inside.

'Eveningwear, please.'

Eveningwear?

He looked at me twice and I felt a creeping warmth stroke the back of my neck, but I didn't dare move. She had a plan and, really, what was the worst that could happen? Would getting thrown out of Selfridges *really* be that bad? It was hardly a place I relied on for groceries. I was starting to enjoy myself. The lift stopped and the attendant glanced in my direction again. Bebba leaned in a little towards him.

'Yes,' she said. 'It *is* her. But please don't say anything. She'd rather not be recognised.'

His eyes widened and he nodded solemnly as he pulled back the metal lattice gate.

'Eveningwear, Madam.'

We stepped out and a sales woman, around my age, spied us from across the floor and started to stride towards us with great purpose. She held her head a little high, as if being led by her nose.

'Stand straight,' said Bebba in Greek. 'And ignore her. I'll do the talking.'

'Ladies?'

She gave us both a slow up-and-down and seemed undecided.

'I'm Miss Hargreaves. How may I assist you today?'

Bebba put her finger to her lips.

'Is there somewhere – private?' she asked. She was using her best English voice. There was still an accent, but she sounded like a person with authority. 'It's a matter that requires a little discretion . . .'

The woman jumped a little.

'Certainly, Madam.'

She guided us to an office just off the shop floor and pointed to a couple of seats, but Bebba declined, so I stayed standing too.

'My friend here,' began Bebba, 'well, strictly speaking my employer, is . . .' (and here she whispered) '. . . a very well-known Greek actress.'

'Oh?'

There was a pause, as Miss Hargreaves leaned in.

'Ellie Lambeti,' said Bebba.

'Oh, er – of course!' said the assistant, glancing at me. She'd obviously never heard of her.

'Would Miss Lambi . . .'

'Lambeti.'

'. . . Lambeti, yes, Lambeti, like some help choosing some outfits?' She looked directly at me now but, as instructed, I said nothing.

'Her English is limited. She prefers to let me speak for her,' said Bebba.

I dug my nails into my palms till they hurt, so I wouldn't laugh. Of course, I'd heard of Ellie Lambeti, but I had no idea what she looked like. I doubted though that she'd wear huge sunglasses in Selfridges like an idiot, but at least they covered half of my face and for that I was thankful.

'We need to see some dresses for her premiere,' said Bebba. *A premiere!*

'A premiere!' Miss Hargreaves took a notepad and started to scribble furiously while Bebba spoke.

'She loves green, something rich in colour, not harsh. And blue, nothing garish. The dress must be long, and we'd like to see your latest styles. Something striking. After all—'

'She's Ellie Lambeti,' she jumped in.

'Exactly.'

'Have a seat,' said the woman. She was slightly breathless now and a light film of sweat had formed on her forehead. Part of me felt a bit sorry for her.

'Do you need to measure Miss Lambeti?' asked Bebba.

'Oh, no.' She eyed me up and down for the second time, but this time with warmth. 'I think I have an idea of Madam's size and we can always alter. I'm going to get a few things together and I'll be back. In the meantime, I'll send in one of the girls with some tea.'

'Oh, and . . .' said Bebba. '. . . if you don't mind, Miss Hargreaves, I need an outfit too. Could we save time and also do that now? I'm accompanying her, you see, as her private secretary.'

'Certainly,' she said. 'You're a little smaller I think, yes?' she appraised Bebba's frame.

'Nothing too showy, please' said Bebba. 'But an evening dress – a dark blue, or a grey? Classic rather than fashionable. Miss Lambeti's the star.'

'Yes, of course, Madam.'

She swept out of the room and I turned to Bebba, finally lowering my sunglasses.

'Ellie Lambeti? What are you doing?' I said, trying not to laugh. 'We'll get into such trouble.'

'Ssshhh! You wanted to have fun, didn't you?'

Just ten minutes later, as I sipped tea from a pretty floral china cup, Miss Hargreaves swept in with a red-faced young girl at her heels.

'Here we are!' she said. 'Would you like to come through, ladies? Your dresses are in the changing room. I'll help Miss Lambeti get changed, and Jenny here will assist you, Miss . . . Sorry I don't think you gave me your name?'

'Papadopoulos,' said Bebba, not missing a beat.

'Miss Pap . . .'

'It's quite a mouthful isn't it. Shall we?'

We walked into the dressing room and I almost gasped. Hanging on both sides of the room were the most exquisite gowns I'd ever seen. Any pangs of guilt vanished at the sight of this finery. On my left were evening dresses, made from silk, velvet and satin. Here was a slippery sapphire dress that reflected the light like a moonlit waterfall. Next to it, a glittering silver number with delicate long white feathers hand-sewn around the neckline. What kind of fantastic beast had feathers like that? But the dress that really caught my eye was a lavish emerald silk robe with hundreds of bevelled beads sewn onto the bodice, like an army of tiny jewelled insects.

I'd never seen anything so beautiful in my life. Who'd have thought that just a few years ago this country had been at war? Perhaps the kind of women who wore dresses like this were immune to hardship, had hardly felt the effects of the war at all? Somehow that made me feel better about the prank we were playing. Why shouldn't I be like them, if only for a day?

The assistant started unzipping one of the outfits but Bebba reached out to stop her.

'Miss Lambeti only lets me dress her. Do you mind . . .? She needs privacy.'

'I understand,' said Miss Hargreaves, 'but usually our clients need a little help getting into these. Some are very heavy.' Then she paused. 'They are luxury items.'

'We'll be very careful,' said Bebba. 'And Ellie – Miss Lambeti – can zip me up, can't you?'

I gave a smile and nodded, having lost track of whether I was supposed to understand or not. I was frantic to try on the green dress. *Come on, hurry up.*

'Well – if you're sure. You will let me know if you need some help, won't you? You see this?' She pointed to a light switch. 'Just flick that on and off and the light outside will tell me you require assistance.'

'Perfect. Thank you so much.'

Reluctantly, Miss Hargreaves left us, with her assistant following. She closed the door behind her – a heavy, wooden door, thick and strong enough to contain our mischief. There was a tiny key and Bebba clicked it in the lock. I put my hand over my mouth and tried to avoid her gaze so I wouldn't dissolve into giggles, but it was hopeless. We collapsed with laughter, incapable of anything else for a minute or two.

Finally, we both calmed down. 'Come on, let's get these on,' she said, wiping the tears from her eyes. She carefully took a dress off a hanger on her side on the room, laid it out on the chair and started to shed her clothes.

I couldn't get my coat and clothes off fast enough. I wiped my hands on my corset before touching the green dress, took a deep breath and stepped into it. Bebba pulled the neckline so it sat flat against my chest and carefully fastened the clasp at the nape. She slipped into a diaphanous navy silk sheath and I fastened the zip on the side for her. The assistant had brought heeled shoes for us to try on, too. We looked at ourselves in the mirror and grinned, turning this way and that.

I let my fingers dance across the precious beetles that marched across my chest. There were perhaps a hundred of them and, caught in the electric light, the effect was mesmerizing.

'You look wonderful,' she said. 'Put the sunglasses back on.'

'Why?'

'For the full effect – go on.'

I picked them up and did as she said, grinning and turning to inspect my profile in the mirror.

'I really do look like a movie star.' I pulled the glasses down and peeped over them. 'How do you do? I'm Ellie Lambeti.'

'And I,' she said, arm up in the air, striking a pose like one of those models in *Vogue*. 'I'm . . .'

'You're an heiress!' I said. 'I mean look at you. You're no assistant. You're filthy rich but simply can't find love.' She put the back of her hand against her forehead, in an exaggerated 'poor me' stance.

'Like Princess Margaret,' I said. 'So glamorous . . .' she swayed to one side '. . . so romantic . . .' she moved again and placed her hand on her heart, '. . . but . . .' I continued '. . . full of terrible sadness.'

She rolled her eyes. 'Oh Lord, Dina – why do I have to be tragic? Can't I just be gorgeous?'

'No – you have to drown your sorrows in gin. That's what heiresses do, when they're unloved.'

She turned her back and started to take her dress off, ready for the next one. 'At least let me drown my sorrows in champagne, darling.'

I laughed.

'Come on,' she said. 'Let's try these other ones before she comes back. You need to try the one with the feathers. It's ridiculous.'

We spent a good hour playing dress up. Eventually Miss Hargreaves knocked on the door and we came out in our own clothes. I quickly slid the glasses back on, not that it mattered much now.

'Well?' asked Miss Hargreaves, her face full of hope. 'How did you find the dresses?'

'Beautiful. Thank you so much for everything,' said Bebba. 'We'll take this beaded one for Miss Lambeti, and I'll have the navy one, please.'

I jumped a little. What was she doing?

'Excellent, excellent!'

'They need a few adjustments,' said Bebba. 'May we come in tomorrow for a fitting when we have more time?'

'Oh, absolutely.' Miss Hargreaves motioned to her assistant, who took our dresses to one side and walked off to the rear of the shop.

'And may we take a contact number?' she asked.

'We're at Claridge's,' said Bebba, not missing a beat. 'Not under Miss Lambeti's name, of course.'

'Of course.'

'Under mine. Papadopoulos.' And she spelt it out slowly while Miss Hargreaves furrowed her brow, wrote it down and showed it to Bebba to check she'd got it right.

'I'll call you first thing tomorrow to arrange a fitting appointment.'

'Perfect,' said Bebba. We walked to the lift and Miss Hargreaves followed us and pressed the button.

'So, we'll see you both tomorrow,' she said, beaming.

The same attendant slid the metal grille open, and we stepped in. As he pulled the gate across and pressed the button, I couldn't help myself. I lifted my hand and, just before the doors clanked shut, I looked at Miss Hargreaves and gave her a gentle wave.

The lift trundled down. Bebba took my hand and pressed something sharp and cold into it, then closed my fingers around it.

She spoke in Greek: 'A memento. Wait till we get out.'

The doors of the lift opened and we walked out across the lobby, through the revolving doors and onto the street. We walked a few yards, then I pulled her to a stop. I lifted my hand and uncurled my fingers. There, nestled in the palm of my hand, was a single, perfect shimmering green insect.

IO

That evening the tiny room in the basement of the Mapleton was jumping. We sat at the bar and jiggled to the music, watching the flailing arms and legs on the dance floor. Every inch was occupied with bodies – men, women, white, black, young, not-so-young – all jostling and gyrating as if a thrill of electricity ran through them.

'See!' shouted Bebba in English, trying to be heard above the band. She had a rule when we were out – always English, so we fit in. She reached across the sticky counter and squeezed my hand. 'Didn't I tell you, darling? The best live music in Soho.'

'It's amazing!' I shouted. 'Look.'

I nodded towards the scarlet-cheeked drummer who, doused in sweat and with his shirt stuck to his chest, was working through a vicious solo.

'He's melting,' I said. 'A human candle!'

She laughed. 'Oh, Dina. You are funny.' I felt a flash of delight.

His bandmates – on sax, piano and trumpet – had already done their solos and were swigging Double Diamonds from bottles.

After our morning at Selfridges we'd had lunch in a tiny Italian café she knew till late afternoon, then wandered through Berwick Street Market. We'd then gone our separate ways to freshen up, but not before she'd pulled out a neatly folded blouse from her handbag for me. She'd thought of everything.

It was the prettiest thing I'd ever worn: French navy chiffon, frill at the collar. I'd been afraid to put it on, worried I would feel like an imposter, but the fabric was so fine and light – like a whisper against my skin. I felt dazzling. Her choice was perfect. I was in the middle of a jazz club in Soho and I felt I belonged.

I reached out for my glass and clinked it against hers. This night would be memorable, I could tell. Four empty Martini glasses were lined up in front us, all bearing ghostly red kisses. It was my first taste of a Martini and it had only taken a few sips before the gin streaked through my limbs, leaving me warm and woozy. I should have eaten something this evening before coming out. Oh, who cared. I would feel awful tomorrow but right now I felt wonderful.

'I love a Martini,' said Bebba, holding the stem of the glass in her fingers and twirling it against the light. 'They slip down beautifully, don't you think? And they're so stylish. What's your favourite drink?'

'I don't really have one.'

'Oh, you have to find a drink you like,' she admonished. 'And always order it.'

She was funny with her silly rules. 'Why?'

'Well, to make you different from everyone else. The same reason you find your style and stick to it. You don't want to dress like everyone else.'

'But I do! I already feel different enough. I want to be the same.'

She smiled. 'You think you do,' she said. 'But you don't.'

A huge roar went up as the drummer embarked on a crescendo of cymbal-clashing, signalling he was nearing the end.

'I thought jazz was meant to be relaxing!' I laughed. 'It's so loud!'

'I know!' She tilted her head back and rolled her left shoulder forwards, then her right, luxuriating in the movement. 'The louder the better!'

Finally, I was on the inside of Soho rather than a spectator watching from afar. And next to me sat this wonderful friend, with her funny ideas and her leopard-skin coat, which now lay like a sleeping animal at her feet.

'Hey, *gori*,' I said, 'are you drunk?'

Her mouth dropped into an O as she pretended to be hurt by the suggestion. 'Me? Never, I'm just merry. You?'

'I'm Mary, too.'

The air filled with cheers and whistles as the band took a break.

She lifted her hands above her head and joined in the applause. 'You mean merry.'

'That's what I said.'

She turned back to me. 'No, it's *merry*. With an "e". You said Mary, with an "a". Like the name.'

'Did I? Then I'm merry Mary. A very merry Mary.'

'Oh, Dina, you kill me,' she said. I started laughing at her laughing and then we couldn't seem to stop.

'I've got a stitch – stop, please!' I clutched my stomach. 'And I'm going to fall.' I pretended to wobble on the revolving stool.

This set her off again and I relished watching her, helpless. Finally, we came up for air. As I dabbed away the tears from under my eyes, trying not to smudge my mascara, a tall, skinny barman walked over.

'There's my favourite customer,' he said. A wide smile, full of sharp baby-animal teeth, broke across his thin brown face.

'Walter!' shouted Bebba, raising her arms towards him.

'Walter!' I cried, raising mine too, though I'd never seen him before in my life.

He laughed and pulled a white napkin from his shoulder, where it had been resting. He began to wipe a glass, then glanced at his watch.

'I thought you were tucked up in bed and weren't coming tonight.'

'Oh Walter,' she pouted, reaching out to stroke his face. It made him stop in his tracks for a second. 'It's cold in my bed. Now, say hello to my friend, Dina.'

He dropped the napkin, took my hand and kissed it. 'Hello Dina.'

I'd never been kissed by a Jamaican man before.

'You can call me Mary if you like,' I said.

Bebba giggled.

'Whatever your name is . . . you're sure pretty. Hey.' He turned to Bebba. 'You got some competition here.'

Bebba gave him a playful slap on the arm. 'We're not rivals, silly. We're best of friends. She's my new partner in crime, aren't you?'

'That's right. Partners. Crime – lots of it.'

Walter laughed.

Bebba reached out and put her arm around my shoulders. 'Dina's the most reliable person I know, aren't you darling? And she also happens to be great fun. Now, be a sweetheart. We need two more drinks.'

'Oh, but—' I shook my head, then stopped as I felt a dull thrum.

'Come on. My treat.'

I hesitated.

'Lovely,' she said. 'Let's see the night off in style. Have you ever had a champagne cocktail?'

'Well . . .'

'Heavens. Two champagne cocktails, Walter.'

He turned on his heels, plucked two champagne saucers from the rack above his head and swirled around to grab the bottle from the ice bucket. We watched as he glided like a dancer on opening night.

'Do you know him well?' I asked.

She put her hand up to fix her hair but barely touched it. 'I haven't slept with him, if that's what you mean.'

'Oh – I didn't mean . . .' That's exactly what I meant.

'Don't worry. I'm not offended that easily.' She smiled.

Walter placed two glasses in front of us. 'On the house.'

'Thanks, darling.' She'd obviously expected nothing less. 'Cheers!' She raised her glass to mine. 'Here's to us. And champagne cocktails, and . . . Soho nights!'

'And friendship!' I said.

'To friendship.'

Our glasses clinked. I'd never been happier in my life.

'Now, drink up. There's something I must show you.'

*   *   *

'Won't you give me a clue? Why's it special?'

I was thrilled she was sharing something that meant so much to her. Up to now she'd told me so little about her life. Perhaps I'd finally find out more.

'You're like an impatient child,' she laughed. 'It's two minutes away. Just wait, will you?'

We turned off Wardour Street and as the crowds thinned out, an alley I'd never noticed before appeared to our left. We edged down it and entered a large open bomb site, where heaps of smashed walls lay like huge broken teeth dropped from the sky. Gingerly I picked a path over the rubble; a misjudged foot would send me toppling.

'Here.' She offered her gloved hand and I held on tight. 'Mind you don't turn your ankle – it's tricky round this part but gets better further on. Tread gently first, like this.' I could make out the shape of her leg testing the ground. 'Then see if it will take your weight before stepping properly. Okay?'

I nodded, more to reassure myself than her as she could hardly see me, and then copied her. The dark was suffocating. When we were children, Peter had teased me for leaving the shutters slightly open at night, to let the moonlight slice through our room. Even now an ocean of total darkness made me anxious, as if I could drown in its depths. I needed to feel the edges of life, know where the world ended and I began.

My eyes had become accustomed to the dark, now, and I could see further ahead.

'Come on,' she said. 'We're nearly there.'

We continued for a dozen or so more steps and then stopped.

'What is this place – or what was it?'

'Sssh.' She stood in front of me, putting her hands on my shoulders. 'Are you ready?'

'I think so . . . but what—'

'Just say "yes".'

'Yes.'

She turned me and nudged me around a corner. 'There.'

The moon, which had been hiding till now, hung low in the velvet sky. Beneath it, bathed in a soft glow, was an old court-yard full of scattered ruins. A Gothic stone arch that had once been a doorway stood tall and proud overlooking a wasteland of devastation. Half-crumbled walls rose like shattered bones from the ground. And windows, with their glass long since blown out, stared sightless into the night.

She walked ahead. 'It's even better from inside, come on.'

I stepped over a rubber tyre. 'What is it?'

'An old church, St Anne's, bombed in the war. Come.'

Inside, the ground was pitted with large craters here and there, as if scooped out with a monstrous spoon. A corner of the building at the far end had remained intact. She made her way towards it, picked up a large piece of cardboard that had been ripped from a box and sat down on it. She waved her arm majestically over the ground. 'Won't you come in?'

I joined her and pulled my coat close.

'Cold?' she asked.

'Bit.'

She put her arm around me and rubbed my shoulder. We had no roof above our heads and most of the walls had disappeared, yet this corner was perfect and solid against our backs. It was the only part of the bomb site that was in complete darkness.

'Look.'

She pointed at the archway. The bricks that had clung devotedly around the doorway created a ragged silhouette, and through the arch itself was the star-strewn sky.

'A door to the world. On a clear night this is the best seat in the house.'

It was enchanting. I tipped back my head and drank in the Milky Way.

'There are hundreds of them,' I said. 'I've never seen stars in London before. I miss them so much.' I sighed. 'What do you miss the most?'

Then I remembered she was an orphan and could have kicked myself.

'Sorry,' I said. 'I wasn't thinking.'

'That's all right.'

'I don't know how you manage by yourself.'

Her arm stiffened and a shot of shame rushed through me.

'I mean, I know you have no choice. It's just that even though Peter is difficult at times, well . . .'

'It's better than being alone?'

I shrugged. 'I suppose it is. I mean, Father is still alive, but he doesn't recognise us. There's a neighbour, she cares for him. Says he barely speaks now. And I miss my mother – is that silly?'

'Why would it be silly?'

'Well, because I never knew her. She died giving birth to me. Sometimes I think Peter's never forgiven me for taking her away from him.'

'Surely he doesn't think that?'

'He's never said it outright. But he had her to himself for three years and then I came along, and she was gone.'

'Do you look like her?' she asked.

'Not really, she had dark hair. There was one photograph at home.' I remembered the round, pretty eyes staring out with a look of surprise, as if she, too, was shocked to leave us so soon. 'My father put it between the crucifix and the *kandíli* lamp, you know – a bit like a shrine. He trimmed that wick every day and would top up the oil to make sure the flame never went out.' I wished I'd brought it with me. 'I've got a small picture of the two of them, but it's blurred. Funny how you can miss someone when you didn't even know them.'

She gave me a squeeze. 'You miss the idea of her.'

'At times other people make me jealous.'

'What do you mean?'

'Mothers, with their daughters. There's an elderly West Indian lady who comes in every Friday with her daughter. Two teas, one teacake, which they split between them. Butter on the side so they can spread it how they want. They don't talk, they just sit, drink their tea and eat.'

I took a deep breath. As I exhaled it hung in the air for a second in front of me.

'You've got Peter,' she said. 'I know it's not the same but it's something, isn't it? And you've always got somewhere to go back to, if you wanted to.'

'That's the dream, isn't it?' I said. 'Make some money, go home, buy some land. But I don't know if I'd want to – not for a long time, anyway. I mean, after Soho . . . it would seem so . . . *quiet.*'

'Dead, more like.'

'Do you think you'll do it one day?' I asked.

'Go home? God, no.' Then she gave a cold, short laugh. 'I'd sooner die.'

I looked up at her, surprised at the bitterness in her voice. 'Really?'

'I'm not exactly welcome.'

'Why not?'

She paused and I could sense her gauging whether to tell me or not. She said finally, 'There was a man.'

I knew it! Of course there'd be a man.

'He was married.'

I actually gasped, then hated myself. 'Sorry.'

'That's all right. You're shocked, I know. You can imagine the fuss when people found out.'

'People found out?'

She nodded. 'We were caught, so . . .'

'You—'

I pressed my lips together to stop myself repeating her words again. I was desperate for details. Who was he? What did he look like? Were you in love? What did your father do when he found out? No. I *wouldn't* demand answers. If I knew anything by now, it was that she loathed people prying. I *wouldn't* be like every other village gossip. She'd tell me when she was ready. *Please tell me. Please.*

She let out a long sigh. 'As you can imagine, there was hell to pay. For me, not for him. He went back to his wife as if nothing had happened. My life, however . . . Oh, listen to me going on,' she laughed. 'That's enough of my sob story. My father died shortly after that so . . .'

'You have nothing to go back to.'

She shook her head. There was a heavy silence between us that throbbed with the words she wouldn't say.

'I can't imagine what it must be like for you,' I said. 'I mean, no brothers or sisters, by yourself. Both parents gone.' I felt a bit mean pressing for more but couldn't help myself. I was intrigued by her.

She drew the collar of her coat tight across her neck.

'I try not to think about it,' she said. 'Waste of time, crying over the past.'

We sat shoulder to shoulder, and I could hear the hum of the traffic as minutes passed. She put her head on my shoulder and it felt so light, like the touch of a child. I let my head drop to rest on hers, the stiffness of her lacquered hair against my face, the tang of Spray Net in my nose.

'You know you have me, don't you?' I said.

'Sorry?'

'I mean, you're not by yourself. We're sort of family now, aren't we? We have each other.'

She paused and then said, 'You're sweet, Dina.'

I nudged her. 'Seriously. Anything you need, I'm here. Hey,' I said, trying to lift the mood, 'we'll be like sisters. Soho sisters.'

She jolted upright.

'Sssh! What was that? Listen – there's someone coming.' She grabbed my arm and squeezed it tight.

I heard it now, too: a heavy-footed crunch, coming towards us. I pulled her hand off my arm but held onto it and, as she squeezed it tight, I could feel a tremor in her fingers.

'What is it?' I whispered.

A beam of light skimmed the ground just in front of us. We both instinctively drew up our legs and hugged our knees.

'Who's there?' A man's voice, middle-aged, maybe older, cross. 'I know you're there!' he shouted. 'I heard you talking.'

I daren't breathe. I pressed my lips together and glanced at Bebba. She'd put her hand over her mouth. A few moments passed but he didn't come closer.

'Suit yourselves,' he called. 'But it's not safe here – you'll be sorry.'

The sound of glass breaking underfoot faded as his footsteps retreated.

'It was just a copper,' I whispered.

Bebba took a few deep breaths but she continued to tremble ever so slightly, a nervous energy running through her. She'd always seemed so fearless.

'Are you okay?'

'Yes, fine. He just gave me a fright, that's all.'

'Harmless enough,' I said.

'How do you know?'

'Well, he was a policeman.'

'Oh, Dina,' she said. 'It's not a cowboy film where the bad guys wear black hats.'

I didn't know what she meant by that and we sat in silence for a while. Finally, I spoke: 'You were right when you said it'd be worth it. This place is beautiful. All these stars.'

'Make a wish,' she said.

I looked up at the sky. 'Hmmm . . . let me see . . .'

What do you wish for when you've hardly lived?

'So many wishes . . .' I said, '. . . if I start, I'll never stop.'

'Just one, then. If you could have one wish that came true, what would it be?'

'To be happy, I suppose. Have something for myself. And not worry about Peter or money. Just to live for myself.'

'Not to find love?' she asked. 'I had you down as a romantic.'

'No, I've tried that – it didn't end well.'

'Really? What happened?'

'Oh, I was engaged in Cyprus . . . but it's a long, sad story,' I said. I didn't want to talk about it tonight. 'Another time, perhaps.' I still didn't understand what had happened myself.

'And there's nobody else?' she asked.

I could tell her about all the tea and cake in Pat Val's. But would it upset her if she realised I'd kept him from her? I didn't want to ruin this perfect evening.

Just the other day she'd jokingly called me her protégée; how would she feel if she knew my attention was divided? I'd tell her everything about him when our friendship was on firmer ground.

'No,' I said, stretching out. 'Nobody else. But tell me, Madam. What will it be for you? One wish. Fame? Fortune? A Hollywood film contract?'

She sat up, suddenly animated. 'Yes, all of those please.'

'Consider it done.'

'And diamonds, of course.'

'Of course.'

'Large ones.'

'The best.'

She paused. 'My real wish would be to start again.'

I frowned. 'But you're doing that now. We both are. That's why we're here.'

'No, I mean *really* start again. No past, nothing. Just rub it all out so nothing showed. Not even a faint outline.'

I looked at her, but she turned away and a gate came down. She straightened her stockings and started to fuss with her hair, tying her scarf over it then untying it and tying it again a little tighter. Then she pulled up the collar of her leopard-skin coat and just as I was about to say something she got up. The temperature had dropped, and a swathe of clouds now covered the stars. Everything that had seemed crisp just moments ago was now blurred around the edges.

'We should go,' she said, offering me her hand.

I clasped it and pulled myself up in one quick move. I dusted down my coat, then we started to pick our way back over the rubble. Once we were out of the churchyard, she linked her arm through mine.

We walked back along Wardour Street and, without looking at her, I asked: 'Was it so very awful in Cyprus?'

She didn't answer at first, and just as I thought perhaps she hadn't heard, she said: 'Long sad story. Another time.'

II

The sulky redhead was in a rare good mood because she'd been given the coveted final spot in the show.

'Just me, five whole minutes,' she said, chewing gum and smoking at the same time. I kneeled on the floor and hemmed silver braid on her cape.

She bent down and whispered. 'There's a man in tonight. Sharp suit, writing things down in a notepad. One of the girls says he's a talent scout, for the movies. Mentioned me – said he was here to see the redhead.'

I glanced up in disbelief. I didn't have the heart to tell her she was almost certainly being ribbed. She flicked her cigarette and the ash tumbled down, missing her bare leg by an inch.

I had just snipped the cottons and was getting up when the music stopped, and I heard shouting outside. What was that?

There were four of us in the tiny dressing room and we all looked at each other, then back at the door.

'That's Billy isn't it?' said one of the girls.

'Is it a robbery?' gasped the redhead.

'Ssshhh!'

I ran to the door and put my ear to it. Then – crash! Something smashed against it, making me jump. One of the girls screamed and the door burst open. We huddled against the dressing table, eyes fixed on the broken chair lying across the threshold.

I crept forwards and peered out. There, lying on his back among the splintered wood, arms and legs at all angles, was Ratface, blood dripping down his chin.

He noticed me and his face filled with hate.

'You . . . *you* . . .'

'What in the—?' And then I saw Peter, rubbing his knuckles. What was he doing here? Had he followed me? My stomach twisted; I'd been found out.

'Peter?' My voice sounded small. 'How—?'

'Get your coat, Dina.' He spoke in English and didn't look at me. 'We're leaving.'

'But I don't understand,' I started. 'I mean . . . how . . .'

Billy sat up and spat blood onto the floor. Something pale flew out of his mouth. It was a tooth. He looked up at Peter.

'I told you she wasn't in the show,' he said.

What had he done?

'Peter?'

'I heard you were here,' he said. 'I thought . . .'

I looked at him and the dozens of faces behind him, all waiting to see what would happen.

'Oh bloody hell, Peter.' A bubble of anger rose inside me. 'I'm a seamstress you idiot.'

Confusion crossed his face, but he couldn't back down now. He leaned towards me.

'*Get your coat.*'

I put my hand down to help Billy up, but he ignored it and shuffled to his feet.

'I feel sorry for you,' he said. 'A brother like that. Bloody liability. Don't bother coming in tomorrow.'

'Billy please—'

'*Billy please!*' he mocked. 'Get lost, both of you.'

No, not like this.

'Billy – please. I can't lose this job. I—'

'Didn't you hear me?' he snarled. 'I said get lost. You're fired! Now get out!'

'But Billy,' I tried to reason. 'Look, I'm sorry – he made a mistake. He's sorry, aren't you Peter? We'll pay – we'll . . .'

'Oh, you'll pay. Get out before I call the police!'

My mind raced. There must be something I could do or say to make him change his mind, but he'd already turned his back and was walking away. There was a moment's silence, then a chair scraped, and someone started talking at the bar. A group of men who'd been sitting nearby laughed at something, then notes filled the air as the band struck up again.

The scene blurred before me and I turned and ran downstairs, tears dripping down my cheeks. I snatched my coat and bag from the workroom and ran back up and onto the street where Peter was waiting for me.

'I hate you,' I shouted in Greek, storming past him. I ran towards the bus stop, but he caught up and grabbed my arm.

'Leave me alone!' I screamed, pulling away. 'I hate you.'

He took hold of my arm again and I tried to get him off. A couple were stood in front of us and the woman nudged the man.

'You all right miss?' he asked.

'I'm her brother,' Peter hissed.

The man looked at his partner, shrugging.

Peter leaned in and spoke quietly.

'I didn't realise you were sewing, *gori*. Why didn't you say?'

He offered me his handkerchief, but I turned away.

'I can't talk to you – leave me alone . . .'

'Dina – what were you thinking? Why didn't you tell me you were there?'

'I was trying to make some money for a deposit. For a bigger place.'

His posture stiffened at the news.

The bus pulled up and we stumbled on. I ran upstairs and threw myself into a seat. He followed and nudged in next to me.

'How was I to know you were just sewing?' he asked. 'Someone told me he'd seen you there. A friend. What was I to think? If you'd said something . . .'

'You would never have allowed it,' I said. 'You always assume the worst. I knew you'd be like this.'

'Dina.' He put his hand on my leg, but I pushed it off.

'I loved that job,' I said. 'And I was good at it – really good. I could have made something of it.'

'You can carry on sewing if that's what you want. I'll ask my boss at Mackenzie's.'

'No, I don't want to work there.'

'Well what *do* you want? Because one minute you want to sew, the next you want to stay at the café.' His voice was getting louder. 'And in the meantime, you're lying to me. Don't do that again. Don't keep things from me.'

'Maybe I don't want to tell you everything, Peter. Maybe it's time you stopped suffocating me and let me live my life.' There. I'd finally said it.

'But I'm in charge,' he said, his voice quiet again but firm. 'You can't come and go like you did at home. All sorts can happen here.'

I let out an exasperated sigh.

'You're my responsibility,' he said, 'till you're married. And you're not married, so . . .'

'You don't have to keep reminding me,' I said. 'I can't help it that Yiannis walked out.'

He jolted when I said his name and didn't speak for a few moments. Then, 'I've never blamed you for that,' he mumbled. 'Let's not get into it now.'

We took a sharp corner and he fell into me, squashing me against the window. We righted ourselves and after a few moments, he asked the question I knew was coming.

'What happened to the money?'

I opened my handbag and took out my compact.

'I spent it,' I lied, as I rubbed at the mascara that had smudged under my eyes. 'I'd only been there a week.'

One lie, two lies – what difference did it make? I'd tried to plan for us both and now he'd gone and ruined it. I wasn't about to hand over my savings. They'd only end up in his bookie's pocket. I clicked the compact shut and slipped it back in my bag.

I rubbed the window, clearing a small peephole. Outside, a fine drizzle had taken hold, wrapping the streets of Soho in a hazy embrace. Dark shapes huddled as they rushed past, but it was impossible to make out details.

Bebba! I hadn't even had a chance to say goodbye and had no idea where she lived. Billy would never let me through the door again. I rubbed at my cheeks.

'Oh, come on *gori*,' he said. He put his arm around me, and I didn't pull away. 'It was just a job – if you really want to sew come to Mackenzie's. There's bound to be something.' I imagined the noise of the huge, dull factory compared to the liveliness of the Pelican's workroom.

'It was different there,' I said. 'I don't want to work in a factory.'

He handed me his handkerchief and this time I took it.

'Not good enough for you?' he joked, pulling me in close.

'It's not that. I can't explain it.' I couldn't look at his face. 'I want to have something that's just for me.' I mopped my nose and stared into my lap.

'What do you mean just for you?'

'You know – something separate.'

His hot, heavy sigh brushed my neck.

'I don't understand you sometimes,' he said.

I pulled away and wriggled out of his embrace.

'I need to breathe,' I said.

'And I'm stopping you doing that?'

I didn't answer and the bus lurched to a halt. After a moment the bell rang, and we set off again.

I turned and looked at him. 'I've racked my brains for months trying to understand what happened with him—' I couldn't continue. The tears came fast and suddenly I was a soggy mess.

'Oh Dina, come on. Shh – shh – here.' He took the hanky and folded it over again before handing it back to me. 'Come on. He's an idiot. Who knows what possessed him?'

'It doesn't make sense . . .' My voice came out in judders. 'I've wondered every single day and still I can't believe it.'

The sun had been relentless the day Yiannis came to the door.

'Hello, this is a lovely surprise.' I reached up to kiss his cheek and he turned slightly so I caught the edge of his ear.

'I have to talk to your brother,' he said, looking behind me. 'Is he in?'

'You should get going, Dina.' Peter came through the kitchen clutching a glass of water. 'Go on, before it gets too hot.'

'You want me out of the way?' I joked.

Yiannis smiled. 'It's just business.' I didn't ask what business, why I couldn't stay.

'I'll see you later,' he said, and I left, bag over my arm. When I returned after a couple of hours, I found Peter sitting, his back to the door. I walked around the table and saw that he was turning something over and over in his hands. His face was ashen white.

'What's the matter? What's that?'

He opened his palm and I saw that he was holding the watch that I'd given Yiannis as an engagement present.

'Peter?'

'He's broken it off.' His voice was hoarse. 'Said to give you this.' He placed it flat on the table.

'What?' I laughed. 'I – I don't understand. What do you mean?'

'There's a girl in the next village whose parents have come into some land. Says he needs to make a better match. Their parents are keen. And as you'd only been engaged a few weeks . . .'

I could hear the blood pumping through my ears.

'But – he can't – he wouldn't – he gave his word. We both did.'

'I'm sorry. I tried, Dina, but he wouldn't listen.'

I made a dash for the door. I had to find him. Peter ran and grabbed me round the waist.

'Don't,' he said. 'He's gone. His father's taken him to visit her. He doesn't want to see you.'

The next day I walked to his house, but as I approached the courtyard the wooden shutters on the windows were slammed shut. I didn't knock on the door. My heart couldn't take it.

Weeks later I gazed at his back as he stood several rows ahead of me in church. She was next to him. She had long dark hair in a thick plait, and when she leaned in to say something the tail brushed against the small of her back. A few of the women along my bench leaned across to see my reaction. Peter gripped my hand and we stared straight ahead. And as the faded faces of saints stared out from the stone walls in their glorious reds and golds, I thought of his hands in her hair later that day, unfurling her plait as they undressed.

I turned away from Peter and rested my head on the bus window.

12

Bebba held her white demitasse cup in one hand and with the other smoothed down her favourite olive-green pencil skirt. She noticed that when she touched her legs Peter made no secret of watching her hands slide down.

'It's cramped, isn't it?' said Dina, reddening. 'We're hoping to move somewhere bigger soon.'

The smell of the backed-up drains had hit Bebba's nostrils as she walked in, and the rotten windowsill that was gently weeping down the wall was truly awful.

'My place is much the same,' she lied. She'd turned up unannounced to deliver Dina's wages and ever since she'd walked in Dina had fussed over her.

She'd thrown a tablecloth – embroidered with a map of Cyprus – over a chair and had placed a plate of *baklavá* on it. Peter had set chairs around it and they had sat and pretended it was a table, dipping down like pigeons every few minutes to peck at the stale crunchy layers of syrupy filo pastry.

Bebba stood and slowly circled the small room. 'Have you been here long?'

Dina came and stood next to her at the window.

'About nine months now, since we came. Peter came a couple of weeks before and found this place. It's a dump, I know. But soon we'll move somewhere better. We just need to save a little.'

Bebba stared down on the scruffy patch of garden: an abandoned vegetable patch, a ghastly moss-covered shed, a rusty

Anderson shelter and a wall that had been bomb-damaged years ago and never repaired.

'Outside space though,' she said. 'Rare in London.'

'We can't use it,' said Dina. 'Belongs to the ground floor, though I've never seen them out there.'

Bebba turned back and looked around. What were those hooks on the wall? Surely they didn't hang that sheet there at night? Good Lord. She walked over and sat next to Peter again.

'It's so good of you,' said Dina, 'bringing round my cards and wages. What did the other girls say, when they found out?'

She put down her cup and took out a packet of Piccadillys. 'Do you mind?'

'Of course not.'

Peter took his lighter from his pocket and flicked it on in one smooth move.

'They were shocked,' said Bebba. She leaned in and held her hand over his as he lit her.

'We were all shocked. In fact . . .' She blew out the smoke and it circled above them. 'Well . . . I've left too.'

'No!' Dina leaned forwards, all big eyes and mouth open. 'Why? What happened?'

She tapped her cigarette into her saucer and took a sip of coffee.

'I told him what I thought of him,' she said. 'That idiot, Billy.'

Peter laughed out loud.

She turned and smiled, the first time she'd allowed herself to look at him directly. His dark eyes shone with excitement.

'He would never have got away with it if Madame Sylvie had been there,' she said. 'So, I told him he was stupid to fire you, and a few other things too.' There was a pause. 'Let's just say I didn't hold back.'

'And then he fired *you*,' said Peter.

She nodded and gave a little 'what-can-you-do?' shrug.

'Oh, Bebba, I'm so sorry,' Dina said.

She picked up the *baklavá* and offered her more, but Bebba refused.

'Don't be. I'm glad to be out of that place.' She paused. 'I get tired of doing the same thing again and again. Don't you?'

She re-crossed her legs and as her skirt rode up a little, Peter shifted in his seat. She set down her cup and addressed him directly.

'I hear you practically knocked him out?' He grinned. 'They say he was in a terrible state.'

'I don't know my own strength sometimes,' he said

Dina nudged him. 'Fighting's not the answer,' she said.

'Depends on the question,' he replied, his eyes not leaving Bebba's the whole time. 'Sometimes people need to be taught a lesson. Don't you think?'

She held his gaze. 'Absolutely.'

Dina put her hand on Bebba's sleeve. 'What will you do? I could ask Harry if there are any openings, but he's almost as bad as Billy.'

'Oh.' She lifted her arms behind her head and stretched. 'I've no idea but I have a little something put by, not much but enough. So I'll just see what turns up.'

There was an awkward pause.

'I should go,' said Bebba. 'I know how precious weekends are.'

'But we haven't had a chance to ask you anything,' said Dina.

'Yes, stay a little,' said Peter. 'You've told us nothing. Where are you from? Which village? Maybe we know some of your people?'

She smiled and settled back. It had been a while since she'd had an audience. She exhaled and her stories swirled into the smoke above her head and enveloped them all.

Well, she was from Limassol, not a village and no, she didn't know their cousin. But it was a big place, so that was hardly surprising, darling. Yes, that's right, her parents had both died, God rest their souls. Just her – no brothers or sisters – did they realise how lucky they were to have each other? She'd come to London to work with an uncle, but he'd returned soon after. So, yes, she'd never really thought about it that way, but you could say she was completely alone.

*   *   *

Not everything Bebba told them had been a lie. Dina already knew she was an orphan, and the details she'd given today had been more or less true: first how she lost her mother, when she'd been eight, to an illness that ate her from the inside out. Then a year ago her father, who'd gone to bed one evening and not woken up.

She stepped off the number 14 and walked up Hornsey Rise, contemplating the afternoon. She'd had a lovely time – despite the squalid surroundings – and it had made a nice change from the usual tiresome empty Sundays. Of course, she knew lots of people in London and could have called on anyone if she wanted, but most of them bored her. She pulled her collar around her neck and hurried along the rain-slicked pavements as she thought about the siblings.

Their warmth and kindness reminded her of the good things back home, before her life had become difficult. They'd been so interested in her, it had been fun. Dina had always been attentive; Bebba had enjoyed going out with her in recent weeks, showing her what was what.

And now she'd finally met that brother of hers with his fading bruises. Imagine marching into the Pelican like that, the way he had. Poor Dina. But then again, it never hurt to have a capable man around.

Bebba pushed open her front door and was welcomed by the smell of curry. She peered up the staircase and there, at the cooker on the landing, stood Mrs Gupta, a blue checked pinny tied over her red sari. Bebba trotted up the stairs, suddenly wanting nothing more than to be in her room with the door locked.

'Aaah, Miss Bebba, are you hungry?' Mrs Gupta's bangles rang out as she stirred the pot. 'We have plenty. Come join us.'

'Oh, that's really kind of you, Mrs G, but I've just been out for dinner with friends.' She didn't stop while speaking but carried right on. Halfway up the spiral staircase she called down: 'Another time perhaps?'

She could hear Mrs Gupta mutter something to herself but too bad. If she accepted, then they'd expect a return invitation. Before she knew it, they'd be poking around.

The aroma of mellow spices chased her all the way to the third floor. As she ran up the stairs, her silhouette grew taller before her in the yellow street light that was flooding through the hallway window. She stretched into a long, thin line, then snapped into nothing.

She stood outside her room and slipped the key in the lock. The door swung open and she looked at the bed, the wardrobe and the table and chair. It was a small flat, but it wasn't that bad, not compared to Dina's. A world apart from what she was used to in Cyprus, but that had been then.

After bolting the door behind her and checking the lock had slid right across, she slipped out of her pointed-toe shoes and placed them neatly against the wall. Then she walked to the battered wardrobe, put her finger under the metal filigree handle and pulled. There it was. She leaned over the grey suitcase and let her fingertips stroke the sturdy, hard shell before closing the wardrobe again.

Suddenly she was aware of a gnawing sensation in her stomach. Was she hungry? Maybe she should eat? But she looked at the loaf of bread on the counter and couldn't bring herself to start cutting and toasting and making tea now. And anyway, the *baklavá* and *kafé* had left her jittery and a little nauseous.

Grabbing the crocheted blanket from the back of the chair, she lay down on her bed and wrapped herself tight in its multicoloured squares, facing the wall. God, being Bebba exhausted her; all that perkiness, all that sparkle. She could never go back, she knew that. As sleep pulled her in tightly, she heard a soft, long wheeze. She sat up with a start.

The door of the wardrobe had swung open and there sat the suitcase, watchful. She slid back down.

13

After Bebba had left, around five o'clock that afternoon, we both seemed to fall into some sort of daze. I could hardly believe she'd seen this mean little bedsit and yet if she'd been appalled, she'd hidden it well. Peter slumped in the armchair with his *Express*, and I started tidying. She'd scribbled down a telephone number on a strip of Peter's newspaper, saying the phone belonged to the woman downstairs and that I should call to meet again. I carefully folded the piece of paper and slipped it into my pocket. We had a phone at the café. I'd wait till Harry was out.

As I gathered the plates I glanced up at Peter. He shifted in his seat, his features pulled tight into a frown. He'd been attentive during Bebba's visit but, as soon as she left, his mood had soured. A few minutes passed in silence, then he dropped his newspaper to the floor.

'I'm sick of this place,' he said, walking over to the window. He swept his hand over the rotting sill, which had started weeping again.

'Look!' He flicked his fingers and grey pearls of dirt rained onto his shoes. 'It's embarrassing having guests when we live in a place like this.' He snatched his coat and hat from his bed, where he'd dropped them earlier.

'Where are you going?'

He shrugged. 'The *kafenio* probably.'

'Okay, but Peter, please – will you promise not to—'

'For God's sake Dina, I'm going for a coffee, not to play cards.'

We both knew that all the cafés he favoured ran illegal gambling dens in the back. He thrust his arms through his coat and tugged his trilby low over his brow.

'How many times? I've stopped. I just need to get out of this dump.'

'We're in this dump *because* of your gambling.'

He went to open the door, then turned back. '*What?*'

I'd gone too far but couldn't stop myself.

'We can't get out of this dump because of your *bellára*,' I said, 'your madness. If you stopped gambling, stopped the poker, stopped throwing your money at the horses . . .'

'Don't speak to me like that.' His voice was calm, but his cheeks had turned pink. 'You're lucky I'm not the sort to force you into marriage. To drag you down the registry office with just anyone off the street and see how you'd like that.'

I have someone, you fool. Someone you know nothing about.

'What's that look for? Do you have something to say?'

I shook my head. 'It can wait.'

He turned his back. 'I'll be home late.'

He trotted down the stairs and the front door slammed, making the whole house judder. A baby's cry started up in one of the other flats.

Bebba's visit had been a bright spark in an otherwise dull weekend, and I'd be damned if I'd let him spoil it. I'd call her tomorrow, make plans to meet. Peter kept a wireless by his bedside permanently tuned to the Light Programme. I turned it on, and breezy piano music swept through the flat.

The water spluttered into the sink and I sprinkled in some washing powder, swilling the tepid suds into a whirlpool before adding the cups, plates and saucers. A thought struck me.

I dried my hands, took the straw broom from the corner and got onto my knees. I pushed the broom under my bed and waved it around once, twice, till I heard the clank of the metal box. I hooked it towards me and dragged it out.

The square red Oxo tin had a dent in one side, and in that dent a bud of rust had started to blossom where it had touched the wet wall. I glanced over my shoulder at the door, then sat cross-legged with the tin in front of me. If he walked back in, I'd just kick it under the bed. The lid was clamped down hard, but after a few tries at the edges I prised it off. I picked up everything in turn and carefully placed each item on the upturned lid. A dozen or so buttons – white ones for Peter's shirts, a couple of brown ones for my mac. A handful of almost-spent cotton reels that still had a little thread wound on them (Peter had brought them back from work saying they'd only get thrown out.) A handmade pin cushion that was intended to be in the shape of Cyprus but looked more like a guitar, with needles and pins stabbed in it at all angles. A pretty pair of steel dressmaking scissors with decorative handles, smaller than my palm but razor-sharp. And, sleeping in the corner, the coiled snake of a tape measure, ready to spring loose.

Under it all was a paper envelope with a drawing of a woman on the front. She was wearing a pretty outfit and looking to one side, as if she knew you were staring and felt shy. It was a McCall's paper sewing pattern for a Simple Summer Blouse that I'd wanted to sew for months. Madame Sylvie had said I could take some fabric from the remnants pile, but the next day Peter had arrived.

I rifled through the tissue paper inside, pulled out the notes and counted. Ten pounds. Three weeks' wages from the Pelican. He could never get his hands on this. He could never even know about it. I'd also added a few coppers here, a sixpence there, the occasional shilling or so he left lying around. He had no interest in the housekeeping so he didn't notice when I returned a little short on change every now and again.

A better home for the two of us, that's what I'd been scrimping for. I pushed the money back into the envelope, placed it in the bottom of the tin and put everything back on top. With the heel of my hand I pushed down hard on the corners of the lid, making sure it was firmly closed. A home with no sodden walls or leaking windows, where the only smells were of my cooking, where I had a room with a door I could close. Somewhere both of us could live side by side.

A thought flared through my mind. I used the broom and pushed the box back under the bed. *Admit it, Dina. What you really want is to leave him behind.*

14

The radio was blaring, and a holiday mood hung around the flat because Bebba was arriving any minute. She'd suggested a day out for the three of us, to cheer me up after losing my job.

The presenter said a few words, then Doris Day's silky voice began to fill the tiny bedsit.

When I fall in love
It will be forever ...

I smiled as I packed the picnic and thought of last night. Was I falling in love? I didn't know. But as we'd walked over Hungerford Bridge to watch the trains go by, I'd certainly felt something. Halfway across he'd stopped, unbuttoned his coat and wrapped one side around me to stop my shivering.

'Is it ready?' called Peter.

He'd taken his time shaving and was finishing off with a generous slap of the woody cologne he rarely used.

'Almost.'

Just a couple of days before, Bebba had come round in the evening when I was working, and they'd had a few drinks together. That's when they'd come up with the picnic idea. By the time I'd returned she'd left. I felt a pinch of jealousy when I realised that she knew my shifts, so had intended to catch him alone.

Looking at him now, combing his hair this way and that in front of the tiny mirror, I dreaded him making a fool of himself. I'd watched him drink her in as she spoke and knew there was no way she'd feel the same about him. She would have told me. As I wrapped wax paper around our *halloumi* sandwiches, there was a knock at the door. Before I could answer, a key grated in the lock and it swung open.

'Oh, Mr Cooper.'

It was our landlord. He never made weekend calls.

'Hello Miss Dina,' he said, and the giant who stood next to him pushed his way in. Mr Cooper followed. I turned the music down. 'Excuse me using the key,' he said, handing it to his friend. 'Thought you might be trying to avoid me.'

Pink-faced and well-fed, Cooper stood there in his starched collar, Liberty-print waistcoat and pressed suit, a man on his way somewhere better. There was a damp patch on our ceiling that had started as a small blob and over time had bloomed into a map of Australia. And here he was, impeccably turned out.

The giant half-sat on the windowsill, arms folded, oblivious to the fact that his thick woollen coat was slowly drinking up the damp.

'What is it?' I asked. 'We're expecting a guest.'

'Won't keep you long,' said Cooper, moving to the middle of the room. 'And you know I don't usually bother my tenants unless there's an issue. You're two weeks late with the rent.'

I turned to look at Peter. He picked up the ashtray and busied himself tipping out the contents and blowing it clean.

'It's not a problem,' he said. He ran the water, gave it a rinse and then wiped it with the tea towel, smearing ash everywhere. 'You'll get it soon enough.' His hands were smudged black.

'It might not be a problem for you,' said Cooper. 'But if I have to—'

'Look.' Peter raised his voice. 'I said you'll have it. I'm just waiting on someone. He owes me you see, then I'll get it to you. So, you can take your thug . . .'

'Hey!'

The giant pulled himself up pretending to be offended, but the gesture was half-hearted, and he leaned back again. At some point his nose had met a hard surface.

Peter put the tap on full, put his hands under and made a show of lathering and rinsing, scattering drops of water everywhere. I could bloody kill him. He shook them, realised the tea towel was dirty, and wiped them down his trousers. He turned to the wireless, twisted the knob so the music blared, and threw himself on his bed.

'Mr Cooper.' I raised my voice. 'Can we speak outside?'

'Dina, leave it,' shouted Peter. 'It's nothing to do with you.'

'With respect, Miss,' said Cooper, 'it's your brother I do business with.'

I looked at Peter, but he stayed where he was. The giant made a move towards him, but Cooper shook his head.

'Ladies present,' he said.

He waited, but Peter didn't make a move.

'Come on then, Miss.'

I followed him and his friend onto the landing and closed the door. It was cramped and, as we shifted to avoid treading on each other, I held the bannister behind me to steady myself. His flunky immediately looked down at my chest and I quickly folded my arms.

'Look,' I started. 'We're really sorry. I know we said it wouldn't happen again.'

'You did – well, *he* did,' said Cooper, milking his moment. 'But your brother seems to think this is a game. You can tell him from me that I had to ask the Wheelers to move out last week. They hadn't paid for months.'

The shock must have registered on my face. He'd evicted a family with a baby?

'They left me no choice,' he said.

'It won't come to that,' I said. 'I'll make sure we pay you back in a couple of weeks. Three at the most.' I thought of the tin under the bed. I wasn't giving that up. Peter would have to find it from somewhere. 'And it won't happen again. I promise.'

He sighed.

'The thing is, Miss Dina, this has to be the last time. I don't want to get heavy-handed, but I will if forced.'

I must have looked shocked.

'Not physically.' He smiled. 'I mean eviction.'

I heard a door slam downstairs and prayed it wasn't Bebba.

'You work, don't you?' asked Cooper. 'Couldn't you contribute?'

The nerve of it.

'He pays the rent, my wages pay for everything else.'

He nodded. 'That brother of yours is – what's the saying? – living beyond his means.'

I wasn't about to get into a conversation about Peter's failings. We'd be here all day.

'As I said, two or three weeks at the most. That's all we need.'

'I'm doing this for you,' he said. 'Because I like you.'

A snort from the giant.

'I appreciate that. I really do.' I needed to get them out. 'You'll get your money. I promise. Sorry, but I really have to go. Thank you so much.'

Without letting him respond, I edged between them both, avoiding all contact, and went back inside. Peter lay on the bed reading the *Express*, feigning nonchalance. I marched over to the wireless and flicked it off. Snatching the paper from his hands, I threw it to the floor.

'Hey!'

'I swear I could kill you. Cooper's given us three weeks.'

'What? It's not up to you to strike bargains with him. It's my name on the rent book.'

'And what a good job you're doing,' I said. 'We'll lose our home. You know he's evicted the family on the ground floor? And they have a baby.'

He looked shocked.

'He wouldn't think twice about kicking us out,' I continued. 'What's the matter with you?'

'I messed up, okay?' He jumped up and walked to the window. 'That's what you want to hear, isn't it?'

He pulled out his Woodbines, lit up, then peered out onto the foggy street below.

'Why didn't you tell me?'

He shrugged. 'Didn't want to worry you. I've been trying to fix it.'

He pulled back the net curtain. 'I tried to win it back. I had a tip. A sure thing.' He stared outside as though the sure thing might be out there waiting for him. Tugging his arm, I forced him to turn around.

'You promised you'd stop.'

He pushed my hand off.

'It's one of my few pleasures, I mean it's not like I'm hurting anyone. Just a few shillings here and there, that's all.'

'But you're hurting *us*. And it's not just shillings, is it? It's now two weeks' rent.'

'But what if a big win was just around the corner? And I missed it? If this one had worked out, it would have solved everything.'

'But it didn't, did it?' I said. 'And now we've got Cooper and his thug at our door.'

Every time I came up for air, there was Peter, his hand on my head, pressing me down. I'd saved enough to pay the debt, but why should I? I'd tried hard, had even got a second job, but that had all come to nothing thanks to him. I wouldn't work more hours now. When would I have time to go out, to see Bebba? To *live*.

'I'm already on lates at the café,' I said. 'You have to fix this, Peter.'

'Don't tell me what to do. I've already said I will, haven't I?'

'I know, but your idea of fixing it is to borrow more. If you do that, I swear . . .'

He rose and held his hands up, like a thief caught red-handed. 'I won't.'

'Good.' I walked to the mirror, checked my face and pushed my hair behind my ears. It sprang forwards again. 'Ask at Mackenzie's tomorrow for more shifts. Or get another job.'

It felt strange giving orders. I shoved the sandwiches in the bag, next to a jar of shiny black olives.

'Here.' He handed me a bottle of lemonade and I caught a whiff of his cologne. 'Don't look at me like that – it's hardly champagne.'

As I was rearranging the contents, there was a knock at the door. It must be her. She'd missed Cooper by minutes.

'You can give it to me on Fridays,' I whispered.

He looked at me, puzzled.

'The rent. I'll pay it, not you.'

'Perfect. So, my own sister doesn't trust me.'

He pushed his hair back, adjusted his posture and opened the door.

Bebba stood there, coat collar pulled up high around her neck, lilac chiffon scarf over her brittle, snowflake hair. She greeted him with a peck on each cheek, then stepped inside and kissed me, too. The sweet tang of lily of the valley filled my nostrils, and I was suddenly pleased we'd be in the fresh air soon; between the two of them it was like being trapped at the Woolworths perfume counter.

'Heavens, it's far too cold out there for a picnic.' She shivered, noticing the bag of provisions. 'The grass will be damp and horrible.'

'But I've made sandwiches,' I said.

'I've got a much better idea, darling. Plan B. You need a ticket, but it's on me.'

Peter shook his head. 'No Bebba, I don't want you paying for us. It's not right.'

'Oh, nonsense – let me do this just once.' She took both of our hands in hers. 'I really want you to see this place. Then perhaps you can take me out another time, okay?'

'Well, only if you're sure we can return the favour,' he said. What was the matter with him? He thrived on false promises. He turned to me: 'What do you think?'

I pulled back the curtain.

'It doesn't look that cold,' I said. It was November, but the sun was shining.

'But it feels like it might turn,' she said. 'And I'm sure I have a chill coming on.' She gave the gentlest of shudders and sank even further into her leopard-skin coat. 'Come on.' She put her arm through mine. 'I've got an idea you'll love. And I promise it will be more fun than a picnic.'

'Sounds perfect,' said Peter.

'Excellent!' She grabbed the bag and handed it to him. 'Carry this would you? We'll eat the sandwiches later.'

*   *   *

'Lions?' asked Peter, as he held up his hands like claws.

We stood in the queue waiting to enter the zoo. He growled and rolled his head full circle.

'Like MGM?'

'Exactly!' Bebba laughed. 'And tigers. And zebras. You won't believe it.' She turned to me. 'Dina, have you ever *seen* a zebra?'

I shook my head and laughed at her expression.

'What is it?' I asked.

Her eyes widened: 'It's the most *curious* thing in the world. It's like a horse but with stripes, like a tiger. But black and white. It doesn't know *what* it is.'

Her enthusiasm was contagious and coming to London

Zoo was a much better idea than sitting on grass eating sandwiches. I marvelled at the thought of this fairy-tale creature. The only animals I'd ever seen – that weren't in a magazine or book – were the sheep and goats back home. And our donkey, Achilles. I turned to remind Peter about him and saw his eyes fixed on her face. She paid at the booth and brushed off the cashier's offer of a map.

'We don't need that,' she said in English. 'We're Londoners. Follow me. Onwards!'

She raised her hand in the air and we trotted behind her, laughing. A zoo attendant wearing a cap and uniform quickly pulled his broom out of our path as we walked past, but if she noticed she didn't care. As we meandered around different enclosures, she stopped and pointed out her favourites, telling us about each in turn, speaking in English and at times attracting quite a crowd. A young couple, holding onto their son with reins, slowed their pace so they could follow and eavesdrop as she explained different things about each creature.

'This is the place I used to visit when I first arrived,' she said, as we neared the chimpanzee cages. 'I'd often spend the day – sometimes right into the evening. I never feel lonely here.'

'But weren't you working at the Pelican?' I asked. She'd said she'd been working there for ages.

'Of course. But I had other jobs before that – a café, a shop, you know how I get bored.'

She rarely spoke about the job she'd taken since leaving the Pelican, except to complain that it was dull; some café across the river where the shifts were so irregular she didn't know if she was coming or going. Funny, but I couldn't picture her as a waitress, serving others. It just wasn't her style.

And now she stood in front of a snowy owl, pointing something out to Peter while he tilted his head towards her. With the other hand she held her shawl collar tight, making her leopard-skin coat stretch beautifully over her shoulders, an assured animal, poised for action. Perhaps she didn't work at all? But how could she afford to dress like that? I remembered how we'd joked in Selfridges about her being an heiress. Perhaps she really was.

*   *   *

The day turned out mild, with no damp or fog; perfect for a picnic after all. After an hour or so, my back began to ache, and I could feel a headache nag at my neck. We'd wandered between cage upon cage of sad-eyed animals and the stench – faeces, fur, too many different species in one place – had begun to turn my stomach.

The deeper we pressed through the zoo, the thicker the crowds grew till they congealed into a slow-moving mass, pushing closer to get a good look. My cheeks and neck felt hot and sticky. I needed to splash my face, to breathe and take a few moments. I started to lag behind and looked around for the exit. Could I break away? I'd find somewhere quiet to sit and meet up with them later. Just then, I felt her grab my hand and pull me towards her.

'Oooh, Dina, look at this!' she said, pointing out a glassy-eyed, scruffy little monkey. 'Have you seen its tail?' She was still speaking English – louder now – and people were listening.

I unbuttoned the collar of my raincoat.

'Poor things,' I said. 'All of them caged up like this.'

Peter laughed. 'Don't be soft! They're animals.' He turned to Bebba. 'It's not like they know they're in a zoo, is it, Beb?' He'd started calling her that.

'Exactly,' she said. She rubbed my arm and gave me a hug. 'But you *are* a sweetheart to care so. They look after them awfully well here.'

I peered through the bars and waggled my finger at the wretched little beast inside. It rubbed its amber face with its paw, showed me its teeth and gave out a high-pitched screech that made us all jump back.

'Well I never!' said a woman next to us, pulling her son closer.

'He's fed up,' I said, loudly, 'that's all. Sick of us standing here, staring.'

Peter snorted.

'She's got a marshmallow heart, that one,' he said to Bebba.

'I'm going to find the lavatory,' I said in Greek. 'I'll see you at the end,' and hurried away.

As I walked against the crowds a voice whispered in my ear: 'Fucking foreigners.' I jumped. 'Jabber, jabber! Monkeys, fucking foreign monkeys!'

I turned to see two men in suits laughing. One of them squatted so his arms dragged on the ground.

'Oo-oo-oo!' he said, and started screeching like a monkey. 'Look at me, I can't speak English. Oo-oo-oo!'

My face felt as if it had burst into flames and, as I spun around and started to run, I could hear them hooting with laughter behind me. My head pounded with fury and utter shame. I ran out of the monkey house into the park and carried on until I was away from the crowds. Why hadn't I said something? But what could I have said? I should have just struck the fool on the head with my bag. Next time I'd be ready, and I wouldn't just hit him once.

I looked to make sure they weren't behind me and slowed down, breathing deeply to calm myself as I strode towards the building behind a hedge. The sign said 'Ladies'. It was the first English word I'd learned to read. There was nobody inside and I stood at the mirror and pulled my shoulders back a little.

What a day. I felt exhausted. It was good to get away from the crowds. Something was shifting between me and Bebba, and all I could think was that Peter made a difference. When we were three, she seemed more interested in him than me. Oh, for heaven's sake, I was actually jealous. And yet I knew that our friendship – the friendship between two women – was stronger than anything they'd ever have. I mean, she could spend an evening drinking with him, yes, but it was me she'd tell her secrets to. Me she'd confide in.

I pushed the cracked pale-green soap between my fingers and scrubbed my hands twice, rinsed and shook them dry. Then I looked in the mirror, flipping a disobedient curl behind my ear. I was determined to switch my mood, to have an excellent day out. My stomach rumbled and I remembered the sandwiches we'd packed. We could stop and have lunch soon, then enjoy a stroll through the park before dusk fell.

As I neared the exit for the monkey enclosure I searched the crowds but couldn't see them.

'Penguins!' shouted a bespectacled girl. She ran and tripped right in front of me, sand streaking her navy duffle coat. I bent down to take her hand, but she sprang back with such violence she almost hit me in the face.

'Careful!'

She didn't even turn, but continued running.

I scanned the park for Bebba's lilac headscarf but still couldn't see her. I'd give it five more minutes. If I didn't find them by then, I'd make my way home.

Just then I noticed a couple on a bench. It was that white halo of hair that caught my eye. I took a few steps closer. She'd slipped off her headscarf and Peter was leaning into her face, saying something.

Slowly, I started to walk towards them, watching as he took a handkerchief from his top pocket and gave it to her. Something was wrong. Was she crying? He looked up, saw me, and stood to wave me over. As I approached, she held the handkerchief in front of her face.

'Bebba? What is it? What's the matter?' I leaned forwards till I was inches away. 'Are you ill?'

'It's my fault,' said Peter. 'I shouldn't have pried.'

She shook her head. 'Don't be silly.'

'What?'

'It seems,' he said, 'she hasn't been completely honest with us.'

Something shifted like a fish in my belly.

'What's happened?' I asked.

'Well – it's more what she hasn't told us, isn't it, Beb?'

He placed one arm very gently around her shoulder, barely touching her, and she hung her head, crying.

I knelt down and took her hand.

'Please, just tell me,' I said. 'What is it?'

She took a sudden breath and her words tumbled out. 'My landlord's kicking me out, isn't he?' she said, her voice breaking. 'Served me notice.' She gulped an unexpectedly ugly sound. 'I have to leave. And I don't know where . . .'

And the rest was muffled as she turned and wept into his shoulder.

He pulled her in tight and I sat back a little on my heels, surprised at the scene before me: Peter so ready to embrace, her so ready to accept.

'Can he do that to you?' I asked. 'I mean, is he allowed?'

Peter nodded.

'They just say they're rebuilding to get tenants out, then charge more to the next lot,' he said. 'They can do what the hell they want. We're just bloody foreigners to them.'

At this her shoulders heaved. I took the handkerchief that was still clasped tight in her hand and started to gently wipe away a mascara smudge from under her eye. Her lipsticked mouth bore the blurred lines of someone who'd just been kissed. The unease in my belly swirled up to my chest.

'We have to do something,' said Peter.

She sniffed, straightened up and edged out of his embrace.

'There's nothing you can do.'

'But you can find somewhere else, can't you?' I said. 'I mean, you have so many friends.'

She shrugged. 'More acquaintances than friends, really. Nobody I can call on for help.'

She opened her bag and took out a duck-egg blue compact, glanced at her face and grimaced. I had the same one in my bag; we'd bought them together in Woolworths.

Then she sighed. 'You don't understand,' she said, 'what it's really like to be alone. I know I always complain about that place, but I like the other tenants.'

She Max Factored her lips and took a long look at herself in the mirror.

'We're always having dinner together, looking out for each other. Me, the Guptas, the others . . .' She dropped the lipstick in her bag and took the handkerchief from my hand. 'It's nice to have company.' She found a clean corner and gently pressed her lips to it, then looked again at her face. 'It's different for you two. You have each other. The truth is – I'm lonely.'

She smiled and dropped the compact back into her bag. 'Pathetic darling, isn't it?' She handed me the handkerchief that now bore her mouth print.

'You've no need to be lonely,' I said. 'We're family. We'll sort something out.'

'But I couldn't possibly live with you,' she said.

'I wasn't suggesting—'

'Your place is tiny,' she continued, 'and it wouldn't be proper.'

Peter shuffled a little.

'No, what I meant was—'

'The flat downstairs!' Peter blurted. 'It's empty. Hasn't it got three rooms?'

She jumped in: 'The flat with the garden? Oh, is it big?'

He nodded, vigorously.

'Do you think we could get it?' she asked him. 'Share the rent between the three of us?'

'Why not?'

'What?' I started. 'Wait. I mean, the rent . . . how would we . . .?'

Peter ignored my protests and addressed her directly.

'You have money, yes?' he asked.

Her eyebrows drew together at the question.

'Forgive me, but . . .' He gestured, indicating the way she was dressed. 'You did say you have a little put by?'

'A little. I saved some before coming here.' Then her face glowed. 'I wouldn't mind contributing half – more if need be.'

'That wouldn't be fair,' I said.

'Well, then we could definitely afford it,' said Peter.

What was he doing? I put my hands on both their arms.

'Look, will you both stop a minute? You don't know how much it costs, Peter. So let's not go making promises that . . .'

He put his hand on my shoulder to stop me talking, then patted it a few times.

'My sister doesn't think I can do anything right, do you? But I know that flat – I knew Wheeler. I've been inside. It has three rooms and a living room. It's perfect for us.'

'Cooper will never allow it,' I said.

'All he cares about is money. And it'll mean more for him.'

'Perfect!' she said.

He addressed her: 'You could have your privacy but still have company when you wanted.'

She looked from him to me, then pulled me into a sudden hug.

'Let's at least find out about it, shall we?' she asked. 'Please? I don't mind dipping into my savings a little, until you get yourselves straightened out. You could even pay me back if that would make you feel better about the whole thing.'

Straightened out? Had he told her about our debt?

'Wouldn't you *like* a room to yourself?' he asked me.

I thought of the tiny space we currently shared, the sheet dividing us every night and morning.

'Well, who wouldn't, but—'

'It's a *wonderful* idea, darling!' Bebba stroked his lapel. 'Let's find out about it first thing tomorrow. Before someone snaps it up.'

What was the point of arguing? It would probably never happen. Cooper wouldn't rent us the flat, surely, when we already owed on the one we were in.

'Your brother is a clever thing, isn't he?'

Peter looked fit to burst.

'Good, that's settled.' Reaching out, she stretched her limbs like a cat luxuriating before an open fire. 'Where's that bag? I'm ravenous!'

She picked it up from the ground and pulled out the bottle of pop. Peter took it, used his Swiss Army knife to clip off the cap and passed it back.

'Damn,' he said. 'We forgot cups.'

She took a small sip, leaving her cherry-red imprint over the top. 'I don't mind sharing if you don't.'

He took a swig without wiping it.

'Look at these!' Bebba pulled out the *halloumi* sandwiches I'd made.

'Oh no!'

The bottle had squashed them into ugly shapes. She giggled, then glanced at him, and he started laughing too, until they were in fits while I tried to remould the packages. Every time I pressed the wax paper, they laughed even harder.

'Don't!' I thought I might cry. 'They're completely spoilt.'

'Oh, darling, do stop fussing.' She took them from my hands and unwrapped them. 'They'll still taste fine – see?'

She bit into one and a piece of *halloumi* shot out of the side into Peter's lap. Shielding her full mouth with her hand, she laughed. He picked up the rubbery slice of cheese and popped it in his mouth.

15

Two days later, there was a knock at the door. I'd barely opened it before she burst in.

'He's said yes,' she beamed. 'Your landlord – he's agreed.'

'Really?' I had half-hoped Cooper would refuse.

'I've paid a deposit.' Then she saw the look on my face. 'Just insurance, darling, to make him feel more at ease.'

'Bebba, we can't—'

'Stop it.' She held a finger up in protest. 'Listen, you're doing *me* the favour. I'll have somewhere to live, and I'll be with friends. What could be better? Where's your brother?'

'At work, look—'

She held up her hand and put her handbag on the table. She rummaged inside and pulled out a slip of paper with sums scribbled in pencil.

'You see, with my share paid it will actually work out cheaper for you than this place.'

'What's that?' I asked. In the corner was a calculation that was underscored several times. Then I realised. It was the exact amount we owed.

'I'm paying it off weekly and then you can pay me back,' she said.

So Peter had told her. Did he have no shame?

'Oh, don't look so glum,' she said. 'Better than owing that shark the money.' She put the slip back in her bag and looked at me. 'Imagine the fun we'll have living together. All those nights out we'll have! Unless you don't want me.'

'Of course it's not that,' I said. She was the closest thing to a friend I had here – my best friend – but the thought of being indebted rattled me. 'I just, I just don't know what to say.'

'It's nothing,' she said, putting her hand on my cheek and giving it a gentle squeeze. 'Don't look so serious,' she laughed. 'There – that's the smile I've been waiting for.'

*   *   *

Within a week, we'd thumped our three boxes of belongings down the creaking stairs and moved into the ground-floor flat. It was a lighter, happier space than the bedsit and the damp wasn't as bad. In the cold morning, as I lay under the covers and the winter sun spilled over my bedspread, I half-opened my eyes and was struck by a feeling that this was a place where good things could happen. Of course, the raised voices of the Jamaican couple who'd been our neighbours still floated under our door most evenings, but wasn't everywhere like that in London? I had my own room and that was delicious. It was certainly small, just six footsteps across, but I could hardly believe it was all mine. There might even be space for a sewing machine, if I could save up to buy or rent one.

Bebba had the largest of the three rooms, which was only fair. She had to walk through mine to get to hers, but it meant she'd have extra privacy and, being the only male, Peter was quite separate. He kept reminding us in a rather stiff way that this was only 'proper', despite the fact we'd just spent several months with only a sheet to separate us.

She'd arrived with surprisingly few belongings: an old suitcase, a number of outfits that she carried in on hangers, a vanity case full of cosmetics and her coat. She didn't have many clothes, but what she had was beautiful and far nicer than anything I owned: a couple of chiffon blouses, a few beaded cardigans, three tailored pencil skirts, one dress, two soft woollen sweaters, a black coat as well as her trusty leopard-skin one, and a couple of pairs of shoes with pointed toes – and she let me look at it all as she put it away. They all had London labels, but I knew not to ask how she'd afforded them because she'd never give a straight answer.

There were no family photos, no mementoes, but that seemed understandable what with everything she'd been through. Although she seemed at ease with Peter, I knew she confided more in me. For instance, she'd never tell him about the married man she'd had an affair with – he would never understand.

She sat me down on her bed and got me to close my eyes while she applied black eyeliner and a ruby-red lipstick, a darker shade than I'd usually wear. When she'd finished, she pulled me over to the dressing table and we put our faces next to each other and stared at our reflections, turning our heads this way and that.

'We're like twins,' she laughed. And although we looked nothing alike, I loved the idea and agreed.

'I look older like this, more sophisticated,' I said.

'Well of course you do.' She patted down my hair to try to get the curls to lie flat. 'You've always had it in you – it was just a case of teasing it out.'

I was stung that she thought I needed so much help. I had to stop being so sensitive.

'Let's go dancing one night,' I whispered. 'Without *him*.' I gestured to the next room.

She started to say something, then hesitated.

'What?' I asked. 'We can still have fun, can't we?'

'Absolutely, but we can't be sneaking about any more and . . . well . . .'

'What?'

'It doesn't matter.'

'What?'

'Well, it's honestly fine . . . but I have to watch my finances – you know, with the payments to Cooper.'

'Oh God – of course.' I was mortified. 'I'm sorry.'

'No, really it's *fine*, darling.' She put her hand on my shoulder. 'I should just watch the pennies for the next few weeks. And when we do go out, wouldn't it be a good idea to include him? After all, living together, all of this – this *was* his idea.'

I let out a sigh.

'Come on Dina, we'll still have the best time ever,' she said. 'All three of us. Just wait and see.'

True to her word, in the weeks that followed, we only went out a couple of times, but they were memorable evenings and we did have fun. Peter was working fewer hours and happily came along.

I put my unease down to jealousy. And yet there was something about our set-up, like a mismatched jigsaw that's been forced into place; a month ago I'd hardly known her and now she'd just rescued us from ruin. It had all happened so quickly. One day, as we were preparing dinner, she mentioned that she'd asked Peter to get her a job at Mackenzie's.

'I'm sick of working in that awful little café,' she said, as she sliced bread.

'What do you actually do there?' I asked, surprised she had mentioned it at all. It was rare that she volunteered anything.

Her knife slipped a little, cutting the slice to a wafer of nothing. 'I'm a waitress, of course,' she said. 'What else?'

I let out a nervous laugh and she stopped, knife aloft, and gave me the severest look.

'Sorry,' I said. 'I just can't imagine it, that's all.'

Her face softened. 'Well, I'm not playing to my strengths, that's for sure. Running around after people all day. I don't know how you stand it.'

We both knew she'd never waited tables in her life. But the money had to be coming from somewhere. I'd even started to wonder if she was on the game but quickly dismissed it when I saw how particular she was about anyone touching her hair. As she continued to slice the bread, I decided not to ask the questions racing through my mind. 'Which café is it? Where exactly? Where's your uniform? And why don't know how to lay a table? How can you be a waitress and always mix up your left and right?'

She'd been so generous, and I didn't want a confrontation. So what if she told a few fibs – she must have had her reasons. Perhaps she was too proud to admit she didn't work at all. She had nobody here, that much I believed. Perhaps her life in Cyprus had been so dreadful she couldn't talk about it.

I took three plates and placed them around the table. All I knew was that she'd been a very good friend. Colleen was fun and I would have been bored to tears in the café without her company, but with Bebba it was different. She understood me. I didn't need to explain anything because she knew what it meant to be a Cypriot woman here. And in time she'd tell me everything, I was sure. So I kept my silence and kept my room. I had a door, a window, a bed without a curtain drawn down the middle of the room. I wasn't about to give those things up.

And every now and then she'd surprise us with a generous treat, as if we were her children. She'd come home with the most wonderful packages: a small tin of sliced apples, some chocolate biscuits (now they were off ration and I had a taste for them, I craved them even more), and once even a pat of real butter as big as my fist. She said she didn't pay for any of it, had friends who knew people.

The three of us fell into an easy routine. She and I took it in turns to cook and wash up, then we'd collapse – me in the wing chair, legs thrown over one side, *Picture Show* or *Life* magazine in my hands, her at the small table with Peter, smoking and playing gin rummy.

I watched as he pre-empted her every need, pulling out a chair, lighting her cigarette. My unread magazine in my hands, I feigned interest in Cary Grant's new film or whatever was that week's cover story as I peered over the top of the page at the performance before me. When Peter lost at cards, she'd let out that bark of a laugh and there-there his shoulder, teasing him. When he won, she'd throw down her cards with a pout. That was his cue to lean across and, with his index finger, lift her chin up a little and make a silly face till she smiled.

They were the two people I loved the most in the world, and yet when they were together something unnerved me. What was it? I couldn't decide. And then, as I turned the page, it struck me. They were behaving as if I didn't exist.

16

I unbuttoned my coat for the third time, ran my thumb inside my waistband and checked it was lying flat against my stomach. The air crackled with anticipation as dozens of people jostled down the stairs to the club. This was our first evening date and, as I waited at the top of the stairs for him, I remembered that night of dancing at the Mapleton with Bebba.

She was going to the cinema with Peter this evening. They'd asked me along, but I'd said that Colleen had invited me for dinner again, although I'd hardly seen her outside work since meeting Bebba.

I'd expected a flurry of questions from Peter – who else was going to Colleen's? Would there be any men there? What time would I be back? – but surprisingly there had been no protests.

'Good evening, beautiful!' I turned at the sound of his heavy accent and he gave me a long kiss on the lips as if he always did this. I was taken aback but liked it.

'So we're speaking English tonight?' I teased. 'That'll be interesting.'

'That's all I know.' He grinned, switching back to Greek. 'Sorry I'm late – bloody weather. Buses gave up and I had to walk.'

I hadn't seen him for a few days and as he embraced me I felt the now-familiar whirl of attraction spin through me. His cheek was smooth, so he must have shaved especially. And had he combed his hair differently or used something to keep it back off his face? The overall effect was even more disarming than usual.

'I wasn't sure this was the right place,' I said. 'There's no sign or anything.'

He took my hand and pulled me towards the dimly lit steps. 'The club's not strictly legal,' he said, over his shoulder. 'They don't want to advertise it.'

Before I could ask more we were trotting down the stairs. An elderly gentleman in a long evening coat pushed past, followed by a younger woman in a rich crimson satin dress. I suddenly felt self-conscious. I was wearing the black off-the-shoulder dress I'd sewn and had added a double layer of netting to create a fuller, more modern skirt. I'd cinched the waist with a wide black velvet belt Bebba was throwing out. The cocktail dress fitted me like a dream and was just as nice as anything she owned. But I still wasn't sure it was glamorous enough for this place.

'Hold on,' I said, and we stopped just before the entrance. 'I just want to . . .' I pushed my hand into my coat pocket and pulled out the jet necklace that I'd picked off her dressing table this morning, quickly fixing the clasp.

'There!'

'Very nice,' he said, 'have I seen that before?'

I shook my head. 'Borrowed it from a friend. I don't think it's real. She won't miss it.'

He raised an eyebrow.

'Oh, I'll put it back – she won't even know it's gone.'

'Come on.'

He pushed through a door and pulled me into the room, a cavernous space with low ceilings and no windows. Dozens, maybe even a hundred people lined the walls, chatting, laughing, all watching as a band in the middle of the room set up their instruments.

'It's so loud!' I shouted about the noise.

'And the music's not even started yet,' he said. 'Welcome to Jimmy's.'

I wanted to know who Jimmy was, but at that moment the band struck up and the crowd surged towards the musicians and started dancing furiously, the kind of dancing that was all arms and legs and totally unselfconscious. He pulled me towards the bar at the far end.

'Let's have a drink first,' he said.

I pulled off my coat and bundled it up onto the stool. He spoke to the barman in Greek and a tumbler with an inch of amber liquid was placed in my hands.

'He's Greek?' I asked.

'Everyone is – all the staff anyway. Jimmy's from my village. That's how I heard about this place.'

'What a mix,' I said. 'Look, everyone is dressed so differently.'

One man near us had his sleeves rolled up, a trilby perched at an angle on his head and his skinny striped tie was already loose. Next to him, a woman sported black feathers on the shoulders of her long white evening gown. Two younger women stood in the corner swirling their full skirts around their waists in time to the music, revealing their petticoats.

'You know the best part?' he asked.

I sipped my drink and felt a warm trickle of happiness work its way down my throat. 'What?'

'Jimmy doesn't pay any rent. Doesn't even know who owns this place. It was locked up and then after it was bombed nobody came back to claim it.'

'I don't understand.'

'Every day he just turns up, books musicians and sells booze. Look at your face.' He laughed. 'Don't tell me you've never broken the law?'

'No, it's just – well – isn't he worried he'll get caught?'

He shrugged. 'It'll happen eventually I suppose. But then he'll pay a fine, move on and start again.'

He clinked the ice in his glass and gestured to the barman for another round.

'You make it sound so easy,' I said. He'd always been vague about his own job, and I had a feeling some of his businesses weren't 'strictly legal' either, just like this bar. But I didn't want to ask, because I didn't want to know; I was enjoying myself far too much.

'He's just grabbing his chance,' he said. 'You've got to make the most of the cards you're dealt. You'd be a fool not to try.'

I supposed he was right. I mean, we were living proof, weren't we, me and him, Bebba and Peter, too. Leaving home, travelling here for better lives. It's what we all wanted, but what nobody told you was how to do it without completely losing yourself. Without losing the person you'd been before. My life was already changing more than I'd have thought possible.

He took my empty glass from my hand, replaced it with a full one, then put his hand just behind my waist and pulled me in a little.

'I don't think I told you, Miss Demetriou, but you look lovely tonight.'

'Why, thank you,' I said.

He leaned down and placed a gentle kiss on my lips.

'You're welcome,' he said.

He kept his hand in the small of my back and pulled me a little closer. I opened my lips a little and he kissed me again, this time slower. Everyone else fell away and it was just the two of us in the room.

I came up for breath and didn't want to do or say anything in case I ruined it all. What were the rules now? What would he expect? Colleen had laughed when I'd told her how apprehensive I was.

'It's just a date, Dee,' she'd said. 'Not your bloody wedding night.'

But I'd barely been alone with a man I wasn't related to, let alone in an illegal club in Soho. And yet here I was, doing exactly that, living my life. Isn't that what Bebba always said? Live your life. My hand went to my neck and I felt the jet beads.

'Look after those,' he said.

He placed his index finger on a bead that was nestled in the spot just under my ear and ran it from one bead to the next, all along the necklace till it reached the nape of my neck. Then he dropped his hand and sipped his drink. 'Your friend will be furious if you break them.'

'Oh, I don't think she'd mind. She'd say, "As long as you had the time of your life, darling!" That's how she speaks.'

'Well, she sounds very reasonable. Now . . .' he put my tumbler on the bar and took my hand, '. . . come on. I've spent enough time trying to avoid it. I'm going to show you what a terrible dancer I am.'

17

Bebba stamped her feet as she stood in the queue outside the Empire. The weather had turned overnight, and a freezing fog now tumbled over Leicester Square. Along with everyone else she was blinded in a matter of minutes. Her bones felt like icicles ready to snap. Oh, what wouldn't she give right now for an hour stretched out under the Cypriot sun? But that would never happen again.

Someone at the front of the crowd must have moved, because the line concertinaed together, shoulder to shoulder, everyone jostling not to lose their place. She edged her way forwards.

If Peter didn't arrive by the time she reached the ticket booth, she'd just go in by herself. She wasn't missing Gary Cooper in *High Noon* for anyone. Dina had mentioned that she was sometimes afraid in this fog, but for Bebba it was just an inconvenience. Yes, she disliked the grime and chaos it brought, but fear? No. There were far worse things to be scared of.

'*Yiasou!*' Peter grabbed her arm and gave her a kiss on each cheek. 'I thought I'd never find you.' He was wearing a new coat, midnight blue with black velvet lapels. Must have had a win. He put out his arm and as she took it, she was surprised at how much she enjoyed feeling part of something: this evening, this crowd, this couple.

'Just the two of us tonight,' he said, grinning. 'Dina said she's having dinner with Colleen, although after that business at the Pelican who knows if she's lying?'

He was fishing, but did he really think she'd tell him if she knew?

'Colleen's a sweetheart,' she said. 'Or so I hear.'

She thought of mentioning how he barely allowed Dina to speak to a man, yet here he was alone with her. But why ruin her night out? It was time Dina learned to fight her own battles.

After paying tuppence extra for the best seats, he led her upstairs.

'Is this okay?' he asked, pointing to two seats at the end of a row.

'Lovely.' She began to slip off her leopard-skin coat and he quickly took it from her and spread it on the back of her chair.

'Thank you, darling.'

His eyes didn't leave her as she lowered herself into the seat next to him. He stretched his right leg into the gangway and leaned across.

'This is going to be great,' he said. 'It's supposed to be the film of the year.'

She nodded. Now that her English was fluent, films were much more enjoyable, though she'd been able to follow them well enough when she'd hardly spoken a word. There was always a good person and a bad one, so it was clear whose side you should be on. In Hollywood everything was black or white; in Soho she lived her life in the greys.

He rustled next to her and she took a sidelong glance as he tore into a bag of chocolate raisins. He was pleasing enough to look at, she couldn't deny. Dina was fun to be around, but Peter was on her level; they understood each other. He obviously liked her too and she couldn't deny she'd missed having this sort of power over a man. It was exciting.

Was it her imagination or had Dina gone a bit cold on her lately? She was jealous of the time Bebba spent with Peter, that much she knew, which made it all the more puzzling that she hadn't come along tonight. Colleen's dinner was probably a fib. Oh, well, let her sulk. She'd get over it.

Opening her bag, she pulled out her ciggies and her holder. Peter scrambled for his lighter, dropping a few sweets into his lap. She looked up at him from under her lashes as he offered her a light.

'Happy?' he asked, picking a sweet from his lap and popping it into his mouth.

She nodded. He moved his lips towards her ear as if to whisper something, but just then the theatre was plunged into darkness and a huge cheer lifted the room. So instead, he put his hand on hers and squeezed it. His excitement was contagious, and she felt a rush of pleasure. The Donald Duck cartoon was next and then the Pathé newsreel began, with the usual footage of bombed-out London being rebuilt. Just as the credits started to roll a few jeers rose up from downstairs.

'Sort it out!'

'Bleedin' useless!'

'What's going on?' she asked.

The noise downstairs erupted into boos, catcalls, swearing.

Bebba got up and looked around. A crowd had formed around the balcony railing and started shouting questions down to the people below. That's when she saw it.

A thick, lazy tentacle of fog had twisted right through the cinema and was starting to shroud the bottom of the screen. The jeers increased and, as if in defiant response, the fog swelled rapidly and rose. In a matter of seconds, the whole screen was obscured.

'How on earth did that happen?' shouted Bebba, trying to be heard above the boos and hisses.

'Must be the windows,' said a woman behind them. 'If they let in draughts, they let in fog. Or some idiot left a door open.'

'It happened last week at Drury Lane,' said Peter. 'They

had to cancel the show because you couldn't see the actors.'

He took her arm. 'Put your coat on. It's going to get ugly. We should leave.' She let out a sigh, exasperated that their evening would be cut short.

Just then, a man directly behind him kicked his seat.

'This is a joke!' he yelled. 'A bloody joke!'

A young lad next to him got up and did the same and others joined in. Soon, hundreds of seats vibrated to the thudding of shoes meeting upholstery.

'Quick!' Peter pulled her out and they ran up the gangway towards the red 'exit' sign. They made it downstairs but then a surge of bodies pushed up behind her as everyone rushed towards the ticket booth. Her arm stretched as far as it could. He was moving too fast and just as she thought she might trip, he let go.

'Peter? Peter?'

The crowd swept her up and she was pushed in the opposite direction. People shouted for refunds while others banged the kiosk counter. One man grabbed a bag of popcorn and threw it across the foyer. The shutters rattled down over the ticket booth.

She glanced towards the exit. There was no way of getting out – too many people were in front of her. Just as she was wondering what to do, a lady in front of her tripped and grabbed at the person in front of her and they fell like dominoes. A small space opened up around them as others bent down to help.

Bebba took advantage of the gap and peeled off to one side and pushed through a side door. She found herself in an empty corridor that appeared to twist around the back of the auditorium. Did it snake into one large circle, or was there another exit that led to the street? She started walking, confident that once she found her way out, he'd be there, waiting.

Aquamarine wall lights cast an underwater glow and she set off with purpose, down the dimly lit passageway. But as the seconds turned to minutes and still there was no sign of an exit, her steps grew hesitant. It was impossible to see clearly in the sea-green shadows. It was simply a corridor, she told herself, and nothing like that dream of being lost in a maze with the old man right behind her.

She pulled her coat closer across her chest and ploughed on. She wasn't frightened at all; it was just an absolute bore. She considered retracing her steps but realised she was probably going to come full circle and any moment now she'd be exactly where she started, so decided to press on. Then she could slip out of that door and back into the foyer.

What was that? She quickened her step. Was that a voice? She hurried around the curve of the corridor and felt a rush of relief when she saw him.

'Peter? Peter!'

He was standing against the wall, hand up to his forehead shielding his eyes. Next to him stood two men she'd never seen before.

'Oh, thank good—'

He looked at her, eyes wide, and shook his head violently. Before she realised what was happening the smaller of the men rushed towards her. He grabbed her by the waist and slammed her against the wall, next to Peter.

'What on earth—'

'Shut up!' he said, standing very close. The skin across his jaw was pitted where something had once eaten his face.

'Let go! What are you doing?'

Confusion swept over her. The old man had sent someone after all, and they were here for her at last. He must be watching from somewhere. All that running and he'd finally found her.

She kicked the thug's shins, but he slammed her harder this time. Something sharp – a light switch? – met her shoulder blade and she cried out as the pain seared through her.

'Leave her alone!' shouted Peter as he dived towards her, but the bigger man threw a punch and he buckled, folding in on himself. He slid down and ended up half-sitting against the wall, legs stretched out in front. Bebba looked down, waiting for him to get up and fight. Then she saw that he hadn't been shielding his eyes at all but rubbing a thick red welt that now bloomed across his brow.

The taller man crouched down next to him. 'Don't try that again. I'm sick of you giving us the runaround.'

The relief stormed through her. So, this was about him, not her.

'Peter?' she called. 'Are you all right?'

The tall man reached into his pocket and threw something past her face. The other one snatched it from the air. It had glinted in the half-light, but it wasn't till she felt the blade pressed flat against her cheek that she realised what it was. A wet shiver shot down her spine.

The thug leaned against her, pressing the whole length of his body against hers. Through her thin skirt she could feel him begin to harden.

'Bastard,' she hissed.

He grinned. 'Just helping you stay upright, sweetheart. Wouldn't want you fainting.' He wiggled the blade in front of her face. 'Not while I've got this.'

She spat at him and with the back of his other hand he hit her cheek. She heard Peter scrabble to get up, and then the sound of another punch landing somewhere soft.

'Your girlfriend has more spunk than you,' said the tall one.

'I'm not his girlfriend.'

They both laughed.

'Oooh, that told you!' said the tall one. 'Now—' He pulled Peter up to a standing position. 'As I was saying. Jerry doesn't like it when people don't pay up. He gets cross. And if he gets cross, he'll have to do something.'

'Yeah,' said the shorter one. 'Like kill you.'

'Or worse.'

'That's funny, Jim. Or worse.'

'Shut up, you idiot. Anyway, you've got a week to pay. That's it. All of it. You know where to bring it.'

Peter didn't speak.

The small one put away the cut-throat razor, straightened his coat and motioned to the other one with his head that they should leave. Just before he turned away, he reached out to stroke Bebba's face.

She pulled away and for a moment she thought he might hit her again, but he leaned in close, put out the tip of his tongue and licked the air in front of her face.

'See you again.'

She heard a loud thud, then a crash. She turned and saw that Peter had floored the tall one. He was out cold. Taken by surprise, the smaller man just stood wide-eyed. By the time he sprang into action, Peter had booted his unconscious accomplice several times.

The small one leapt on Peter's back, but Peter was too quick for him. He turned, knocked him to the ground, then bent down and rained three, no four, punches on his head.

'Tell Jerry,' Peter said, punching him again, 'I'm paid up in full. I don't pay interest, understood?'

The only response was a whimper.

'I said understood?' asked Peter.

The small thug tried to sit up, nodded and fell back again. Peter dusted down his new coat, straightened his tie and walked over to Bebba. He put his hand on her cheek and stroked it.

'Are you all right, Beb?' he asked, gently.

'I think so.'

He took her arm as they walked away, and she felt a twinge run right through her; she'd never felt more attracted to a man in her life.

* * *

They were outside now. The fog had lifted a little and the streets had emptied fast. Peter stormed through Covent Garden market, kicking the rotting mess of fruit and veg in his path, while Bebba held his arm and trotted alongside, trying to keep up with him.

'Wait!' she called. 'Peter, will you slow down?'

He stopped abruptly.

'How much?' she asked.

'It's interest – like I said, I'm not paying it.' He continued to walk, slower now.

'Peter.' She grabbed his arm. 'I've just had that creep put a knife to my face, so please answer me.'

'Fifty, okay?' His cockiness had left him now and she could see dark shadows rimming his eyes.

'They won't let it go,' she said. 'I mean, he deserved what he got – they both did – but you've probably made it worse.'

He shrugged. 'Maybe you're right,' he said. 'But I can't get it – not in a week. And there's nobody else to ask.'

She didn't say anything.

'I'll just have to make sure they don't find me,' he said.

'Dina was saying just yesterday how she hoped you'd given up gambling. She worries, you know. About money.'

He furrowed his eyebrows. 'I have given up. It's an old debt. But not a word, all right?'

'It's between the two of you.'

'Anyway,' he said, 'she always worries about money. And she nags. But show me an immigrant who hasn't got money troubles. The difference is, I do something about it.'

Bebba thought of saying something in Dina's defence, and stopped herself. They carried on walking, her arm linked through his. She looked up at him and wondered if he was a liability or an asset. He'd certainly been fast with his fists. She pulled him to a stop.

'Your head looks sore. Is it bleeding?'

He reached up under his hat and touched it, then checked his fingers for blood.

'No. I'll just say I got into a fight or something. It wouldn't be the first time.'

He reset his hat and pulled back his shoulders.

'I'm sorry about that,' he said, indicating her cheek. 'You've got a red mark there. Does it hurt?'

He put out his hand, but she pulled away.

'I'm fine. But we can't *both* go home looking a mess. She'll know something's up. Let's stop somewhere so I can Max Factor it.'

He frowned. 'What?'

'The miracle of make-up, darling,' she said, and linked arms again as they set off.

They walked in silence for a few minutes, then, before they entered a small tearoom near Shaftesbury Avenue, he turned to her.

'Are you used to doing that?'

'Doing what?' she asked.

'Covering up? I mean ... has someone done that to you before?'

She placed her palm flat on the glass door and pushed it open.

'I'll take a black tea. Back in a minute.'

18

'Dina, slow down.'

I pulled him by the hand towards the black railings.

'Come on,' I said. 'It's here.'

A rusted chain was threaded through the gate and on the other side the trees could just be seen in the fading light.

'A park?' he asked. 'I thought I was taking you to Lyons' Corner House for dinner?'

'Oh, you are. Don't worry about that.' I ached to visit the Corner House. They had different rooms, each with its own menu depending on what you felt like eating. My ambition was to try each one.

'But you have to see this first,' I said. 'You've never seen anything like it.'

I pointed to a couple of railings on the far left that had been prised apart.

'You'll fit through,' I said. 'It's easy, look.'

I went first and reached my hand through as he followed. Then he stopped.

'I'm stuck, I'm stuck!'

'No you're not.' I laughed. 'I can see you're not. Come on.'

He laughed and clambered through behind me. Sticky, waist-high weeds grabbed at our coats and legs. Once in, we walked half a dozen steps to the edge of a small woodland. Although it was not yet evening the fog had grasped the city and squeezed the life from it, leaving behind a fairy-tale glow.

'Look,' I said.

There, around a scruffy patch of grass, stood a circle of young saplings, silver limbs raised up like watchful guardians.

I pointed further in. 'Do you see it?'

He didn't at first, but then realised what he was looking at.

'That's spectacular,' he said, gazing up. In the middle stood a cathedral oak, arms raised to the sky.

'Isn't it beautiful?' I said.

'You are,' he said, and leaned in for a kiss, pulling me towards him.

Beneath my feet I could feel the tree's roots. They'd burst up through the ground and had continued to grow, all of them eventually leading to the mammoth tree, gigantic veins feeding a colossal heart.

I leaned my head on the rough wool of his grey coat, breathing deeply. The nap of his lapel, the smell of his cigarettes mixed with vestiges of Old Spice; these were all familiar sensations that flooded my body and made me happy in a way I didn't understand.

'Don't you love it here?' I said. 'And that's not all.'

I led him round to the other side of the tree.

'What about that?'

He let out an astonished laugh.

'Isn't it crazy?' I asked.

The bottom half of the trunk had been whittled away to form a beautiful bench that sat inside the tree itself. It was perfect, as if nature had created it this way. I dashed to the seat and he squeezed in by my side. I let my fingers trace the wood above my head where the interior of the trunk had been polished to a smooth finish.

'We're *inside* the tree,' he said. 'Swallowed whole.'

'What a funny thought.' I looked around in awe. 'Swallowed by a tree. You know it's still alive.'

He reached in front of me and knocked the wood right next to my face.

'See,' I said. 'Half of it has been cut away and yet it still lives.' He rubbed at the wood near my face. 'It's a love seat,' I said. 'That's what the English call it. A seat made for two.'

He stared at me and suddenly I felt shy.

'Though, I'm not sure about that,' I said, elbowing him playfully. 'There's no room for you here.'

He jostled me a bit to play along, then became serious and took my hand. He pulled off my glove, kissed my palm, then kissed me on the mouth. We turned, somewhat awkwardly, trying to hold each other in the tight space.

'What? Why are you laughing?' he asked, bemused. 'I'm trying to make passionate love to you.'

'Sorry, it's just that I keep hitting my head.'

He smiled and rubbed the back of my head. 'Poor pretty head.'

He leaned in and kissed me again, forcefully this time, and the desire coupled with an equal measure of dread corkscrewed through my stomach. Slowly, his hand began to travel down from my shoulder to my breast.

'Don't, not yet.'

He sighed and put up his hands, surrendering.

'Sorry, sorry.' Then he slumped back into the seat. 'It's just that it's difficult keeping my hands off you.'

I smiled, embarrassed and delighted.

'You know it's killing me, don't you?' he said.

'Oh, stop that,' I said, and gave him a gentle nudge. 'I don't believe you for one minute.'

'You have no idea, my love.'

We sat in silence for a while and watched the fog as it twisted through the trees like smoke from an invisible fire.

'I want to,' I said, 'you do *know* that don't you?'

He nodded but didn't speak. I pulled off my other glove and placed it next to the one on my lap, a pair of empty hands on my knees. I curled my fingers round his.

'It's just . . .'

'I know,' he said. 'I'm asking too much of you.'

He pushed his fingers through his hair and let out an exaggerated long sigh. I watched his breath cling in the cold air for a second and then fall away. He avoided my gaze as he spoke, looking into the distance instead.

'I just thought . . . if we were serious about each other. What difference would it make when we did it?'

'I just need some time.'

'Do you feel guilty about all this sneaking around?' he asked. 'Is that it? Is that what's stopping you?'

'God, no!' I laughed. 'Anyway, what else am I meant to do? Take you home and tell Peter about us? That would be a disaster.'

He turned to look at me.

'Not because there's anything wrong with you,' I said, 'he'd be thrilled. But he'd be sending out wedding invitations by the time you'd left.'

'It's all right,' he said, smiling. 'I don't want to make things difficult. I'll wait.'

In that moment, I felt closer to him than I had to anyone, even Yiannis. And his kindness and gentleness meant everything to me. I decided then and there that he was worth it. I told myself that he'd be the first after all. I had no idea what would happen in the future, but right now I didn't care; right now I just wanted to be with him.

'You're funny,' he said. 'Most Cypriot girls would be pushing to get engaged by now . . .'

'Well . . .' I shifted. The wooden seat was starting to dig into my back. 'Getting engaged isn't always the answer. Anyway, we're having a good time, aren't we? Why can't we just see how things go? We're in London, for heaven's sake – it's made for us!'

I couldn't think of anything worse than the pressure of a commitment, and I could tell it wasn't what he wanted either, he was just surprised.

'You know I have some money, right?' He brushed down the sleeves of his coat in mock pride. 'Fancy dresses, nights out . . . you name it.'

'Well you can start by taking me for that meal. I'm starving.'

He took my hand. 'I'll buy you all the meals you want,' he said.

'You'll live to regret saying that—'

'Do you ever stop joking?' he asked. 'Seriously, though – I just want to be close to you.'

'I know.' I pressed my lips together but said nothing.

'But if,' he began, 'if it's because I'm a bit older, or because you don't feel the same way, then just tell—'

I leaned across and put my lips full on his, stopping the words from coming out.

'Soon,' I said as I pulled away. 'I promise.' Then I blurted: 'I'm sorry,' and immediately despised myself for apologising.

Oh, I wished it didn't matter but it did; I'd brought more of Cyprus with me than I'd thought. It had to be the right moment. I'd never been with anyone and I'm sure he'd guessed as much. I bet Bebba didn't falter over moments like this; I could just tell that she'd done it.

He reached out, pushed back my hair and brought my face towards his. He kissed me on the mouth.

'I'm falling in love with you,' he said. 'I'll be in love with you tomorrow and the day after that. So I can wait.' Then he kissed me with such a fierceness that I felt I would drown. It felt both reckless and comforting to be craved like this.

I slid onto his lap facing him and returned his kiss with urgency.

19

I balanced the bar of Lux on top of my towel and looked at Bebba, who was hugging her wash bag and towel to her chest. We'd been waiting for twenty minutes, and I shivered as the damp breeze crept under my collar and chilled my bones.

'Have you got your two shillings?' she asked. 'And a change of clothes?'

I stopped myself rolling my eyes.

'Of course.' I indicated the bag on my shoulder. She was annoying me more frequently these days, the way she always assumed she knew the ropes and I knew nothing. And I was finding it harder to hide my feelings, which made me feel worse. I had to admit that, thanks to her, my life had perked up considerably in the past couple of months.

A light drizzle fell on us but at least the fog had cleared. Looking up at the monstrous red-brick building I read the name carved in fancy stone letters across its face: Kentish Town Public Baths. Scores of steamed-up windows, like cataract-clouded eyes, glared down at me. She'd insisted these were much nicer than the Soho baths I visited weekly. They were certainly far grander, that was for sure. Two long queues – one for men, one for women – coiled into separate doorways.

'Dina?' Bebba gave me a quizzical look. She was wearing her sky-blue chiffon headscarf, the same one she'd worn the day we met. 'Is there something wrong? Between us?'

I shook my head.

She leaned into my face and frowned.

'You've been off with me all day. What is it?'

I edged forwards a few inches. A pigtailed girl in front of us dropped her towel and her mother picked it up, shoved it back in her arms and gave her a clip around the ear. The child started to wail. Bebba moved a little closer so she could be heard.

'Is it the flat?' she asked.

I didn't respond.

'I knew it! It's too small, isn't it, and I'm in the way.' Her eyes were suddenly shiny. Was she tearing up? Perhaps it was the wind.

'It's nothing of the sort,' I said.

She shifted her towel. 'I'm not sure I believe you. It is awfully cramped. I just don't really want to be by myself.'

I reached out and put a reassuring hand on her arm.

'No, it's fine. Honestly.'

She laughed softly. 'You're a terrible liar, darling. But I won't forget how kind you've been. You and Peter, taking me in.'

Did she want me to thank her again for paying such a large share of the rent?

The child in front of us was snivelling now and, although she'd been handed a handkerchief, preferred her mother's absorbent tweed cuff. Bebba screwed up her nose at the sight.

'Anyway,' I said. 'It is a bit cramped, but it's so much nicer than the other place. It's not that at all.'

I waited for her to probe but she didn't. I may as well give it a try.

'It's Peter,' I said.

'Really? Have you argued? You seemed fine this morning.'

'No. It's just . . . I think he's gambling again.'

The woman pushed her daughter along and moved up. We nudged behind her. Bebba looked over her shoulder then, after what seemed like ages, turned towards me.

'What makes you say that?'

'So, he is!' I grasped her arm. 'I bloody knew it! He'll ruin us.'

'No,' she said, gently pulling her arm away. 'I didn't say that.'

'But you *do* know something, don't you? About Peter.'

She looked around uneasily.

'Oh, come on, you can tell me. I have a right to know and I won't say it came from you.'

She swapped her towel from one arm to the other but said nothing. She was infuriating at times.

'I know he talks to you,' I continued. 'He tells you things he wouldn't tell me. I *know* he does.'

'It's only natural,' she said, 'now that I'm at Mackenzie's.'

I waited a little. Whose friend was she anyway?

'So . . . what do you talk about . . .?' As soon as I said it, I cringed.

'Don't pry.' She pushed a strand of her hair back under her headscarf. 'It doesn't suit you.'

'But has he said anything about it?' I couldn't stop now. 'The gambling? It's like a sickness with him.'

'Dina, please. This isn't fair.'

'Yes it is. We're friends, aren't we? Come on. You're *my* friend, not his. I met you first.'

She jerked a little, as if I'd kicked her, and I knew I'd made a mistake. She loathed anyone needing her, making her feel hemmed in. That was the thing I'd realised about Bebba. She just wanted you to adore her, and once you did, she pulled away. She'd never say a thing now. I crossed my arms.

'Look, forget it. Forget I said anything. Keep your secrets.'

I'd been so sure she'd admit it, but we were almost at the entrance now and I was none the wiser. When would I have a chance to speak to her alone again? He was her constant shadow.

'It's fairly obvious anyway,' I said. 'That new coat of his, a bottle of beer the other day, packets of crisps yesterday—'

'Crisps!' she mocked. 'Hardly a luxury.'

'Well, we don't all have your money, or the right accent or lovely clothes.'

'What do you mean?'

'I'm just saying it was only a few weeks ago we almost lost our home and I could barely buy bread. Things might be better now but it can all go in an instant, you know that. Why do you think I'm so worried about his gambling all the time?' There was a silence. 'Perhaps you've never had to worry about money.'

She'd never understand. Not what it was really like to feel scared about losing what little we had. We edged towards the ticket booth in silence, I paid my two shillings and pushed through the turnstile. Did she really value her friendship with him more than ours?

'Anyway, whether he admits it or not,' I said, over my shoulder, 'I know he's back to his old ways. That's why that man's been watching him.'

She turned. 'A man?' She frantically looked all around. 'Where?'

'Not here, silly! A man I've seen hanging around near the flat. He walks up and down. Peter probably owes him.'

'Well, what does he look like, this man?'

I shrugged. 'Just a man.'

'Is he old?'

'I've only seen him from the window.'

'Is he Greek?'

I shrugged. 'How would I know? He might be. As I said, I've only seen him from the window.'

A large woman wrapped in a floral housecoat stood in front of us.

'Number three is ready, miss.' She pointed to a cubicle at

the far end with her mop. 'And number four for your friend.'

Bebba and I separated as we entered the adjacent rooms. I shed my clothes and sank into the water.

She'd been right about this place. These slipper baths were deep, and the pale-green tiling on the walls was scrubbed clean. Much nicer than Marshall Street. The gas lamp flickered on the wall and I closed my eyes against the steam. Voices rose over cubicle doors, chatting and calling out for 'more hot, please'.

I lay there thinking about what had just happened. Something was wrong. Not just Peter's gambling, something else.

There'd been no man; I'd lied. I thought if I bluffed then maybe she'd admit to what she knew. But she'd admitted nothing.

All she'd done was turn completely white, as if every last drop of blood had drained away.

*   *   *

The loud knock above her head made Bebba jump.

'Time please! Finish up ladies!'

She was on the floor, her back against the door with her legs pulled up. Her skirt felt heavy and wet and her legs were clammy. She must have been crouched in a puddle. It had to be the old man or someone working for him.

Slowly, she pushed herself up and peeled off her clothes. There was no time for a bath now, she'd just have to get changed.

But perhaps it wasn't him at all, she told herself. Perhaps it was like Dina said, just another thug trying to squeeze money out of Peter. But why not just come up and collect? Why hang around? The old man would wait. He'd waited this long already.

The steam had evaporated, and she now stood damp and naked, her towel on the floor. She must have dropped it after locking the door. Picking it up, her hands searched for a dry section. There was one corner that wasn't soaking, so she used it to pat herself dry. Then she pulled her clean clothes out of her bag. Thankfully, they were still dry, and she dressed herself quickly.

Think now, think. She hadn't dragged the suitcase from Cyprus to lose everything in a panic.

She had two choices: do nothing or run. Where would she go? And what if he caught her when she was alone? No, stay, sit it out. Peter would look after her. She'd have to come up with a story, though. Or perhaps even tell him the truth soon. But not yet.

Stick with him, that's what she'd do. Carry on catching the bus every day to that factory full of dead-eyed women, cutting cottons, checking buttons. Never be away from him. If something happened, he'd be there, ready with his fists.

Shoving her damp clothes and towel into her bag, she took a breath before reaching for the door.

He was smitten by her, he'd protect her. As long as he felt there was something in it for him, which was easily done.

She'd relied on worse men than him, so it really wasn't such a big price to pay.

20

A few days later, I woke to an eerie silence. I crept out of bed and peered out of the window to see that everything had been draped in a cloak of snow. The city lay before me, transformed into a sugared wedding cake. I'd never stepped on snow before – had only ever seen it on the Troodos mountaintops. I had to get out there while it was still fresh and new. I thought about waking Bebba, but she hated early mornings and would probably think me childish. Peter had been out late and wouldn't be up for hours.

I dressed, pulled on the sheepskin-lined ankle boots that she'd helped me choose and left the flat. Shopkeepers were pulling back grilles and rolling down awnings, preparing for the day's trade. As I walked the length of Charlotte Street, the glinting snow squeaked under my feet. I turned to look at my footsteps and could see them trace right back down the road. At times, I'd felt I could lose myself in the fog, but here in the snow I could see who I was.

I cut through Soho Square, where the grass was covered in a sheet of white, and wandered down Rupert Street for old times' sake. All the nightclubs were closed, but I could hear the muffled sounds of metal shutters coming from somewhere. I walked around the corner and saw there was a lorry parked up, its back open, with rolls of fabric stacked high. A man was carrying the long heavy tubes through a small door that was propped open by a crate. It was a delivery for the Pelican.

Before I could think twice, I walked inside. The corridor was badly lit and it was freezing.

'Not much left.' It was a man's voice coming from the cutting room.

From the top of the stairs I could see a soft light in the workroom below. I started to walk down slowly, and countless memories flooded back as the smell of machine oil hit my nostrils. A clothes rail gradually came into view with nothing on it but two pearl-coloured leotards. I shouldn't be here. But I had to see them. I stepped down quietly till I was standing in front of them, took off my gloves and carefully touched one. The material was exquisite, so thin it was practically see-through except for the sequins that had been dusted here and there in crucial spots for modesty's sake. Two black satin bow ties hung on each leotard, ready to be tied in place. Those Wayward Twins always had the best outfits.

'Who's there?'

I peered around the corner.

'Dina?'

'Madame Sylvie? Sorry – I was passing and . . .'

She was standing in a corner, a red chiffon blouse in her hands, her glasses halfway down her nose. Across her shoulders she'd thrown a fern-coloured crocheted shawl and a jade oval pendant hung just below her throat.

'Hello, I saw the door open and . . .'

'Come in, *entrez*.' She looked puzzled rather than cross. I glanced around the workroom; the covered machines sat like sleeping cats. In a few hours this place would be full of the whirr of metal and the chatter of the seamstresses.

'What are you doing here?' She motioned to me to sit and I did, and she did too.

'I was passing, and I heard the lorry,' I said. 'I don't know, I just couldn't help but come in.'

She smiled as if she understood.

'Are you here to ask for your job back?' she asked. I sat forwards and realised I was, but she gave a quick shake of her head. 'I'm sorry, I can't, *chère amie*.'

I felt the smart of the dismissal all over again, made worse by the fact that I was here now, in the very place I'd been so happy.

She folded the delicate blouse she'd been holding and put it to one side, then reached across to my hand. 'It's not my decision – if it were, I'd take you back today. You're by far the best seamstress I've had in years. Billy was a fool to dismiss you – you can't imagine how we fell out over it – but he owns half of this place and without him I'd be in trouble.'

I nodded. 'It's all right. I understand.' How did an idiot like Billy end up with a place as wonderful as this? 'I'm sorry about my brother.' I made to get up. 'I just thought it was worth asking – you know. Take a chance.'

'Of course,' she said. 'It's always worth taking a chance.'

'If you hear of anything else?'

'Yes, yes – give me your details.'

She took a small black address book from her handbag and scribbled down the phone number that I gave her for the grocer's a few doors down. Then she took a quick glance at the stairs. She wanted to say something, but I could see she wasn't sure.

Then she whispered, 'I might be starting a new venture, on my own.'

'Really?' So, it was true. Bebba had said as much.

'Yes, a club – like this but with real singers and more high-class.'

'That sounds wonderful. What will the clothes be like?'

'More a couture evening gown look,' she said, 'rather than revue bar. And certainly no cowgirls. But keep it to yourself.'

Pink spots had blossomed high on her cheeks.

'I'm just securing the money,' she continued. 'I'll need someone I can rely on, someone excellent. *Qu'en penses-tu?*'

'Sorry?'

'What do you say? Are you interested?'

'Well, yes – yes I'd love that.'

She sat back and smiled. 'Well, I'm so pleased. Here.' She opened a thin silver case from her bag, took out a card and passed it to me. On it was printed her name, a drawing of a reel of thread with a needle stuck in it and her telephone number. 'What is it now? November? Call me in a month or so,' she said. 'I should know by then. What about your brother?'

'Don't worry, I'll figure something out.' I had no idea how. But I wouldn't let him ruin this again. 'Thank you.'

I stood and she gave me a hug. As I hugged her back, I caught a sharp hint of lemons in her hair and felt a rush of warmth towards her.

We said our goodbyes and I was about to leave.

'Oh, by the way, Dina.'

'Yes?'

'Whatever happened to that blonde?'

'Sorry?'

'Short hair, *très belle* – Betty?'

'You mean Bebba?'

She nodded.

'Well she—' I was about to say that we were living together when she interrupted.

'Just upped and left without a word.'

My mouth went dry. What did she mean? She'd been fired, hadn't she?

'Billy was particularly cross,' she continued, 'seeing as he'd got her the job as a favour.'

'*Sorry?*'

'*Oui.* They were good friends – he was adamant I employ

her. Said she knew nobody, and we simply had to help. I imagine he thought he had a chance with her . . .'

I didn't say anything.

'And, well, judging by how furious he was when she left, I don't think she kept her side of the bargain.'

'Bebba and *Billy* – but why would she . . .?'

She gave a shrug. 'Perhaps she thought he'd splash his money about. I've been partners with the man for years and I could have told her she was wasting her time.'

I couldn't believe what I'd just heard. What about that night we met, when I'd saved her from him?

'You *did* get your wages, didn't you? She collected them for you. *Dina?*' She touched my hand. 'The money – did you get it?'

'What? Yes, yes she brought it round.'

'Well that's good, because as I say that was the last we saw of her.' She put her hand to her throat, adjusted the jade pendant, then pushed her shoulders back a little.

It was too late to say we'd become friends. And why would I tell her now? She might decide not to offer me the job after all.

'Anyway, you'd better go,' she said, 'because the man himself is due any minute and he'll explode if he finds you here. It was lovely seeing you.' She reached across and hugged me. '*Au revoir.* And don't forget – December, yes?'

I nodded and walked up the stairs. My brain was a jumble of confused thoughts. Sewing again, especially with Madame S, was all I really wanted, but instead of feeling excited I was unnerved. What she'd said about Bebba had rattled me. As I crunched my way to Lina Stores, I turned it all over in my mind. Why would Bebba say she'd been fired if she hadn't? Maybe she'd had enough and was trying to make me feel better about losing my job? And had she *really* been friends with Billy? Or perhaps he'd been trying to get close to her

– she'd said he was all hands, remember? – and she'd rejected him. Yes, maybe he *had* fired her but didn't want to tell Madame Sylvie. That must be it.

I bought bread and milk and then walked the short distance to Old Compton Street, where I bought her *Vema* newspaper from Moroni's. Just a few doors away was Valerie's, and I stopped to peer inside. A few early-risers were out in this weather, but mostly it was empty. He wouldn't be here today; he'd already told me he'd be busy with work for the next day or two. I contemplated going in for a tea, but she'd be awake soon and there was nothing for breakfast. I'd ask her what had happened at the Pelican. If Peter was still asleep, she might tell me the truth.

Back at the flat, I slotted my key into the communal door and strains of gentle jazz floated across the hall. Peter was the only one in the building with a wireless.

Once inside, the music seemed so much louder. It was only just after eight and she wouldn't thank him if he woke her this early. I dropped the shopping onto the table and glanced through my room to hers. Thankfully, she was still asleep because her door was closed. He was so inconsiderate sometimes. The music swelled to a crescendo. *Banayía mou*, Mary mother of God.

I stood outside his room and, just as I put my hand up to knock, the song ended. Above the chatter of the radio presenter's voice I could hear Peter's urgent tone. He was speaking to someone, repeating something again and again, but I couldn't make it out. I put my ear to the door. I listened again, then – oh! I jumped back: a single groan, long and low, like an animal. My hand shot to my mouth as I realised what I'd heard.

I ran to my room and slammed the door. *Why are you crying, you stupid girl?* He'd never brought anyone home before. I was mortified but furious, too.

How dare he flaunt it? I knew he was no saint – all those late-night returns weren't 'overtime', that was for sure. He'd always been so strict with me and now here he was, having sex in the next room while I couldn't so much as look at a man in his presence.

At least he hadn't woken Bebba. I turned my head towards her room and frowned. I hadn't noticed before, but her door wasn't quite shut.

My eyes dropped down and there, at the bottom of her door, lay a golden pool. It was her silk dressing gown. As I walked across the room to pick it up, the door creaked open to reveal just a slice of her bedroom. I pushed it a little, then a little more, until the whole room was exposed.

Her bedclothes were tangled, empty, and on the floor next to the bed were her lilac marabou slippers. One of them had been knocked over.

A laugh came from his room and I heard him shush her. They didn't even care that I knew. I let her dressing gown slip through my fingers onto the floor.

Grabbing my handbag, coat still on, I made for the door. I didn't want to confront them. What would I say? There was only one person I wanted to see, and he'd be working. No, I'd spend the day out alone. I turned back to the shopping that I'd left on the table and took her newspaper. Closing the door behind me, I stepped onto the street, imagining what they would do when they saw I'd returned and left again. Let them feel embarrassed. I shouldn't be the one to feel awkward, and yet I did. It was as if I'd been lifted and shaken to pieces. I set my shoulders back and walked the way I'd come, towards Soho and the streets I knew. The place that would never let me down. My head was full of the conversations we might have next time I saw them. Perhaps I'd say nothing and see what happened. The embarrassment waned and now anger crackled through me. They knew I'd heard. I was sure.

There were voices ahead and I looked up to see two men standing in a doorway, heads together, smoking. As I walked past one of them made a loud kissing noise. He was dressed in a tuxedo, the bow tie unfastened, and he wore red lipstick. My mouth must have fallen open in shock.

The other one laughed and grabbed his friend's arm.

'Oh, poor love! Look at her!' he shrieked. 'She's never seen a queer before.'

The laughter continued and they tumbled through the door. Sometimes I felt so stupid, so young. Everyone could be whoever they wanted to be here. Why not me?

I looked up and found myself outside Valerie's again. It was only half full and I slid into a corner table and ordered a tea and some toast.

'No Romeo today then?' asked the waitress, placing my cup and teapot in front of me. It was Irene, the waitress who'd served me last time.

'No,' I said, 'on my own today.'

'Best company there is, if you ask me,' she said, and turned away to serve someone else.

A minute later she returned with the toast. She'd given me an extra square of butter on the side and I felt my eyes fill. I blinked back the tears, picked up the knife and pushed it with some force into the dry bread.

A few weeks ago, I would have sworn that Bebba and I were the best of friends. Now things would never be the same. How could she choose *Peter*? Peter, who we'd laughed about and who she'd given me advice on how to handle. I felt stupid for not realising this would happen, and completely undone by her betrayal. She'd tugged at the stitching of our friendship and ripped it beyond repair. I had to get away from them both.

I laid her newspaper flat on the table and started reading, letting butter drip from the toast without caring.

21

Through the tiny window of the bathroom on the landing, Bebba could see a small square of ink-black night sky. She stood at the sink, soaping her hands. A quick glance over her shoulder and she turned back and continued to scrub at her fingers. The grime had lodged in her knuckles and, she suspected, under her painted nails. What a nuisance. She'd have to take it all off and reapply in the morning.

'What are you doing up here?'

She jumped, and water ran down her arms to her elbows.

'God, Dina, you startled me.'

The girl looked sleep-drunk, and there was a crease along her cheek where the bedclothes had left their mark.

'What are you doing?' she repeated. 'Why didn't you put the light on?'

'I didn't want to wake you,' said Bebba. Could she do nothing without being watched?

Dina came and stood next to her, peered at the swirls of dirty suds in the cracked sink, then looked at her.

'You've been out in the *garden*?' she asked. God, she was like a child at times, always stating the obvious.

Bebba rinsed her hands and shook them, though they were far from clean.

'But it's night-time,' she said.

'I'm well aware of that,' said Bebba. 'No law against it, is there?' She took a deep breath and edged out a smile. 'Helps me relax.'

Dina gave a snort.

'Gardening in the dark helps you relax?'

Bebba shrugged and wiped her hands on a hand towel, saw she'd left a grey smudge and folded it over so only the clean side showed.

'The mint and the coriander are coming along really well,' she said, as if that explained everything. 'You'll thank me when we can start using them.'

Dina stared at her as if she were mad.

'Anyway, I'm off to bed,' said Bebba. 'It's late. *Kalinihta.*'

She hung the towel on the side of the sink and returned to her bedroom, aware that Dina's gaze was boring into her back.

22

I paused outside the flat and took a deep breath, excitement and fear running through me.

'Come on Dina.' He started kissing the back of my neck. 'Let's get inside.' He pulled me towards him, his arms circled around my waist, then started tickling my ribs.

'Stop it!' I squirmed. 'I'm trying to find the key.' I knew the flat was empty, but nerves sparked through my fingers as I rummaged in my bag. 'What if someone sees us?'

'I bet there's no one in the whole building.'

I slid the key in the door and pushed it open. I'd seen them both leave for work that morning but still made him wait on the landing while I peeked into each room.

'All clear.'

He glanced around the living room and nodded.

'This isn't so bad.' He peered through the doors to the other rooms. 'It's big, isn't it?'

'It's all right. It feels cramped when we're all here, but upstairs was a dump.'

I slipped off my coat and before I had a chance to turn around, he'd come up behind me and pulled me onto him, his hands hanging over my belly. Every muscle tightened, and I tried not to pull away. This was it. He crossed his hands and slid them down, so they rested on my hipbones. I could feel my petticoat rising a little under my skirt.

'Can we slow down?' My voice sounded high. 'How about a drink? Do you want a cup of tea first?'

He laughed softly and turned me round to face him.

'You're turning into an *Englésa*,' he teased. 'Offering tea.'

I didn't say anything and suddenly felt too shy to look him in the eyes, so I stared at his ear instead.

'Listen,' he said, as if reading my mind. 'It'll be lovely.' He pecked me lightly, a pitter-patter of kisses across one cheekbone then the same along the other. 'I promise.'

'I know.' Then I smiled. 'I know – it's just, well, you know.' I wasn't going to spell it out.

My ears pounded with the whoosh of my blood as everything converged on this moment: the meetings, the kisses, the secrets. It's what I wanted. After that day in the park, I knew it wouldn't be long till we found ourselves here.

As he kissed my lips, he gently pushed his tongue inside my mouth, then nipped my lips with his teeth. Something fluttered deep inside.

'You know I'll take care of you, don't you?'

I nodded. 'You've got the thing?'

He tapped his pocket. 'Don't worry.'

The only sound I could hear was the ticking of the clock on the mantelpiece. This room that was never silent, with its gurgling pipes and scurrying mice under the floorboards, was now holding its breath.

'We'll be close at last,' he said. 'And, you know, we don't have to do anything that—'

'Can we just get on with it?' I smiled. 'You're making me anxious.'

'Sorry, sorry.'

And so he took over, gently at first, then less so. He slipped off my blouse, unbuttoned my skirt and pulled my petticoat over my head. I started to fumble with his shirt buttons, but he gently pushed my hand away.

'Not yet,' he said.

He nudged down my brassiere strap and flicked open the

clasp at the back. I dug my elbows into my sides to stop it falling off.

'Let me undress you,' he said. 'I want to see you.'

'But ... what about you ... aren't you taking your clothes off?'

He smiled. I felt like a foolish girl, standing there in my girdle and stockings while he was still dressed in trousers, shirt and tie. Gently, he pulled my arms away from my body and my brassiere fell to the floor, but he kept his eyes on my face.

'There's plenty of time for that. Is that your room?'

I nodded. He picked me up and walked towards my bed, closing the door behind us.

*   *   *

Coming home from school, clouds of dirt puffed into the air as I scuffed my shoes along the track. I'd outgrown my sandals and every few steps the heel of my foot touched the bone-dry earth beneath.

Demi, the baker's daughter, had been babbling for ages. She'd started walking home with me at the end of each day. We both knew it was because she liked Peter though neither of us said so. If she was lucky my father would invite her to stay for a glass of triantáfyllo. *She sucked the milky rose cordial through a twisty straw, making it last for half an hour, sometimes longer.*

She hugged her tattered mythology book to her chest and skipped along backwards so she could face me, long ponytail swinging in the air.

'I bet you don't know this, Dina,' she said, eyes widened. 'If you do it before you're married, you bleed for days.'

'That can't be true ...'

She nodded, violently. 'It is, it is!'

I sped past her.

'Dina Demetriou, it is true, too!' she shouted.

She was chasing me now, trotting behind me.

'*There was a girl my cousin knew,' she continued.'From Lapithos. She wasn't married when she did it and guess what?*'

I wanted to hit her. Punch her in the gut and watch as she doubled over onto the dry red dust.

'*I said guess—*'

I stopped dead.

'*What? If you're going to tell me just tell me!*'

Her mouth tightened and she scrunched that silly turned-up nose of hers.

'*I'll tell you all right.' She spat out the words like bullets. 'She wasn't married, and she bled for days and days and days ... and then she died.*'

'*You liar!' I shook my head and picked up my pace again.*

'*It's true!' she shouted. 'And that wasn't even the worst part.*'

And just as I was about to turn and tell her how stupid she was because surely nothing could be worse than bleeding to death, she ran down the path and shouted, 'The worst part was that everybody knew!'

*   *   *

I could tell from his breathing that he was asleep. I put my hand between my legs but couldn't feel anything wet. I didn't think I'd bled a lot, hardly anything at all. But it had stung for a moment, like soap pushed into a cut, and I hadn't been ready for that.

I must have gasped because he'd pulled back and looked at me and said, 'It's okay'. Or perhaps he'd asked, 'Are you okay?' I wasn't sure, so I'd pretended not to hear. When he'd finished, he rolled off me and I waited a little before I leaned up on my elbow.

'Was that all right?' I'd asked.

He'd laughed. 'Of course! You did fine. And next time you'll enjoy it more.'

I hoped so. Ever since I was a little girl, I'd been told that lying down with a man outside of marriage was an *amartia*, a sin of the gravest kind. But I was still here, and the walls hadn't crumbled down on top of us, the bed hadn't cracked in two. I felt almost the same as I had an hour ago, when I'd slipped the key in the lock, let him in to the flat and he'd taken my clothes off. Perhaps I was more myself now than I'd been before.

I leaned across to kiss him, but he turned over in his sleep. I looked at his shoulder blades now. They were covered with the finest black down, almost invisible. The only other man I'd seen up close was Peter, and he hardly had any hair on him at all. On his upper arm was a long scar and I wondered what had happened. I must remember to ask him.

They'd be home in a couple of hours. I had to get him out, pick up my clothes. Should I change my sheets? We always went to the laundry on Saturdays. I'd wait till then.

He'd said I'd enjoy it more next time. Had I enjoyed it? I hadn't expected to, but I hadn't disliked it either. It wasn't as frightening or bloody as I'd feared. I'd simply wanted it over and done with, so that the next time and all the times after would never be the first again.

He'd kept thanking me when I'd agreed to it, and now I'd taken that step I was relieved. We'd made love – I could say it to myself now, we'd made love – and this afternoon was almost over. And he'd been right, I *had* felt closer to him. And really it had been fine. I'd wanted it too. I chose the day and he'd suggested coming here. Easier, he'd said. Perhaps his flat was worse than this place, and he didn't want me to see. He was proud, quite old-fashioned really.

A wave of loneliness lapped over me. Was it normal to feel this lost immediately afterwards? I stared at his back. He was snoring gently, and I put my hand on his hip, but he pulled away and clamped the blanket under his arm. Rolling onto my back I looked up at the ceiling. There was a crack that ran diagonally from the top right corner of my room across to the middle, where the dusty glass lampshade, an amber honeycomb hexagon, hung from copper chains. I'd always loved that lampshade and the way the light hit the edges, reflecting onto the ceiling, filling the room with a whisky light. How had I never noticed the crack before?

23

All day at work, Bebba had been stifling yawns. She'd hardly slept since Dina had mentioned the man watching the flat. It didn't make sense; if the old man had come all the way from Cyprus, why hadn't he approached her by now? It probably wasn't him. She'd tell the others that she was coming down with something and skip dinner. All she wanted to do was kick off her shoes, close her bedroom door and sleep.

As she pushed open the front door, she sensed that something was different. Then she saw a trail of dark, shiny beads on the hall linoleum that zigzagged from the threshold of the flat to the bathroom. Was that blood?

'There you are!' It was Peter, ashen-faced.

Behind him, Dina had just stepped out of the bathroom, her hand wrapped in a checked tea towel. Down the length of her arm ran a rusty smear and the skin around her eyes was as puffy and pink as a baby rabbit's.

'Darling! What is it?'

Dina held her hand up slightly up in front of her, so the blood wouldn't make more mess.

'What happened?'

Peter embraced his sister, who was looking furious rather than upset.

'She cut herself,' he said, 'trying to tidy up. It's pretty bad. Prepare yourself.'

'Let me see,' said Bebba, making a move to look at her hand.

'No,' he said. 'I mean the flat is bad. Didn't you *see*? We've been burgled.'

A thousand ants on a slow march prickled across her skin. It was happening; he was here. She turned to look at the door. The cheap wooden frame had been ripped through like paper, and a frenzied forest of splinters had burst from it. The door hung from one hinge now, threatening to fall at any moment.

'Oh!' She couldn't find any other words as her mind whirred.

He was a sinewy old man, with a strength that belied his years, but he couldn't have done this himself. He'd brought along some muscle.

'I can't see what they've taken,' continued Peter, as they stood outside, 'but it's a bloody mess.'

Using her wrapped hand, Dina pushed the door to one side, and they all walked in.

'Did anyone see him? Them?' Bebba asked. 'How did they get in?'

Dina spoke for the first time, her voice sharp: 'I've asked the people upstairs a hundred times not to leave the front door open, but do they listen? I found it like this when I got back.'

Bebba's throat was parched. She took a few breaths and slowly looked around the room. A fury of clothes gesticulated: hollow sleeves and trouser legs, emptied-out corpses. An overturned chair, a photo frame on the floor, smashed – the siblings as children.

She stepped over the shards.

'What about in there?' she asked, pointing to Dina's bedroom. Inside she could see a similar mess of clothes, cosmetics on the floor, an old Oxo tin emptied out – cotton reels everywhere, tissue paper from a paper pattern strewn around – the sheets pulled off the bed.

'The same. Yours is probably the worst. They've ripped some clothes and sheets. Broken a few things.'

Bebba walked to the door that led to the garden. They always kept the key in the lock on the inside but when she tried the handle it swung open.

'What? They've been out there, too?' asked Peter.

She stepped onto the stone step. The half-fallen wall seemed the same, as did the splintering shed. The old vegetable patch looked like it might have been disturbed but it was difficult to tell. The pot of mint had been knocked over. It could have been a cat.

'What is it?' asked Peter.

'Nothing – I just wondered if this is how they left – over the fence.'

She came back, locking the door behind her.

'Doesn't look like anyone's been out there,' she said. 'We probably just forgot to lock it.'

'You're the only one who goes outside,' said Peter. 'Do you remember locking it?'

She shrugged. 'I'm not sure, but they obviously came in through the front.'

She watched as Dina unwrapped the towel, wrapped it tighter and walked to the door. 'The grocer's shut now so I'll go to the pub. They have a phone we can use.'

Bebba reached out as if to stop her, holding her good arm. 'What for?'

'To call the police of course.'

'No!' Peter said. 'No police. I don't want them snooping round here.'

'He's right, darling,' she said. 'It'll be an awful waste of time, and they won't be able to do anything.'

Dina stared at her as if she were mad.

'Are you serious? I mean, we have to. Just look at it.'

'No,' said Peter. 'I don't want the police meddling in my affairs.'

Bebba took a cigarette out of her bag and lit up, hoping that would be the end of it.

'Peter, think about it,' said Dina, tugging at his sleeve. 'Why should these, these . . . bastards . . . get away with it?'

She'd never heard her swear before.

'Even if you report it, they won't find them,' she offered. 'They never do. They probably did it hours ago – they'll be miles away by now.'

'Bebba's right,' said Peter. 'Come on, let's just clear up, okay?' He started to push the glass to one side with his foot. 'The police aren't for people like us.'

Bebba saw her give him a long look full of contempt.

Finally, Dina said, 'I'm going,' and made a start for the door.

He ran and stood in front of her. 'I forbid you to report it,' he said. Then, in a much quieter voice, realising how ridiculous he sounded. 'No police.'

Dina practically spat out the words: 'Well, *there's* a surprise.'

'What do you mean?'

'My law-abiding, everything-by-the-book brother.'

'Shut up, Dina.'

'You don't want the police because you know who did it.'

'That's ridiculous.'

'And *you*,' she said, turning on Bebba, 'you're just as bad. Backing him up.'

What had got into her?

'Me? Now hold on—'

'Oh, spare me the speech, Bebba. You didn't even seem surprised. You know more than you're letting on. You both do.'

Peter gave an incredulous laugh. 'I've no idea what you're talking about. You live in a fantasy land.'

Dina pointed at him with her injured hand.

'It's one of your gambling buddies, isn't it?' she said, jabbing him. The tea towel around her hand slowly began to unravel in his face.

'Stop it, Dina!'

She jabbed him again. Bebba had never seen her behave so aggressively.

'Someone you owe.' Jab. 'Looking for money.' Jab. He raised his hand above her head.

'Oh, very nice,' laughed Dina. 'You're going to hit me? Show me that you're the man of the house?'

'You're talking rubbish, *gori*,' said Peter, letting his hand fall. 'That's not how they operate. And anyway, I paid them off days ago.'

'How though?' she asked. 'By borrowing from someone else? I bet you don't just owe one person, do you? How many people are after you? Do you even *know*?'

He didn't answer. Perhaps he was trying to add it up in his head.

Dina continued: 'You're getting in deeper and deeper, Peter, and one day there'll be no saving you.'

She unwound the tea towel and let it fall to the floor. Her hand had stopped bleeding but there was a deep, jagged cut across her palm.

'It's *just a burglary*,' he said. 'It's London. Things like this happen. It's just bad luck.'

She stood by the door and turned to face him. 'There are six flats in this building. Why did they only come to ours?'

'For heaven's sake, Dina. Think,' she said. 'Perhaps because we're on the ground floor? And they didn't want to risk going upstairs?'

'Why did they only take – why didn't they take anything they could sell? They left your jewellery and your good lighter, and, Peter, they didn't take your old watch.'

'Maybe they got scared and ran off?' he said.

'Or maybe it's a warning,' said Dina. 'Telling you to pay up or else.'

Using just her good hand, she made a show of struggling to button up her coat, then grabbed her bag.

'Where are you going?' asked Bebba.

'Well not to the police station. You're right, there's no point. *He'd* raise more suspicions than any burglar. And that's before they even start on you.'

Bebba took another drag of her cigarette, then picked up an overturned ashtray from the floor and stubbed it out, even though it was only half spent.

'I don't know what you mean,' she said.

'Look at you,' said Dina. 'You're scared, but you're not surprised. You're hiding something – both of you. I'm going to the hospital.'

She turned and started to walk away, then called: 'You can tidy up.'

The house shook with her exit. Two seconds later, the door came away from its hinge and fell, narrowly missing Peter.

24

The following day, at Mackenzie's, Bebba sat alone. Her station was set apart from most of the machinists, between two large crates. To the right were the blouses she'd finished, to her left the ones that were still to be done. Once she'd snipped off any loose threads and checked them, the garments were bundled, bagged and sent off in thundering lorries. Just as the bottom of the crate reappeared, another pile would be hurled on top.

The air was laced with the tang of hot metal and grease, and every few seconds, steam puffed up from the presser's irons. The constant whirring of the motors filled her ears, but what she hated more was the incessant chatter and laughter from the other women, a cacophony of Maltese, Greek and Punjabi, with a dash of broken English in thick accents.

Peter had often talked about getting her a job here, so she'd finally agreed, and he'd seemed thrilled to be able to do this for her. He said it was his way to repay her for getting them the bigger flat. The pace was relentless compared to the Pelican, but she couldn't deny she needed the money. The last thing she wanted was to keep dipping into the suitcase. And, although at times he was so attentive it irritated her, she had to admit that she liked having him there all day. She felt safer.

Laughter broke out behind her. She knew the other women disliked her, but she didn't care. She despised them. The way they hunched over their work, jabbering all day, none of them bothering to learn English properly. Most of them kept slippers under their machines, which they changed into at the start of their shifts, and sat on their own cushions, too. As if this were home.

She'd heard the comments about her dyed blonde hair, her accent, the exact nature of her and Peter's relationship. Her nickname among the other Cypriots was *Ee Vasilissa*, The Queen.

She yawned and glanced at her watch. Dina hadn't returned from the hospital till past midnight, and the tidying up had taken hours. Peter had spent all evening fretting that she'd gone to the police, but Bebba suspected she'd been deliberately late to make them suffer. When she did finally return, the girl was tight-lipped and puffy-eyed, though what she had to cry about was a mystery. It wasn't as if she'd lost anything.

She'd made a big show of her bandaged hand and Peter had poured her some tea and made a fuss over her, which was clearly what she'd wanted.

The lunch bell rang. Bebba pushed everything off her lap and stood to slip on her coat. Two of the Irish women near the clocking out cards eyed her.

'Excuse me ladies.' She grabbed her card from the slot on the wall and shoved it under the machine to stamp the time.

'Going anywhere nice?' asked Mary, who worked on cuffs.

Hardly anyone went out at lunchtime. They usually dragged chairs together and ate food they'd brought from home – sandwiches, koftes, day-old chicken and samosas, seeping through the greasy wax paper that they held on their laps for plates. If they stopped for longer than fifteen minutes, they'd be docked half an hour's pay.

'Just a bit of shopping,' she said, slotted the card back in place and ran out.

On the street, she hailed a taxi. 'St Pancras, please. And can you hurry?'

The weary-faced driver sat up straight, opened the door for her and then pulled down the 'For Hire' sign. He took a tight U-turn and they wound their way through Bloomsbury, round Russell Square then Euston. She looked at her watch. Ten to one.

He glanced over his shoulder. 'Whereabouts love?'

'This is perfect, thank you.'

She stepped out and looked around, half expecting to see someone following her.

'Would you mind waiting? I'll be back in a few minutes.'

He frowned. 'Well I don't usually . . .'

'Please?' She offered one of her smiles. 'There'll be a tip for you.'

'Go on then,' he grinned, 'but the meter's ticking so be quick.'

She ran into the station, her heels clacking as she hurried across the concourse. At the far side was a small room, which she entered. Scores of lockers lined the walls. She looked to her left, then her right and felt for the key in her bag.

Locker 37. She pushed the key into the slot and twisted it open. The grey suitcase stood there, just as she'd left it last week. Thank God for Dina. If she hadn't mentioned that man watching the flat, Bebba wouldn't have moved it from the old shelter. And it would have all been for nothing. Even though Dina had crept up on her as she'd washed the soil from her hands afterwards, she hadn't seen a thing.

She had an impulse to open the case, to run her hands over it all. Instead, she held the handle and slowly lifted it off the bottom of the locker, testing the weight. It felt reassuringly full.

'You need a hand, miss?'

She jumped, letting go of the handle. A wiry-haired man in a dark railway uniform stood behind her.

'Oh, I didn't mean to startle you. Sorry. I thought you might need some assistance?'

He pointed at the case, which now lay half in, half out.

'I can summon a porter, miss.'

'No, no.'

She kicked it twice with her foot and it finally wedged back inside. Hurriedly, she shut the locker and turned the key.

'Thank you. I was just checking.'

'Sorry?'

'It's fine. I'm not taking it anywhere. But thank you all the same.'

* * *

Just outside the gates of Mackenzie's she shielded her mouth with her hand and forced herself to drop the smile. She handed the taxi driver a five-bob tip and he looked at her in disbelief, then sped away before she could change her mind.

Inside, she grabbed her card, clocked in and quickly sat down. She glanced at her watch and realised she'd forgotten to bring her lunch today. Six o'clock was ages away, but never mind. She'd grab a G&T on the way home, to celebrate.

'Let's have a look then,' asked Mary.

'What?'

'Your shopping – did you get anything nice?'

Bebba plucked a blouse from the pile on her right and sat down. 'No, couldn't find a thing.'

There was a pause.

'Expect nothing's good enough for you,' said Ayesha, the woman on hems, and a flurry of laughter followed.

25

Bebba looked up at the wicked sky. A glutinous yellow-white smog had slithered over the city. She was used to London fog now, didn't mind it in fact, but had never seen anything like this. It had started as freezing December fog and now it pressed down hard, obliterating all shape and life. She swallowed and tasted the soot, every mouthful a slug of poison.

She pulled Peter's arm a little closer as he steered her towards the flat. He'd tied his handkerchief over her nose and mouth, making an outlaw of her, while he only had a gloved hand to protect himself.

Yesterday, feeling the weight of the case in her hand had bolstered her confidence, but her self-assurance had seeped away overnight. And if she'd been right about the burglary then what would stop the old man returning? The dread coated her. In her mind he was the blackened core at the heart of every swirling shadow, and every muffled step she heard was the sound of his shoe shuffling along the pavement.

She told herself to stop being silly. If most of London had ground to a halt – even Mackenzie's had shut early so they could get home – how would a wrinkled old bastard like him ever make it outdoors? And if he came, she had Peter. He'd look after her. She tried to take in shallow sips of air, but the grit made her retch and she was forced to stop while she was overcome with a coughing fit.

'You all right?' he asked, peering at her face, his expression full of concern.

She nodded, gasped, then coughed again. The filth of it ran down the back of her throat.

A few buses crawled through the streets, but most people had given up waiting and trudged along the pavements. When Bebba could walk again, they moved along with the crowd, shifting like sleepwalkers.

'Won't be long,' said Peter. 'We're lucky to live so close.'

Searching the fog for something familiar – the post office on the corner, that Lifebuoy advert she walked past each day – she found nothing. All the comforting details had been erased. The bus stop had disappeared, the bench that she was sure was there became a wall or something else entirely. Everything had shifted.

The only thing that was solid was Peter's arm, but how reliable would he be? Could she count on him? She jerked as an orange tongue of flame licked the air just ahead of them.

'What's that?'

A silhouette stepped out of the shadows: long, dark coat, peaked helmet, flare held in outstretched hand.

'Poor sod,' said Peter, nodding towards a policeman who was directing a trickle of cars that moved like blood through clogged arteries.

Finally, they turned a corner onto their street and Bebba could just make out the Italian grocer's shop a few doors from their flat. Shutters had already been sealed over the windows, eyes screwed tight against the chaos.

'Do you think Dina will be all right?' she asked.

He looked at her, bemused.

'I'm sure she'll be fine,' he said. 'She's on till eight and that Harry's a tight one. He won't close up early and this might have cleared up by then.'

They entered the hall and Peter quickly closed the communal door, keeping back the fog that threatened to creep over the threshold.

'Come on, Beb. She won't be home for ages.' He put his arm around her waist and pulled her towards him. 'Now how can we spend the afternoon, and stay warm at the same time?'

She laughed and slipped away. He quickly followed, opening the door to the flat and pushing her through.

*   *   *

Hours later, Bebba ground her Piccadilly in the metal ashtray and shook the pack before flicking open the top. Damn, just two ciggies left. She'd save them. No, she'd have one more then save the last one. She placed it in the holder, lit up, then went through the lining up ritual with the Vestas, ciggies and ashtray. She tilted her head slightly, then gave the ashtray a gentle nudge, lining it up exactly.

Outside, the fog had congealed and all that was visible were the feeble yellow pinpricks from street lights. She felt anxious for Dina. If she didn't finish till eight, she probably wouldn't be home before ten, and that was assuming she didn't get lost. Next to the hob sat a covered saucepan of *fadgi* lentils that Dina had prepared the night before, but up to now neither of them had made a move to eat. Three empty bowls and spoons were stacked on the side.

Bebba glanced through to Peter's room. After they'd made love, he'd turned over and fallen asleep. She'd lain awake for a while before getting up and dressing. Now he was awake, arranging cards on the bedspread in a game of solitaire. He was right, Dina had walked in the fog several times. She could look after herself.

A bang – was that the front door? But then nothing. It must be the elderly sisters next door. They were rarely seen, but she often heard their nocturnal scurrying followed by loud whispers as they lay in bed. She imagined them as two wizened rats in floral nightgowns, lying under the covers on the other side of the wall.

She walked to the sink to turn on the tap. The water dribbled pathetically, so she took the spanner they kept hanging from the pipes and banged once, twice, till it gushed out. As she was filling the kettle there was a knock at the door.

'She's forgotten her keys again,' said Peter. He threw the cards on the bed and got up.

Harry had let her leave early after all. Relief swept over Bebba and the unease she'd felt that something awful may have happened seemed ridiculous. She grabbed the pot to get dinner ready.

'Dina! I'm just putting—'

She turned at the exact moment that Peter opened the door and her two worlds collided and collapsed. The pot fell to the floor.

'What is it? Bebba? What's the matter?'

Her gaze crept slowly, like she had all the time in the world when in fact the opposite was true.

Propped against the threshold was a dark figure in a hat and coat with the collar turned up. Tall and strong, not old and shrivelled. He moved closer and came and stood next to Peter. He leaned in towards her and just as he cocked his head to one side she screamed.

'Oh, come on,' said Rico. 'That's no way to greet your husband.'

Bebba stood behind Peter, trying to keep her whole body from shaking by clutching him tight. They both watched as Rico tapped the pack of Craven 'A's on the side of the table, took one out with his teeth and lit it.

'So, Elizabetta . . . tell me. How have you been?'

A pounding had started up in her left temple and her blood roared in her ears. Her breath caught deep inside, snagging somewhere between heart and ribs.

'What's going on?' demanded Peter.

Rico ignored him, flicking ash on the floor.

'You look like you've seen a ghost,' he said, and moved to touch her hair. She stepped back so quickly she almost fell over.

'Steady!'

'I don't—' she began. 'How?' She'd seen his photo with her own eyes, read the words printed beneath: *Beloved son . . . Rico Antoniou . . . passed away from malaria . . . funeral to be held at All Saints . . .*

Peter looked back and forth between them several times.

'What *is* this?' he asked, staring into her face 'You're *married*?'

She didn't speak.

Peter yelled: '*Bebba*?' She jumped and looked from one to the other.

'I . . .' she struggled to find her voice. 'He's dead,' said Bebba to Peter. 'He's meant to be dead.'

'And yet,' said Rico, throwing his arms wide, 'here I am.'

'I – I don't understand.'

'Beb?' asked Peter. 'Tell me this is a ridiculous joke.'

She took his hand and held it tight inside both of hers. She could feel Rico's eyes on her.

'Very cosy,' he said, gesturing to Peter.

'Well?' Peter asked her.

'I thought he'd died,' she croaked. 'It was even in the newspaper . . .'

Rico shrugged. 'We lied. Knew you'd be easier to find if we put that in the English paper. You wouldn't think we were looking.'

Peter peeled her fingers off his hand, then pushed her away and moved across the room.

'Darling, please.' She rushed after him. 'I *was* going to tell you. It's not what it looks like.'

'Oh, come on! It's exactly what it looks like.' Rico crossed his arms and leaned back against the table. 'She ran out, didn't you? After a week. She buried her old man, packed a case and left without a word.'

Peter fell into a chair and leaned forwards, elbows on legs, head hung down. Then in a tiny voice he asked, '*You were married*? There was someone else? All the time we were together you were married?'

She knelt beside him and put her face close to his.

'Listen,' she started. 'I *hate* him, do you hear? I was forced to marry him. It's over. It never even began. I don't want him,' she said, looking at Rico. 'That's why I left.'

'You married him,' said Peter, 'but now you hate him? Well, that's convenient.'

'I didn't have a choice.'

'She'd been a naughty girl, hadn't you?' said Rico.

'Shut up!' she spat.

'She had to marry fast – to protect the family name.'

Peter looked at his rival properly for the first time. 'I suppose I should be flattered. I lasted longer than a week.'

Rico took another drag of his cigarette. 'I imagine you're useful to her,' he said. 'That's why she's still here. Let me guess how she's shown her gratitude . . .'

Peter stood and squared up to Rico. He was a good two inches taller. 'This is my flat. What do you want? Why are you even here?'

'She knows,' said Rico.

'I'm asking *you*,' said Peter. 'Why come all this way to find someone who left you? Who – she says – can't stand the sight of you? And this, this ridiculous charade, pretending you're dead. What's that for?'

Rico ignored him and dropped his cigarette to the floor, killing it with a twist of his brogue.

He strolled over to Bebba and scrutinised her hair and clothes, tilting his head this way and that to take her in completely. She felt like he was touching her all over.

'Well, look at you,' he said. 'The hair, the whole thing. You don't look Greek at all.' He paused. 'But I'd know you anywhere, Elizabetta. Spotted you weeks ago.'

How? Where?

He leaned a little closer to her. She felt herself start to shake again and tried to control it.

'I'll always find you.'

He walked to the door and knocked on the new wooden frame.

'You never really feel safe after a burglary, do you?'

'What?' asked Peter.

'Bring it tomorrow. Piccadilly, by that statue, Eros.'

'Bring what?' asked Peter, but they both ignored him.

'I'll take your passport now,' said Rico.

'But—' she began.

'I'll give it back when you bring the money.'

Peter jolted at the mention of the word.

'The passport, come on,' said Rico. 'In case this fog clears, and you get any ideas about leaving.'

Bebba didn't move, so Rico went to her bedroom. She heard him rummaging around and a few moments later he emerged with her passport in hand and slipped it inside his coat.

'Eros, one o'clock, or you don't get this back.' He tapped his breast pocket. 'And don't even think of running away again.'

'Who do you think you are?' asked Peter, in a rush of anger. 'This is my flat, my town. And you come in here making demands. What makes you think we'll do what you want? I don't answer to you.'

Rico kept his eyes on Bebba the whole time. 'I'll get it anyway, in the end.'

'But you don't know where it is,' he said, 'or you'd have it by now.'

'There are ways of finding out – I just hope it doesn't come to that.'

'Are you threatening me?' asked Peter. Then he realised that Rico was still staring at Bebba. 'You wouldn't hurt her.'

Rico glanced at him now. 'You don't know what I will and won't do. But she does. Just look at her face.'

27

The smog that had crept in after lunchtime killed any chance of customers, but Harry refused to close early.

'Bloody hell, Dee,' said Colleen, using her sleeve to wipe a circle clear on the window. 'It's all gone yellow out there.'

'It's all right for him,' I whispered. 'He's only got to go upstairs. How are we meant to get home in *that*?'

'You never seen fog before?'

We both jumped. Suddenly he was behind us, a sour sweat rising off him like vinegar.

'Not like this, no,' I said, moving away. 'It'll take hours, Harry – *please*?'

He lifted his chin, his oily face catching the light.

'It's half seven Harry,' said Colleen. 'No one will come in now.'

Pursing his lips, he made a show of looking at his watch. Finally, he gave a dismissive wave, 'Go on then.'

We rushed to turn the chairs on the tables.

'But be here on time tomorrow,' he called as we grabbed our coats.

'You're not opening up, surely?' said Colleen.

'It's Saturday. We'll be busy.'

'But Harry – they say it's going to hold and there's no way anyone will come out in this.'

He shrugged. 'Turn up or get fired. Up to you. You're both on till four.' He put his fingers in the till and dropped the day's paltry takings into a small bag.

Sta anáthema, curses on him and this job. I'd have to get home through this muck, and be up at dawn to battle my way through it all over again. He tied the bag of coins with a string and held it in both hands, like a tiny, fragile child.

'Now you have a lovely evening, Harry,' said Colleen, in her best sarcastic voice. Then she opened the door wide. 'You coming, Dee?'

'And shut the door,' he yelled, 'or the fog will get in!' She held it open while I bent over and took my time straightening my stockings.

'Girls!'

Finally, we walked out and let it slam.

I pulled a handkerchief from my pocket and tied it over my nose and mouth. We moved slowly down Wardour Street, arm in arm.

'It'll be unbearable when you leave this place,' said Colleen.

'I won't be leaving for a while,' I said, holding up my bandaged hand.

'Did you call her? Madame Sylvie?'

'Yes, but when I said I'd cut myself, she told me to wait till it was better. I can't be bleeding all over the silks, can I?'

'True.'

'Anyway, she still needs to sort out the details,' I said. 'She asked me to keep it quiet. You won't tell anyone about the new club, will you?'

'Course not,' she laughed. 'Who am I going to tell? Harry?'

I looked down at my hand.

'I hope it doesn't open up again. It still hurts.'

'Poor Dina.'

'Don't.'

'What?'

'Don't feel sorry for me.' I thought about my savings, which had been stolen in the burglary. I'd make the money again, somehow, then I would move on. Between the break-in and them being so cosy, the flat didn't feel like home. And it would be lovely to have my own place, somewhere I could be with him without worrying they'd walk in.

'I'll be all right,' I said.

'Oh, I don't doubt it. You're as tough as old boots, you.'

'Old boots?' I frowned.

'It's a compliment,' she laughed. 'It means you're a survivor. I'd bet my life on you always being all right.'

'Really?' I pulled her in a little tighter. 'Are you trying to get me to cover your late shifts or something?'

'No, I mean it,' she said. 'You're smart, Dina – you have a cool head. Whatever life throws at you, you'll throw it right back.'

There was a lull in the conversation as we continued to thread slowly through the backstreets of Soho.

'Well, you'll be okay too,' I said, more for something to say than because I really meant it.

'I don't know,' she said. 'I'm almost twenty-eight, I can barely make ends meet and my love life, well – it's a state of emergency. Like this fog.'

I laughed.

'I feel as if I'm waiting, you know?' she said.

'For what?'

'That's the thing – I'm not sure. Something big. Happiness I suppose.'

'You can't wait for happiness, Coll. You have to find it yourself.'

'Oh, and would *your* happiness look anything like Loverboy?' she teased.

I gave her a dig with my elbow. Ever since I'd confided that we'd had sex, she couldn't help bringing him into the conversation. It was a relief to have someone I could be open with; months ago, that would have been Bebba, but not now.

Ahead, a policeman with an orange flare lit the way as the road split into two. Colleen dropped my arm.

'This is me – good luck getting home, doll. Take care of yourself.'

I pecked her on the cheek. 'You too.'

I turned down Oxford Street and took my time feeling my way along buildings, running my hands along railings, the post box on the corner, making sure I recognised each landmark. The fog was heavier now, thicker than I'd seen before. It barely shifted, stuffed full of smoke and filth and hiding goodness knew what. And yet, unlike other nights when I'd had to return in this, tonight I wasn't afraid. It was just weather. I was a Londoner now, and we just got on with it.

More than an hour had passed by the time I finally turned into Hampstead Road. Wrung out, I fished in my bag for my key as I wondered how to avoid tomorrow's journey. Harry would never believe me if I sent a message to say I was sick. Could I ask Peter to call him tomorrow? Harry would believe him over me any day. Or perhaps I could—

'Oh, don't give me that!'

Peter's shouts came from behind the closed door. They were followed by a quieter voice, Bebba's. A thrill of excitement shot through me. They were arguing! I tiptoed so they wouldn't hear the creaking floorboards and put my ear to the door.

Just the other day she'd floated out of his room, with that bold grin and hardly wearing a stitch. What had changed? Her voice was soft and though I couldn't make out sentences, I could tell from the tone that she was pleading. What did she want now? I held my breath.

'I don't believe you!' I jumped back a little. His voice juddered, a thread of hurt ran through it. What had she done to him? 'Why should I believe anything you tell me?'

Her words were muffled. I could only make out a few of them.

'Please Peter . . . promise . . . future . . .' *God, speak up, won't you?*

About a minute's silence followed and, just as I was about to walk in, I heard him ask, 'What about Dina?'

Me? What did this have to do with me? This time her voice was decisive and clear. There was no mistaking what she said.

'We mustn't tell her. She doesn't need to know.'

His laugh was harsh, and he said something under his breath.

As I pushed the door open, they quickly turned away from each other.

'What are you two arguing about?' I asked, taking off my coat.

He wouldn't look at me.

'Peter.' I walked towards him, but he went to his room and slammed the door. I was about to follow him but decided to try to get something out of her.

'What's happened?'

'It's nothing,' she said, emptying a large can of Heinz beans into a pan.

'Where's the *fadgi*? I made dinner last night.'

'It's ruined,' she said. 'I dropped it.'

Had she thrown it at him? Had *he* thrown it at *her*? Oh, hell, why had I missed this? I took a quick glance around: no food smears on the walls, no evidence of a fight.

Peter put the radio on loud and she turned her head to look at his closed door. When she turned back, I saw that her face was blotchy and her eyes bloodshot. She'd been crying but there was something else. A rigidness about her face; she was petrified. My heart pitched; I'd seen that look before, that day at the public baths. Suddenly I felt ashamed of myself.

'Bebba? What is it?'

I reached out to hug her, but she moved away and busied herself with laying the table for dinner.

'Bebba?'

Silence.

'You can tell me,' I said. 'What's happened? Have you two argued? Is it money again? I promise I won't nag.'

She stirred the beans over and over in the pan.

'Bebba?'

It was as if I wasn't standing there, as if I didn't exist. I had an urge to reach out and slap her, to shock her into saying something, anything. I stood close, and spoke right into her face.

'Well if you won't tell me what's wrong, tell me this then. What don't I need to know?'

'Sorry?'

'I heard you say, when I was outside, "She doesn't need to know." What is it I don't need to know? You said my name – what were you talking about?'

She'd chased the beans round and round the pan till the wooden spoon had turned them to an orange mush. Every time she moved her arm her elbow touched my side. Eventually, she gave a sharp little shrug and looked me straight in the eye.

'I haven't a clue what you're talking about. Now move out of my way.'

28

That night, Bebba was frantic. Should she run? What if Rico found her? Then she'd be alone with him. Who knew what he would do? But that money was hers by rights. She'd die before she'd hand it over.

No, she had to think of something. She looked at Peter's closed door and realised he was her only hope. She took two glasses from the shelf, a half bottle of gin that they'd been saving for Christmas and walked into his room without knocking, closing the door behind her. There was no ice but no matter, they'd drink it neat.

She poured them each a drink, sat next to him on the bed and took his hand. She sat there for hours, pleading, explaining, whispering, while he barely responded. Outside she could hear Dina sweeping loudly, deliberately knocking the door with the broom while she moved about.

After they'd finished most of the bottle, he finally looked at her and said: 'I need to feel I can trust you again.'

She searched her mind for the one thing she could say to convince him. That would make him agree to help her and come to her side. Finally, she'd pushed her pride aside, got down on her knees and begged.

'I'll give you anything you want. What do you want?'

She saw his face soften. Realising she almost had him, she told him that he may as well know that she loved him. He frowned as if he'd always thought she had anyway.

She was expecting him to say, 'I love you, too,' but instead his words were: 'I need more than that, Beb.'

So, to give him the final nudge, she revealed how much was in the suitcase at St Pancras. If he stayed with her, she said, he'd have both her and the money. She'd lined him up for the ultimate jackpot and, sure enough, he thought about it for less than ten seconds before grabbing her and kissing her hungrily.

When they finally pulled apart, he said he wouldn't let anything happen to her. Then they'd made love.

Outside, Dina had banged around, furiously clattering plates, thumping the broom and scraping chairs as she exhausted her vile temper on the housework.

'Maybe we should we say something?' said Peter later, as they lay on top of the bed.

'No. She'll only worry. And anyway, it's best she's not involved.'

'But what if he turns up and she's here?'

'Then we'll tell her. But not till then.'

'Really? You don't think we should say something now?'

'I don't see the point – it won't get us anywhere and we'll have her moaning at us.'

After another gin, Bebba dozed off. But just as she'd sunk into sleep, she heard a loud crash that made her sit bolt upright.

'My God! What's that?' Her heart hammered in her chest.

'Ssshh.' He pulled her back down. 'It's nothing. Just Dina. She's just leaving for work.'

'But it's dark. It's night, surely?'

'It's the fog. It's morning,' he said, shifting onto his side. 'It'll take her ages.'

Mackenzie's had ground to a halt. It would be days, perhaps a week, before the rolls of fabric, piled high like honeycomb, made it through on their lorries. They'd been told not to come in till the fog cleared. That meant no pay, but she didn't care. She couldn't contemplate snipping cottons while her future unravelled, so she turned over and slept.

When she finally got up, she started to tidy the room, straightening the chairs and realigning old newspapers so they were neatly stacked on the edge of the table. Every few minutes her gaze was pulled back to the second hand as it travelled around the face of the cheap gilt carriage clock. She shifted it slightly so that it sat exactly in the middle of the mantelpiece. Twenty-five past one. How long would Rico wait before he realised she wasn't coming? Then he'd come straight here.

But this time she was ready. This time she wouldn't show fear as she raised her chin, looked at him and said, 'No.' He terrified her, but this wasn't Cyprus and she wasn't alone. He had no power over her now. And if he wouldn't return her passport, there were ways of getting a new one.

That was something Peter *was* good for. As if he could read her thoughts, he came now and stood behind her, his hands on her shoulders, giving them a light squeeze. She tried not to tense at his touch. He began to nuzzle her neck, planting tiny kisses along the nape where hair met skin.

'It's all right,' he mumbled, between kisses. 'Everything will be all right.'

She sighed inwardly as he started pawing her, but without him she'd have to run again. (How *had* Rico found her?)

She took a deep breath and let her shoulders drop, trying to relax as she closed her eyes. Still standing behind her, Peter pushed his fingers through her hair – she'd previously declared it off limits, claiming he'd wreck the style – and continued kissing her neck, his breathing quickening a little.

'He'll know by now,' he said. 'It's one thirty. He said one o'clock.'

A door slammed somewhere in the building. She jolted at the sound of footsteps, but they were light, fast. Someone else. Still behind her, Peter slid his hands to her waist now and pulled her in tight. 'Don't worry. If we stick to the plan, we'll be together. We're doing this for both of us now, aren't we?'

He pressed against her like a randy mule.

'Careful – my ciggie.' She determinedly pulled his hands off her and moved to the mantelpiece, where she rubbed at the clock face and blew imaginary dust off its casing.

'You'll stay with me, won't you?' he asked. 'When this is all over?'

On the wall hung a mirror, and she placed her hands on either side to straighten it.

'Of course, darling,' she said. Then she stubbed out her cigarette. The last bloody one.

29

I was hiding in the ladies, reading about Grace Kelly's 'delightful family' in *Picture Post*, when there was a thump at the door.

'Hey, Dee!' It was Colleen. 'Quick!'

I jumped and shoved the magazine behind the cistern.

'Is he back?'

Harry would kill me if he caught me skiving. I straightened my pinny and released the bolt. She was standing on the other side, eyes wide.

'Guess who's come to see you?' she asked. Then without waiting for an answer: 'Loverboy,' she said. 'He's *here*.'

I hurried into the café and there he stood, leaning against the counter like a Hollywood heart-throb waiting for a bus. He lifted a hand in a wave and beamed. Rushing over, I gave him a quick kiss on the cheek.

'Hello!' I felt my face flush. 'This is a nice surprise.' People turned to look. I quickly changed to Greek. 'What are you doing here?'

'I've come to rescue you,' he replied. 'I remembered you were working today. Then I saw this weather and thought . . .'

Colleen started to half-heartedly wipe a table next to us, very slowly, even though she couldn't understand a word.

'Well it's horrible out there,' he said. 'I'll walk you home. You finish at four, don't you?'

I glanced at the clock over the door.

'But, it's only three.'

He shrugged. 'I'll wait.' He moved to sit down.

Colleen looked from the clock to me then him.

'You want to go?' she asked.

'Really?' I was thrilled at the thought of getting out early.

'Go on. I'm sure I owe you a few hundred favours.'

'What about Harry?'

'I'll think of something,' she said. 'I'll say you were ill. Hurry up before he comes back.'

I grabbed my coat and bag from the peg then ran back to give Colleen a quick squeeze.

'You're a doll, Coll!' I said, mimicking her cockney accent.

'Yeuch, get off.' She laughed, pretending to wriggle away, 'or I'll change my mind. You Greeks – always hugging and kissing.'

I took his arm as we stepped outside. It may have only been three o'clock, but the fog had thrown a heavy cloak over the day, and it felt like night was coming. It was thicker even than yesterday and as it swirled and shifted, a terrible yellow tinge revealed itself.

'It's all right,' he said, pulling me in. 'It's closing in fast, but just hold on tight.' That was fine by me; right now, there was nowhere I'd rather be.

'It's so nice to be out of that place,' I said, as we crossed the road.

'Did you speak to that woman again?' he asked. 'About the job?'

'This comes off tonight,' I said, showing him my bandaged hand, 'so if it looks all right, I'll call her in the morning.'

I felt a surge of happiness at the thought of working with her again.

'Oh, I didn't tell you – there's a room in Colleen's house that might be free soon. It's cheap and they're not asking for a deposit.'

'That's great,' he said, hugging me tighter. 'Everything's changing for you.'

'I know. It could be a fresh start.'

The lamplighters hadn't even tried to come out today, so the usual pale dots of hope that guided everyone had vanished. Carefully, we navigated the chaos as we helped each other from kerb to kerb and crossed Frith Street.

'I'm so glad you came today,' I said, looking up at him, although I could only just make out his face. 'Yesterday was horrible.'

'Why? What happened.'

'Oh, it's awful at home. Something's up, but they won't say a word.' I thought about the night before and how I'd spent hours by myself, shut out.

'My brother and Bebba – that girlfriend of his – they had some sort of row and locked themselves in his room, whispering, completely ignoring me. And I know it's got something to do with me because I heard my name.'

The searing loneliness I'd felt just hours before returned and my voice caught a little.

'You know, sometimes I feel I don't matter,' I said. 'It's as if I'm out in this fog and they can't see me.' I'd been feeling this for weeks, since that day I'd heard them having sex.

He stopped and put his hands on my arms, making me face him. 'Don't say that, *agápi mou*. Of course you matter, my love. You matter to me.'

He always said the right thing.

'And you're not invisible, far from it.' He held out his arm and I linked mine through his as we continued picking our way along the pavement. 'The first time I saw you, I couldn't take my eyes off you.'

'Really?' I couldn't help smiling and my spirit immediately lifted as we carried on walking. Nobody else could make me feel like this.

'Really,' he said, laughing, pulling me even tighter.

'So, you liked me on first sight?' I was fishing for compliments but didn't care.

'More than liked you, if you know what I mean.'

I laughed, embarrassed and delighted to be desired, to have this strange magical power over him.

'Now, come on.' He pulled me by the arm. 'Let's have a drink before I walk you back.'

'What? Oh, I don't know.' I looked up at the sky. 'I mean – this will only get worse.'

'So, what's the rush to get back? Come on, you just said how much you hate it at home.'

He was right. What was waiting for me there? Guarded glances, whispers and closed doors. They were so wrapped up in each other, they probably wouldn't notice if I didn't come back at all.

'Okay,' I said. 'I suppose it's going to take ages to get back anyway. An extra half hour won't matter.'

In the Dog and Duck, I climbed onto a bar stool and waited while he bought me a half of shandy and a whisky for himself. An elderly woman appeared next to me, her face weather-beaten, two spots high on her cheeks the colour of strong tea.

'There you are!' she shouted, patting my arm.

A tin rattled under my nose and she gave me a wide smile; there wasn't one tooth in her head.

'Leave her alone,' he said, not unkindly, placing the drinks down on the bar. 'Here.' He dropped a few coins into the can.

'We thought you were lost, didn't we?' she said.

He put his hand out and pushed her gently away.

'What's she talking about?'

He shrugged. 'She doesn't look like she's been sober for a while.'

Glancing over my shoulder, I saw her kneel next to a table, her tin already upended as she counted out pennies.

'Stupid war,' I said. 'All those people's lives ruined.'

Since arriving, I'd seen many injured people on the streets – men who'd lost an arm or a leg, some who'd lost their minds.

So many men, ruined or gone. So many women left behind to stitch their lives together again. Even those who'd survived were lost.

'I wonder what she was like?' I said.

'What?'

'Who she was. Before.'

He shrugged, knocked back the whisky and pulled a face.

'Hey, you'll get drunk! And then what use will you be? You're meant to be escorting me, remember?'

He reached across, pecked me on the cheek, then lit a cigarette.

'Tell me what you thought when you first saw me,' I said, tugging at his coat.

He laughed. 'You like this game, do you?'

I stroked his collar. The fabric was damp from the fog and I let my hand trail down his lapel and rest just above the buttons.

'Well.' He reached across towards me and caressed my neck before picking up his drink. 'When I first saw you, I thought, how can I get her to speak to me?' He looked into his empty tumbler.

I sighed, exaggerating my disappointment, and let my hand drop. 'Is that it?'

'No.' He took my hand. 'I thought, how can I get her to speak to me? Then how can I make her . . .' he brought my hand to his lips and kissed it '. . . mine.'

'Yours?'

He nodded. There was a glint of mischief in his eyes.

'You *are* mine, aren't you?' he asked.

I shrugged, teasingly. 'Maybe. I'm not sure. Are you mine?'

'Definitely.'

But he said it with a smile as if still playing a game and I felt cross with myself for squeezing it out of him, because it meant less this way. *Don't be silly, Dina. He's here, isn't he?* And really, what was I expecting? A proclamation of undying love in this awful place?

I took off my coat and swivelled on my stool. Apart from the old woman and a man sleeping by the fire, we were alone. The bar boasted a lattice of sticky ring marks, ghosts of previous drinkers. Several dirty glasses were scattered on various tables in the manner of a party that had been abandoned once terrible news had arrived.

'What a sad place,' I said. 'It's so neglected. Have you been here before?'

He nodded. 'I like it. None of the usual craziness of Soho.'

Finishing my drink, I slid off the stool. 'It's the craziness I love.'

I leaned over and kissed him on the lips, lightly and slowly, the way I knew he liked.

'I'm going to powder my nose,' I said. 'Then we should probably go. Before it gets even worse.'

As I carefully washed my hands at the sink outside the lavatory, trying not to wet the bandage, I leaned in and gazed in the mirror. I looked older, which was good. My jawline was definitely sharper than before, and I looked more serious somehow. So much had happened in the past few months, it was bound to have left its mark. Bebba and I hardly spoke now and there was a distance between us I didn't think we'd ever bridge.

I rinsed my fingers and pictured myself telephoning Madame Sylvie tomorrow to say I was ready. I wasn't asking Peter's permission; I'd just tell him. No more secrets. He had no say in my life now.

Pushing my good hand through my hair, I squeezed the curls in my fist, trying to get them to behave. When we first met, he said the colour of my hair reminded him of the sand on Paramali beach. I'd been fishing for compliments earlier because I'd actually wanted him to say he loved me. And if he had, I would have said it too.

He was the best thing in my life right now – him and the prospect of a new job. And after we'd made love that first time, I was worried he might lose interest. I'd heard stories from girls about men who'd turned nasty after sleeping with them, ignored them or treated them meanly. But we'd done it several times now and he'd only grown more attentive and kinder – like the way he'd turned up today.

Exhaustion set in. I needed to get home. I opened my bag to get my lipstick and my hand brushed a photo. I glanced down, not letting myself pull it out completely. It had been taken before I was born. It showed my father when he was much younger, sitting on the beach, waving into the camera, hair caught in the breeze. Next to him my mother, but I kept her half of the photo hidden in the darkness of my bag. My throat tightened and I could feel that the tears would come if I let them. *Oh, come on*, gori. I pushed the photo back in and focused on applying Poppy Rouge to my mouth.

As I approached the bar, I saw that he'd lined up more drinks.

'Andreas, I'm shattered.'

'Just a quick one, I've paid.' He pointed to the glass. 'It's only grapefruit squash. You like that, don't you?'

'Okay. But I really have to go after this. I was up at five today.'

Sitting on the stool, I took a big gulp and then another, in an attempt to finish it quickly. A bitter tang washed around my mouth and I scrunched up my nose.

'Has it gone off?' I offered him the glass.

'Mine's fine.' He took a long drink from his and wiped his mouth with the back of his hand.

'I don't want any more,' I said, and stood up. 'Come on. You don't need to walk me. I'll try and get a bus.'

'Don't be silly, I'll take you.' He held out my coat for me and I slipped my arms into the sleeves. 'I said I'd look after you and I will.'

I picked up my bag, turned my head to speak but all that came out was a gentle wheeze, a gasp of life escaping. As my mind tried to catch up, my legs folded.

When I was a girl of eight, I spent many summer hours jumping into the oncoming waves at the beach in Kyrenia. I'd look out for the next swell, trying to ride the wave and let it carry me out to sea a little. One day an undercurrent took me by surprise, kicking me right off my feet. At the same moment, a larger wave crashed through, sweeping me further out than I'd ever been. I remembered it now, the split second of confusion, the realisation of what had happened and then the panic and heavy dread that I'd be forever lost.

Peter had saved me, that day. He'd put one arm across my body, lifted my head out of the jade water and swum to shore.

Now, thousands of miles from that clear, green sea, in the middle of a pub in the middle of Soho, another strong arm held me as I dropped into nothing. He reached right across my back, under my arm, and lifted me up slightly.

'Dina, listen,' he said, as his tobacco-laced breath kissed my ear. 'Listen, it's all right. I'm here. I've got you.'

30

Bebba had been so sure Rico would come, but it was now twenty past ten in the evening. Peter would wear through the lino with all that pacing up and down, the boards creaking under his feet, and she needed something, anything, to distract her. She turned on the wireless by his bed. Each of the three stations was reporting on the weather:

As London enters its second day of what is now being called the Great Smog, there seems no indication that the weather will change, and the terrible consequences are becoming all too apparent. Hundreds of people have been admitted to hospital and for many the effects of the thick, relentless fog have been fatal. The government recommends—

She switched it off. To hell with their terrible consequences – she had her own to consider. All of this waiting felt like a death of sorts. He'd said Eros, one o'clock. As the clock had gone past the hour, the seconds had seeped into minutes until the day collected like a poisonous pool at her feet.

Every sound corroded her courage: the hiss of the gas shooting through the pipes, the call of the paperboy on the corner ('Fog chaos! Fog chaos!'). All of it plucked at the threads of her thoughts until her mind was a frayed mess.

Her head throbbed. She'd taken the last of the aspirin yesterday so now, along with ciggies, she was clean out. On any other day, she'd shoot down to the newsagent on the corner. But he'd be shut now, if he'd even bothered to open at all.

Anyway, she couldn't leave this room, not yet. What if Rico caught her in the corridor by herself? Or on the street? Thank God she wasn't living by herself in her old flat. Imagine if he'd found her there.

Her scalp itched and she put her hand up to her hair and pushed it behind her ears; she hadn't washed it for two days and, as she examined it in the mirror, she saw that it needed dyeing too. The snow-bleached tips had started to turn yellow, like crystallised honey. Who'd have thought she'd unravel so easily?

Peter looked out of the window and gave an exasperated sigh.

'Maybe he won't come?' she said. 'It's practically impossible to get anywhere. They said so on the wireless.'

'He wants that money. I doubt the fog will stop him.'

She turned her back and closed her eyes, knowing he was right.

'Where on earth is Dina?' he said.

She hadn't thought about her for hours.

'She should have finished at four today,' said Peter, raising his voice. 'That's – that's six hours ago – six! – and she's still not home. This is ridiculous. I'm not letting her work there any more. He's taking liberties, that Harry. Making her walk home in this.'

'Calm down, will you? My nerves are terrible as it is.'

She picked up his Woodbines from the table, flicked the top open, then saw he had none left either. Scrunching up the pack, she threw it back. She doubted she and Dina would ever be friends again. Too much had happened. But she had once been so fond of her; she'd been the closest friend Bebba had ever had. How easy things had been in those early days, when the only decisions they'd had were which bar to go to and what to wear.

The door swung open. Rico stood there, blocking out the light from the hall.

'How did you get in?' asked Peter, moving between the two of them.

Rico stepped around him and stood just a couple of inches from Bebba's face.

She told herself that he couldn't touch her, that Peter was right here.

'What are you doing, Elizabetta?'

She felt the patter of her pulse quicken at the base of her throat but kept her eyes on his, defiantly holding his gaze. Clenching and unclenching her hands, she lifted her chin a little.

'Why didn't you do as you were told?' he asked.

His face was so close that for an awful moment she thought he might try to kiss her.

Instead he blew onto her cheek, gently.

'Are you scared?' he asked.

Now would be the time for Peter to act, she thought, but he did nothing. She drew her arms across her body, gripped her elbows to steady herself and glared back at Rico.

Finally, Peter seemed to wake from his stupor. 'The thing is,' he said, his voice a little higher than usual, 'the thing is we've decided not to give you the money.'

His attempt at matter-of-factness came across as ridiculous, and the tremble in his voice gave him away.

Rico raised his eyebrows, amused.

'The thing is,' continued Peter, hands on hips and stretching arms back to widen his chest, 'we've made a decision. It's hers and we're keeping it.'

Rico walked to the table and leaned back, half sitting on it.

'Ah, you've decided, have you?' he asked.

Peter nodded, then wiped his forehead with the back of his hand.

'*The thing is,*' said Rico, 'you don't get a choice. The money is a dowry, a payment for marrying her. It's mine and *she's* mine.'

'Rico?' She tried to make her voice soft. 'Rico, please? I'm sorry about the way things happened. Me walking out. It was wrong, I know that. But it *is* my dowry and we're not even together any more.'

He didn't respond. She put herself in his line of vision.

'Please. It's all the money my family have – had. You know that. You don't need it. Your family has so much already.'

He stared at her blankly.

Anger filled her. He was going to make her beg.

'*Please*, Rico,' she said, louder. 'When you changed the amount of the dowry, at the last minute – when you squeezed every last penny out of my father . . . he . . . we had to sell everything. The olive groves, the fields, the animals. *It killed him.*'

He pulled a mocking face.

'Oh, you're breaking my heart.'

She raised her hand, but he was fast, in the way that only someone who's done it several times can be. He hit her hard with the back of his hand and she stumbled, knocking over the chair and falling on top of it.

To her utter surprise, Peter ploughed in and hit the soft spot of his stomach with perfect precision. Rico's eyes widened and he fell to his knees next to her, bent over, winded. He coughed and coughed and pulled a handkerchief from his pocket. He spat into it, trying to compose himself, fighting for a clean breath of air.

Peter offered her his hand and pulled her up.

Finally, Rico stood, his face red, his hair flopped over his forehead.

'That was a stupid thing to do,' he gasped.

'Well . . .' Peter didn't seem to know what to do now. 'There you are. That's just for starters. Now . . . now get out, or . . . or you'll be sorry.'

He was almost convincing.

'All I have to do,' he continued, 'is give the word and you will get hurt. I know people. Locals. Gangsters, some people call them, but I call them friends.'

Rico looked at him is disbelief. '*You're* threatening *me*?'

There was a film of sweat on Peter's forehead and he dabbed at it again.

'All they need is the word from me,' he said, 'and they'll hunt you down and mess you up so badly ... so badly that you'll be crying for your *mama*. You won't even make it back home.'

Rico smoothed down his coat. 'So that's the best you can do?'

Something wasn't right.

'I'm not bluffing,' said Peter.

'Oh, I believe you,' Rico reached inside his pocket and Peter took a step back.

Rico noticed and shook his head, then pulled out his cigarettes. 'Now let me give you some advice.'

He tapped them on the table, took one out and lit up.

'If you're going to threaten someone the stakes have to be high.'

He inhaled long and hard and blew the smoke directly at them. 'The other person has to risk losing something big or it doesn't work. I don't have anything left to lose. But you do.'

She glanced at Peter. He looked just as confused as she felt.

'I want the case,' said Rico. 'And I want . . .' he made a circle with his finger and finally pointed at Bebba, 'you. You're coming back with me to Cyprus.'

'No!' She shook her head and backed into the corner. 'No, you can't force me.'

'Won't have to,' he said. 'It'll be an exchange.'

'An exchange for what?' asked Peter. 'You don't have anything I want more than her.'

Rico laughed. 'That's touching, but I think I do.' He paused then frowned a little. 'Are you *sure* you're related? Because she's much cleverer than you.'

His words hung in the air for five, maybe six seconds. Then Bebba realised.

'You can't—' A wave of nausea rose in her stomach and her hand flew to her mouth.

'But I have,' said Rico.

'What?' Peter didn't understand.

'A fair exchange, I'd say.'

'Will someone tell me what's going on?' asked Peter.

Rico sighed: 'Like I said – much smarter than her brother.'

Peter still didn't understand and then, suddenly, he did.

'*Dina?* But how – I mean – you can't know Dina . . .'

'She finishes at four today,' said Rico. 'She would have been home by now, wouldn't she? Even with the fog – I mean it's almost eleven. She was right when she said you two didn't care.'

Bebba leaned over the chair to let the blood rush to her head.

'How . . .?' she asked, her head still upside down. 'What?'

Rico came and put his arm around her shoulder, lifting her upright. 'We're so alike, me and you. We'll do anything to get what we want.'

'How could you know her?' said Peter. 'You're lying.'

Rico pointed to the left. 'That's her room there, isn't it? The bed's surprisingly comfortable, but it does creak a bit.'

Peter shook his head. 'No . . .'

'When she gets going.'

Peter's hands became fists. 'No . . . shut up! Dina wouldn't do that . . .'

'It's a nasty cut she's got on her hand. I've taken that bandage off and it's healed. Though,' and here he gave an awkward, half-embarrassed shrug, 'the rest of her is a bit of a mess.'

'I swear,' said Peter. 'If you've hurt her . . .'

Thoughts raced through Bebba's mind. Peter would want to give him the money now. Could she get to St Pancras first? Even if she could in this fog, there'd be no trains. The world had ground to a halt. And how on earth did he know Dina?

'Rico, listen.' She grabbed his arm. 'Just let her go. Please, just let her go. I'll do anything.'

Peter was still in the middle of the room, mouth slightly open, face the colour of sour milk. He walked to Rico and grabbed him by the shirt.

'Where is she?' he asked. 'Tell me – take me to her now. I have to see her.'

Rico looked down at his shirt.

'Get your hands off me.'

Peter let go.

Rico slipped off his coat and held it out to Bebba. She took it and put it on the back of the chair. He sat and instructed Peter to do the same.

In a daze, Peter did as he was told.

'Bring the money on Monday and you'll get her back. Don't bring the money and you'll never see her again.'

'We'll bring it,' said Peter. 'We can give you it tomorrow, can't we Beb? We don't have to wait till Monday. Can we get her back tomorrow?'

'I said Monday. You should have brought it today so now you can wait another day. And don't do anything stupid like involving the police. I'll get the tickets and then we can leave.' He looked at Bebba. 'Two tickets.'

'Why not tomorrow?' asked Peter.

'Are you stupid or deaf?' yelled Rico. They both jumped. 'I've already said Monday. I'm not running around in this fucking fog on a Sunday for your convenience.'

Nobody spoke.

'You've forced my hand. Your sister's life is at stake now and it's all your fault.'

The only sound was the ticking of the clock.

'Her *life*?' asked Peter. 'You wouldn't . . .'

'Of course I would.'

'You'll get the money,' said Peter. 'Just don't hurt her.'

And while the men sat and Rico told Peter where to meet on Monday, Bebba had one question, but she couldn't bring herself to ask. How long did she have before they left for Cyprus?

31

When I woke, I was on the floor, hands tied behind my back and something tight around my mouth. There was an itch at my cheek – wool carpet? At home there was lino. An ache drilled deep into my bones and I twisted to try to take in my surroundings.

Next to my head, the carpet's crimson and silver pattern changed from flowers to feathers then grasping hands, all in time with the fitful smack of my heart.

Under the bed sat two shiny black brogues, as fat and wicked as cockroaches. I closed my eyes for a second and when I opened them again, I was sure they'd crept towards me, heel-toe, heel-toe. On the floor to my left was a metal ashtray; in that, a pyramid of cigarette butts. Next to it, a crushed packet, red and white. I stared at the box. Craven 'A's. How could something so familiar be in a place like this? *Come on, just get out.* I struggled to sit up but fell back down. I pulled at my wrists, trying to loosen the knot, but when I shifted my weight my left shoulder ripped deep inside, and the hungry red mouth of the carpet rushed up to kiss me.

I don't know how long I lay there, slipping in and out of consciousness. Every time I opened my eyes, I teased the knot a bit more while the night gradually ate all the light. I tried not to panic; I hated the dark but at least the gag wasn't too tight, I told myself. At least I could still breathe. I shivered and realised my skirt was bunched up around my waist, my legs exposed.

Digging my heels into the carpet, I moved myself around, till my foot hit a wall. Slowly, I shuffled against it and managed to sit up. The pulse in my ears knocked out two words, over and over: *get out, get out.* With my back against the wall I was able to look around the room. Sloping ceiling – an attic. Voices in the street below and a car. Could I still be in Soho? Still close to home? Every so often a shaft of light sliced through the room and illuminated objects in turn: a thin pillow, a chrome desk lamp, a doorknob. My eyes darted from one to the other, drinking them in, trying to understand how they fitted together and how I fitted with them, all the time tugging at the knot behind my back. I could hear my breathing as it became heavier, and I felt consumed by the night. *Come on, stay calm, slow shallow breaths.*

Another beam of light slid slowly across the room. It must be traffic struggling through the fog. Look, there was a wardrobe. And a table, and a sink in the corner. A wide beam, softer than the rest, crossed the room and then stopped on a patch of shiny brown wall. I could hear the familiar thump of an engine. A London bus. There were people down there. The snake of light slithered along the wall and I turned my head to keep it in sight for as long as possible.

The door opened and I let out a muffled scream. He walked in and stood with his back to the wall, the white of his shirt just visible in the half-light. Between his fingers he held a cigarette and the orange-red tip raged as he put it to his lips and sucked. Slowly he blew a perfect smoke ring into the air. I didn't know he could do that, but there was a lot I didn't know.

I froze as he came towards me, put the cigarette in his mouth and bent down. I thought he was going to pull off the gag, but instead he pulled off my shoes, scooped me up in his arms and threw me on the bed. I bounced and my head thwacked on the wall. Something pulled in the side of my neck.

Tears rolled down my face. He walked to the door. Where was he going? He couldn't leave me like this. I started thrashing my legs, shouting in a panicked garble.

'Shut up,' he said.

He closed the door and locked it.

*   *   *

Hours passed and a sickly daylight soaked through the room. I'd loosened the knot and managed to slip my hands out, but I kept them behind my back. I'd pulled down the gag and practised dipping my chin and edging it back up quickly, in case he burst through the door.

Sitting on the bed, I leaned against the wall trying not to fall asleep. But now a tiredness gripped me and all I wanted to do was lie down and extinguish the questions rushing through my mind. *Why was this happening? Why would he do this? Did he think I had money? Was he going to kill me?* I didn't understand any of it, but I knew I needed to get out. I remembered a staircase. Being carried. *She's used you, that's what she does.* Crying, pleading. Him shouting.

Something else. What was it? Me and Andreas, Peter and Bebba, each of us linked in some terrible way. A thought whipped at the edge of my mind, flitting backwards and forwards, like the ocean teasing the shore.

Cramp shot through my leg and I pointed my toe and flexed my foot. Pain and relief collided. I shivered. When I exhaled, I could see the ghostly vapour of my breath. Do the dead know they've died?

Next to my face the wall was melting, drips of shiny brown paint dried halfway down. My eyes searched for the familiar line of drawing pins that kept the paper from curling. How I would have loved to run my finger from one end to the other. Don't be stupid, *gori*, that was in the bedsit, before it all began.

I looked up. A single window of milky yellow-grey stared

down, a Cyclops watching from the slanted ceiling. Too high to reach and, even if I could, too small to squeeze through.

What was wrong with my arm? I twisted it around and saw the grey flesh above my elbow, a bracelet of finger-shaped bruises. My hand was no longer bandaged. The cut had left a neat scar.

Two ladders clawed up my nylons where they'd been ripped. Hesitantly, I put my hand up my skirt and checked – my underwear was still on. I pressed my thighs, my groin. I didn't feel bruised. Why would he? He'd had me already, willingly. But he could have if he'd wanted. He still could. I leaned over the bed and a dry, empty heave shook my body. Tears dripped off my chin.

Exhaustion flooded through me, but I fought sleep; what if I drifted into nothingness, lost myself completely. I searched for the bruises on my arm. I needed to bring myself back to something that was real. I found them, placed my fingers on top, where his had been, and pressed down gently. It hurt. I didn't understand any of it. I pressed harder.

I hated them all. Sleep snatched me and pulled me down.

* * *

I stared, blinked and stared again. There it was, a slice of light running down the side of the door. It was open. *Get up, do it now.*

I willed myself to move, but my body stayed still. I wanted to try, I wanted it so much, but what if he was waiting outside? Who knew what he was capable of? I felt sure I hadn't seen the half of it.

I shook my head so the gag fell to my chin and slipped my left hand from under the knot. He'd used his navy necktie to bind me. I swung my legs off the bed and the carpet felt rough under my stockinged feet. I looked around for my coat, my shoes and bag. *Forget them, just go.* I stood, for the first time in how long? Slowly I took a step. I didn't fall. I took another, and another, silently, quickly towards the door. Beyond here were the stairs. Beyond the stairs, the street. And beyond that? Home.

I placed my hand on the doorknob and pulled it slowly without turning. It didn't squeak. Standing on the threshold, I glanced to the left. Empty corridor. To the right nothing. Then a clatter. Was he there? *Wait. Stay still ... don't move.* Several seconds passed. It was nothing. Another step down and I'd be on the landing. There. My blood thumped out a tune in my ears: *get out, get out, get out.*

Hand on rail down the stairs. Steady. Don't fall or he'll hear. Come on. Take a step. Good. Now another. Yes. And another. Quick. You are almost there. Almost. I turned and stopped. Another door? How could that be? A door on the landing closed off the staircase. I put my hand on the knob. It turned but wouldn't open. I tried it again. And again. And—

'What are you doing?'

I cried out.

He was standing behind me in a vest, towel slung over one shoulder, hands dripping with water.

He reached for my arm but I rushed at the door and started banging, shouting frantically.

'Let me out! Help!'

'Stop it.' His voice was calm, but he grabbed my arm with such force that I yelped. 'The building's empty. Nobody will hear you.'

'No – let me out!'

The slap came from nowhere and I fell to the floor.

'I told you to stop it, Dina,' he snapped. 'Now look what you made me do.'

He dragged me by the arm back into the room.

He pushed me onto the bed then wiped his hands on the towel.

I could feel the sting of his fingers on my cheeks as I shuffled against the wall. I searched his face for a sign that he was changed, but it was the same face I'd known all this time, the face I'd loved.

He came to the bed and leaned his fists onto the mattress, making me slide towards him. Then he leaned in a little closer.

'Try that again,' he said calmly, 'and I will kick you all the way back.'

Fear buzzed through me as I pulled back. My breath caught in my chest and I hugged my knees in close. Throwing the wet towel next to me, he produced a small tube from his pocket and started rubbing cream between his fingers.

'Andreas, please.' My voice sounded croaky. 'Why am I here? What's happening?'

He glanced up.

'You can blame *her* for all of this,' he said. 'She brought it on herself.'

'*Who?*'

I had a feeling I knew but hadn't a clue why.

He walked to the desk, unlocked the drawer and took out a brown envelope. He held it out to me, then pulled it back.

'Wipe your face first.' He threw me a handkerchief from his pocket. 'You're a mess.'

I wiped my eyes and blew my nose, then took the envelope. Inside was a passport.

I opened it and stared at the photo. A young woman with long dark hair. She was less polished, but I recognised the defiant tilt of her chin.

'Why do you have Bebba's passport?'

He motioned to the envelope and I slipped my hand in again and pulled out a piece of thick paper.

'Be careful,' he said. 'Are your hands clean?'

I unfolded the rectangular sheet. Emblazoned across the

top, in a beautiful bold italic Greek script were the words **Certificate of Marriage**. My eyes dropped to the dotted line where two signatures floated in the air.

'She's your *wife?*'

I felt sick. Everything I thought I knew about her – and him – had been a lie. Who *were* they?

'The bitch stole my money after the wedding,' he said. 'The dowry.'

'And she left you?'

'Over a year ago.'

'What did you do to her?' I asked. 'Why did she leave?'

'I didn't do *anything*. I'm her husband.' Some spittle had flown from his mouth onto the bed and the tendons in his neck tightened. 'She's mine, she can't just leave. Can you imagine the shame that brought on my family?'

I didn't say anything.

'You might want to ask what she did to *me*.' He pointed to the scar on his shoulder. 'She's vicious. And she practically ruined my reputation when she left.'

He picked up the certificate, folded it again and took the passport, dropping them back in the envelope.

'Why me?' I asked. 'What's this got to do with me?' He didn't answer but turned the envelope over in his hands, then put it on the bed. 'Andreas?'

'Rico,' he said.

'What?'

'Nobody calls me Andreas. And I hate Andriko. The old man calls me that. Makes me feel about ten.'

'You even lied to me about your *name*?'

'It's the same name, stupid. Andreas, Andriko, Rico.'

I shook my head. She was married, he wasn't who he said he was, and I was tangled up in the middle. I rubbed my face with the hankie.

'And you came here to find her?' I asked. 'All that way?'

'I looked for months.'

He sat down and I rearranged myself, shifting further away.

'She always talked about London – the jobs, the opportunities, all that bollocks – so I knew she'd be here somewhere. Showed her photo around all the Greek areas but nothing.'

'Because she'd changed her hair.'

He nodded.

'She changed everything,' he said. 'It was you who helped me find her. I recognised you from the café, then I saw who you were with.'

'What? You saw us together? Where? When?' It could have been any of a dozen of our Soho haunts.

'Does it matter?' he said.

I tried to think of the places we'd been together. There'd been so many.

'*Where?*'

'Some dive on Rupert Street – terrible acts.'

I hesitated.

'You . . . you mean *the Pelican*?'

He shrugged. 'I recognised you from the café.'

'So, you decided to get to know me,' I said, 'to get to her?'

'I'd always liked the look of you. I'd even been thinking of asking you out . . .'

'Oh my God!'

'Calm down, *gori*. I was here for *her*. If I'd met you another time, who knows?'

I cried out. 'You think I'd want to be with you? After all of this?'

'Of course not, I'm married. I'm just saying . . .'

I hurled a pillow and the corner hit him in the eye. He flew across the room and slapped me with such force that I fell onto the bed and hit my head on the wall. I pushed my face into the bedclothes and shouted.

'I can't make out what you're saying, you idiot,' he yelled.

I turned towards him, 'I said I want to go home.'

'We all fucking want to go home.'

I took some breaths and tried to calm myself.

'Why didn't you just take her?' I sobbed. 'That night you saw us? You could have taken her with you and none of this would have happened.'

'Without knowing where the money was? And in a public place? She'd raise hell. Anyway, I couldn't find her again. Then when I did spot her, she was with him. Stuck to your adoring brother like glue.'

'So, what was I, then? Your bargaining chip?'

He shrugged. 'You can call it that. Or a last resort. Or a naughty Greek girl desperate to lose her virginity.'

I kicked the envelope off the bed.

'If you rip that I'll—'

'What? *Kill* me? You need me, Andreas, Rico – whatever your bloody name is.'

He bent over and picked it up, then said, calm as anything,

'Don't make me hurt you. Because I will.'

'You won't. If you do you won't get your money back.'

'You want to bet on that?'

'Do you?'

He put the envelope back in the drawer and locked it. I stared at the carpet, my eyes following the sickening pattern of red and silver.

'They know I'm here?'

He nodded.

'And you'll let me go once you've got the money?'

'As long as they don't do anything stupid. She's coming back with me, and then you can go – to hell for all I care.'

Peter would be sick with worry. And her? She wouldn't give up the money without a fight, let alone go back to Cyprus with him.

Then as if he knew what I was thinking he said, 'Let's hope for your sake they pay up, eh? Now do you want some food?'

I didn't reply.

'Suit yourself.' He leaned across and tied my hands behind my back, tighter this time. 'I'm locking the door. The Fifi downstairs is away so save your breath.'

I slid down the bed.

'You know, Dina—'

'Shut up! I don't want to listen to you any more.'

He leaned across and tugged the gag across my mouth, tighter this time. 'Works both ways.'

A few hours ago I'd thought I was in love and now I loathed him. Almost as much as I loathed her. Peter was the only one I could trust now. The only person I could count on.

32

The following morning, Bebba stood under an arch at St Pancras, a French-navy headscarf wrapped around her unruly hair, a handkerchief across her mouth. The smog was in its fourth day and had turned wetter and denser overnight, refusing to let go. Although it was only just after ten, the paltry daylight was already losing the fight. The air lay around them solid and noxious as a bloated carcass. She pulled the handkerchief down and turned to Peter.

'Can I have a ciggie, darling?'

'You want to smoke, now?' he asked, but still fished in his pocket and pulled out a new pack of Woodbines. She took one and he lit a match for her. She'd only smoked Piccadillys since arriving, it had been one of her things, but she'd forgotten to buy some, and frankly was thankful for anything. She'd also left her cigarette holder at home. It seemed that everything that made her Bebba was coming undone. Fear and a lack of sleep did that to a person; you forgot who you were. She took a long, hard drag and enjoyed the kick of nicotine as it reeled through her body.

They'd left at eight that morning, knowing it would take ages to get through this mess, especially as they had to stop frequently to check where they were going. As she'd walked with him gingerly to the station, the boldness of her previous journeys through the fog was a distant memory. All she'd thought about for the past two days was whether Rico expected her to leave with him today. She hadn't asked and hadn't packed. Why make it easy for him? She'd have to return to the flat for her things and perhaps she could give him the slip then. She'd considered leaving in the dead of night, taking the money from St Pancras and disappearing. But this blasted weather had made moving around impossible, especially alone. And anyway, she'd be foolish to walk out on Peter now; she might need him in the coming weeks. She'd stick around for a little while at least.

They entered the station and went to the left luggage, where she picked up the case. They waited outside the office, as he'd instructed. In a few minutes, they'd have Dina back. Bebba stamped her feet to help the feeling return to her toes. What would she say to her? Had he told her everything?

When she'd first found out that Rico had kidnapped Dina, a switchblade of guilt had sliced through her, but since then the worst of the feeling had simply dissolved. After all, how could Dina possibly blame her? It was Dina's own fault for keeping secrets in the first place. If Bebba thought she could retrieve the case and escape them all, she'd have left Dina to her fate. They'd been friends, some would say good friends, but the way she saw it she didn't owe either of them anything.

Peter kicked the suitcase with the toe of his shoe. 'Is that it, then?'

She nodded.

'My sister's life in exchange for this?' He kicked it again.

She opened her mouth to say something conciliatory but closed it again as she saw a solitary figure approach.

'*Kaliméra*,' said Rico, with a sarcastic tip of his hat. 'I see you brought it this time.'

'Where's Dina?' asked Peter, looking around frantically. 'You said you'd bring her.'

'Calm down. She's safe. You'll get her when I've had a chance to look inside.' He looked at Bebba. 'Check that you haven't filled it with old newspapers or rubbish.'

'We wouldn't do that,' said Peter, squaring up to him. 'It's my sister we're talking about here.'

Rico shrugged. 'Well, you didn't do as you were asked before, so I'm not taking chances. If it's all there, I'll get the tickets and tomorrow we'll swap.'

He leaned down and picked up the case.

'No. Hold on,' said Peter, his hand on Rico's arm. 'You said today.'

'I know.' He pushed his hand back off his arm. 'I lied. Platform three tomorrow at five o'clock. She'll be there.'

'How do I know that you're not lying now?'

'What do you take me for?' said Rico, as if greatly offended. 'I'll bring her.'

Bebba stepped forwards.

'Listen, Rico, I'm sorry. But I . . . I had to spend some of it.'

'*What?*'

She flinched.

'Not much,' she said, hurriedly. 'Well, quite a lot. But I had rent to pay and – well, I had to get by. Food and . . .'

He took off his gloves and she stopped talking, not sure what he was about to do. He reached out and sank his fingers into the fur of her leopard-skin coat, ruffling it like a pet.

'Fake?'

She nodded.

'Like you,' he said. 'Well, you'll have to replace the money.'

'How?'

'Earn it back. I'm sure we can think of something.'

Pushing his hand back into the glove, he took her arm. She instinctively tried to pull away, but he held on.

'Stop that. You're coming with me. There's something I need you to do.'

She shot a panicked look at Peter.

'Don't worry,' said Rico. 'I'll bring her back.'

Peter stepped up to his face. 'No, I don't think so,' he said. 'You've got my sister and now this? You don't get to walk away with the money and the girl.'

Rico laughed. 'Here. I'll leave the case. Now you know I'll be back.' He put it down at Peter's feet. 'Won't be long.'

'Where are you going?' asked Peter.

'We'll be fifteen, twenty minutes at the most,' he said. 'I have them both now, so just you remember that.'

Rico linked his arm through hers and, as they walked away, he pulled Bebba in tight, like any adoring husband might. On the corner stood a newspaper vendor, a boy, barely fourteen. He held a large sheet displaying the day's headlines: FOG! TRAM AND COACH COLLISIONS.

'*Daily News*! Paper mister? Read about the fog chaos.'

Rico gripped her tight and pushed past without a word. Could she pull away? Kick him and run? He'd catch her. And where would she go? He was walking so fast she didn't have time to think. She had to half run to keep pace with his long strides and her shoes pinched at her toes as they hit the pavement.

They made their way around the eastern side of the station, along Old St Pancras Road, then stopped. Looking up, she could see fragments of the monstrous building: blackened Gothic arches like giant arms thrust up, hands clasped in celebration of the smog.

Beneath each arch lay a secret world of workshops, coal offices and stores, some of which were still open. He pulled her past the thin but steady trickle of people. He was now holding her so tight that her face was right up against the coarse grey wool of his lapel. Claustrophobia engulfed her; he was everywhere.

'Rico please.' She tried to pull back a bit. 'Where are we going?'

'Shut up.' He practically spat into her face. 'Just do as I say.'

They walked to the end of a row of arches and, just when she thought there was nowhere left to go, he turned into a hole in the wall. A man inside jumped up from his seat, knocking his sandwich to the floor. He was old, maybe seventy, and in shirt sleeves despite the freezing cold. Torn between picking up his food and shaking hands, he ignored his snack and reached out.

'So, this is the lucky lady is it?' His handshake was strong and reassuring. 'Mondays are usually busy, but the fog has put a stop to that.'

Bebba looked from one to the other. 'What?'

'We're having our photo taken,' said Rico in Greek. 'To send back to my father, in Cyprus.'

She looked at him, incredulous. 'Are you *mad?*'

She'd said it in English and the photographer coughed awkwardly. Then he bent down, picked up his sandwich and blew on it before taking a bite. Something yellow oozed out of the side. He turned and pretended to rearrange some photos on a shelf.

'Whatever for?' she asked, in Greek this time.

Rico pulled her outside and put his mouth to her ear: 'To show that we've reunited. To prove that I've found you. Now shut up or—'

'Oh!'

Once she realised, she was surprised she hadn't seen it before. This hadn't just been about the money or his love for her (if that's what it was). It had always been about more.

'The land. Your inheritance.'

He nodded.

'You get nothing from your father's estate if you're not married.'

'Exactly. And the old man's not well.' His hand held her arm like a vice. 'I'll be damned if it goes to some cousin on the other side of the island. Come on.'

He pulled her back inside.

So she stood, like a fool, in the middle of the tiny studio while the photographer fussed around her, placing a chair just so, then fiddling with a camera and flash. Then he took her coat and pointed to her head.

'Headscarf, please. You need to take that off.'

'Oh no!' Her hand shot up to her head. 'My hair. It looks shocking.' She couldn't bear it, not on top of everything.

'Yes, yes, all okay. Take off,' said Rico, as he untied the knot under her chin. He pulled off the scarf and pushed her hair back.

'You look perfect, Madam,' said the photographer.

After some fussing with different backgrounds Rico finally settled on an alpine setting of cerulean sky and snow-capped mountains.

'It's black and white,' said the man, 'but I hand tint it.' She couldn't have cared less. 'It'll look very convincing.'

She was sat down. Rico stood behind her, a hand on each shoulder.

Could the man help her? Could she say something in English? But Rico would hear, he'd realise. Perhaps she could pass him a note? But what could she say? *He won't let me go. He's got my friend held prisoner.* Who'd believe such a thing? The man was old. Rico could knock him down in an instant.

Rico posed this way and that, enjoying every minute. When they were finished, he took out a slip of paper that had his father's address written neatly in English. The man copied it for him onto the form, handed it back and Rico paid.

'How long?' asked Rico. 'One week? Two?'

'Well, it'll go Express,' said the man slowly, trying to make himself understood. 'Quick you said, yes?'

Rico nodded. 'Yes, quick. Must be very quick.'

The man held his hand out and showed his fingers. 'A few days.'

'Maybe we get home,' said Rico. 'Before picture.'

'You're going back?' asked the man.

She took a deep breath and tied her headscarf on.

'Don't like it here?' he continued.

She couldn't speak.

'This blasted fog I expect.'

'Yes, fucking fog.' Rico laughed as he helped her into her coat again.

The man flinched a little, shocked at the swearing. He looked at Bebba and realised she didn't care one way or the other, so he laughed, too.

'You've got that right, mate.'

She stood still while Rico quickly did up the buttons on her coat for her, the way he would if she were a child, got her handbag off the floor and handed it to her. Then he took her by the arm.

'It'll look grand,' said the photographer. 'Lovely surprise for your old man. Your father.'

Rico nodded.

'And when it arrives, think of me,' he continued, 'while you're sunning yourselves, think of me in grey old London, stuck in this . . . this . . . fucking fog.'

Rico slapped him on the back, hard, as if it was the best joke he'd ever heard. The photographer was still chuckling as they walked away.

33

Later that day Bebba sat on Peter's bed, feet tucked to one side. She'd finally bought some Piccadillys and had already got through half a pack. For hours they'd talked and smoked and downed shots of Gordon's. The emerald green bottle now lay empty on the floor, but she'd never felt more sober in her life.

She shifted a little closer, put her hand on his leg and left it there.

'I'm not doing it,' she said. 'He's got my money and now he wants me, too? I'm not going back to him.'

She looked at him for a reaction. He'd taken to repeatedly running his hands through his hair, searching for something there, an idea, an opinion – anything. And his eyes . . . had he been crying?

'I don't want you to go, either, Beb. But he's got Dina.' His lip showed the ghost of a quiver. 'What choice do we have?'

God, she wanted to shake him.

Instead she moved even closer and asked, 'Do you love me Peter?'

'What a question!' His voice was breaking. 'Yes, of course I love you, but she's my sister.'

She dropped back on the bed, exasperated.

'For heaven's sake, I'm not asking you to choose – I'd never ask you to choose between the two of us.' She'd win outright, surely?

'Good, because you know I couldn't.'

She squirmed closer till she was practically in his lap. 'Of course we'll get Dina back, but I'm saying that if you love me, and you want me to stay, to be with you forever, then the solution is simple.'

He frowned, so she told him. The one outrageous act that Rico would never expect. He took some convincing – about the same amount of time as it took for her to lift her arms, pull off her dress and roll down her stockings. He frantically helped her shed the rest. His lovemaking was even more rushed than usual, as if a large clock was above them and their time was ticking away. When it was over, she whispered all kinds of ridiculous promises about their future and told him again why her idea was really the only way out. Yes, he agreed, it was a simple solution. Perfect in fact. But they'd have to be quick. He'd make some calls. They'd act tonight.

* * *

That same evening, every inch of Bebba's body fizzed with nervous energy. He'd wanted to go alone, but she'd insisted. The smog outside was as thick and wet as treacle. With handkerchiefs tied around their mouths, they'd set off immediately. Arm in arm, he led her along fog-wrapped Dean Street, the muffled sound of their footsteps echoing the pounding in her head: this-time-tomorrow, this-time-tomorrow. This time tomorrow it would all be over. A cocktail of dread and anxiety swilled through her, and she could taste the bitterness on the back of her tongue. But she also detected a drop of hope.

'You're sure he'll be here?' she asked, as they approached the club. 'Your contact?'

'He's always here. It's his office. Anyway, he knows we're coming. His associate said he could help.'

'Do you have enough money?' She couldn't believe that Rico had taken the suitcase.

'Don't worry. It's sorted.' He stopped and pushed open a dark door. 'Here we are.'

They pulled down their handkerchiefs. The hallway stank and she felt all the confidence of the past few hours seep away. On the wall was a sign painted in a thick olive green: 'Colony Room Club, 1st Floor, Members Only'. She could hear the melancholic strains of jazz float towards them.

'But we're not members.'

Peter sighed. 'Will you stop worrying?'

He'd never grown irritated with her before.

'He's not in the Colony. He runs the Cypriot club, on the second floor.'

This was his sort of place, his corner of the world and he seemed at ease, comfortable even. As she followed him up, the light bulb threw a sickly, yellow stain over the cracked lino, grubby walls and splintered skirting. Something sticky had clung to the sole of her left shoe but she didn't want to stop and look. As they ascended, the smell of urine and tobacco grew stronger. Just outside the Colony Room, a couple stood, kissing. The man, in a black sweater, had his back to them but the woman saw them, and she stared as they walked past. Her hands were draped around her lover's neck, casually crossed over, cigarette between her fingers. Bebba wished she was her.

There were no windows in the Cypriot club. There was no real club to speak of either, just a desolate room with three battered long tables at one end, a dozen or so chairs and a bar. Men in dark, crumpled suits clustered like flies, buzzing with Greek conversation, playing cards, gambling and arguing. Even the deadliest smog couldn't stop truly dedicated losers. Most of them were drinking shot glasses of what looked like liquid fog – *ouzo* mixed with water.

There was only one other female in the room, a washed-out middle-aged woman behind the bar, but still nobody glanced at Bebba. Either she'd unravelled more than she'd realised or these men were losing hard.

'There he is,' said Peter. They walked towards a dishevelled, portly man who reached across and shook his hand.

'Hello, Peter. Who's this?'

'A friend,' then to her, 'This is *Kyrieh* Vasos.'

The man began to reach out to greet her, but she nodded a hello and used her hands to smooth down the back of her skirt before she sat.

He rubbed the grey stubble on his chin, and she noticed the skin on his knuckles was flaking as if his fingers were made of *filo*. Down the front of his shirt were the remnants of a long-forgotten meal. Here was a man who'd fought with life and lost. Tinny *bouzouki* music played from a gramophone in the corner and they all leaned in to avoid being overheard.

'So, can you help us?' Peter asked.

'What? Not even the offer of a drink?' He wheezed as he said it, then gave a laugh, pretending it had been a joke.

'You're being paid so let's just get on with it shall we?' Peter's business-like tone surprised her. It seemed she had a habit of underestimating people.

'I can't do it myself but—'

Peter jolted in his seat. 'But – I was told—'

'I'm not taking the risk.' Mr Vasos put his thumbs under his lapels and straightened himself up. 'Can't afford to. Just got out, you see.' Then he looked at Bebba and spoke to her directly for the first time, in an exaggerated hush, 'from prison'. He raised his eyebrows. Was she meant to be impressed?

Peter banged his hand on the table, and she jumped.

'Steady!' Mr Vasos grabbed his empty glass.

'I was told you could help me. Can you or can't you?'

'I didn't say I couldn't help you. I just said I couldn't do it myself.'

Bebba spoke: 'What . . . so . . . so you mean you know some-one *else* who could do it?'

'Yes. But it's your timing, you see. The gentleman I'd usually use is in hospital at the moment. His lungs don't like this fog. And everyone else is busy – this weather opens up all kinds of . . . opportunities.'

'*So?*' Peter's impatience was growing.

'So . . .' Mr Vasos put down his glass, coughed twice without covering his mouth and leaned in. 'I can still supply the item. For a price. Of course, I don't want it back. That would be stupid, wouldn't it?'

'But I don't understand?' Peter's confusion scrunched up his face. 'If your man is in hospital—'

'He means for *you* to do it,' said Bebba.

'*What?*' Peter's face lost all its colour. 'That's ridiculous. No. I can't.'

Mr Vasos gave an exaggerated shrug. 'Your choice.' He shifted in his seat, picked up his glass again and looked into the bottom of it, but it hadn't refilled magically.

Peter shook his head. 'I just can't.'

There was a pause and Mr Vasos sighed then moved again, making as if to get up.

'I can do it,' said Bebba.

They both looked at her and Mr Vasos burst out laughing.

'Don't be stupid,' said Peter.

She leaned in close to Peter's face and spoke in a fierce whisper. 'Why not? You think I wouldn't? I'd shoot him in a heartbeat.'

Mr Vasos' smile slid off his face and he sat back to take her in fully. There was an awkward pause of a few seconds and then he said, 'I don't care for details, really. None of my business. I just need to know if you want my services or if we're wasting our time here.'

'We do,' she said.

'No!' said Peter.

'Definitely,' she countered.

'Well I can only sell to ...' he nodded at Peter, '... your husband ...'

'*Excuse* me? What do you mean?'

'Those are the rules.'

Bebba laughed, incredulous. 'Rules? Wait – you don't mind selling guns or hiring out thugs, but you have morals about selling to a *woman*?'

He turned and addressed Peter. 'We can't have ladies running around out of control with, well, this kind of equipment, can we?'

'No,' said Peter.

'For heaven's—' Bebba began

Mr Vasos stood. 'Now, I'll pop off to the gents,' he said, 'give you a minute, and when I come back you can let me know what you've decided.'

Peter nodded, solemnly, and as he passed, the man slapped him on the back as though he was about to commence a challenging dance at a Cypriot wedding.

As she watched the old man walk away, Peter grabbed her arm. 'What are you thinking, *gori*?'

'Get off!' She pulled her arm from his grasp. 'If you won't I will. You'll get Dina and I'll get what I want.'

He shook his head. 'You can't. Look, let's go to the police instead. We can go right now.'

'Oh, don't be ridiculous.' She lit a Piccadilly and took a deep drag. 'It's far too late for that. We're up to our necks. Just get it. I'll do it. It's the only way.'

Peter shifted in his seat and leaned so close, the smell of stale sweat hit her nostrils.

'What if,' he whispered, 'what if something goes wrong? If you hit her by mistake? Or get hurt?'

She didn't reply.

'I mean,' he spoke quickly and quietly now, 'do you even *know* how to use a gun?'

'I grew up on a farm. Find your target, point and shoot.'

'What? A rifle? For God's sake, Beb. This is completely different.'

He was right, but what else could she do?

'I can't let you do it. I won't. It's a huge risk,' he said. And just as she thought he was about to change his mind and say he'd do it himself, he put his arm around her shoulder and pulled her in to kiss her cheek. She moved an inch away and he ended up with a mouthful of hair. He spoke into her neck: 'A gun is too risky, too noisy. You'd be seen, heard. In this country, they *hang* people for murder.'

Her chair scraped on the wooden floor as she moved a little.

'Still better than going back.'

She tapped the filter of the ciggie with her thumbnail, flicking ash onto the floor.

'Anyway,' she continued. 'You've changed your tune. Last night this was all a good idea.'

'When someone else was going to do it, yes. Sorry, Beb, but no. I'm not using a gun, and neither are you.'

Anger flared inside her chest. She'd worked on him for so long, and here he was, at this crucial moment, saying no to her.

'So, what do you suggest?' she hissed.

They heard a loud cough and both looked up. From the far end of the room they saw Mr Vasos trundling towards them. In his hand he held a refilled glass.

'It's not the only way,' said Peter.

34

I lay on the bed and watched Rico count the money. He arranged the contents of the suitcase onto the table in parallel rows. I'd never seen so many Cypriot notes before and, from the way he handled each packet – delicately picking up each bundle with the tips of his fingers like it might explode – he hadn't either.

Once he'd placed it in rows, he took a silent count, pointing at each stack in turn. I counted with him, watching how many times his finger went up and down. I made it five, with a few extra notes on the side that he stuffed into his pocket. We both counted again. Definitely five. Then he opened each pack and counted the notes one by one.

That's when I realised these weren't stacks of tens – they were blue notes, not green. Could they really be twenties? He licked his thumb and counted and counted. He came to the end and started over. I counted with him. Twenty-five notes, all twenties. That was, what? Five hundred Cypriot pounds.

My mind raced as I quickly calculated it in my head. I earned just over three pounds a week at the café. That was, say, £150 or thereabouts a year. This was over three years' money. Imagine. Three years' hard work all there on that table. More, once it had been changed into sterling. All the things a person could do with that: buy anything, go anywhere, be whoever they wanted to be.

He looked up and caught me staring. Neither of us spoke and I rolled over. After a few moments I heard him place it all back in the case, then click it shut.

35

When I woke I'd been untied. I quickly pulled off the gag and saw a glass of water on the floor next to the bed and a plate with the heel of a small loaf. I gulped down the water, then picked up the crust and started to devour it, trying to ignore the rancid smell of the greyish substance that had been spread over it. How many days had passed? Had I eaten anything since he'd brought me here? I couldn't remember, but it felt good to chew something solid and swallow it, feeling it go down into my stomach, proving that I existed.

The door opened and he walked in. I stopped, bread halfway to my mouth, and instinctively pulled myself into a corner. He threw a brown paper bag onto the bed.

'What's that?' I asked, mouth full.

'Stockings,' he said. 'Get dressed. We need to get going.'

I didn't move.

'Well, come on,' he said, straightening his tie. 'Don't just sit there with your mouth hanging open. We need to leave in twenty minutes. Make yourself presentable. You're a mess.'

Was it a trick? I dropped the bread on the plate and quickly wiped up with the back of my hand. Relief rose in my chest and I battled not to let it take hold; I wasn't safe yet.

'*Really?*' I asked. 'I'm going home?'

'Really – now get moving.'

I put down the plate and swung my legs out of bed.

Rico walked to the wardrobe, pulled out the case, sat it on the table and opened it, looking at the money again. Then he held it open at an angle so I could see the notes neatly tucked next to each other, a row of sleeping angels.

'Quite something, isn't it?' he asked.

I shrugged and pulled the paper bag towards me.

'It's just money.'

'It's never *just* anything. Use your imagination. It'll get you everywhere you want to be.'

'It got me here,' I said, opening the packet of stockings. 'So excuse me if I'm not that excited.'

He closed the lid and clicked the case shut.

'That's where you're wrong,' he said. 'The money didn't get you here. She did.'

He was about to return it to the wardrobe, then had second thoughts and slid the case under the bed. The stockings were darker than I usually wore, too tanned for my pale skin. He was right. If it hadn't been for Bebba, he'd never have come to Soho, we wouldn't have met and there wouldn't be this: me, here, now.

'Where did she keep it? The money?' I asked.

'St Pancras, left luggage. But to begin with the garden. Outdoors. Imagine that.'

'She *buried* it?' I remembered her washing dirt off her hands in the middle of the night.

He shook his head. 'Some old shelter, she said. Silly cow, anyone could have taken it.'

I thought for a moment and then it all came together.

'What?' he asked.

'Nothing.'

I remembered how keen she'd been to move into the garden flat. Had she noticed the shelter when she'd come for coffee that day? I bet she hadn't got kicked out of her place at all. How much of what she told us had been true? Was any of it? The sob story about her parents, our friendship, her relationship with Peter? Everything had been built on brittle lies, and now they began to snap one after the other.

I watched as he walked to the mirror and checked his tie, pushing it over slightly with his thumb. To think, once I'd believed the two of us were inseparable; Soho sisters on a wonderful adventure. Soon she'd leave with him and I'd never have to see her again.

'Can I go to the bathroom?' I asked. 'To fix my hair?'

'No.'

I looked him square in the face. 'Well let me at least wash. I need privacy.'

He considered it for a moment and let out a sigh. 'Five minutes.' He left the room and I heard the key turn in the lock.

Standing at the tiny sink, I avoided looking too closely in the mirror. I gulped some more water thirstily, straight from the tap, then splashed my face and wiped myself on the grubby towel that hung from the side. This would be the last time I stood here. I wet my hands again and used my fingers as a comb, trying to detangle days-old knots.

Pulling at my waistband, I straightened out my uniform skirt and blouse and had a quick sniff under my arms. I didn't want to undress in case he walked in. I unbuttoned my blouse, wet my hand again and quickly rubbed my armpits. I took off my knickers, did the same between my legs and dabbed myself dry with the clothes I wore. Then I turned my knickers inside out and quickly put them on. Without bothering to knock, he came in as I was straightening my stockings. I turned my back.

'Let's go.'

'Where are my shoes?'

He opened the wardrobe and took them out from a high shelf, along with my bag. I slipped them on and looked down. After days of wearing nothing on my feet they felt hard and unfamiliar. I opened my compact and powdered my face a little, keeping my gaze on my cheeks, nose, chin – anything but my eyes. Then I applied a slick of Poppy Rouge to my lips. The last time I'd done this was the day he'd met me from work. I placed the compact into my bag and saw the photo. If I looked at it now, my heart would split open. As I picked up my mac from the bed, he moved to help me put it on out of habit.

I dodged away.

'I can manage.'

Not much longer, gori. I buttoned up my coat. *When you take this off, you'll be safe, at home.* I took the belt and tied it tight. *She'll be gone and it will be just you and Peter. Like before. Like it should be.* I'd missed him. I was surprised to realise it, but it was true.

Rico moved to the door. 'Come on, or we'll be late.'

As he pulled the keys from his pocket, he turned to me and asked, 'Your brother?'

'Yes?'

'How stupid is he?'

'Sorry?'

'Would he involve the police?'

I shook my head. Peter was many things, but he wasn't disloyal.

'He'd never do that,' I said. 'He'll be worried sick.'

We started down the stairs, past the damp-stained wall-paper and the anaemic painting of a woman in a poppy field.

'He loves me, you know,' I said, perhaps convincing myself as much as him.

Rico held my arm tight and unlocked the door.

'I don't doubt it,' he said. 'But he's *besotted* with her.'

*   *   *

We stepped out of the flat and the smog kissed my face slow and thick, like a drunken uncle. Had this chaos really lasted all these days? A few yards in front of me I could just make out the Dog and Duck. *So he lived just across the road?* He'd only had to carry me a few steps after slipping something in my drink. I turned back and looked at his flat. An unremarkable blue door, nothing more. I pulled up my collar against the muck.

Traffic was barely moving so he decided we'd walk, but the fog meant we had to stick to main roads. It was a slow, difficult trudge up to Holborn and through Southampton Row, all the while him steering me along. I'd hardly slept for days but, despite my exhaustion, the thought of returning home kept me moving.

Finally, we turned right into Euston Road and there it was: St Pancras Station, regal and terrible, a crown of fog wrapped around its spires.

On seeing it, he tugged at my arm.

'Will you stop it?' I said, loudly. 'You're hurting me.'

A woman pushing a pram came towards us and threw him a filthy stare. I could shout out. *Do it now.* I opened my mouth to speak but she'd scurried past.

'Well you hold *me*, then,' he said and stuck out his elbow.

Reluctantly, I slipped my hand through his arm and he pulled me in tight, trapping me against his side. The wool of his coat brushed against my cheek. I'd once loved the touch, smell and taste of him: the coarse nap of fabric, the whiff of Old Spice, the aftertaste of Craven 'A's when we kissed. Every sensation I'd associated with him was now heavy with hate.

Inside the station, steam shifted and mixed with the fog above our heads, and every few seconds another rib of the monstrous arched roof appeared, only to disappear again. It was nearly five o'clock, and the concourse and platforms were soaked in a grey half-light with acid-yellow spots where the lamps shone.

A train groaned to a halt and dozens of passengers rushed to board as others spewed off. Twice we were almost knocked over. Families, couples, young and old – people everywhere but nobody was looking. Frantic thoughts scuttled through my mind: I thought again about screaming for help and I must have slowed down because Rico, irritated, drew me closer. There was only a scrap of life left in me, not enough for a fight. And if I did escape, what then? I'd have to find Peter and then *she'd* get away too, because Rico would have nothing to bargain with. No, I would wait a few moments; I'd be free, and she'd be gone forever.

He stopped, coughed, then coughed again, hard, wild things trapped in his throat. Bending over his handkerchief, he retched up something black and disgusting.

'Where are we meeting?' I asked.

Another retch, then he stood upright.

'Jesus Christ . . . this city is a hell hole.' Sweat beaded on his forehead. 'End of Platform 3,' he said, pointing just a few yards away. 'And don't try anything, or I swear it'll be the last thing you do.'

We side-stepped the crowds along the platform,

'Look,' said Rico. He nodded to the far end. 'They're here.'

36

Bebba stamped her feet to get her frozen blood moving. It was Dina she spotted first, sliding in and out of the fog, and for a moment she thought she'd come alone. Then a dark shadow appeared next to her and she knew from the size and shape that it was Rico guiding her, pushing her forwards.

'Peter – he's brought her!'

She realised she hadn't quite believed he would. She turned to say something to him, but he wasn't by her side. Where the hell . . .? He was several paces behind, his mouth twisted, his body unable to move any faster, as if walking to the gallows.

'Come *on*,' she hissed.

He'd been so sure he could do this, and now the idiot would ruin it all. She'd tried to think of everything – worn her dark coat and hidden her hair under a black headscarf – but here he was, faltering, drawing attention with his awkwardness. She quickly glanced at Rico and Dina; they'd slowed down, too. Did they sense something was wrong?

Eventually, like a man on a tightrope, Peter took a few tentative steps towards her. His coat was slung over his arm and he kept patting it. If he let her down now, she'd rip him apart. Finally, he stood next to her.

'All right?' Her voice was sharp.

He took a deep breath then nodded.

'Yes. I can do this. For us.'

'Quick and decisive,' she said. 'Remember?'

They continued walking along the platform as Dina and Rico approached. They were just close enough to make out each other's faces. Dina's was a jagged portrait of her former self, all the prettiness stamped out.

'Does she look all right to you?' asked Peter.

'She looks fine.'

Then a voice, over the speakers, apologising about a platform change. They were forced to stop as dozens of passengers swarmed towards the platform, and Rico and Dina stopped too. She saw Peter's arm shake as he reached under his coat.

'All these people,' he said, his voice tight. 'What if someone sees?'

A gust of loathing swept through her.

'Keep it *hidden* until you're right next to him. If you can't, I can take—'

'No.'

Steam belched from the train and as it mixed with the fog, a bitter, yellow smog billowed over them. She lost sight of the others, then the cloud blew away and there they were again, a few yards from where she stood. A train whistle shrieked, and they all took tiny steps towards each other.

Then Peter's voice cracked: 'She looks awful.'

She really did, but there was nothing to be done about it now. Rico said something to Dina, let go of her arm, and she took two steps towards them.

'Go on,' said Peter to Bebba. 'He's let her go. Remember what we said.'

'Don't *you* forget,' she said. 'We have an agreement.'

'Go.'

She started walking. Peter stayed close behind her. Dina took another step towards them. Passengers milled around, oblivious to the deadly dance playing out.

As the women approached each other, a thought came to Bebba: what if Peter didn't manage it? If he changed his mind?

In a few seconds Dina was next to her, eyes spilling with hate. Standing shoulder to shoulder, they faced opposite directions. Bebba turned her head and said two words, but a train door slammed, and Dina frowned. She hadn't heard.

Bebba repeated it, urgently: 'Run. Now!'

Peter swooped towards Dina and knocked her out of the way. In a heartbeat Bebba felt a hand tug at her wrist. Rico had her. *No!* Her stomach heaved. She tried to pull and twist away, but his hand tightened. *No!* Peter was meant to be right behind her.

Her throat seized. He pulled at her and she twisted this way and that, a hare caught on barbed wire, trying to shift to one side. But Rico moved too, and there he was, in front of her now, and there again, in front of her, always there, perhaps for life. His grip slipped up to her arm now, a stronger hold, and his other hand grasped her shoulder.

Move to one side. That's what Peter had said. *Move to one side so I can slice him quick and deep.*

37

I ran towards my brother. I didn't know what was happening, but I knew that if I ran towards Peter everything would be all right.

'Stay there!' He hugged me quickly, then pushed me away and started to run in the opposite direction. What was he doing? Why was he chasing Bebba and Rico and leaving me behind? What the hell was going on?

'Peter! Come back!'

I bolted after him, along the length of the platform. Through strands of fog I could just make out Rico striding away, Bebba wedged in the crook of his arm.

Come back, damn you, Peter. I'm here. Let them both rot in hell.

He was right behind them now, though they hadn't seen him. I caught up and grabbed his arm.

'Peter!'

Rico spun round at the sound of my voice. Peter shoved me with such force that I stumbled and fell to my knees. I quickly got to my feet but stayed where I was. The veil of fog weaved and twisted around the trio, making them invisible one moment then visible the next.

Rico let go of Bebba and took a swing at Peter, but he jumped back, and the right hook missed. Surprised, Rico was thrown off balance. He put out his hands and clutched at the air, trying to hang onto the fog itself. He'd just righted himself when, quick as anything, Bebba grabbed something from Peter and rushed towards her husband, giving him a long, awkward hug. They looked like lovers saying goodbye. Her headscarf had slipped, and a white tuft of hair shone brightly against his dark coat. A cloud of smoke went up and I strained to see. Suddenly, it cleared, and I saw her let go of Rico. He was bent over as if staring at his feet. Then Peter appeared again in between them and pushed Rico towards the platform edge. Rico lost his balance; he stumbled backwards, grasping at the air. Peter gave him a second shove, harder this time, and Rico fell onto the tracks.

In an instant Bebba was next to me, pulling Peter by the hand. I watched, waiting to see if Rico would climb back up onto the platform. An almighty whistle screamed, followed by a deafening hiss as a train juddered to a standstill where Rico had fallen.

'Come,' she ordered. Then calmer: 'We have to go.' She took my left arm, Peter my right, and they started to drag me in the opposite direction. 'Now walk,' she said. 'Quickly.'

My pulse drummed in my ears. What had just happened? I wanted to look back, see for myself. Through the fog up ahead I caught a glimpse of a man wearing a dark uniform. He was running straight towards us. Getting closer. I stopped and tried to move, to twist and go another way, but they held me tight.

He was practically upon on us when I saw the familiar badge worn by train staff on his chest. He pushed right past us in the direction of the chaos.

Within a minute we were on the Euston Road, walking through the wreaths of fog that coiled in front of us. Peter pointed to the soft yellow light of a taxi up ahead. He took out his handkerchief and waved to hail it. Not sure if the cab had seen us, he ran into the road.

He cried out and fell to the floor as the cab pulled up next to us, missing him by a matter of inches.

'What is it?' asked Bebba.

'My bloody ankle, I've twisted it.'

He stood, wincing as he tried to put weight on it, and almost fell again.

'Need a hand, sir?' asked the cabbie.

'No, no, we'll manage,' said Bebba. She opened the taxi door, practically threw me inside, then grabbed Peter's arm and pulled it over her shoulder.

'Lean on me,' she said. 'Come on, that's it.'

She was perfectly calm and in control. She settled on one side of me and gave the cabbie our address, while Peter wedged himself on the other.

'Not a word,' she whispered in Greek. Each of them clasped one of my hands tightly.

Our taxi inched along, the smog making the journey home torturously slow. Exhaustion crashed into me and the loud chug-chug of the taxi added to the ache, which was gripping my neck with increasing pressure. My body was trembling. I kept seeing it over and over in my mind. Peter pushing, Rico falling. He had to be dead, surely? There was no way he'd survive that.

I stared at the back of the cab driver's head. His soot-smudged collar was just visible above his black jacket. Everything had been clean once, before this all began.

38

When we finally got home Bebba pushed me into the flat, and Peter hobbled in as quickly as he could. She locked the door behind us, and I fell into the armchair.

'What are we going to do?' I asked. My breath came in short, rationed gasps and I could feel the panic rising. 'We could tell the police. What he'd done – taking me like that. They'd understand if we said it was an accident. You pushed him to get to me. That's what happened, isn't it?' I almost believed it myself, although I could still picture Peter's decisive shove.

Peter lowered himself onto the lino and she unlaced his shoe. His foot had swollen so much there was no discernible anklebone at all, just a fleshy sausage on the verge of bursting. He shuffled towards me and reached up to stroke my hair. I stared from his face to hers: they seemed so calm.

'It's so good to see you safe,' he said. Then, 'We're not saying anything to the police.'

'But why?' My voice was raised now. 'It could have been an accident.'

'Be quiet,' said Bebba, her tone quiet and flat. 'The neighbours will hear.'

'She's right,' said Peter. 'Keep your voice down.'

I leaned forwards, incredulous. This time I whispered: 'We have to do something.'

'You're in shock,' she said. 'I'll make some tea.'

He rearranged himself near my feet, unbuckled my shoes and took them off.

'Peter? What if he's alive? What if he comes back?'

'Put your bag down, Dina,' he said, 'and take off your coat.'

I did as he said and unbuttoned my mac. I shrugged off the sleeves and let it fall around me. He pulled me down next to him on the floor, and I leaned against the armchair.

'It's all right,' he said. 'He's gone. He won't come back. You're safe.'

'But how do you know?'

'I just do. I did what I had to. We both did. Now let me look at you.'

He twisted round and his eyes searched my face and my body, looking for answers to questions he'd never ask.

'You're home and that's all that matters,' he said, quietly. 'I was worried sick.' He gave a broken smile.

Bebba came over and placed a cup of tea on the floor.

'She'll be fine, won't you Dina? She's tougher than she looks.'

Peter took a handkerchief out of his pocket and dabbed at my wet cheeks.

'I thought I would die,' I said.

His face crumpled.

I grabbed his hand. 'I thought I'd never see you again.'

Bebba crouched and rubbed my arm. 'But you're here now, darling, aren't you? And you're safe. Now have some tea. I've put sugar in it.'

'Peter. What if someone saw? Let's go to the police station. We could do that, couldn't we? Tell them how he fought you – you were defending yourself, weren't you? Defending me. We were just trying to get away.'

Yes, I was sure that's what I'd seen. Rico tried to punch him, and Peter had simply fought back. I could make that story convincing, for Peter's sake.

Peter held his hand out and he winced as Bebba helped him up and into the armchair now, his swollen foot extended in front of him. She pulled a kitchen chair across to him and lifted his leg onto it.

'We had a plan and we're sticking to it,' he said. 'Forget the police.' He lit a Woodbine and took a long drag.

'But if we go,' I said, 'then they'll think we have nothing to hide. It was an accident. A terrible accident. But we must go *now*.'

A look passed between them.

'What?' I asked.

Peter flicked his ash onto the floor.

'They can't *prove* it wasn't an accident, can they?' I asked. 'There must have been so many accidents in this fog. Even if someone saw ... it would be their word against ours. And after what he did, taking me—'

'Don't you *get it*?' she asked.

'What?'

She took her handbag from the table and opened it.

'Don't,' said Peter, half getting up, then wincing. 'Don't show her that.'

Bebba carried her bag to the sink and turned on the tap. With her back to us, she busied herself for a moment, then faced us, holding a kitchen knife, dripping wet. Our kitchen knife. The one we used for everything. She pulled the tea towel from the hook on the wall and gave the knife a careful wipe. Then she opened the kitchen drawer and slipped it in.

'All that matters is that he's gone,' she said.

I closed my eyes; the truth of what I'd seen rattled through my head.

'She's right,' said Peter. 'We need to lie low for the next few days – all of us.'

'A knife?' I asked. 'I mean, you went there intending to ... to ...'

'Oh, for goodness' sake,' she said, exasperated. 'What difference does it make? The point is he's dead. Who cares how it happened?'

I ignored her.

'What were you *thinking*?' I turned to Peter, but he looked away.

I stared at her. She lit up, her hand shaking a little. I went and stood next to her, leaning in close, my lips an inch from her ear.

'*You.*'

'Actually, it was his idea, but when it came to it,' she said, drinking down her smoke, 'he couldn't see it through. Could you?'

Peter didn't speak.

'Don't tell me you're sorry,' she said to me, 'because I won't believe you.'

'Look here, *gori*,' he said, all his gentleness already dissolved. 'You're back, aren't you? You're safe? And so is Beb.' He held out his hand and she sat on the arm of the chair. He stroked her back.

'She's free of him – we all are. We did it together, didn't we? I gave him that final shove.'

'You did.' She nodded.

He smiled at her, a man who'd just played a perfect hand and won. If it wasn't for Peter stepping in, she'd be on her way back to Cyprus now. She'd owe him for the rest of her life. The bag of stones in my chest sagged heavily as I realised that what I'd been imagining all that time in Rico's flat, that she'd be out of my life, wasn't going to happen. At St Pancras he'd gone back for her. She was here to stay.

'Dina – you're safe,' he repeated.

'How dare you,' I whispered. 'Don't sit there and tell me I'm safe now. Are you expecting a thank you? I almost died, and all because of *her*.'

She walked to the gas ring and, cigarette still in mouth, started stirring some food.

'Look, Dina . . .'

'Do you *know* what you've done, Peter? Because you can bet *she* won't be blamed if it comes out. She'll find a way. She'll say it was all you, and that *you* stabbed him then pushed him, just wait and see. And what if someone did see you? Did you think of that?'

'No?' He said it like a question. 'No. It was so busy. And the fog, the confusion—'

'Listen,' I said, 'don't think they won't find you, they will. Then they'll hang you.'

'You're not helping,' Bebba said.

'And don't think you're safe either,' I said, 'because – because if they get him, even if he decides to cover up for you and says he did it all – which he's stupid enough to do – I – I will tell them.'

She stopped stirring but didn't say anything.

'I'll tell them it was you. It was all you from the beginning.'

I wasn't sorry Rico was dead, but if Peter was caught, I'd make sure he wasn't the only one to hang. As if he could already feel the noose, he unbuttoned his collar and loosened his tie.

'We'll lie low for a few days,' he said. 'Can't go anywhere with this bloody ankle anyway. They'll never find me.' He rubbed the back of his neck. 'And even if they did, they can't link me to him. I mean, how could they? I don't have a motive, don't even know him. It's perfect.'

I couldn't believe what I'd just heard.

'Are you stupid? There's your link.' I pointed at her. 'And your motive.'

His hand stopped mid-air and his expression dropped. God, he really hadn't considered it at all. He pulled his tie off and let it fall to the floor.

'We don't need your lectures right now,' said Bebba. 'He did this for you, you know.'

'No,' I said. I picked up my bag and my coat and walked towards her. 'He already had me. Rico let me go and we could have left, but he chased after *you*.' I turned to look at my heroic brother. 'Because he thinks he loves you. And – this is the ridiculous part – that you love him, too.'

I stormed into my bedroom, dropping my coat and bag on the floor. Well, if she wasn't leaving then I would. If the room at Colleen's had gone, maybe she'd know of another that was as cheap.

A weariness flooded through me. First, I needed to rest, then I'd collect my wages from the Coffee Corner and leave. I rummaged inside my bag and pulled out Madame S's card, staring at the familiar drawing of a cotton reel with her name and number on either side. I slipped it into the inside pocket to keep it safe. I picked up a few things and walked to the door.

'Stop!' Peter's voice was thick with panic. 'Where are you going?'

'I've been locked up for days, so if it's all right with you I'm having a bath.' I thrust the towel and soap towards him. 'Or do I need your permission for that, too?'

39

I lay in bed that evening and drifted in and out of sleep, obliterated by the relief of being home. I saw the events of the past few months thunder through my mind, unreeling like a film at the Empire. There I was, dancing with Andreas in Jimmy's, sitting with him in that huge oak tree in the park, lying next to him in my bed. It looked like me but surely it was someone else. I turned in my sleep and a now-familiar twinge strummed along the left side of my neck, telling me this hadn't happened to another Dina, but to me. I massaged it gently, willing it to repair. If my body forgot, perhaps my mind would too.

There he was, towel over his shoulder, hands dripping wet. I felt him, too: his finger pushing my hair off my face, his hands slung over my hips as he came up behind me that first time, here in this flat, on top of me in bed. His grip on my elbow tight as he pulled me through St Pancras. The moments all shuffled against each other like a pack of cards, Andreas, Rico, Andreas, Rico. Arranged, rearranged, no matter how many times, the final scene that landed face up was always the same: Rico hugged by Bebba then folding into nothing. A disappearing act. The perfect conjuring trick.

An anaemic winter light bled around the edges of the curtains, making it impossible to tell the time. Sometimes I'd wake and forget, then my hand would go up to my left arm and press the pale-yellow ghost prints on my skin, where his fingers had gripped. I was sure that even when those marks had faded to nothing, I would still feel them.

A door closed and I jerked into a sitting position, heart pounding. *It's all right, gori, you're all right now. He's gone.* There was a glass of water on the bedside table. She must have put it there. I took it and drank every drop. She'd left a bowl of *avgolémoni* egg-lemon soup on the floor. How long had I been in bed?

I lay down and looked up at the ceiling crack, the one I'd noticed the first day he was here. *You know I'll take care of you, don't you?* A long, crooked spider's leg that stretched and twitched from the corner of the room to the amber lampshade.

'He's dead,' I said quietly, to myself. 'He's dead.'

As I stared at the leg, in the corner of my eye I saw another long, pointed leg twist to meet it above my head. From the edges of the ceiling, other legs burst forwards, rushing to the centre, meeting in a vile, dark knot. The huge misshapen spider throbbed, and I held my breath, not daring to look away. Then, quick as a finger-snap, the whole wicked mess burst open and rained down on me, drenching me in a thick sleep.

40

I opened my eyes to find Bebba perched on the edge of my bed.

'How long have you been sitting there?' My voice sounded croaky and I reached out for the glass. She'd refilled it.

'Sorry, darling.' She helped me sit up. 'I did knock but you were asleep. You've been drifting in and out.'

'Have I?'

It felt like just a few minutes ago that we'd returned from St Pancras. 'What day is it?'

'Thursday.'

'Not Wednesday?'

'You slept through it – on and off.'

I could hear the voices of a news broadcast from the radio in Peter's room. That's what the tinny sound was. I had heard it in my dreams.

'Your brother's been out of action, too,' she said, leaning over me. 'Ankle as black as an aubergine – I wondered if he'd broken it.'

'What? Did you call a doctor?'

'Of course not. Don't worry – the swelling's started to go down, but he still can't walk. He's in a filthy mood, being cooped up all this time.' She rolled her eyes and smiled, trying to make light of it. There was a weariness about her mouth. 'He hasn't slept a wink and is full of demands – never knew he had such a rotten temper. I haven't had a minute to myself.'

'It's really been two days?'

She nodded. 'I've only been out once to the grocer's on the corner for a few minutes. I daren't leave you. You were hallucinating, I think. Do you feel hot?'

She put the back of her hand against my forehead.

'Heavens, you're burning up.'

My nightdress had stuck to my chest. I pulled it away from my skin and blew down my front.

'Hope it's not flu,' she said. 'Maybe you should sleep a bit more. By the way, the Jamaican woman upstairs was asking after you.'

'What?'

'Wendy?'

'Winnie.'

'I was emptying the bin,' she continued. 'Said she hadn't seen you for ages. I told her you were poorly and then she turned up with some rice dish, can you believe it? Bloody nuisance. I said I'd heat it up for you but I didn't let her in.'

I squashed the pillow behind my back and sat up properly so I could look her in the eye.

'What do you want?' I asked.

She averted her gaze and looked down at the candlewick bedspread, tracing the pattern with her finger as if touching it for the first time.

'Why were you sitting here, waiting for me to wake? It wasn't to tell me about Winnie, was it?'

'Just to talk. When you're well enough – though it *is* urgent ... so ...' Her smile quickly turned into a frown. 'I have to ask you to do something.'

'Go on.'

'It's for all of us.' She pulled a pack of cigarettes from her pocket, changed her mind and pushed them back in. 'I need your help. I need to get the case – with the money.'

'What?'

'The case in Rico's flat. I don't know the address, and I'm sure you remember where—'

'No.' My chest felt tight and I started to cough. It took a few moments for the wheeziness to subside and she waited for me to catch my breath. 'I'm not going back there, I just—'

'Oh, I know,' she interrupted, putting her hand on my arm. 'I *know* it's difficult. But if we don't get it, then it would have all been for nothing, don't you see?'

I pulled my arm away. The thought of returning terrified me. A slick of sweat had cooled on my skin and a shiver spun through me. I tried to yank up the bedspread for a little warmth and she half-stood, tugged it up for me, and sat again. I held it as a barrier against her.

'How do you know it's still there?' I asked. 'In the flat?'

'Why wouldn't it be? It's only been a few days. They won't have rented it out already. I doubt anyone's even noticed yet that he's . . .' Her sentence tapered off. 'Look. It's not just for me. I promised your brother a share, so I'm sure he'll do something for you, too . . .'

'I don't want any of the money.'

'He won't deny you anything now. He'd even buy you a ticket back to Cyprus if you want.'

'Cyprus?'

She smiled brightly.

'What are you talking about?' I asked. 'Why on earth would I want a ticket for Cyprus?'

'Well – I just thought you might want a different kind of life now. With everything that's happened here . . .'

I couldn't believe it. *Did she think Soho was just for her?*

'No.' I said. 'I'm staying.' It was one of the few things I was certain of.

She gave a little suit-yourself shrug.

'But I am right,' she said. 'If we get the suitcase you'll benefit, you know. He'll give you anything. Think of that.'

Her stories, her reasoning, her bargains – it was all so exhausting. But I knew what I wanted, and it was something only she, not Peter, could give me.

'And you'll be where?' I asked.

She shook her head. 'What do you mean?'

'Once we have the suitcase – *if* we get the suitcase – you'll be where? What's your big plan, Bebba?'

She sat up a little straighter and gave a bright, cold smile.

'Well, I'll be with Peter, of course.' I didn't believe a word. Why would she stay with him once she had the money? She was saying what she thought I wanted to hear. That's how she got what she wanted, making you feel she was doing something for you when it was really the other way around. I reached out and took her hand and a look of pleasant surprise came over her face, and then shock as I dug my nails in a little.

'Ouch!' She pulled away with some force.

'You listen to me,' I said. 'I'll go and get your suitcase on one condition.'

'There's no need for that.' She rubbed her hand.

'*You* leave,' I said.

'But . . .'

'Anything you want, you said, and that's what I want. We go and get the suitcase when I'm better. I choose the day, because right now I feel dreadful. And you sort out the money between the two of you and then you leave. I don't care what you tell him or if you just disappear into the night, but you walk away and don't look back. Get out of my life, and his.'

There was a pause for a few seconds, and her face hardened. Surely this was what she wanted too – to be shot of us both. She shuffled her feet then she stood up, smoothed down her skirt and pushed her shoulders back. She held out her hand and in a cold, flat voice, she said: 'Deal.'

41

I lay in bed for days, too weak to do more than visit the bathroom. It struck me that Rico had been pasty-faced on that day we went to St Pancras, and I wondered if he'd had the flu. Is that what was reeling around inside me now? Rico's flu? What a parting gift. She kept coming into my room, pretending to care how I was, but really she was furious because she wanted to go and get the case.

At one point she'd started questioning me about where his flat was, but I pretended to fall asleep and rolled over. If I told her, she'd run off with the money and then Peter would get nothing. After everything he'd done for her.

They'd started arguing more. I heard him say something about a pair of crutches so he could meet friends for a game of poker at the *kafenio*. He hadn't placed a bet for days, and it sounded like it was killing him. She told him he was being ridiculous and where did he expect her to find something like that.

Finally, on Tuesday – a week to the day after Rico had been killed – I felt well enough to leave the house. It would be the beginning of the end for us, and soon the shadow she'd cast over our lives would disappear.

The Dog and Duck was as miserable as I remembered it. The dark, shadowy room was empty, save for an old man snoring in the corner. I sat at the table in the window and waited.

The fog had lifted and from here I could see straight across the road to his flat. If I could do this – go in there with her, get the money – then she'd go. I was doing this for Peter too, because he didn't stand a chance with her in his life. He'd been in better spirits today because his ankle had finally healed.

I watched the people stream by and wondered if he'd fall apart without her. I hadn't told him yet that I was moving out. I'd wait till I had it all lined up: the flat and the new job. Finally, I felt strong enough to work again, and I was determined that Madame Sylvie wouldn't forget me.

'Here.' Bebba pushed a glass across the table. 'I got us both a grapefruit squash.' She sat next to me. 'What's that look for?'

I pushed it away. 'Nothing.'

She sipped hers and peered through the greasy window pane.

'The blue door?'

I nodded.

We sat in silence until the light began to fade. I was getting up to go to the ladies when she grabbed my arm, spilling cigarette ash on my sleeve.

'Careful!'

'Look,' she said.

A woman with a brown bag of groceries in her arms and a silly little dog by her feet stood at the door, struggling to get in. We were out of the pub in seconds.

She was still on the doorstep when Bebba spoke.

'Hello, do you want some help?'

She turned and looked at us, puzzled. She was very young; eyes ringed with black liner, hair blonde and stiff as a week-old meringue.

'We're going up too,' said Bebba. 'Let us help.'

'Oh, thanks!' she said. 'This bleedin' lock is so stiff.'

Bebba took the key from her hand and pushed hard till it clicked into the lock. I held my breath as the torn, stained wallpaper came into view. Something brushed against my ankles, making me jump.

'Oh, Betsy! Stop it!' she called to the poodle. 'I'm sorry about that,' she said, as she ran up the stairs, slingbacks clip-clopping on the lino.

Bebba turned to me and mouthed, 'Which floor?'

I pointed to the top. We followed her up and she stopped on the flight below Rico's, placing her shopping next to a scuffed door. Her dog scratched at it, desperate to enter. Its tiny nails had been painted fuchsia pink, just like hers.

'Betsy, behave! She's not usually like this,' she said, turning to us. 'She's a bag of nerves with strangers. She's fine once she knows you.' She smiled expectantly. I didn't know what to say so I mirrored her smile and tried to edge around her and continue up the hall.

'She's more highly strung than I am! Is it Rico you're after?'

We froze.

'Because I don't think he's home. Haven't seen him for days. I got stuck at my sister's during the fog and, well – I hope he's all right.'

'No, I mean yes,' said Bebba. 'He's gone now. Back to Cyprus.'

'Oh.' She looked disappointed. '*Really?* That was sudden.'

Neither of us spoke.

'Without saying goodbye?' she continued. 'I mean I know we couldn't really say much to each other . . .what with him not speaking English . . . but . . . I mean we got on so well . . .'

Bebba walked back to stroke the dog.

'It was a bit of a rush,' she said. 'Family illness. He had to go back.' The dog licked her gloved hand. She straightened up. 'I'm his wife. Bebba. We've come for his things.'

The woman suddenly reddened. 'Oh . . . I . . . oh . . . Your English is very good.'

Bebba smiled. 'He didn't mention me, did he? Don't worry, that's Cypriot men for you.' And she rolled her eyes in fond exasperation. 'I'd only just arrived with my sister,' she motioned towards me, 'when he had to go back.'

'Well, that's a real shame,' said the woman, as she unlocked her door. 'So the room's going to be free, is it?'

'Yes.'

'Because it's paid up for six months, you see. Rico told Mr Panayio – Panay – the landlord, he's Greek too – maybe you know him?'

Bebba shook her head.

'Oh.' She seemed disappointed that we didn't know every Greek in London. 'Well, Rico didn't want to be bothered every week for rent.' She peered up the stairs. 'A pity to waste that money ... what with it being paid for. I've got a girlfriend, Cynthia, who'd love that room. I mean she could be out before the six months is up and Mr P would be none the wiser ...'

'She can have it,' said Bebba. 'We'll just clear it out.'

'Really? Will you want money for it? Because I don't think Cynth—'

Bebba shook her head. I could sense her patience was wearing thin. 'Don't worry about that. As you said, it's paid for. Consider it a leaving gift, from Rico.' Then she pulled off her glove and put out her hand. 'It was nice meeting you.'

'Likewise, I'm sure,' she said, grasping Bebba's hand. 'I can't wait to tell Cynthia!'

Once she'd closed the door behind her, we climbed the final few stairs. We turned the corner and almost walked into the door on the landing.

'Is this it?' whispered Bebba.

'Oh, no.' I couldn't remember if he ... I put my hand on the doorknob to turn it and, unlike that day when I would have given anything to find it unlocked, it clicked open. 'He must have forgotten.'

She hurried me through and closed it behind us. A few more stairs and we were standing outside his flat.

'What now?' I asked.

She opened her bag and pulled out a small black screwdriver.

'What on *earth*?'

'Shush.'

'Bebba. You can't. She'll hear you!'

'Calm down, *gori*. How did you think we'd get in?'

She placed the screwdriver between the door and the jamb, just where the lock was, and slowly levered it till the wood sighed and the lock cleaved away. It took all of five seconds to break in. The lock now hung off, threatening to clatter onto the floor. She dropped the screwdriver back in her bag, tugged at the lock till it came off and gently placed it down by the skirting.

'Come on,' she said.

I couldn't move.

'Come *on*.' She took my hand. 'It's all right. He's gone.'

Inside, an appalling odour hit me. Rotting food. Everything was as we'd left it. The bed was unmade, crumpled sheets half on the floor. A balled-up brown paper bag lay on the covers and next to it a piece of card with *Ladies' Stockings* in italic type across the top. I felt his presence all around. Maybe he wasn't dead. Maybe he'd just stepped out to buy the newspaper, or was washing in the bathroom and would return at any moment?

'Let's be quick.' She opened the wardrobe, pushing clothes out of the way. 'Where is it?'

'Under the bed.'

Bending down, she pulled out her grey suitcase and opened it. She ran her hand over the contents then shut it again.

'Find his case and pack up his clothes.'

'Why?'

'Because we said we were coming for his things. We can't leave a trace here, in case anyone comes looking.'

I pulled an empty suitcase from the top of the wardrobe and threw in his trousers, shirts and ties. A tang of his after-shave rose up. I took the black brogues from under the bed and his cologne, razor, comb and toothbrush from the tiny sink in the corner and packed those, too. He had very little and, even when it was all together, the case was barely half full.

Bebba looked around the room. She tried the drawer to the desk. 'Key?'

I shrugged. 'I think he kept it on him.'

With a twist of the screwdriver she opened the drawer and pulled out a large brown envelope. I watched as she tipped it onto the desk: two passports fell out and she quickly opened them to check one was hers. Then she pulled out the folded paper, opened it and looked at the marriage certificate. She put everything back in the envelope and slipped it into her bag.

The smell of his aftershave suddenly filled my head, as if he was stood right behind me.

'I can't . . . I want to go.' I put my hand out on the table to steady myself.

'All right – one moment.'

She took a second look around and leaned over to pick up a piece of paper sticking out from under the bed. She unfolded it and stopped dead.

'What is it?'

She showed me the photo – it was the same as her passport. Her, but much younger. Dark hair, no make-up.

'The good old days,' she smirked.

'Bebba, *please*, can we go?'

'Come on then.' She dropped it into her bag and took me by the arm.

We heard heels run up the stairs.

'Excuse me!'

Bebba quickly stood in front of the splintered wood.

'Sorry – I forgot!' said the woman. She pulled a face. 'Ooof! That's a bad smell.'

'I know,' said Bebba. 'He left some food out. We'll open the windows before we go.'

'Jeez, it's awful! Anyway, I forgot. Here.' She handed her a pale-blue letter with the *Par Avion* motif in the corner.

'It says Express. Came today.'

'Thank you,' said Bebba and pushed it into her pocket without a second glance.

'Looks like it's from home,' said the woman.

'Yes. Thank you.'

There was an awkward pause. She clearly expected us to open it in front of her. When she realised that wasn't going to happen, she smiled brightly.

'Happy to help,' she said, and turned back down the stairs. 'And thanks again, for the room.'

42

I watched as my brother stood in front of the mirror and admired himself in a dead man's shirt. It was the first time he'd been on his feet without help for a week.

'It's perfect,' he said, buttoning up the collar.

'It's small. Look at the sleeves. He was shorter than you.'

'You can fix that, can't you, Dina?'

I shook my head. 'Cuffs are difficult. There's not enough material to let them down.'

'What about the trousers?'

I took the trousers out of the case and looked at the hems, already deciding I wouldn't do it even if I could. 'No, not enough fabric.'

'Well, never mind,' he said. 'I'll keep what I want and ditch the rest.' He grabbed a red silk tie from the suitcase and hung it around his neck. 'I thought there'd be more,' he said, tying a Half-Windsor. 'Wasn't there a coat?'

'That's all of it.' I folded up the discarded clothes.

'I think I left mine at the *kafenio*.'

Bebba walked in, saw Peter and stopped dead.

'Don't wear his stuff. Let's get rid of it.'

'I'd like to keep the ties,' he said, excitement in his voice. 'They're snazzy.'

'They belong to a dead man,' I said.

'Exactly,' he grinned. 'He won't be needing them, will he?'

He walked a slow circuit of the room, like a gentleman about town.

'No limp!' he exclaimed. 'The human body. Amazing how it heals itself. I'm going for cigarettes.'

'Like that?' she asked.

'Why not? I'm almost out. I'll get you some too and pop them back – then I'm going to see some friends.'

'Friends?' I asked. 'You mean bookies.'

He gave me a look but said nothing.

I folded the discarded clothes and put them back in the case.

'Here, keep this in your room till we figure out what to do with it. I don't want to look at it.'

He took the case, slung it in his room, then picked up an old mac and a trilby from the back of the chair. Was the hat his or Rico's?

'I need air! I haven't been outside for days.' He peered outside and looked at his watch. 'God, it's dead out there. Might walk round the block to get used to it.' He flexed his foot. With the hat perched on his head, he turned and laughed.

'You two look so worried,' he said. And he walked up to Bebba and gave her a kiss on the cheek. 'They're only clothes, Beb. See you in a bit.'

He'd been gone a few minutes when there was a knock at the door. We looked at each other but neither of us moved.

Bebba pointed upwards. 'Winnie?' she whispered.

I shrugged.

She went to open it, but I held my hand out.

'I don't want to see her.' I barely knew her, but I couldn't trust myself not to blurt everything out.

There was another knock, this time more insistent.

Just when I thought she'd gone away, a voice called out.

'Miss Demetriou?' It was a man. English. I looked at Bebba in a panic. 'Christina Demetriou?' Another knock. 'It's the police, miss. Can you open up?'

Bebba grabbed my arm. It was happening.

'It's important,' he called. 'I know you're in there. I heard you. We need to speak with you.'

'I'm . . .' my voice quavered. 'I'm coming,' I called.

She tried to block me, but I nudged her away. What choice did I have?

'Don't admit anything,' she whispered. 'Nothing, do you hear?'

I opened the door. Behind it stood a hefty, middle-aged man in a dark raincoat and a smaller, scrawnier man, in a pale coat that swamped him. They both took off their hats at the same time.

'Miss Demetriou?' the older man asked.

'Yes?'

He held out an identification card.

'I'm Detective Inspector Harrison,' he said, 'and this is DC Steele. You're Christina Demetriou, sister of Peter Demetriou?'

I nodded. My head pounded. They'd caught him. Someone had seen and they'd been waiting for him to step out of the house to arrest him.

'May we come in, please?'

I hesitated for a couple of seconds, dumbstruck, wondering what to do, then I let the door fall open. They already knew. What was the point? Bebba was by my side.

'And you are?' asked Harrison.

'Bebba . . . Bebba Antoniou. A friend.'

'Do you live here too?' asked Steele, glancing around the flat.

'Yes. What's the matter?' she asked. 'Is there something wrong?'

Steele wrote something in a notepad, ignored her question and turned to me.

'Sit down please, miss.'

My mouth trembled and I didn't know what expression to set my face in, if that was even possible. Bebba would know what to do. I looked at her and she gave my arm a tiny squeeze of reassurance as she gently guided me into the chair.

'Your brother,' he said. He pointed to a small photo of the two of us in Cyprus that leaned on the mantelpiece. 'This is him?'

I nodded.

My breath quickened and I looked up at Bebba. Her face didn't betray the slightest hint of worry as she looked at the inspector. What should I do? He'll be hanged, and what about me?

You're his sister, surely you knew, miss?

There was so much to explain. Would my words come out in the right order? Would I be able to make them understand that it was her fault, not Peter's?

'Can we ask you when you last saw him?' asked Harrison.

I opened my mouth, but nothing came out.

'Miss,' started DC Steele. 'When did you last see him?'

'He . . . he just went out for some cigarettes,' I said.

Steele flicked through his notebook.

'Was it last week during the smog, miss? Around the ninth of December?'

'What?'

'That was seven days ago,' said Steele, 'but you didn't report him missing? Why is that?'

I stared at him.

'He just went out for cigarettes.'

'But when he didn't return – why didn't you contact the police?'

He'll walk back in any moment now.

'I – he's not—'

'She's been ill with the flu, haven't you?' said Bebba, quickly. 'I couldn't leave her, you see. And what with the smog and everything, we could barely get out. She's only just up today.'

'I see,' said Harrison, nodding. Then he perched on the side of the table and gave me such a soft, sad look that I immediately began to cry.

'I'm very sorry miss,' he began, turning the brim of his hat in his hands. 'But we have some very bad news.'

Suddenly, my right leg started to shake violently. I couldn't make it stop. Bebba knelt next to me and squeezed my hand. I rubbed at my eyes but couldn't stop the shaking.

'I know,' I said. 'I wanted to say something . . .'

She squeezed tighter and put her other hand on my leg to steady it.

'Please miss, let me speak,' he said. 'It's easier that way. Then you can ask me anything you want.'

My hand throbbed under hers. I looked down and her knuckles had turned white.

'It seems your brother, Peter Demetriou, had an accident at St Pancras. On the ninth.'

I looked at Harrison's impenetrable face.

'No.'

'He . . . he fell onto the track,' said Harrison. 'I'm very sorry miss. He died.'

'Oh, Dina!'

Bebba grabbed and hugged me with such force I heard my breath expel. Her face buried in my shoulder, she muttered, 'Dina, I'm so sorry!'

What was she doing?

I pushed her away. 'No – that's not true,' I said.

'I'm afraid he didn't stand a chance,' said Harrison. 'There was a train coming in.'

'That's awful,' Bebba said, dabbing at her eyes with the edge of her sleeve. 'Just awful.'

She put her hand on my shoulder, but I shrugged it off angrily.

'No!' I shot up. 'No! That wasn't Peter.'

Harrison grimaced. 'It's a shock, miss.'

He took my arm and gently guided me back into the chair.

'I know it's very distressing to hear this,' said Harrison, standing over me. 'But the evidence points to it being him.'

'Take a deep breath, darling,' said Bebba. 'Try and calm yourself.'

'My brother's not dead,' I said to Harrison. 'It's not him. It's someone else.'

Steele scribbled something in his notepad while Harrison knelt down so that he could look me straight in the face.

'I know you don't want to believe it. And we do apologise for taking so long to inform you. This terrible fog has caused havoc with all of our investigations.'

'It's chaos,' said Steele. 'Normally we'd be more efficient than this.'

From the corner of my eye I could see Bebba nodding.

'There's no easy way to say this, miss,' said Harrison, 'but the body is . . . unidentifiable.' He paused. 'There was considerable impact, you see. But I'm afraid we found this in his coat pocket.'

He reached inside his mac and pulled out a dirty pale-blue scrap in a transparent bag. It was Peter's identity card. He'd never stopped carrying it, even though it was no longer the law. The card was creased and dog-eared, but it was definitely his. His name and address were clearly visible.

Perhaps they were right. Perhaps there'd been an awful mistake and it was Peter who'd died and Rico who would walk through the door any minute. Had I been right when I'd felt him just behind me at the flat?

'I'm afraid we need to hold on to this. And the coat . . .'

Bebba's fingers stroked my hair.

Harrison stood up and let out a sigh. 'Never seen anything like this fog. Silent killer, that's for sure. You wouldn't believe how many accidents there've been.'

Steele flipped a page over on his notepad, his stubby pencil poised.

'Too right, sir,' he said. 'Young, old, even the animals at Smithfield's – dozens of them. Poor buggers.'

Harrison shifted a little. 'We'd better get on.'

Steele didn't seem to want to go.

'Can you just tell us again why he wasn't reported missing?' he asked.

'I . . . er . . .'

'He didn't always come home,' said Bebba. 'So we weren't overly worried.'

Steele frowned.

'He's a gambler – was,' she said. 'Played poker through the night. He'd sometimes be gone for days so we didn't think it was that unusual.'

Steel wrote down her words.

'He'd be gone for days on end?' he asked.

'He sometimes stayed with friends, slept wherever he found himself. You know the kind of thing.'

'I thought you didn't report it because Miss Demetriou was ill? That's what you said . . .' he flicked back a page and read out her words. ' "*She's been ill with flu . . . and what with the smog and everything . . .*".' He looked up again.

'That's right,' said Bebba, facing him square on, 'and there was the fog, too. Like you said yourself, everything's in disarray. And once he'd been gone for a day she fell ill and then I couldn't possibly leave her.'

'Is that right, miss?' asked Steele, looking at me.

I didn't speak and all that could be heard was the ticking of the clock on the mantelpiece. Then I nodded.

'Well, we'll be in touch,' said Harrison. 'We need you to come to the station, identify the clothing. Come on, Fred.'

'Oh, I can do it,' said Bebba. 'The poor thing doesn't need to go through that, do you Dina?'

'No, it has to be next of kin,' said Steele, then turned back to me. 'There'll be an inquest, then the death needs to be registered.'

'Rest assured,' said Harrison, 'we'll get things moving as quickly as possible. Releasing the body and so on.'

I must have looked shocked.

'For the funeral, miss,' he continued. 'You can still give him a funeral, you know.'

'Though there's a bit of a backlog at the undertakers right now,' said Steele, 'as you can imagine.'

Harrison gave him a look.

'What he means, miss, is that you may have a bit of a wait.'

'Thank you,' said Bebba, getting up and walking to the door. 'Thank you for everything.'

Steele frowned. 'We haven't done anything, miss. Apart from give you bad news.'

'No, I know. I just mean, thank you. For the considerate way in which you've done it. That's all.'

He tilted his head back like a dog deciding if you're friend or foe. Harrison extended his hand and I shook it, dumbly.

'She's in shock,' he said to Bebba. 'Only to be expected. You need to keep an eye on her. I'm afraid I need this,' he said, taking the photo. 'Just for our records. We'll have a copy made and return it. Give them our details, Fred. I'm all out.'

Steele patted his trouser pocket and drew out a rectangular cream card. Bebba reached to take it but he pulled it back and handed it directly to me.

'Steele,' he said, looking into my face. 'Please call if I can be of any assistance.'

I turned it over in my hand and held it tight.

'Goodbye miss,' said Harrison, as he opened the door. 'Our sincere condolences.'

'Oh, one last thing – you're not going anywhere, are you?' asked Steele.

'What do you mean?' said Bebba.

He pointed to the suitcase of money by the table. It had been there all this time.

He buttoned up his coat. 'We may need to ask you both a few more questions, you know. Just standard procedure, to fill in any gaps.'

'No, we're just clearing some things out,' she said.

He nodded and we said our goodbyes. We walked to the corridor together and watched in silence as they left. Then I heard a loud creak and I twisted around to see the bathroom door inch open.

'It's just the wind,' said Bebba.

But as she reached for the handle to close it, the door swung open and we both jumped back. There, stepping out of his hiding place, was Peter, his face as grey as spoilt meat.

43

Later that evening, Bebba drew the curtains against the cold, dark night as Peter poured a third shot of whisky. It had taken a while, but his hands had finally stopped shaking. She caught his eye and bestowed on him her special smile, the one that promised all kinds of things. At that point she knew she had him.

'It's impossible,' said Dina, mouth rigid.

'It's very possible. Think about it. Who'll miss him?' She turned to Peter. 'No offence, darling.'

He leaned forwards in his chair, twisting the tumbler round and round in his hand.

'I see what you're suggesting,' he said, 'but I'm still not sure *why*.'

His fidgeting was driving her mad. She leaned across and put her hand over his.

'Look,' she said. 'They think it was you who died, right? In fact, they're convinced of it, yes?'

He nodded.

'So, we *bury* you. Tie up your affairs – everything.'

He shuffled. 'But – then I'll be dead. What happens to me then?'

She paused. He really was slow sometimes.

'You pretend to be Rico,' explained Dina. 'That's what she's saying.'

He frowned. 'Why would I want to be *him?*'

'It works in your favour, darling,' said Bebba. 'Your debts

will disappear. Remember those thugs at the cinema? You'll never be bothered by them – or anyone like them – again.'

'What thugs?' asked Dina.

He lifted his head a little.

'Okaaaay, but if I wanted to do that, I could just become someone else. Why would I want to be *him*?'

And still he didn't get it.

'It's much easier than creating someone new. We have his passport, his clothes. Think about it – it's by far the best option we have.'

'Or,' Dina said, 'we could just say it's a mistake.' She turned her back on Bebba and addressed her brother directly. 'Listen, Peter, we could say you turned up after the police had left.' Her voice quickened. 'It was a mix-up – it wasn't you under the train. We don't even have to mention Rico at all. It could have been a complete stranger who died.'

'So why is Peter's coat there?' asked Bebba. 'And his papers?'

'She's right,' he said. 'If we did that, they'd realise it wasn't an accident. Thank God they can't tell he was stabbed.'

'Stroke of luck,' said Bebba, pulling a Piccadilly from a pack on the table. 'What was it? "Considerable impact."'

She placed the ciggie in the holder and lit up.

'I suppose if someone's under a train,' she continued, 'you assume that's what killed them.'

Peter chuckled, then suddenly stopped.

'But, if I'm him,' he said, 'that means we're . . .'

She blew smoke to one side and waited for the penny to drop.

'That's right.' She tried to make her voice light. 'We'll live like a married couple. Of course, we'll have to move. After the funeral, once things have settled. We'll leave without anyone knowing. All three of us. We should stick together and go somewhere nobody knows us. Until then, you *mustn't* leave the flat. We can't risk anyone seeing you.'

Dina stood up and her chair fell to the floor, making Bebba jump.

'But you promised,' she said, her voice whining. 'You were going to leave, once you had the money.'

Bebba didn't respond.

'What are you talking about?' asked Peter.

'We had a deal,' said Dina. 'She agreed. She'd go – disappear – if I showed her where the money was.'

Peter looked at her and she shook her head, pretending the whole thing had been a misunderstanding.

'You promised,' shouted Dina. Red patches had sprung up on her cheeks.

'Keep your voice down,' Bebba hissed. 'You're not thinking straight. If I leave, they'll suspect something – you heard Steele. He said we should stay put. They could be watching. Once the funeral's done and Rico is buried, we'll wait a while till they lose interest and then we'll leave. He's just another foreigner to them. They'll let it go. But we have to be careful, be sure they're not watching. And in the meantime,' she said, turning to Peter, 'stay indoors. We'll have to put a notice in the Greek paper, do everything properly, as if you'd really died.'

Dina turned to Peter.

'You can't! What about Father? Are you really going to let him believe you're dead?'

He rubbed at his face.

'Peter!' Dina grabbed his arm.

'He's half-dead himself,' said Peter. 'He doesn't know who we are. Face it, Dina. It won't make any difference to him.'

'But it's wrong,' said Dina. 'It's vicious and wrong.'

'Oh, really!' Bebba couldn't help herself.

'Shut up,' said Dina, 'I'm not talking to you.' Then turning back to him, 'You'll never be able to go back.'

He shrugged.

'No,' she continued. 'I'm not doing it.'

Bebba walked to the mirror and straightened the collar of her dress. She'd never really considered Dina much of an obstacle before, let alone a risk. But it seemed she had a thread of steel running through her.

'You don't have a choice,' she said. 'I know it's awful, but you have to go along with it.' She watched their reflection in the mirror as she continued: 'If you want to save him, that is.'

Dina walked up behind her, making Bebba turn. Then she spat – *ptoo!* – next to Bebba's feet, like a village elder bestowing a curse.

'That's what I think of you.'

It was as if she'd been slapped. Bebba quickly stood a little straighter to try to compose herself. 'Curse me all you want, but don't tell me you hate your brother, too, because I won't believe you.'

Dina didn't speak. 'And it's all very well being self-righteous,' continued Bebba, 'but one of us has to think of something. Unless you want to see him swing.'

'Listen,' said Peter, getting up. 'Beb's right. It's the only way.'

At last, thought Bebba, he was going to come and stand next to her, show a united front. But he went to Dina and put an arm around her. She whacked it away like a live ember.

'Dina,' he pleaded. 'Why would my papers be there if it wasn't me who died? They'll know I had something to do with it. I have to do this, don't you see?'

'Who *are* you?' she asked. 'Because I don't recognise either of you any more. You sicken me.'

'Oh, change the record, will you?' said Bebba. 'And cut out the high-and-mighty act because, frankly, you're hardly an innocent, are you?'

That shut her up. She didn't respond for a few seconds, then finally she said, much quieter: 'What do you mean?'

'Well, let's just say you're not blameless yourself,' said Bebba. 'An *unmarried* girl . . . having *sex* with her *boyfriend* when her brother's out of the flat? Tut tut.'

There. It was said. Peter hadn't uttered a word, so it had come down to her.

'Rico only found out where we lived thanks to you,' she continued. 'Go to the police about him and see if they believe you. Go on.'

'No.' Dina started to shake her head. 'It wasn't like that!' She was trying to speak over Bebba.

'Tell them he was your boyfriend,' Bebba ploughed on. 'That you were courting.'

'Shut up, Bebba!' said Dina.

'See what they say to you then.'

'But . . .' Dina seemed at a loss. At last. That would teach her. There was a long pause and Peter coughed awkwardly. 'I didn't know who he was . . .' said Dina. 'I didn't mean for any of this to happen . . .'

'I don't recall you putting the police straight, either,' said Bebba.

'I tried to, you know I did!'

'Yes, but not very hard. You went along with it because you knew it was the only way.'

'No, that's not true.'

Bebba walked to the table, poured herself a shot of whisky and dropped into the chair.

'Peter, did anyone see you today when you were out?' she asked.

He shook his head. 'Don't think so. Shop was closed with a sign on the door saying Thompson was ill.'

'It's a gift, can't you see that?' Bebba's voice was softer now. 'With his ankle he hasn't been out for days. It's perfect. Come on, you don't want to see your brother arrested, do you? He won't stand a chance. It'll be the death penalty.'

On cue, Peter pulled at his collar.

Dina's face turned red. She walked to the window, peered out, then after a while turned and said: 'All right.'

'You'll go along with it?' asked Peter.

Dina nodded. 'For you, not for her. But this time I'm getting what I want in return. No backing out.'

'Name it,' said Bebba.

Dina put her hands on her hips, bracing herself. 'I'm staying. Here – in Soho.'

Peter laughed, then realised she was serious.

'Don't be ridiculous. You can't live by yourself. Can she, Beb?'

Dina continued: 'After the funeral, you can both go – wherever you want. Scotland, Ireland, as long as it's not in Soho I don't care where, because I'm not coming with you.'

Peter stood up and folded his arms. 'No! Absolutely not. I'm not allowing that, Dina. Beb, talk to her.'

She put up her hand to stop him. 'Hold on,' said Bebba. 'She's an adult, Peter.'

'No.'

'She is, and you can't stop her. And you can't stay here – it's too risky.'

Then she turned to Dina. 'None of us can leave straight after the funeral. We'll draw attention to ourselves. Let's take a few weeks – a month, say, after he's buried. If they're watching they definitely won't keep it up that long, will they? And we'll need to find somewhere to go.'

'All right,' said Dina. 'But no longer.'

Bebba gave a little nod. She had to ask her – if not now, when? 'And the money?'

Dina shook her head. 'I don't want anything to do with it.'

Bebba bit the inside of her mouth to stop herself smiling.

'What?' asked Peter, two steps behind as usual. 'But you can't stay in Soho, all alone. How will you live?'

Dina shrugged. 'How do people live? I'll go back to the café for now, till I get back on my feet. But there are lots of jobs out there, Peter. You just never let me try anything before. I was offered a sewing job before all this happened.'

'But where will you live?' he asked.

'Colleen has a cheap room at hers. I'll take it if it's still free.'

Bebba was surprised. It sounded like she had it all worked out. When had that happened, and how hadn't she heard about it before?

'Now don't go asking questions about jobs and flats,' she warned her. 'Not yet – none of us can make a move till a month after the funeral, agreed?'

Peter sniffed and Bebba had to turn away as Dina went to put her arms around his shoulders.

'I'll be fine, Peter, honest.'

'But ... but ... I was meant to find you someone,' he protested. 'To marry.'

He blew his nose, and all Bebba could hear was his erratic breathing as he took in huge gulps of air and tried to compose himself.

'I'll be fine.'

'And ... I ...' he was trying to get the words out, but they got stuck in his throat. 'I promised *Pappa* ... that I'd look after you. I should have been a better brother.'

Finally, he managed to compose himself and it was only then that Bebba turned around.

He let out a loud, long sigh. 'Bugger it, Dina,' he said. 'I really made a mess of things, didn't I?'

She lifted her head and stared at Bebba.

'I think we all did.'

44

On Christmas Day I lay on my bed sketching dresses on my notepad. I was bored. I hadn't worked for a couple of weeks now and though I never thought I'd say it, I actually missed the Coffee Corner. More than that, I hated being cooped up indoors with the two of them. Bebba had said I shouldn't return for a few weeks – after all, who went back to work straight after their brother had died? She was right, of course, so I stayed indoors with Peter and she was the only one who stepped outside for essential groceries.

Peter had brought the wireless into the living room and it had been on for much of the day. The Queen's young, shy voice filtered through, and I felt a kick of sadness as I caught snippets of her speech:

. . . Many grave problems and difficulties confront us all, but with a new faith . . . strength to venture beyond the safeties of the past . . . worthy of our duty . . . keep alive that courageous spirit of adventure . . .

She'd had an awful year, losing her father, her life changed in an instant, but she'd no choice but to push on. And I had to do the same.

I let the pad drop to the floor. What on *earth* was that smell? Heady, sweet and slightly familiar, it had seeped under the door and begun to fill my room. I got up to investigate.

In the living room, Peter knelt by the hearth while he tried to attach yellow paper chains to the damp walls.

'Where did you get those?' I asked. They looked pathetic.

'Beb made them,' he said. 'From some old wrapping paper. She's resourceful, my girl, aren't you?'

Bebba gave me a sidelong glance, daring me to laugh. I pressed my lips together and said nothing. He got up and, as soon as his back was turned, the soft plaster spat out a couple of the drawing pins and the decorations sagged towards the floor.

Bebba walked to the tiny gas ring and poured a glass of red wine on top of a pale lump. She looked at me over her shoulder.

'It's ham,' she said. 'I wanted chicken, but, of course, there aren't any.'

She pushed the whole thing down with a wooden spoon. The saucepan was too small, and the white fat kept bobbing up over the rim.

'It won't be ready for a while. Not sure how the English cook these things, but wine has got to help, don't you think?'

'That's okay. I don't want any.'

'But it's Christmas dinner,' she said, looking genuinely upset. 'Why ever not?'

'She's right Dina,' said Peter. 'Come on. You have to have Christmas dinner.'

I pulled a face at the saucepan. It was so easy to annoy her these days.

'Looks so pale.' I shuddered. 'Bland.' I took an olive from the bowl on the side, leaned against a chair and popped it in my mouth.

'Suit yourself,' she said.

The suitcase of money sat next to the table, like a fourth member of the family. Bebba had left it there after checking its contents when we'd returned, as if to prove that it belonged to us all. She couldn't deposit it in a bank or withdraw it again without a man's signature. And anyway, what with it being Christmas, everything had been shut.

Peter picked up a pack of cards and sat at the table.

'Dina, a game of *bastra*?' he asked, shuffling them like only a pro could.

'No,' I said.

'Oh, come on, you love that game.'

'I don't fancy it.'

'You're in a funny mood,' he said.

I shrugged. I couldn't pretend this was a normal Christmas.

One side of the paper chain fell with a rustle. We all turned and looked at it and the other end did the same. Peter half stood but before he'd had a chance to do anything, Bebba stormed towards the decorations, picked them off the floor, scrunched them into a ball and dropped them in the bin.

* * *

An hour or so later, there were carols on the radio and I could hear the two of them laughing and chatting, clinking their glasses practically every time they took a drink.

Eventually the singing stopped, and the flat fell silent. There was a knock on my door, but she didn't wait for a response before walking in. I'd been painting my nails, Golden Rose, and I held out my hands as I blew on them to dry the polish.

'This is for you,' she said. She pushed a rectangular box towards me. I shook my head. I hadn't bought her a thing.

'Take it. I got it for you weeks ago.'

'My nails,' I said. 'They're wet.'

'Oh, okay. I'll wait. I want to see if you like it.'

Before I could protest, she sat on my bed, took my magazine and started to flick through it. After a few minutes she gestured towards my hands.

'Dry yet?'

I touched a fingernail gently to test it and nodded. I didn't want to open the gift while she watched, but it seemed the only way to get rid of her. She picked up the box and placed it into my hands. It felt light.

'Go on.'

'I didn't get you anything,' I said.

'That doesn't matter. I saw this ages ago, before – well, I just loved the colour.'

I pulled at an edge of the brown paper wrapping, careful not to use my nails. Underneath was a beautiful purple box; it was from Liberty's and I felt my cheeks flush. Whatever was inside must have cost a fortune. I unpeeled the rest of the wrapping and slowly lifted the lid.

It was the most exquisite green silk scarf I'd ever seen. I didn't even want to touch it. The sheer brilliance of it reminded me of the rain-soaked hills back home after a summer storm. I'd seen one of the girls at the Pelican wear one just like it and had often wondered how she could have afforded it.

'Well?' she asked, an expectant smile on her face.

'Did you buy it?'

'How else would I have got it? I wanted to give you it a while back but then everything happened.'

I pushed the box back towards her. 'It's too much.'

'That's okay. Go on.' She placed the box in my hand.

It *was* lovely. I think she expected me to put it on, but I placed the lid on top and held it in my hands like a delicate relic. A vestige of our friendship. I wanted to thank her, but the words wouldn't come out.

She made no move to leave.

Eventually I spoke. 'I'd like to read my magazine now,' I said.

She looked around the room like she hadn't heard me.

'You know Rico killed my father, don't you?' she asked.

'I don't know why you're telling—'

'Well, as good as,' she continued. 'He increased the price of my dowry at the last minute – demanded more than we had – and my father went along with it. By the time I found out it was too late. He'd sold the land, everything. He went to bed the evening of my wedding and never got up again.'

She was staring past me at the wall, as if in a daze.

'What's that saying? No fool like an old fool. Well, that was him all right. Forced me to marry for "family honour" and made things even worse.'

'If this is all to make me feel sorry—'

'Who needs sympathy?' she bit back, and I flinched at the change in her tone. 'I'm just saying all men let you down in the end, Dina. Even those you're related to. If you were me that day at St Pancras, you'd have done the same.'

'You really believe that?' I asked. 'You're always trying to make out we're the same but we're not. I'm not like you.'

She placed her hand on mine and stared straight at me. 'We're more similar than you know,' she said. 'Look, I know it was terrible the way he took you like that, keeping you in that flat . . . I could tell the moment I saw your face at the station what you'd been through.'

I pulled my hand away. 'I don't want to talk about it.'

'He was vile. He won't be missed,' she said.

I remembered how mean he'd been to me in the flat.

'Darling,' she said, 'he tried to break us both, but he can't. Because we're stronger than that, you and I? Aren't we?'

I turned my face to the wall. I was so close to crying, to hugging her and telling her I wanted things to be the way they were before. I missed her. And she *was* trying to make amends. Just as my heart started to soften, she spoke.

'Of course, you don't understand.' Her voice was brittle as glass. 'That money is mine, my birthright and he took it. And so what if I took some wedding gifts too.'

'You took the *gifts*?'

'Only the silverware. I sold it – what? You think I'd leave it for him? Don't look at me like that.'

Money. Always money. Getting her money, then having some more. That's what this was about; that's what it had always been about. She didn't care about us at all.

'When is the funeral?' I asked. 'I want it over with. Then you can go away, and I can put this all behind me.'

Her face hardened. 'I'm trying to book it for next week.'

'Make sure you do,' I said.

'There's a huge backlog with the smog, it's not that easy.'

'I don't care. Get it done. Make the plans. I want this over with.'

'I know, but let's not talk about it today.'

'Why not?'

She sat back and put her hand up to her neck, feigning shock.

'Well for goodness' sake, Dina. It's Christmas Day, that's why not.'

I turned and stuffed the Liberty box in my underwear drawer, beneath my knickers and stockings.

'We had a deal,' I said. 'The funeral, then a month later, the two of you leave. So, don't go thinking you can back out.'

She stood.

'I wouldn't dream of it,' she said, her voice cold now. 'Frankly, I'll be glad to go.' She looked around at the walls, then at me. 'It's all turned out a bit shabby, hasn't it darling?' And then she walked out.

I went to the drawer again and opened the box. Whether she'd bought or stolen it, the scarf was a beautiful thing. I lifted it to my face and caught a faint fragrance. I dropped it back into the box and shoved it to the bottom of the drawer.

45

My brother was buried on Friday 9th January, 1953, a month to the day since he'd died. As his only relative here, I'd had no choice but to identify some scraps of clothing, attend the inquest (death by misadventure) and register his death. By the time his body had been released, I was sick of the whole charade. The lie felt all the worse for being at the start of a fresh new year, sullying any optimism the coming months might hold.

I wouldn't help her organise the funeral itself, so Bebba saw to the detail. All I had to do, she said, was turn up on the day.

'I'm not going,' I said, as I sat on her bed and watched her pulling on her dark stockings.

'You have to.' She checked the seams were straight, then looked up. 'What would it look like, if his own sister wasn't there?'

Peter trudged in, stubble-faced, dressing gown open revealing his vest and faded striped pyjama bottoms. He had nowhere to go these days, so rarely bothered to dress.

'Come on, Dina, please?' he asked. 'For me? If you don't turn up, it all falls apart. Who knows – the police may even send someone along.'

I went to my room and grudgingly pulled out a dark dress.

'It's not even a proper funeral,' I shouted. 'Not a Greek one, anyway.'

'It doesn't matter,' she called. 'Probably better this way. We'll just say we couldn't get a Greek priest in time.'

She walked into my room and I instinctively turned my back as I got ready.

'And what with all those funerals after the fog, it's chaos,' she said. 'We can't be blamed for not sticking to the rules.'

She started to zip me up, but I pulled away.

'I can manage. Get off.'

⋆   ⋆   ⋆

We were the only mourners there. Peter knew so many people in Soho and yet no one bothered to attend. Even the police hadn't thought it worth the effort.

The English priest said a few words, then led us outside to the churchyard as four gravediggers in mud-smeared clothes carried the plain coffin to the graveside. I stood on the sodden edges and watched as the box was lowered into the gaping hole in the treacle-black earth. I remembered another box of lies, one that Rico had given me: small, gold, tied with a brown ribbon.

Once it was over, I felt relieved and exhausted. Bebba linked my arm and, I'm not sure why, I let her keep it there. She pulled me along to the bus stop.

'That went well, don't you think?' she asked, as if discussing a tea party.

I shrugged. 'As far as sham funerals go, I suppose it did.'

She hailed a number 29 bus and before it stopped, she turned to me. 'Strange how nobody came, though. I put the notice in the paper. I'd have thought a few of his pals would have been there at least.'

We boarded.

'Not really.'

I walked to the downstairs seats, even though I knew she'd want to go up and smoke. I sat down and she slid in next to me.

'They're just users,' I said, 'like him. He doesn't have any real friends.'

She didn't respond so I stared out of the window. The buildings were streaked with the fog's dirty long fingerprints where it had groped the brickwork for days. *Just ask. You need to know.* I turned to her.

'Did you ever even want to be my friend, or was the whole thing planned from the outset?' Once I'd said it, I couldn't look at her.

'Dina – please.'

We were speaking Greek, but she still turned to check who'd heard. The seats behind us were empty. I started to fiddle with the clasp on my bag.

'Because I've often wondered, you know. All those evenings we spent together, the bars, the cinema visits, shopping trips.' I opened my bag for no reason and closed it again. 'Did any of it even *mean* anything to you?'

She didn't say anything, and I forced myself to look at her. I saw her face fall a little, but how did I know what was real any more?

'Of course it meant something,' she said, quietly. 'It meant a lot to me. I was lonely. Don't give me that look – it's true. When I met you, everything changed. I thought perhaps we could be good friends.'

I shook my head. How could I hate and love her at the same time?

'Well, a funny thing struck me the other day,' I said. 'About the flat – where we are now.'

The bus turned a corner and we both grabbed the rail in front of us.

'Tickets, please.'

A uniformed conductor took her coins, pulled two tickets from his holder and punched a hole in them.

'Remember how you told us your landlord was kicking you out?' I asked. 'Renovating or something?'

'It was an absolute godsend moving in with the two of you.'

She folded the tickets again and again until they were deadly bullets. The bus stopped and an elderly couple got on and sat in front of us.

'Not really though, was it?' I asked. 'I don't think God had much to do with it.'

She faced forwards and didn't speak.

'A place with an old air raid shelter in the garden that nobody would ever think to look in. Perfect spot to hide something.'

She turned and stared out of the window.

'The first time you came for coffee,' I continued. 'All those months ago – you saw it then. A scruffy little garden that would hide your scruffy little secret.'

The woman in front of us shifted.

'Ssssh. Dina, please.'

Perhaps she was Greek and could understand every word. Perhaps she'd go to the police. What did I care?

'You didn't even get fired from the Pelican,' I said. 'Madame S says you just disappeared. Says you and Billy were mates – he'd got you the job in the first place.'

Her mouth dropped.

'She says you just upped and left. I've no idea why you lied about him – or how you left – but it seems you can't help yourself. Did you think I'd like you more if you'd been fired because of me?'

Bebba shrugged and her tone was cold when she spoke: 'I don't see what difference it makes now.'

'You really don't, do you?' I asked. 'It makes a world of difference. If you were fired because you stood up for me, that's the kind of thing a true friend does.'

She let out an exaggerated sigh as if she was bored.

'But if you just left of your own accord,' I said, 'and made the whole thing up? Well, then you're a barefaced liar, someone with no morals at all. So, which are you?'

46

Finally, a month later, I stepped back into the world as I walked towards the Coffee Corner. I'd planned to avoid Rico's flat but as I walked near there for the first time since his death, instead of turning off, I went past after all. I stopped for a moment and stared. Scabs of flaking paint surrounded the blue door. Just a door, just a flat. Nothing more.

I moved on, happy to be heading back to something familiar and looking forward to seeing Colleen again. I also needed to earn some money, quickly. It was already February and I hadn't called Madame Sylvie about the new club because I'd been forced to lie low.

But today, finally, I'd get in touch. I wasn't sure if she was still at the Pelican, but I didn't want to turn up unannounced and put her in a difficult position. And I couldn't risk bumping into Ratface. I'd call her on my way home and just pray she hadn't already found someone else.

The fog had more or less disappeared and the streets hummed with life. Someone had a radio blaring and the voice of a male tenor drifted down. I turned off Berwick Street and started down Wardour. I'd really missed the push and pull of Soho life. London was my home now and nothing could change that.

I dropped my smile and frowned, trying to look like an exhausted grieving sister, not someone thrilled to be back. The tiny brass bell on the door rang as I entered and Colleen rushed towards me, almost knocking me over.

'Dina, oh Dee, I'm so sorry!'

I'd asked Bebba to let them know so I wouldn't have to explain anything. Tears had already pooled in her eyes and I felt a terrible bite of guilt. We hugged.

'Are you all right? I wanted to come round but I . . . well . . . I didn't know what to say.'

Thank God she hadn't.

'Really, I'm fine.'

She hugged me long and hard. I'd forgotten how good that felt.

'Come on, Coll.' I smiled. 'You'll set me off.'

Harry trundled over and, rather formally, shook my hand. '*Sillibidiria*, Dina,' he said. 'My heartfelt condolences.'

The pink V of skin on his chest seemed paler than usual and he had a washed-out look about him.

'Thanks, Harry.'

He leaned forwards, too close as usual, and I smelt the whisky fumes spark off him.

'Terrible business,' he said. 'I can't believe it. We didn't know a thing until your friend told us, then that very same day I saw it in the paper.'

Bebba said she was putting a notice in.

'I saved it.' He went into the back and returned with a tattered copy of the *Vema* in his hands. He jabbed at a corner where a small box was outlined in black. The words read:

Peter Demetriou, died aged 29 on Tuesday 9th December, 1952, in a tragic accident. Funeral to be held at St Saviour's on Friday 9th January. No flowers.

She was smart. She'd been close-fisted with the details: no mention of our village or surviving relatives. News might spread to Cyprus, but the only family was our ailing father. He wouldn't know Peter if he shook his hand. There were just a few acquaintances and neighbours in the village now, but nobody who'd be heartbroken. My brother was a scoundrel and, for once, it would work in our favour.

'I didn't know him that well, but he'd always struck me as a decent man, your brother,' said Harry. 'Sit down, sit down.' He pushed me into a seat. 'I'm sorry I couldn't come to the funeral, but I was suffering—' he banged his chest, '—with the fog.'

'You look awful, Dee,' said Colleen.

'Thank you.'

'You're so thin. Harry, can we get her something to eat? A full English or something?'

'I'm not that hungry.'

'Some soup then,' she said, taking charge. 'Tomato soup and bread and butter – or whatever it really is. On the house, Harry – yes?'

He hesitated, then waved a hand in the direction of the kitchen.

'Go on,' he said. 'Tell chef, "on the house",' pronouncing the words with care, because presumably he'd never spoken them before in his life. Then he pulled out a chair and sat opposite me. He reached across and suddenly clasped my hands in his warm, pudgy fingers, pulling me towards him.

'You can have your job back,' he blurted. 'No problem.'

'Er . . . thank you.'

I had no idea I'd lost it. I shifted and he let go.

'I had to fire you,' he explained, 'when you didn't turn up during the fog.' He pursed his lips. 'But, of course, you couldn't come to work then, could you?'

Rico, the bed, me on the floor.

'Can I start right now?' I asked. 'After I've eaten. I can't go home. It's awful there.'

'Yes, if you're sure.'

'I'm sure.'

He got up just as Colleen came back with a bowl of orange-red soup and a double portion of bread and butter.

'Get that down you,' she said.

'Whenever you're ready,' said Harry, walking away. 'There are spare pinnies and caps in the back.'

Colleen slid into the seat. 'You coming back?'

I nodded, lifted a spoonful of soup in front of my mouth and blew. 'For now.'

'Oh, that's wonderful Dina!' She turned to check he wasn't nearby. 'It's been *hell* without you. I reckon you could get away with murder now.'

The spoon trembled in my hand.

'Is that bedsit still free?' I asked. 'In your house?'

'Oh, no – it went ages ago, sorry,' she said. 'I hadn't seen you for so long, and someone else wanted it. I did ask the landlady to wait but she wouldn't.'

'Oh.' It was the only room I'd come upon that I could afford, but surely there'd be others?

'I imagine you want to leave it all behind?' she continued. 'Move out of the flat you had with Peter. Must be weird still living there by yourself.'

I ate some soup and she let out an exaggerated sigh.

'Poor Peter. I cried buckets when I first heard,' she said. 'I had a soft spot for him, you know. I'd never really stopped liking him, after that evening out . . . I don't know if you knew that.'

The whole of Soho knew that. A thin film of grease had collected around the edges of the spoon. How could tomato soup be greasy?

'But it wasn't to be.' She sighed, reached across, nabbed a triangle of bread and start munching. Then with a full mouth she said, 'Whatever happened to him?'

I looked up from my spoon.

'What?' I asked. 'He died . . . it . . . it said so in the paper.'

'No, not Peter, silly! Loverboy. Whassisname? Andreas.'

'Oh, *him*.' I let the spoon slide into the greasy pool and pushed the bowl away.

'Don't know.' I shook my head. 'Just disappeared.'

She took another triangle of bread.

'Typical. Bloody men.'

47

Madame Sylvie settled down opposite me and started to saw into her ham.

'It's lovely to see you, Dina,' she said. 'I'm so glad you called.'

We were 'lunching', as she'd put it, at the Lyons' Corner House. She'd chosen the one on the Strand rather than our local, so we wouldn't see anyone we knew.

'And I'm so glad you suggested coming here,' I said. 'I haven't been to this one.' I forked some spaghetti into my mouth.

'Forgive me for saying, but you look very tired, *ma chère amie.*' She tilted her head slightly. 'I was so shocked when you told me about your brother. Losing him like that – it must have been awful.'

I swallowed hard and thought of everything I'd never be able to say. Without a word she opened her bag, took out a handkerchief and offered it to me.

'I'm all right,' I said, shaking my head. We both took a sip of tea and returned to our food.

'I didn't mean to upset you,' she said, 'but I didn't want to ignore it either.'

'No, it's fine. Really.' She held up the pot, I offered my cup and she filled it.

'Terrible shock losing someone so close,' she said, 'but you *will* come through this. In time.'

I nodded and pushed my food around. 'I know. He's gone and I have to think of myself now.' As I said the words, they felt true. 'Anyway, what about you? How have you been, Madame?'

'Oh please, it's Sylvie, *oui?*' She popped another piece of ham in her mouth. 'Well, life has been difficult, but nothing compared to you. Just business.'

My heart skipped and I put down my fork.

'I'm afraid my investors have let me down.'

I felt my face drop and checked myself. She eyed me with concern.

'I'm sorry Dina, but there's no new club, no job. I wish I had something I could offer you, but I don't.' She reached across and placed her hand on mine. My breath snagged. *What was I going to do?* First the bedsit and now this.

'You were counting on this opportunity, weren't you?' she asked.

I looked down and nodded, willing myself not to cry, and resumed eating my pasta.

'I was too,' she said. 'But, what can I tell you? Men can be very unreliable. Remember that. Especially the rich ones.'

I tried to smile. 'They're fools.'

'Perhaps,' she said, 'but this isn't a lifelong dream to them, it's just business. And you'll find something else, I'm sure. I'll see if there's anyone I can put you in touch with.'

I nodded my thanks and we carried on eating for a while. After a minute she pulled a face at her cup.

'*Mon Dieu,* it's stewed,' she said. 'And I thought the English were experts at tea. The ham's a little dry, too – how's your spaghetti?'

I scrunched my nose. 'Not so good.'

She pushed the plates to one side.

'I have an idea,' she said. 'Let's get some coffee and move on to dessert. My treat. The patisserie section looked wonderful on the way in. Shall we?'

We walked to the counter and eyed the cakes while the

waitress cleared our plates. Back at our table, Sylvie gazed at her layered cake in anticipation.

'I love cake, don't you?' she said.

A sadness swept over me as I remembered a similar conversation a lifetime ago. So much had changed since then.

I gave a tight smile. 'I'm definitely a girl who appreciates cake.'

'Well then, we're kindred spirits.'

She looked at me over her glasses. As long as my tears didn't fall, we could both pretend everything was all right.

'Dina,' she said, gently. 'Do try not to let this disappointment pull you down. You have talent – you'll be all right.'

'I know.'

I watched as she set about ploughing her fork into the layered sponge.

'Mmm . . . that's better.'

'So,' I tried to sound cheerful as I cut my cake into pieces, 'what will you do? Will you stay at the Pelican?'

She nodded. 'Yes, I suppose I'll have to, for now . . .' she paused as she licked her fork clean, '. . . it's not the end of the world, but it does mean, of course, that I'm stuck with Billy for a while longer.'

I sipped some tea and shook my head sadly.

'*Mon Dieu,*' I said.

'What?'

'Now I really *am* going to cry.'

48

I allowed myself a few tears that night. Now the possibility of a job with Madame Sylvie had disintegrated, I needed something else fast. Any day now Peter and Bebba would leave and, unless I wanted to go with them, I'd be homeless. Every landlord wanted a deposit and I still couldn't afford a room of my own along with the bills.

What I'd told Peter was true, there were lots of jobs – at garment factories and other cafés – but the wages were always the same if not worse. The manager at Lyons' – where the Nippies were always so well turned out and better-paid, too – took one look at me and shook her head. Did I really still look so bad?

So, I volunteered for extra shifts at the Coffee Corner, and slipped the money into my red Oxo tin. In my lunch break I scoured the newsagent's window for a room.

I soon discovered that the ones I could afford were derelict. There was one I visited on Windmill Street where, on opening the door, I was greeted by a long, grey curtain dividing the tiny room in half. I turned around and ran down the stairs.

At least there'd been no more police visits and I was starting to think that we'd got away with it.

Unable to step outside, Peter had taken to playing solitaire for hours on end. When he wasn't playing cards, he'd pace up and down, dragging himself around the flat like a wounded animal, his dressing gown gaping open, the tail of his belt trailing behind him. I felt claustrophobic just looking at him, and Bebba must have felt the same because she soon decided to return to Mackenzie's.

Harry used up his supply of kindness in a matter of days. And once the regulars had expressed their condolences, nobody mentioned Peter again. Except for Colleen.

'It doesn't feel real, does it?' she said, staring at the clipping that Harry had kept, even though she couldn't read a word of Greek. 'I just can't believe he's gone.'

I scraped some dried crusts from one plate to another and added it to a stack.

'I'd rather not talk about it.'

When I returned from the kitchen, she had her head on one side, all wistful.

'Of course you don't want to,' she said. 'I mean, he's your brother.' A pause. 'Was.'

She pinned the tatty square of newsprint back on the notice-board outside Harry's office.

'But I still can't quite believe it.' She sighed. 'Oh! Did I tell you? I saw him the other day.'

'What?'

'Peter.'

The menu fell out of my hand. Her cap had slipped a little and she pulled a grip from her hair and jabbed it in again with some violence.

'Well, someone who looked so much like him I had a bit of a turn. I swear it was his double.'

He didn't, did he?

'It was on Regent Street. Tuesday – or was it Wednesday? That day it was pouring.'

She sat on a table and started to swing her legs. I moved the cruet set to one side and straightened the paper napkins in their holder.

'I was waiting for the bus and there was Peter, across the road, no coat, nothing. And it was filthy that day. His suit was soaked. I remember thinking how strange it was that he wasn't wearing a coat.'

I stared at the table and rubbed at an invisible stain in one corner.

'Then he took off his hat and ran his hand through his hair – you know the way Peter does? – used to? And . . . well . . . it looked *just* like him. I almost dropped right then and there. Made me go all peculiar.'

I couldn't speak.

She gave a soft, sad laugh.

'Strange,' she said, 'how you see what you want to.'

Keep moving, don't stand still. She'll see your hands shaking. I fussed with the chairs and tried to compose myself. The bell above the door rang and a man holding a whippet with a lead around its neck walked in. He sat down, put the animal under the table between his feet and put his finger to his lips.

'Shhh!'

I passed the man a menu, took a few deep breaths and walked to the back of the café. My forehead had broken out into a sweat and I rubbed it with the back of my hand. She'd see it in my face, surely. Collen came over and leaned next to me.

'Dee?' She cocked her head.

'Mmm?'

'So . . . I mean, I don't mean to sound morbid, but . . . how exactly *did* he . . . you know?'

I didn't say anything.

'How – I mean – how did he . . .'

I couldn't look at her.

'Die?' she asked, in case I wasn't sure what she was getting at.

'Colleen, please.'

The old man motioned to me and I hurried over and scribbled down his order.

She'd been piling one question on top of another for days now. How did I hear? What was it like when I found out? Did I sometimes forget? Because she did, and then she was sad when she remembered. Was it like that for me? After handing chef the slip, I turned and jumped. She was standing right next to me again.

'I mean, the notice in the paper said "tragic accident". Well, that's what Harry said.'

She tugged at her cap again, and instead of straightening it set it off kilter.

'Was it the fog? I heard a terrible story about a woman who was run over by her own car. Her husband went right into her and didn't see her. Can you imagine? Was it a tram?'

I rearranged some chairs, then pulled off my pinny and cap. Instead of hanging them up I bundled them into a ball and threw them on an empty table.

'He *fell*, Colleen, okay? In front of a train. He was crushed and killed. Squashed to pieces. Nothing left of him.'

There. She had what she wanted, the whole slippery lie. I didn't look at her while I pulled on my coat and tied the belt tight around my waist, but then I turned back and saw that she was still standing in the same spot, eyes wide, hand in front of her mouth.

'Oh, Dee . . . oh . . . I'm so sorry.'

'Get table six. I'm going for lunch.'

49

I stormed out of the café. Bloody Peter. He was going to ruin it all and for what? To go outside in the rain? Who else had seen him that day? Rico had once asked me how stupid my brother was and now I had the answer.

I sucked the damp air deep into my lungs as I walked down Wardour Street. A weak February sun fought through the grey clouds. Thankfully Colleen had doubted her own eyes, never even entertained the idea that what she'd seen might have been real. But had she been on the other side of the street, had the weather been better, had she been closer, that would have been the end of it, the end of us. I had to tell them how close we'd come to being found out. If Bebba still had any feelings for him – if she ever really had any feelings – this might kill them off.

Avoiding the main roads, I weaved my way through Piccadilly and up Jermyn Street, past shops I would never enter. Shops reeking of tradition with their thoroughly English names: Dunhill, Floris, Geo. F. Trumper.

The burden of knowing had started to weigh heavy and I ached to shrug off the secrets along with the whole sordid business.

Keep your head, gori.

I'd seen Bebba circling adverts for flats to rent in the newspaper. Soon they'd be gone for good.

'Excuse me, miss!' I heard a man's voice behind me. I didn't look around, but continued walking towards the park, sure he was talking to someone else.

'Miss! Miss Demetriou.'

I spun around and my blood ran cold.

'Oh. You startled me.' He was the last person I expected to see.

He patted his chest. 'DC Steele. Remember?'

'Yes, yes, of course.'

'Can I walk with you?'

Could I say no? Without waiting for a response, he fell into step beside me.

'But – I'm in a rush, on my lunch.'

I wanted to run. *Don't be stupid.*

'It really won't take long. And it would be an immense help.'

We continued walking, side by side.

'Sorry for sneaking up on you like that, but I didn't want to come into the café. Where you work.'

Was he going to arrest me? I'd done nothing except keep quiet, but perhaps that was enough?

'The Coffee Corner?' he continued.

My voice sounded feeble: 'How do you know where I work?'

He smiled. 'Well, it's not a state secret now, is it?'

Calm down, gori. I tried to smile back. 'No, of course not. Sorry.'

Someone else must have seen Peter. Maybe someone he owed money. And they'd gone to the police. I put my head down and picked up my pace a little.

'I don't have very long for my break. I just came out to clear my head.'

'Well it won't take long. Actually, do you mind?' He pointed at an empty bench. 'It might be easier if we sit. Quicker that way.'

I hesitated, but he sat so I did the same. He pulled a note-pad and pencil from his pocket.

'Oh, don't look alarmed!' He laughed, and flicked back a few pages. 'My memory's not what it used to be. Now, your brother – Peter?'

At the mention of his name I pictured him in his vest and dressing gown, sulking around the flat. *Peter's dead. Remember that.*

'Yes?'

'I was wondering if . . . as far as you know . . . he was in any kind of trouble?'

A thread pulled tight around my heart.

'What do you mean?'

'You know, something illegal perhaps? Owed someone money, dealing in stolen goods, that kind of thing?'

'No, nothing like that.' My voice was indignant, suggesting the very thought was an insult. 'He had a job, he brought home a wage—'

'Oh, I know. But you also said he was a gambler.'

He flicked back another page and pointed at his notes.

'He worked at Mackenzie's as a pattern-cutter? Same place that . . .' he pursed his lips while he found what he wanted, '. . . your friend, Elizabetta . . . also known as Bebba . . . Antoniou works.'

He'd been digging around. I dug my nails into my palms. He would put it all together, matching piece to piece, until the whole ugly picture stared him in the face. Shifting in his seat, he lowered his voice a little. There was nobody listening, but I leaned towards him all the same.

'The reason I ask – whether he may have been involved in something . . . illegal,' he said, 'is because I think, and it's just a theory at this stage mind, I think that something else was going on that day.'

I stared at him. *Speak, you idiot. Ask the kind of question a sister asks about her dead brother.* He kept his eyes on my face as heat rose up my collar and I felt my cheeks redden. I dropped my gaze, opened my bag and pulled out my compact.

He continued. 'Do you know where he was going? Why he was at St Pancras? Was he meeting someone?'

'No. I mean I have no idea.'

I peered at my face in the mirror. My mouth trembled slightly but I had to do something, so I twisted the lid off my lipstick and put it up to my bottom lip.

'You see,' he said. 'I don't think he was alone.'

I spread Poppy Rouge on my lips, trying hard not to let my hand shake, and pressed my mouth together. What would Bebba do? She'd give him nothing.

'I can't prove this, miss, but I suspect foul play.'

I twisted down the lipstick, snapped the compact shut and dropped them both into my bag, then raised my chin a little as I looked him full in the face.

'I don't understand.'

'It's an expression. It means things aren't what they seem.'

'Yes, I know what foul play means,' I said. 'But I don't understand what you're getting at.'

'Well,' he flicked back another page, 'at the scene, we had – forgive me – the remains and pieces of what now appears to be *two* overcoats. We've only just realised.'

I looked at him blankly. Two coats? Of course. Rico had been wearing a coat that day, too. My guts churned as I tried to maintain a look of boredom.

'It's difficult to tell,' Steele continued, 'after . . . an accident like that . . . there's so little left. But a witness has come forwards to say she saw another man there. When he fell. She thinks she saw a struggle, but she wasn't close enough to be sure, and what with the fog . . .'

I opened my mouth to speak but decided against it.

'The station was particularly crowded that day,' he said. 'Her description is sketchy, but I think there may be something in it.'

I looked at my watch.

'I still don't see what that means,' I said, 'and I really need to get back.'

'Miss Demetriou.' He put his hand on my arm and left it there. 'I can't prove anything, but the two coats don't make sense. Now if you know a reason – any reason – why someone might have wanted to hurt your brother . . . a feud, a debt . . . Well, then I need to know.'

'I honestly don't know,' I said. 'He was a terrible gambler. He probably owed someone money, but he didn't tell me anything. Greek men are very proud.'

He nodded like he knew all about it. My mouth was parched.

'Before you go,' he said, 'I just want to read you this description. From the witness.' He flicked on to another page in his notepad. 'She described the other man as youngish,' he continued. 'About thirty at the most. Dark – and by that she meant olive-skinned – about five foot ten, a slim man, verging on skinny, black hair slicked back, in a suit. Does that ring a bell?'

He'd just described Peter.

I shrugged. 'Sorry, no – I mean yes.'

'It does?'

'Well, only because she's described every Mediterranean man in London.' I stood up. 'I'm sorry not to be of more help.'

He stood up.

'May I go now?' I asked. 'I'll be late, and my boss will dock my wages.'

'Oh, of course.'

I picked up my bag, turned and started to walk away.

'Oh, hold on!' he called, and ran after me.

'Yes?'

'Do you still have my card?'

It was in my pocket right now. I'd looked at it so many times.

'Here.'

He handed me another one.

'You never know when you might remember something. There's the address of the station and my number. I'm always available. Even if it's something little, something you think just doesn't fit, get in touch.'

'Thank you. I will.'

I dropped it into my pocket with the other card and walked away, head down, mind racing. First Colleen and now this. We were fooling ourselves thinking we were safe.

Should I tell them about DC Steele? If I did, Bebba would insist we stuck together. She'd postpone everything and I'd never be rid of them. And if I didn't? Would Peter be stupid enough to go for another jaunt, and come face to face with the detective or Colleen or someone else we knew?

I ran my fingers over the edges of the cards, wondering what to do.

*   *   *

I'd never seen Bebba so furious.

'You're an imbecile,' she hissed. 'After all of this you go for a walk? On one of the busiest streets in Soho?'

Peter got up and paced around the room, rubbing the back of his neck.

'It's all right for you. You don't know what it's like, being cooped up in here. I'm going mad.' He stood at the window and looked outside. 'I just needed to get out. I thought, what with the rainstorm, it would be safe – everyone would be rushing home.'

I dropped into the armchair and flung my legs over the side, letting them swing back and forth. So much for their cleverness. We'd been just moments from it all falling apart. 'You're so lucky Colleen didn't see your face,' I said. 'Imagine if she had.'

'And what if she'd called your name?' asked Bebba. 'I bet you would have turned round.'

Peter took a packet of Woodbines from his dressing gown pocket.

'Where the hell did you get those?' Bebba asked.

'Bought them that day.' He lit up. 'I'm fed up of smoking yours. I want to *smoke* what I want and *go* where I want. I can't go to the pub, the bookies or even the *kafenío*.' Ciggie in mouth, he slapped the windows. 'I need to get out.'

'Oh, drop the melodrama, will you?' she said. 'I'll find some places before the weekend and maybe we can move next week. It's time we did. We would have heard if the police were still investigating.'

I stood up, walked to my room and closed the door behind me.

50

I was sat on my bed, sewing a narrow beaded trim onto the cuffs of my lilac sweater while Peter rummaged in the next room.

'If you're touching anything on her dressing table, she'll kill you,' I called.

'I need some matches.'

A few seconds later he came in, sat on my bed and handed me an airmail envelope addressed to Rico. It was the one the woman with the little dog had given us the day we took the suitcase. I'd forgotten all about it. Why hadn't she opened it? Printed across the flap on the back was the name 'Yiacoumi Antoniou', and a return address in Cyprus.

The front door opened, and we looked at each other.

'What are you doing with that?' Bebba demanded, snatching it out of my hand. 'Where did you get it? Going through my things, I see.'

'No – I didn't . . .'

'It was me,' said Peter. 'My lighter's broken. I was looking for matches in your room . . . you didn't tell me the old man had written to Rico.'

'Ages ago,' she said, folding the envelope and pushing it into her pocket. 'I meant to say. The time wasn't right.'

'Why haven't you opened it?' I asked. 'You've had it for weeks.'

'I forgot. Anyway, who cares what the old man has to say?'

'If you don't care why did you keep it?' asked Peter.

She didn't speak for a few moments, then sighed.

'I almost tore it up so many times,' she said. She pulled it from her pocket and stared at it. 'I didn't know what to do. I thought it might be more bad news. I couldn't bring myself to open it . . .'

I'd never seen her so conflicted.

'Well go on,' I said. 'Read it.'

She hesitated, then put the crumpled sky-blue envelope on the bedspread and we all stared at it.

'What do you think he wants?' asked Peter.

She shrugged. 'He's a horrible man,' she said. 'Mean as anything. And still hanging on – must be over eighty.'

I grabbed it and tore it open. There was a single sheet of paper inside, folded into four. As I opened it something floated onto the floor. She picked it up and gasped. It was a money order for fifty pounds. She rubbed it between her thumb and index finger as though feeling the quality, to check it was real.

Peter actually laughed.

'Oh, money from the old man!' he said. 'That's just wonderful.'

He reached out to touch it, but she pulled back.

The letter I held was covered in a neat, tight script. It had been written in a heavy hand, and the black ink bled through the onionskin paper. Someone who wasn't used to writing letters had spent time over this.

'Well, thank you, *betherós*! I take it back. What a father-in-law!'

She had perked up immensely. She took the letter from my hand and sat up straight. She began to read in a mocking voice.

My son, Andriko,

I hope this finds you and your wife well. You cannot believe the joy I felt when I received the beautiful photograph this morning of the two of you. I thank God that you have reunited and put your differences to one side, and I trust that you have our money now, too. Be patient with her. With firm handling – here she raised an eyebrow but continued – *I'm certain Elizabetta will make an obedient wife.*

I'm enclosing a wedding gift to be used for your return journey. I look forward to showing you the workings of the estate before it is too late. Doctor Savvidis tries to feed me medicine and says I should rest but, as I tell him every morning when he comes to check on me, he is a fool and knows nothing.

Your father, Yiacoumi

'What photograph?' I asked.

'He forced me to have one taken,' she said. 'To send to the old man and prove how happy we were now we'd reunited. The old bastard was going to cut him out of his inheritance otherwise.'

I pictured a weary man sitting on a porch, skin as parched as the red earth and trammelled with age.

'Poor thing, out there waiting for him,' I said.

'Oh, please,' said Bebba. 'He's a mean old man who raised an even meaner son. If you knew him, you'd not feel any sympathy.'

Peter reached for the money order, successfully this time. 'Do you think he'll send more?' he said, wonder in his voice as he gazed at it. 'If we ask him?'

'Who knows?' said Bebba, smiling. 'It's worth a try. Let's write and see if he responds.'

I leaned forwards and put my hand over Peter's.

'You can't. He's expecting Rico to go back.'

'But,' he peeled my fingers off, 'what if Rico needs some cash?'

'What if he comes upon a business opportunity?' she said, warming to the idea. 'Somewhere outside London? Then he'd stay, wouldn't he?'

Peter sat up. '*And* he'd need some money.'

I hadn't seen either of them this animated in weeks.

'I'll write it from me,' she said. 'He knows Rico's handwriting. And to think, I almost threw this out.'

'No! Please don't. You said it was over. That you'd both get out of Soho.'

She folded the letter and slipped it back in the envelope, while keeping the money order on the table.

'For heaven's sake, Dina, stop whining. We'll be gone soon enough, but let me see if he bites. A little extra cash for the journey, that's all. The more we get the further away we can go – isn't that what you want? Never to see us again? I'm sure Peter will give you some of this, too.'

'I don't want any of it,' I said. 'How much more money do you need anyway? If you wait for more money from him, it will just slow things down – you must have enough by now.'

'Every penny counts. Me and Beb are planning to open a café,' he said, 'aren't we, Beb?' He smiled brightly. 'A small *kafenio* in the day but with drinks and singers in the evening. Greek, of course.'

I looked at her face and knew that this was his dream, not hers.

'The old man can afford it,' she said. 'I'll write again – let's see if he sends more in a week. He might send another fifty pounds – can you imagine? That's, what, easily two – three months' wages.'

'But when does it stop? Don't you care that you're pretending his son is alive when we know he isn't?'

'So what? Better that than the truth.'

Peter nodded. 'She's right.'

Folding her arms, she sat back with a satisfied smile.

'But it's not fair,' I said.

Peter gave an ugly smirk. '*Fair?* Life's not fair – it's down to luck and nerve.'

'Anyway, you don't know the half of it,' she said, 'his family took everything.' She folded the money order and tucked it in with the letter, then put it in her pocket. 'They owe me. So don't talk to me about fair.'

'It's cruel,' I said, 'and you know it. And you,' I pointed at Peter, 'I can't believe you'd go along with it.'

'What do you mean?' he asked.

'The Peter I know wouldn't do this.'

'But it's fallen into our laps,' he said. 'We can make a bit more cash. What's the matter with you? Why can't you see that?'

I pulled on my coat, grabbed my bag and ran out of the flat into the cold March air. I had no idea where I was going, but my fury propelled me forwards. Their lies would bind us together for life and drag me down with them. Unless I stopped it all right now.

The rain fell straight and hard, sheets of glass slicing through the night. Brushing the tendrils of wet hair off my face, I pulled up my collar and hurried along Goodge Street. The moon had wrung its light over my path, washing everything in a milky glow. As I turned the corner, I could see the blue lamp flicker outside the police station.

I stood across the road and watched as a taxi swished past, its polished carcass reflected in the rain-slicked road. I wanted to step into a puddle and fall through to another London, where life made sense again. A life before her.

I would do it. I'd had enough, even if it meant getting into trouble myself. I crossed the road and began to climb the stairs to the police station. An exhaustion had crawled into my bones and I grasped the metal railing tightly; it was good to hold something solid. I pushed open the wooden door and a waft of heat hit me as I walked into the tiny reception area.

Behind the counter was a policeman speaking into a

telephone and taking notes. He saw me and lifted a finger in acknowledgement.

Do it. Tell him everything.

Would I be arrested? Quite possibly. Almost certainly.

Finally, he placed the receiver in its cradle, screwed the lid onto his pen and looked up.

'Sorry to keep you waiting, miss. Still raining, is it?'

He looked a steady person, exactly the sort I could tell everything to. He was forty at the most, handsome in that pale, muted English kind of way. A smile skimmed his lips and there were creases around his eyes; he must laugh often.

'Miss? What can I do for you?'

My voice snagged in my throat and I tried again, taking a deep, noisy breath. A searing heat rushed over my neck.

His smooth, happy face turned serious and he rushed out from the counter and took my arm. 'Miss? What is it? Are you unwell?'

'I . . . I . . . n . . . never wanted to . . .'

'Maybe you should sit down?'

He began to lead me to a corner where a single straight-backed chair stood.

'No!'

I pulled my arm away with such force that he stepped back, shocked. I needed to breathe.

'Miss. Please.'

'I didn't know—'

'Miss, calm yourself.'

He stood inches away, my eyes level with his chest. Deep-navy uniform, silver buttons, a star-studded sky. A summer night somewhere far away. 'Come on, now.'

He put his hand under my elbow and gripped it tight. And suddenly I was stumbling through the fog again. *I'm warning you.* The sound of the trains, as we hurtled along the platform with his hand firm, pulling my body in so close to his that we moved as one. *Don't do anything stupid, Dina. Or you'll be sorry.*

'Come on now, miss,' said the policeman, 'let me help you.'

I turned to tell him everything, so I could breathe easy and be free of it all. I saw his mouth move but all I could hear was the roar of blood in my ears. Then a black shape flapped across my eyes like the wing of a terrible bird and the darkness pulled me back.

PART TWO

51

Liverpool, six months later

I shivered as a brisk autumn wind picked up and a flurry of leaves darted between my feet.

'Wait a moment,' I said. Bebba stopped pushing the pram.

'Oh, surely not,' she said. 'This must be a mistake.'

We both looked up at the soot-stained house that teetered before us. What a dump. I checked the scribbled note I'd held in my hand since Lime Street Station. Yes, this was it, Earle Street.

'Come on,' I said. 'This is the place.'

'I don't know if I can live here,' she said. 'I mean look at it. It's falling down and . . .'

Just then the baby let out a screech.

Bebba gave an exasperated sigh and bent down to the pram.

'I'll do it.' I lifted my daughter out and held her to my chest, rocking her slightly.

'Ssshh . . . there's a good girl,' I whispered. 'Mama's here.' Her cries softened.

A middle-aged woman burst from the front door and rushed down the steps. She wore a lavender-and-yellow floral housecoat and had rollers in her hair.

'Lord, look at her,' said Bebba in Greek.

'Are you the new tenants?' asked the woman. 'I've been waiting on you all morning. I'm Mrs Fitzpatrick, your landlady.'

'Hello.' Bebba put on her best English accent and offered her hand, but the woman came straight to me and the baby.

'Ah, would you look at him?' She waggled her finger in front of the baby's face. 'He's a wee angel.'

'He's a girl,' I said, stroking the baby's face. 'Athena.'

'Ath – what?'

'Athena.'

'Well you're very welcome, I'm sure. Now, I live on the ground floor.' She waved her hand at the large, battered windows. 'Ask for anything you need. I get on grand with all of my tenants. You Maltese?'

'No, Cypriot,' I said. 'I'm Dina.'

'Well, as long as you pay the rent, that's all I care about.' She folded her arms, providing a shelf for her bosom. 'But you look the decent type.'

Bebba shuffled. She hated being ignored.

'I'm Bebba,' she said, but she hardly got a glance.

'It'll be grand to have a wee one around the house,' said Mrs Fitzpatrick, stroking the baby's cheek. 'Your man's already here.'

'*My* man – husband, actually,' said Bebba, and reached out for Athena. '*My* baby.'

The woman frowned at her and then at me.

'Oh, sorry,' she said, flushing. 'I thought her – well . . . Mr Rico's here and settled in.'

'My sister here isn't very well,' said Bebba, 'so she'll be looking after the baby while I'm at work.'

The words rang so false in my ears, but the landlady seemed to take it all in her stride. Why wouldn't she believe it?

'That's a pity,' said Mrs Fitzpatrick, concern all over her face. 'Your wee 'un looks young to be away from her ma. Needs must, I s'pose.'

Bebba plonked Athena back in the pram as if she was depositing a bag of shopping.

'The sacrifices mothers make, I could tell you some stories—' started Mrs Fitzpatrick.

Bebba cut her dead. 'We must get on, so much to do.' And with that she clasped the pram and tried to push it through the hall, hitting the threshold a few times, having to rear up and try again. *Tilt it up for heaven's sake!* Her cheeks had gone pink and just as I was about to go and help, Mrs Fitzpatrick called out.

'Hey, love, you'll never manage it like that,' she said. 'Will you carry her up, and get your man to come down for the pram. It's a tight squeeze and there's an awful lot of stairs. Top floor. Bannister's a bit shaky.'

Bebba picked up the baby and started at a fair pace up the narrow stairs, leaving the pram blocking the hall. I moved it to one side and followed her past the battered black phone that squatted like a splattered insect on the wall, and up the dingy staircase. The faded wallpaper was shredded in places, and in others it had come off completely. Underneath, the walls looked slimy. I remembered following her up another derelict staircase on Frith Street months ago where, at the top, resided a secret – and surprisingly smart – nightspot for gin-lovers. If only a scene half as enchanting was waiting for us today.

This was worse than anywhere we'd lived in Soho. Peter had arranged this all and had come ahead the day before. Was it really the best we could do?

As we turned the corner there he stood, just inside the doorway, sweating in his vest and trousers as he unwrapped plates, discarding the newspaper onto a heap on the floor. Once over the threshold, Bebba handed me the baby and lit a cigarette. I turned and took in the same faded wallpaper from the hallway, with damp patches under the window frame.

Bebba stood in the middle of the room, elbow in hand, cigarette upright, and slowly turned a full circle, taking it all in. Then she shot me such a vindictive look it was clear she blamed me for this situation.

'Hello!' Peter embraced her and planted a kiss on her lips, then came and gave me a hug.

'So, this is the living room,' he said, with a majestic sweep of his hand. There was a grey sink, two chairs and a table. I squeezed past and peered into an open room.

'That's your room, Dina,' he said. I held the baby to my chest, peered in to see the single bed, small wardrobe and chair and then looked at him and made a face. 'It's tiny. What about the pram? I don't think we can leave it downstairs.'

'Leave it in here. For now. Maybe we can get one of those folding ones?'

He looked at Bebba, as he always did whenever there was talk of spending money. She'd bought the train tickets and paid the deposit for the flat. He kicked a box to one side and took her hand.

'And this,' he said, with as much pride as if he'd built it himself, 'this is our room.'

She peered through the door and I put my head around too. A sagging double bed with a washed-out slippery blue bedspread, a battered wardrobe, which was definitely tilting, and a chair. I took a sidelong look at her face and watched as she tried to contain her anger.

Her voice was flat: 'I was rather hoping to have a room of my own.'

He laughed, then realised she wasn't joking.

'But we're married,' he said. 'Wouldn't it look odd?'

She shrugged. 'I suppose so.' She pulled her leopard-skin coat a little tighter, and it was the first time I thought she looked silly in it and out of place.

'It's just, well, I'm used to sleeping alone every now and then.'

He pulled at the neck of his vest. 'This was the best place I could get . . . not unless you were going to—'

She shook her head. Of course she wasn't.

'No. Not yet,' she said. 'We're saving up for the café, remember?'

She leaned towards him and gave him a long, noisy kiss on the cheek. 'Don't worry, darling. This will do just fine. Do you mind if I have a lie-down? I'm getting one of my headaches.' And with that she went into their room and closed the door.

52

Bebba had drawn the thin curtains against the fading light. She lay on her back as she stared at a stain on the ceiling, too furious to sleep.

So, this was Liverpool: all the grime of London with none of the glamour. She'd suggested they come here because the city was teeming with immigrants. Lazy ones straight off the boat, who didn't have the resourcefulness to travel elsewhere. Three more Cypriots would hardly stand out. Well, four including the brat.

'Nobody will find us,' she'd said, 'we don't know anyone in Liverpool.' The added bonus, of course, was that Peter's contacts wouldn't reach this far. In Soho she'd itched to take the suitcase and run, but he'd stuck to her like glue day and night, talking about how he'd saved her from Rico. And when she was out, the suitcase was with him in the flat. If she tried to leave, he'd find her. She couldn't go through that again, constantly looking over her shoulder, listening out for the creak on the stairs. In Liverpool, she was safer and she'd get her chance.

She'd establish a routine, wait till he felt secure, then one morning he'd wake, and she'd be gone. Last week, he'd suggested they deposit the money in the bank once they'd got here, but she'd refused, said it was too risky because of the questions they might be asked. She knew she couldn't open an account without him, which meant she couldn't withdraw without his say-so either. No, best to leave the suitcase in the wardrobe and feign nonchalance when it was mentioned, although, in fact, it was all she thought of. Then at least it would be to hand when she needed it. She wasn't running from Rico now, so she could take her time. She'd waited so long already. She had to be sure she had enough because her new plan, though wonderful, was expensive.

She swung her legs off the bed and stood up. This time it would be different. This time she'd go somewhere no one would dream of looking. And that was another reason Liverpool was perfect. She'd seen the signs for the docks on her way to the boarding house and her heart skipped at the thought of how close those huge ocean liners were.

53

I stood in my new bedroom and peered out of the window. Athena began to grizzle, and I pulled her a little closer, till I could feel the warmth of her breath on my skin. Despite being so high up, I could only just make out the rooftops of Edge Hill. So, Liverpool had fog, too, but here it hung over the city like delicate lacework; there was no toxic yellow core. Perhaps that was a good omen.

I looked down at her drowsy face and my mind was wrenched back to the evening I fainted, back in the spring. As I woke in hospital, a freckle-faced doctor had leaned over me, his hand on my arm.

'Is there any chance you might be expecting, miss?'

Sometimes, when you're falling, you think you've reached the bottom and there's nowhere left to fall, but then you realise that you're only halfway. You've stopped because you're trapped on a ledge. And you look down into the abyss and fall some more.

I had blacked out before I was able to utter a word to the police. And everyone had assumed I'd stepped inside the station because I'd felt faint. *How clever of you, Miss Demetriou.* The pay packet in my bag meant they had my address and, thankfully, nobody had looked in my coat pocket.

For weeks, knowing that a part of Rico grew inside me made me numb. How could I be a mother? I didn't want this, this life sentence that felt so undeserved. What had happened to the Dina I'd wanted to become? The one who'd be free of them both, have her own dress shop and say yes to adventures? The one who'd never hear the names Bebba and Peter and Rico again. The life I'd imagined for myself was like a fine garment I'd painstakingly sewn but that didn't fit me and whatever alterations I made, never would.

In the early hours I'd wake with a strange hunger in my stomach, but it wasn't lack of food that woke me. I was hollowed out with grief, a yearning for a future I'd never know. The pain scraped against my chest, and as the baby pushed and grew and stretched inside me, I thought I couldn't go on. But my heart had other ideas.

From the living room a clash of metal rang out as something fell to the floor. Bebba's unpacking was tinged with careless resentment, but I wasn't surprised. As much as the baby had changed everything for me, this set-up hadn't been part of her grand plan, either. In fact, I was often surprised to turn and find her still there. Perhaps she really did care about Peter? After all, a couple of times now she'd mentioned how Liverpool was the 'perfect spot' for this café of theirs.

The clattering took me back to that woman in Soho, a few days after I'd found out, fishing in the depths of her Gladstone bag for the right implement to 'fix' the problem. Bebba had arranged it all, though Peter insisted we pay extra and have her come to us.

Weary-eyed and gently spoken, with a tendril of grey hair hanging down by one ear, she was in a terrible rush. A solid, metal utensil fell from her hands and she hurriedly picked it up, gave it a quick blow and wiped it on her rubber apron before slipping it into a large pocket on the front. She unfolded a frayed square of hessian and spread it on my bed.

'Now come on Diane, be a good girl,' she said. 'If you do as I say it really won't take long at all.'

'It's Dina.'

'Yes, well lie down, love.'

I climbed up, feeling the rough hessian on my bare legs. Bebba had placed a tin bucket to one side, as instructed, and a couple of towels.

Peter had carried the table into my room, and on it lay the tools of her trade, lined up in a neat row. A pair of tongs, a long-handled metal spoon, some heavy, rusted scissors and a brown glass bottle containing small tablets.

'All off down below?'

I nodded.

'Good. Close your eyes.'

A cold sweat flicked over my body. Blood thumped in my ears.

'Wait!' I tried to sit up. 'Will it hurt?'

She pushed me down gently.

'I won't lie. It will a bit. But as long as you rest for a few days you'll be right as rain.'

The door creaked and I looked towards the wedge of light that had fallen into the room.

'I don't want her watching.'

The woman got up, walked towards Bebba and muttered something. She shut the door gently and came back, giving me a tired smile. I wondered if she had children of her own.

'We're all set, now, Diane. Shall we get on?'

Perhaps she was right, and I wasn't Dina any more.

'Now come on, stop crying. Try and relax. That's it – deep breaths. Good girl. I don't want to rush you, but I've got another girl straight after, then I can get off home.'

*   *   *

I leaned down and kissed the top of Athena's head as I remembered the look of disbelief on Bebba's face that day. The colour had leached from her skin in a matter of seconds.

'You don't know what you're saying,' she said, leaning over me as I curled up in bed. The woman had long since left and she'd had to pay her anyway.

'I can't do it,' I said.

I pulled the covers over my head.

I felt the bed sink as Peter sat down.

'Come on, *gori.*'

He gently pulled the bedspread down, so he could see my face. 'We've been through all this, haven't we?'

'I'm not doing it. I've changed my mind.'

He smoothed my hair back.

'Peter,' I said, 'women *die.*'

'Do you think I'd let you do it if it wasn't safe?'

He stroked my cheek and Bebba let out an exasperated sigh as she shifted her feet. 'Oh, for heaven's sake!'

I ignored her. 'And it's illegal,' I said. 'What if I get found out?'

She crouched down next to the bed and tried to hold my hand, but I pulled it away.

'Dina, look at me.' Her voice was softer now. 'Look at me.'

I turned towards her, our faces just inches apart. She'd changed; the beauty was still there but she'd lost that freshness, that spark that had made her so irresistible, so Bebba.

'You *must* do it. It's awful, but you don't have a choice, do you darling?' she said.

I sat up on my elbows. 'But I do,' I said. 'I could have it.'

'Don't be ridiculous. Then what?' she asked. 'One of those awful unmarried mothers' homes?'

I shook my head.

'Because you know those places are dreadful, don't you?' she continued. 'They're more like prisons than anything.'

'I know. And anyway, they make you give up the baby once you've had it, to women who can't have them.'

'Well, of course they do.' She gave a little laugh then her face dropped as she realised what I meant.

'You don't actually intend on *keeping* it do you?'

'Well, yes. I want to have it *and* keep it.'

'But it's Rico's,' she said. 'You'll see him every time you look at it.'

'It isn't his,' I said, furious. 'It's Andreas's, and he never existed. So it's all mine.'

'Oh, that's perfect!' She stood up. 'You have well and truly lost your mind. Just listen to yourself.'

She walked out, slamming the door.

There were a few moments of silence, then Peter spoke.

'Don't take any notice,' he said. 'She'll get over it.'

'Do you understand? Why I want to keep it?'

He shook his head.

'Not really, but I'm glad. Something good to come out of this mess.'

I circled his chest with my arms and squeezed him tight. I couldn't remember the last time I'd felt this close to him. We sat like that for a few seconds and then he broke away, taking my hands in his.

'But you can't have it here, Dina, you know that, right? Someone will notice. Ask questions.'

A sadness settled on me as I guessed what he was about to say.

'We'll leave Soho,' he said. 'Come on, don't cry. We were going anyway. You'll come with us, that's all.'

He smiled. It was what he'd wanted all along.

'You'd never be able to manage on your own,' he continued. 'And it's not so bad, is it? Being with your brother?'

All three of us together again. Four. I'd imagined life without them and now this. The baby was the only thing that felt completely mine. I couldn't get rid of it, even though it meant I needed Peter now more than ever.

'We'll go somewhere they don't know us,' he said, 'till you have it. I've known girls in trouble before, and they've rented places in the East End – short-term. No questions asked.'

I rubbed my hand across my eyes. 'What happens afterwards?' I asked. 'Once the baby's here? Nobody will rent me a room if they know the truth.'

I fell back on the bed and stared at the ceiling and he lay down next to me.

'People believe any story you tell them,' he said. 'I'll think of something.'

54

Mrs Fitzpatrick had let me use the ancient iron mangle in the backyard and, after a day of boiling and wringing nappies, I was exhausted. I rubbed the small of my back and glanced up at the patch of sky overhead. All the houses backed onto each other, leaning in on the small, ruined courtyard.

Although it was still mild for October, the violet clouds threatened to erupt and there was another storm brewing indoors. I'd heard them squabbling this morning, and there was a deep satisfaction in being able to close my door on their bickering. She hated sharing a room, but that was too bad. He'd been good enough for her when she'd needed him.

As I folded the damp nappies, I imagined what my life in Cyprus might have looked like. Since Athena had been born, my mind had often wandered back there. If the wedding had gone ahead, perhaps Yiannis and I would have a baby by now. I'd certainly have stayed there and would never have met Bebba or Rico.

If my own mother had lived, I think she'd have visited every morning. We'd have sat on the veranda drinking *kafé*, while talking about the baby. How was the little one today? Had she slept? What was I cooking for dinner later on? The things mothers and daughters talk about. She'd give me advice and reassure me that I was doing just fine. She'd have crocheted Athena a blanket, the way Greek grandmothers often do.

A breeze picked up. How could I be a mother when I'd never known one myself? One of Bebba's blouses snapped on the washing line and the sleeve hit me in the face. Yesterday she'd practically thrown her dirty washing at me, saying she needed it for work and didn't have time to do it herself. She was a sales assistant at Lewis's, and Peter had got a packing job at the Tate & Lyle factory. Now I wasn't earning anything, they helped out even less at home. I could feel rain in the air, but I left her blouse where it was and walked back inside with the basket of nappies.

She was at the table brushing crimson polish on her nails. Peter sat in his vest reading the *Echo*. Dirty breakfast plates and coffee-stained cups were stacked next to the overflowing ashtray and the room smelt like a pub. So, this was it? This was my life from now on? Doing their washing, clearing up after them? Well, I wasn't having it.

I dropped the basket onto a chair.

'Don't smoke in the same room as the baby,' I said. 'It clings to her.'

'I've just got in,' he said. 'I need a smoke.'

Athena was grizzling and I walked to the pram, picked her up and stopped dead.

'What's that?' I asked. I sniffed her again and presented her to Peter.

'What? I can't smell anything.'

I held her out to Bebba, but she turned her head away and shook the pot of nail polish before starting a second coat.

I sniffed again, more deeply this time.

'It's alcohol,' I said. I sniffed again and then I saw it, a small yellow-brown stain on the front of her cardigan. I put her back in the pram and took a deep breath to steady my nerves.

'Bebba?'

'Hmmm?' She was looking at her nails.

'Did you give her *whisky*?'

Peter let out a laugh. 'You didn't did you?'

'Well she wouldn't shut up.' She blew on her nails. 'Just a drop. To keep her quiet.'

I lunged forwards but Peter was fast and grabbed me by the waist. Bebba yelped and jumped back, almost falling off her chair. The baby started crying.

'Dina, calm down for heaven's sake!' Peter had me round the waist.

'I swear,' I said, 'if you do that again . . .'

'Look what you've made me do!' Her nails were smudged. 'Do you hear?'

'I heard you, all right? It's just a drop of whisky.'

'No harm done,' said Peter. 'Everyone does it.'

She had started furiously taking off the nail polish.

'It wouldn't stop crying . . .' she said, 'just like now.'

'*It* is a *she* and she's teething, she's not doing it to spite you. She's a baby.'

'Well I couldn't take it any more. Anyway, technically she's mine, so I can do what I want.'

I leaned into her face. '*She's not yours,*' I said. 'Do it again and you'll see what happens.'

'Will you both stop?' shouted Peter. Then, lowering his voice, 'We don't want everyone knowing our business.'

I picked Athena out of the pram and jiggled her around, trying to calm her. From now on, I'd have to make sure I never let her out of my sight.

'It stinks in here,' I said, opening the window. 'And these dirty dishes have been here all day.'

Nobody said anything. On the floor was a scrunched-up ball of yellow paper, a betting slip. He saw me look at it and shifted his chair. I didn't have the energy to say anything. What was there left to say? Ardana, Soho, Liverpool, it didn't matter where we lived. His pockets would be stuffed with the remnants of sure things gone wrong. In thirty years' time, he'd still be the same.

'There's no point getting so cross,' said Bebba, working the polish off her nails. 'It's all your own doing, after all.'

'What?' I asked.

'The baby, playing house . . . all of this was your idea, wasn't it? You and . . .' she motioned towards Peter with her head. 'What did you think it would be like? It could have been much simpler if you'd—'

'Don't.'

His voice was stern. He rarely cut her off. She looked surprised, then gathered her nail polish and cotton wool and stalked to her room, kicking the door shut behind her.

He stared after her and sighed.

'Come on, let's not argue, Dina, okay?'

I put Athena back in the pram and sat next to him.

'What she did was wrong, you have to see that?' I asked.

'You overreacted,' he said.

'She's *my* baby, Peter. She can't do that without asking.'

I took the paper from him to force him to look at me. I thought he was about to agree with me, but he patted my shoulder half-heartedly.

'Everything will be all right,' he said. I'd never been less convinced of anything. 'You'll see. Liverpool's not so bad you know. Lots of opportunities here.'

'Did you speak to her?' I asked. 'About what we discussed? You didn't, did you?'

He picked up the paper and smoothed it out.

'I will, I just have to choose the right time.'

He tried opening it again, but I put my hand out.

'Look,' I whispered. 'Everything that's happened – all of this – is because of the money, isn't it?'

He nodded.

'Then I don't see why we can't *spend* some of it. I know I said I didn't want it before, but Athena needs some new clothes and that pram is impossible with those stairs.'

'I know.'

I leaned in and lowered my voice even more.

'She *will* let us spend it, won't she?' I asked. 'I mean, eventually. It's not just for her, is it?'

He looked appalled, like the very idea was inconceivable.

'Of course not. It's *ours.* We're opening that café together. She's as excited about it as I am . . . I mean, that was the deal. I help her with the . . . the situation . . . and . . .'

I wanted to believe that as much as he did and, after all, she was still with us, wasn't she? Our lives here were far from happy and she could have left ages ago.

'Good,' I said. 'I just wanted to make sure.'

Athena started squirming, so I went to my room to feed her. Settling in my chair, I unbuttoned my blouse, unclipped my brassiere and put her to my breast. She looked up at me with his eyes and my mouth went dry. I'd sometimes forget and then all of a sudden there it would be, the reminder, and it would jolt me every time. Bebba had been right. I did see Rico in her.

We never discussed what would happen – in one year, two, five, ten – who my baby would know as her mother, let alone her father. She snuffled a little and I pulled away to let her breathe. It clawed at my heart every time Bebba pretended to be her mother, pretended to care in front of others. But for now, it was the only way I could keep her close.

I'd phoned Madame S twice the day before, when they'd been out of the house, but the number just rang and rang. I knew it was unlikely, but I hoped she'd have some contacts here in Liverpool. Maybe a nightclub owner who needed someone to hand-sew garments. Work I could do in my room at night and they'd be none the wiser. I needed my own money to build a future for me and Athena, but I was also desperate to sew again. I missed the Pelican so much and ached for those dazzling days.

The phone rang and rang into an empty corridor somewhere in Soho. Nobody answered, but I'd try again as soon as I could.

55

We stared at the new pram, which stood like a shiny monument in the middle of the room.

'Look Athena! Your uncle's bought you a present!' I turned her round so she could see.

'And this is the best bit,' Peter said, and he pulled at levers on each side, making the whole thing collapse onto itself. 'It's really light, try it.'

I picked it up while still holding the baby.

'How much did it cost? Did you have a win?'

He pulled it up again and fastened the clasps.

'Don't worry about that. Put her in. Let's try it out.'

He picked up her pillow from the old pram and put it in the new one.

'Go on.'

I lowered her into it and wheeled it a few feet one way, then turned it and wheeled it the other. It was so much lighter than the old contraption.

'Thank you so much. I can't wait to take her out in it.'

'I bought you this, too.' He handled me a small bundle wrapped in brown paper. I ripped it open and saw it was a pretty pale-yellow cotton fabric. 'So you can make something for her. Mrs F has a machine you can use.'

I unfolded the material and let it drop open – there was enough here for a couple of outfits.

'I noticed it when I helped her with her shopping the other day,' he continued. 'It's just sitting in the corner of her living room collecting dust. I told her you sewed, and she said you can borrow it if you like.'

'Really?'

He nodded. 'Says she'll get Tony – her "gentleman friend" as she calls him – to bring it up.'

'I don't know what to say, Peter.' A rush of affection overwhelmed me, and I gave him a big hug.

At that moment Bebba walked in and came to an abrupt halt. She looked from the pram to him, her mouth open.

'What on earth—'

'It folds down,' I said. 'Look.'

I gave Peter the baby and demonstrated.

'Ta-da! Isn't it wonderful? It'll be so much easier getting it up the stairs.'

Her face blanched and she rushed to the wardrobe. She yanked at the case, threw it on the floor and knelt beside it. She was all thumbs as she tried to undo the clasps and eventually it clacked open. Quickly, she ran her hand over the neat stacks of Cypriot pounds that stared back at her.

'I didn't pay for it with that,' he said, his voice cold. 'I wouldn't. I told you we should put it in the bank, but you won't listen. Well, tomorrow we're going to left luggage at Lime Street. I don't want it in the house any more.'

She opened her mouth to protest, perhaps, but then just said, 'So where *did* you get the money?'

He handed me Athena, plunged his hand into his trouser pocket and pulled out a piece of paper. It was a familiar sky blue.

'You had no right opening that!' she hissed.

She jumped up and tried to snatch it, but he held it high. With the other hand, he pushed her back, gently.

'Well, of course, I have a right,' he said. 'After all, it's addressed to me.'

'*It's addressed to Rico.*'

She tried to snatch it again, but he pulled back.

'That's what I said. Me. I sorted the ID out weeks ago.'

I recognised the writing on the front.

'From his father?' Athena wriggled and I settled into the armchair and rocked her a little.

'Yes, but not just a letter,' said Peter. 'Money, again. And from the sound of it, on a regular basis.'

Peter poured himself a whisky and sat down at the table.

'So, you're still writing to him?' I asked her. 'Here? In Liverpool?'

She didn't deny it, just folded her arms and leaned against the wall. Was there no stopping her? Someone had to.

'So, Beb, tell me,' said Peter, his voice thin, 'what's happened to the rest of it?' I could tell by the way his neck was thrust forwards that he was trying hard to smother his temper. 'It sounds like he's been sending money for a while now.' He paused for a moment, mopped his forehead with the back of his shirt sleeve, then started again, this time in the tone he often reserved for her, as if she were a disobedient child. 'Beb, you know that money's not yours, don't you? It's for both of us – Bebba *and* Rico.' He hesitated. 'What I mean is, all of us.'

The baby squirmed in my arms.

'So, you carried on writing and the old man coughed up?' he said, trying to lighten the atmosphere. 'I mean it's good, right?'

She looked at the floor. 'Yes. I should have said.'

I couldn't believe it – was she actually going to apologise?

'Look, I haven't cashed any of the money orders,' she said. 'After all, they're in Rico's name.'

So, she hadn't worked out how to cash them, in other words. She needed Rico's ID for that. She took her handbag from the hook by the door and flicked open the clasp.

'Here. It was always for all of us – I can't believe you'd think otherwise.' She tipped her bag and half a dozen slips of paper floated down onto the table. 'You make out we're a family but we're not, are we? It's always the two of you against me.'

Peter walked towards her, but she pulled away.

'Spend it all on the baby,' she said, furious now. 'I don't care. He probably won't send any more anyway. He's a tight old bastard.'

Athena grabbed at my blouse. She pulled a fistful of fabric to her mouth and started to whimper.

Bebba slammed the door behind her and the baby started to bawl. Her shoes rang out on the staircase, getting quieter and quieter, and then the front door crashed, making the windows shudder in their frames.

Peter rubbed the back of his neck and stared at the floor.

'I don't know what to do,' he said, as the baby continued to cry. 'I just can't get through to her.'

I rocked the baby back and forth for several minutes while he sat at the table, head in hands. After a while, Athena wore herself out and her eyelids grew heavy. I put her in the new pram and sat down next to him.

'She doesn't trust you,' I said. 'Did you see how she thought you'd dipped into the money?'

His eyes glistened and, using his knuckles, he rubbed them and then blinked several times.

'That's not true,' he said. 'I mean, if she didn't trust me she wouldn't have kept it here for so long.'

She was obsessed with money, any fool could see that, and probably wanted to look at it every day.

'What?' he asked. 'Why are you looking at me like that?'

I put my hand on his arm. 'Listen to me,' I said. 'Truthfully. Do *you* trust *her*?'

He pulled his head back a little. I knelt down next to him and put my hand on his. Perhaps I could still make him see.

'Let's just stop this now,' I said. 'We could leave. Just me and you, and the baby. Forget her and that bloody suitcase.

We can cash in those money orders now you have the ID. We could go back to the way things were.'

He shook his head, 'No, we couldn't. Bebba said you'd try to make me choose between you and her. It's not right.'

'I'm not, I'm asking you to think for yourself.'

'I can't leave her and, anyway, where would we go? That money won't last long. And the baby, how would we explain that?'

'Come on. You're just looking for reasons not to go. We'd figure something out. We always do. Just *look* at her.'

I got up and pushed the pram near him. He peered over the side and watched her doze.

'Look at her, Peter, and tell me she doesn't deserve better than this.'

'My place is here. With her. I'm her husband.'

'But you're not! You're not anything to her, don't you see? She's used you and will drop you like that.' I snapped my fingers and he jerked.

'No, no . . .' he faltered. 'No, that's not true.'

'Peter, please . . .'

He laid his head on the table and covered it with his arms, like a man shielding himself from shrapnel. Then, a muffled voice rose. 'I love her,' he said. 'And, in her own way, she loves me.'

56

The following day, Bebba sat at the table in the empty flat. She'd risen early and gone with Peter to Lime Street, where they'd locked away the suitcase of money as he'd insisted. She'd held out her hand for the key but he'd slipped it in his wallet and had said, in a matter-of-fact tone, that it was all right, he could look after it. She had to remind herself that this was Peter. Peter who was infatuated with her, and would never think of double-crossing her. Anyway, it should be easy enough to retrieve when the time came. For now, let him think he was in charge. He went off to the factory and after an hour at Lewis's, she'd feigned illness and returned home, knowing Dina would be at the market. Now she pulled an airmail form from her bag and began to write.

To my dearest, beloved father-in-law, Kyrieh Yiacoumi,

I pray this finds you in better health. As we sit and read your letters together, they never fail to lift our spirits during these exhausting days.

The baby is growing strong and married life suits us. Rico works hard: the new building venture we wrote to you about, developing the bombed land here in Liverpool, is coming along well. It's a slow, expensive process (our heartfelt thanks for your generosity) but the rewards will be immense.

We miss Cyprus and hope it won't be too long before we're able to return. Life in England can be difficult. The hours are long and everything is so expensive. And yet we are so pleased to be here, because the opportunities are plentiful. We'll soon bring our fortune home to Paramali and make you proud.

It's probably not a good idea to come for a visit, even though I understand how much you must miss your beloved Rico, and that you'd like nothing more than to surprise him. Forgive me if I sound inhospitable, but we live in cramped conditions and, with this damp weather, I do fear for your health. Please be patient, father, and one day soon we'll be drinking ouzo together on your veranda and telling you stories of our time in England.

And do forgive Rico for not writing. He's working every hour God gives us and has no time to himself. I've enjoyed getting to know you and the fact that you call me your daughter makes me so happy; I thought I was an orphan, but it seems I am to have a father once more.

With all our love, Elizabetta, Andriko and baby Athena xxx

PS By the way, would you mind sending any future money in cash, please? Rico's hours mean he doesn't have time to visit the post office and, of course, I'm not allowed to draw out the money without him. Thank you so much. With love x

57

'It's so lovely to hear from you, *chère amie*. Where have you been?'

The sound of Madame Sylvie's voice finally floating down the line made my throat tighten. It was rare to have the house to myself and I'd called on impulse.

'I'm not in Soho any more,' I said.

'Really?' She sounded puzzled, as if the very thought that someone would leave was ridiculous.

'I – I wanted to get away.'

'Where *are* you?'

'After everything, with my brother. Dying.' Neither of us spoke as the lies bounced off the walls of the damp corridor. I realised I hadn't answered her question. 'Oh, I'm in Liverpool.' It sounded ridiculous to my own ears.

'*Liverpool?* But why so far?' she asked.

I didn't say anything. I'd had no choice but to come here, so I'd tried not to think about Soho and what I was leaving behind. Now something inside me lurched.

'Oh Dina,' she sighed. 'You really *did* want to get away, didn't you? I suppose it was all too painful here.'

I was silent for a moment and rubbed at my wet cheeks.

'I was wondering,' I said, trying to steady my voice, 'I was wondering if you knew anyone here, in Liverpool, who might give me some work.'

'In a club?' she asked.

'No – piece work, from home. I – I have to stay home really. I'm . . .'

'Are you ill?' she asked. 'Do you need help, *chère amie*? Is everything all right?'

Why hadn't I thought she'd ask questions? My lies would be my undoing.

'I'm all right, really.' I said. 'I just want to sew from home, till I feel like going back to a workroom again.' I had the feeling she knew I was lying. After all, I'd always loved the camaraderie of the workroom.

'Well ... er ... I don't know anyone in Liverpool myself, but I can ask a friend. I do know someone near St Helens – that's close, isn't it? She's a seamstress too, and—'

Athena started bawling. I put my hand over the mouthpiece. Perhaps she hadn't heard.

'What's that?'

Her wails got louder. *Please not now.* She'd been in such a deep sleep.

'Is that ... is it a *baby*?'

'No – yes, I don't—' *For God's sake, Dina.* 'I'm sorry ... I have to go – I ...' Athena sounded distressed. What could I do? I should just hang up. 'Sorry ...'

'Dina? Dina! Calm down and listen.' Her voice was firm but full of kindness. 'Dina, I'll wait – go to the child and I'll stay on the line.'

I left the receiver hanging next to the wall and ran upstairs. Athena was red in the face and her skin was warm to the touch. Her bedclothes were in a tangle. I picked her up, dipped my fingers in a glass of water on the bedside and stroked her cheeks. She grizzled and I went to put her down, but her crying started up again. *What are you doing to me?*

'All right, all right,' I said, carrying her downstairs, 'you can come with me.'

She whimpered and I held her up to my shoulder as I picked up the receiver again.

'I'm back,' I said. 'I'm sorry about that.'

There was a silence on the line.

'Sylvie? Are you still there?'

'Is it a boy or girl?' she asked.

'Girl. Athena.'

'That's a lovely name,' she said.

I didn't reply.

'And that's why you left? So suddenly?'

I couldn't tell her more lies.

'Yes.'

'But Liverpool – so far. The father . . .?'

'He left me,' I said. 'I can't say anything else about it, please don't ask.'

Athena started crying again.

'Sorry,' I said, 'do you mind holding on?' I let the phone hang down again and carried her into the kitchen, where I knew I'd left her rattle. Picking it up I showed it to her, and she grabbed it and started shaking it enthusiastically.

I hurried back.

'I'm sorry, Sylvie. Maybe I should go – she's woken up properly now and—'

'Have you got a ring?'

'Sorry?'

'A wedding ring,' she said. 'Have you got one?'

'No, why?'

'Well, that would take care of the questions,' she said. 'So many people died in the fog. Who's to say he didn't go the same way?'

There was a silence on the line.

'Thank you,' I said.

'What for?'

'For not being horrible about it.'

She gave a gentle laugh. 'If you haven't made mistakes in life, you haven't lived.'

'She's not a mistake,' I said. 'She's the best thing I have.'

'Well, I'm glad to hear it. In that case, I shan't feel sorry for you. I'll be happy for you.'

We talked for a while and she made me promise not to disappear again.

'I'll give you my new address,' she said. 'I'm moving – a smaller place. No phone yet.'

'You're staying in Soho, though?' I asked.

'Well, of course. I can't imagine being anywhere else.'

I felt the same, and yet here I was in a boarding house in Liverpool, with two people who didn't care about me.

I grabbed a pencil and paper and sat on the floor, resting Athena in my lap while I scribbled down her details. Then I gave her my address.

'It's better to write, not call,' I said. 'It's . . . well, it's a bit awkward here.'

'I understand.'

'Where's the place?' I asked, 'that you're moving to?'

'Around the corner from the Pelican. I'll never go far.'

58

A week later, I watched as Bebba fell ill. I'd never seen her look so helpless. Forehead clammy, her sweats drenched the sheets and soaked through her champagne-coloured nightie, making it resemble a greying dishcloth.

The papers had been full of headlines about the flu sweeping through Europe, and many had lost their lives to it. When Peter was home, he'd fuss over her, bringing her cups of tea or the latest edition of *Picture Post*, although she was in no fit state to read.

Infuriated by her own helplessness, she kept trying to get up, but she could barely stand unaided. And as the flu dragged on, the anxiety hollowed her cheeks and carved a deep crease between her brows. I had no choice but to care for her while Peter went to work.

Morning and night, I rubbed Vicks decongestant paste on her chest and back; the whole flat stank of menthol. When I wasn't cleaning or looking after Athena, I'd try to tempt her with a bowl of *avyolemoni*, the same soup she'd brought to my bedside all those months ago.

Whenever I leaned over to rearrange her bedclothes or dab her face with a damp flannel, she avoided my gaze, embarrassed she wasn't invincible after all. Every morning she'd say she felt better only to be racked with exhaustion by noon from all the coughing.

That Thursday, Athena had fallen asleep in her pram and everyone else was out. A hush had fallen over the house. I'd just put my feet up when I heard the torturous mucus-filled cough explode in her chest. She was struggling for air. I rushed to fetch a glass of water. Gently, I propped her up with a pillow. Gradually her breathing evened out and she regained composure. Looking down, I realised that we were holding hands.

She clasped my fingers tightly. Her voice was as fragile as ice: 'This is awfully good of you.'

She closed her eyes and I saw her eyelashes moisten. I looked away. I didn't want to feel sorry for her. I wanted to let go of her hand, but she held on so tight. Then she looked at me.

'I know we're . . . well, we're not exactly friends any more,' she said, 'so thank you for this.'

She smiled at me and, for a second, I caught a flicker of the girl I once knew, the one who threw her leopard-skin coat on the floor at jazz clubs and taught me to drink Martinis. Gently, I pulled my hand away from hers and smoothed out the extra blanket I'd spread over her bed.

'Can you pass me my robe?' She motioned towards the gold robe that was at the end of the bed. 'I need the bathroom . . . do you mind?'

'Hold on.'

I went to my room and grabbed my pink dressing gown from my bed.

'Here. It's warmer.'

I helped her into it and tied the belt. It looked wrong on her, too bright and homely.

As we walked down the corridor towards the bathroom, I was surprised by how my robe swamped her tiny frame. She'd always been smaller than me, but the illness had made her so insubstantial.

'Careful,' I said.

I placed my arm over her shoulders and felt the angles of her bones as sharp as a small bird, ready to snap. We walked past the loose bannister and I hesitated for a moment at the top of the staircase.

She looked up at me and frowned.

'What?' she asked.

'How long?'

'Sorry?'

'How long do you think you can get away with this?'

She frowned.

'What do you mean?'

'All of it. Killing Rico, pretending to be married, money from the old man, the whole charade. At some point you'll get found out. *We'll* get found out. Where does it end?'

She clutched the bannister. It shook.

'Remember that night in the bombed-out church?' I asked. 'Just me, you and all those stars. I often think of that night.'

She nodded. 'Those were good days.'

'You asked me what I wished for more than anything in the world. I can't remember what I said, something stupid like love I imagine . . .'

Her voice was a whisper. 'Can we get to the bathroom, now?'

'But I remember what *you* said. You said you wanted to rub it all out, so nothing showed. Start again.'

She looked at me.

'I didn't understand what you meant at the time, but I do now. Because that's how I feel. That's how *you've* made me feel. Made me wish I was someone else.'

I sensed her watching me as I gazed down four flights of stairs.

'You wouldn't,' she said, but it was more a question than a statement. 'You're a good person, Dina.'

I laughed. 'Am I? Maybe. I used to be good, but I'm not sure who I am any more.'

'You can be whoever you want to be. Don't you know that by now?'

'It's so easy for you, isn't it?' I said. 'Just moving on, regardless. You don't care about anyone. I wish you'd disappeared after Rico died, just walked out and left us both alone. Peter would have had a better chance without you, you know. He'd have made something of himself if you'd let him go.'

She stood up a little straighter, gathering strength from somewhere. 'It wasn't a magic spell, Dina. He *chose* to be with me, he *begged* me to stay. Anyway, he never would have let me just walk away.' Her face hardened. 'He just couldn't get enough,' she said. 'And what was the alternative? Going back to a miserable existence with his whimpering little sister? Hardly appealing.' She let out a vicious laugh. 'He was never going to choose you over me.'

It was the cruelest thing she'd ever said to me and I felt as if this was the real Bebba, the one she'd kept hidden from us both.

'Don't go thinking you're more important than you are, Bebba. I mean more to him than you do.'

'Can I suggest, darling, that you never make him choose? Because you really don't know him at all.'

'And you *do*?'

'I know things he's done. Things you have no idea about.'

Anger fizzed off me. 'You're a liar. Everything about you is a lie. The hair, the voice.' A surge of vindictiveness flooded my chest. 'I mean, just look at you.'

'Don't be spiteful.'

'I'm sick of you telling me what to do,' I said. 'The day I started listening to you was the day everything started going wrong.'

'You really are a little bitch, do you know that?'

'What the hell is going on?' It was Peter. He ran up the stairs, taking them two at a time, and I took a step back on to the landing, pulling Bebba with me.

'Don't call her that,' he said. 'What's the problem with you two?'

Bebba looked from him to me. 'Ask him. Go on. Ask him about Yiannis.'

For a moment I thought I hadn't heard right, but when I glanced at Peter the colour had drained from his face.

'*Yiannis?*' I asked, frowning.

'Shut up,' Peter said to her. 'It's nothing.'

'Ask him why Yiannis really left,' she said. 'Why he broke off the engagement. Go on Peter, tell her.'

A weight dropped in my stomach. 'Peter? What's she talking about?'

He looked at her. 'You shouldn't have done that.'

She shrugged.

'What's she talking about?' I repeated. 'Why did he leave? You said it was that girl, the one with the plait . . .'

He lit a cigarette. 'Let's go back inside.' He gesticulated towards the flat.

I crossed my arms and stayed put. 'Tell me.'

'Look, I'm sorry . . .'

'You said she had more money . . .' I paused, hoping he'd start talking.

Eventually, he did. 'She did have more money. His parents wanted her because of it, that part was true, but *he* wanted you.' He flicked his cigarette ash and looked at the floor. 'He always did.'

He always did.

'So, what happened?'

'I didn't know how to tell you,' he said. 'I was trying to make it easier for you – okay, for both of us – when we came here . . . so I didn't say . . .'

'It wasn't the money that made him leave?'

Bebba piped up. 'Oh no, it *was* money all right, I mean, when is it not? Let me help you out, Peter.' Her voice was bright now; my misery had given her a shot of energy. Then, addressing me, she said, 'Your brother borrowed a small fortune from Yiannis. And when he couldn't pay it back, and Yiannis's parents found out . . . well – bye bye Dina's future!' She smiled and waved her fingers. 'See. *That's* how well you know him. He told me ages ago but couldn't bring himself to say anything to you.'

'I wanted to, but . . . I'm so sorry . . .' He reached to touch my arm, but I rushed to my room. I could hear that bark of a laugh from the bathroom and his stern voice, admonishing her.

I threw myself onto the bed, waiting for the tears to come. For almost two years Peter had lied to me, made me think Yiannis hadn't cared when in fact *he* was the reason it had all fallen apart. But the tears didn't come; instead of sadness, I felt relief. He'd always wanted me. And if *he'd* wanted me, there'd be others too.

59

The day we got found out seemed like any other day. I'd been pushing the pram for hours and, irritable and exhausted, I dropped the shopping by the door and laid Athena on the bed.

They wouldn't be back from work for a while. After splashing my face, I wiped hers with a damp flannel and she wriggled. Now that the memory of his features had started to fade, all I saw when I looked at her was the way her cheeks rose when she smiled and the reddish tone of her hair. Not for the first time, I wondered what she would have looked like if Yiannis had been her father.

I settled in the striped armchair in my bedroom to feed her. We were so high up that I could look out of the window and daydream without being seen. She clamped on quickly and began to suckle, the rhythm of her hunger and my steady breathing merged into one.

Closing my eyes, I let myself settle into daydreams. What was he doing right now? Definitely married. I saw her now, that dark, thick plait snaking down her back, in a red-and-white gingham dress and worn leather sandals. After work, he'd change into that soft white cotton shirt and those frayed shorts and sit close to her, their legs touching. They probably had a child, too – it had been almost two years. Outside, the crickets would argue incessantly, and he would watch as she flicked open a couple of buttons on the front of her dress and took out her breast to feed their baby. Let her have him, I thought. He deserved an uncomplicated life. We would have dragged him down with us.

A door slammed. I jumped. Athena looked at me and started to grizzle. Had I fallen asleep? No, my watch said four o'clock – much too early for either of them to be back. Her cries rose and I heard a voice.

A knock at the bedroom door. Had I locked it? Torn between getting up and rearranging my blouse, I did nothing. Mrs Fitzpatrick walked in.

'Sorry, love – I do beg—' Then her mouth made an 'O' as I quickly pulled down my blouse to cover my breast.

'Mrs Fitzpatrick, you startled me. How are you?'

She stood, eyes wide in disbelief.

Athena was still crying, and I stood and rocked her a little. Fuss over her, that's it. Maybe she didn't see. Was that possible?

'I . . . I did knock,' she said, her eyes fixed on the baby. 'I thought you were all out, so I had my key . . .' she held it out to show me, 'to empty the meter.'

In her other hand she held a drawstring bag, heavy with coins.

'I must have fallen asleep,' I said. 'Do empty it – do what you need. I was about to make a cup of tea – would you like one?' *Shut up. What are you doing? Shut up and get her out.*

She folded her arms and looked at me from under the solid line of her brows. She didn't say anything, so I didn't either. If I didn't speak, perhaps she'd think she imagined it.

She shifted her feet and spread her legs a little, like a boxer preparing for a fight.

'So.'

I didn't reply.

'The child is *yours*?' Her voice was all edges. 'I said, the wee 'un is *yours*? Not your *sister's*?'

'Well ... I ...' I could lie. I had a baby, you see, and it died ... and then my sister had a baby and ... Oh, what was the point? I nodded. 'I'm sorry. I didn't know what to do.'

'So, you've been lying to me?' Her eyes travelled the length of me and back, then stopped in a cold stare. 'You're not married?'

I hesitated.

'He died. But, no. Not married.'

She nodded.

'Too bad,' she said, and sniffed. Perhaps she'd show compassion. 'She's a bastard *and* an orphan.'

I flinched. In an instant my cheeks were a wet mess. I placed the baby on the bed and sat next to her.

'I'm sorry, truly,' I said, trying to breathe properly. 'But it's impossible if ... you knew ...'

She sat down heavily next to me, and the mattress rose a little.

'I detest liars,' she said, 'making a mockery of me.'

'I didn't mean to.'

'I'm no fool.' She put her hand up to her headscarf and pushed at the rollers beneath. 'I'm too kind-hearted for my own good, that I know, and people take advantage. Like I'm an eejit or something. I'm sick of it.'

'I ... I would never want to offend you, it's just ...' I stopped talking. After all, what was there to say? My arm began to tremble, and I held it with my hand so she wouldn't see.

'You'll be going, of course,' she said.

'What?' Panic surged through me.

'Well, you can't stay.'

'Please ... I don't have anyone ...'

She hesitated. 'What about your sister and that man of hers?'

I didn't say anything, just looked down at my hand.

'I see. So, she's not your sister? Is that what you're telling me?'

I shook my head. Let all the lies unravel, let the truth unfurl.

She let out a huff. 'I knew it! So, what are they to you? Those two?'

I hesitated. I honestly didn't know any more.

'*Friends?*'

I began to nod, but something made me stop. I was sick of the lies.

'Actually, he's my brother,' I said. 'She's – she was – a friend. But he's . . . what's the word? Besotted with her. I hardly know him any more.'

'I see.' Her face softened and she sat in silence for a while.

'If you throw us out,' I said, 'maybe they'd think it was too much trouble, dragging me and a baby around . . .' What if they didn't want to move again? Bebba would cast me off in an instant, I was sure. I felt my throat tense as I realised that Peter was so blinded by her, his loyalty towards me had dried up long ago. Don't make him choose, she'd said.

'I have nothing,' I said. 'Otherwise I'd offer you something. For your trouble. But . . .' I looked around the room '. . . most of this isn't even mine.'

My tears started up again and it seemed that they'd never stop. I pictured myself, pushing the pram up Mill Hill. How would I live? The baby started crying now and I reached out and picked her up.

My voice was thick with emotion when I spoke: 'The last year has been awful. If I told you the half of it . . . you wouldn't believe . . . and now this . . .'

'Will you stop your crying now.' She put her hand on my shoulder. 'Come on, stop that blubbing.' She handed me a handkerchief from her housecoat pocket. 'You're not the first to be in this situation and you won't be the last. I'm not going to throw you out this very minute, now am I?'

I dabbed at my eyes then blew my nose. How long did I have?

'Well, would you credit it,' she muttered. 'Never thought you were poorly. Not for a minute. Up and down the stairs all day with that pram. Strong as an ox, that's what I was thinking.'

'I'm really sorry, Mrs Fitzpatrick.'

She took a deep breath and let it out in an exaggerated huff.

'I won't lie. I knew something wasn't right from the start,' she said, and prodded a curler back under her headscarf.

'What do you mean?' A hard pebble settled in my stomach.

She shrugged. 'Call it what you like. A notion, a sixth sense, I s'pose. A gift and a curse.'

She leaned across and pushed her little finger towards Athena's mouth and wiggled it while I waited for her to explain.

'It makes sense now. I've heard the way they speak to you – her especially. Nothing sisterly there.'

We thought we were so clever, but a complete stranger had seen through us.

'But you'll still have to go, mind. I can't have gossiping. A story like this. It'll get out eventually.'

Athena grabbed at her pinkie and began to suck.

'They'll be furious,' I said. 'When I tell them what's happened. That you know all about it, and that it was my fault.'

She pulled her finger away and the baby whimpered.

'Well, it's a nuisance, to be sure,' she said. 'Highly inconvenient, finding new tenants.'

Was she softening?

'Yes, I'm sure.'

'I've got a decorator in next week, to paper the sitting room, and before that, Tony – my friend – was going to move the furniture. So the house will be upside down, what with the packing, never mind this carry-on.'

'I – are you saying we . . .'

She took a deep breath and her bosom lifted, then she turned to look at me.

'Well, it might take a little while to find someone else for the room. Until then we'll say nothing to them. No point you getting an earful for longer than necessary, is there?'

'Mrs Fitzpatrick – I don't know how to thank you.'

'It's Kathleen, and none of us is perfect. It's the lying I mind more than your . . . predicament. We'll speak again, but until then we'll carry on as normal . . . all right?'

I nodded.

'Though if you ask me,' she said, standing up, 'any eejit can see she's not hers.'

I picked up the baby and studied her briefly.

'What do you mean?'

'Can you not see it for yourself, love? She's the spit of her ma.'

60

The floor of the Scala was sticky with spilt drink and I could hear my shoes lift with every step. I glanced at Bebba and noticed that she sat down tentatively, placing one leg over the other, her back very straight. Peter sat in the middle, and I shuffled down in the seat next to him. She and I had barely spoken since our fight on the landing that day, and Peter had been at pains to bring us all together tonight.

It was his thirtieth birthday and we'd both agreed to come out and 'try and have a nice time'. I was surprised I wasn't angrier with him about lying to me all that time, then I realised it was probably because I expected so little from him. Nothing surprised me any more about his behaviour, and when it came to money and gambling and borrowing and losing, it was part of him; I knew he couldn't change. If anything, I'd been more upset with her for the vindictive way she'd told me, the way she'd obviously relished it. I hadn't chosen him as my brother, but I'd chosen her as a friend, and that somehow made it worse. Our broken friendship would never be mended. The hateful words we'd said had been stitched into the air between us and were impossible to unpick. And all the time that blasted case had sat in her wardrobe, and was now locked away at Lime Street. Peter wouldn't talk about it and it galled me that all of this had been for nothing.

Peter had bought me a box of Rowntree's Fruit Gums, and I set about picking out the green ones first. Bebba had suggested I might want to stay home with the baby, but I wasn't about to miss a rare night out. Mrs Fitzpatrick had happily agreed to babysit, and I was ecstatic to be out for the evening. She, however, seemed determined to sulk. I got the impression she'd wanted Peter to herself tonight. He'd not paid her much attention. He pulled the *Echo* from his coat pocket, folded it into a small square on his lap and tried to follow the words in the half-light.

The film was a 'howl-raiser', *A Night in Casablanca*, featuring the Marx Brothers. It was several years old, and we'd seen it before, but along with the rest of the theatre we found ourselves laughing hard at the antics of Groucho and his idiotic brothers. It wasn't even that funny, but the atmosphere, the crowd, the music and the sheer silliness of it all was contagious. A couple of times I noticed her jump a little as everyone burst out laughing.

The leading lady wore a captivating plunge-necked sequin gown with heavy pearls draped in her hair, and I could almost feel the fabric under my fingers and hear the whirr of the machines at the Pelican.

I offered Peter a sweet, then stretched over him and shoved the box under her nose. She stared straight ahead, stony-faced, palms flat on her handbag. She was somewhere else entirely.

*   *   *

'Did you enjoy it?' asked Peter, linking arms as we walked along the road. He was glowing with happiness.

'I loved it,' I said, perhaps overstating it. I was just glad to be out.

'What about you, Beb?' he asked.

She shrugged. 'Three grown men acting like fools.' She stood and lit a cigarette while we waited. 'I can see that in any bar on any street in England.'

'Oh, don't be like that,' he said, and dropped my arm as he grabbed hers.

As we made our way home, I turned up the collar of my mac and walked ahead. I could hear him recounting scenes from the film, quoting lines to her despite the fact she'd just sat through it. I heard him shuffle through a dance routine and she laughed, thawing at last as he grabbed and kissed her under the street light.

I wandered on past a row of closed shops and looked at the shoes and hats in the windows. My eyes stopped at a stylish navy beret with white flowers made from long beads, sewn into one side. With a shorter hairstyle, that look might suit me. They were walking slowly, talking intensely now, so I turned down Church Street and stopped outside Woolworths. The bunting and flags were still out, despite months having passed since the Coronation. Dozens of cups, postcards, plates, badges and ribbons, were crammed in the windows, all with the letters ER and the face of Queen Elizabeth smiling out. She wore a dress that sat perfectly on her trim waist, and a cobalt-blue sash fell from her left shoulder across to her right hip. We'd been born in the same year but a world apart, had both started a voyage that would change our lives. She had a man by her side, but a look in her eyes said that when it came down to it, we all stood alone.

Peter tugged my arm. 'Come on,' he said. 'It's getting late.'

*   *   *

The three of us slowed down when we saw him.

'Who's that?' I asked. 'In front of the flat?'

The young man, a boy really, of about eighteen, was leaning against a motorbike, cigarette in hand. He jumped up as we approached, dropping his goggles. He dipped down to pick them up and held out his hand to Peter, awkwardly, at the same time.

'Hello sir,' he said, ignoring me and Bebba. I noticed his uniform and cap. He was a telegram boy, and had obviously been waiting for our return. He flicked his cigarette to one side and stubbed it out with his heavy boot.

'Are you Mr Andreas Antoniou?'

Peter shook his head. 'No – he's . . .'

'Yes, he's Rico,' said Bebba. 'What is it?'

At that moment Mrs Fitzpatrick came to the door, holding the baby.

'Oh, thank God you're back,' she said, rushing down the stairs.

I walked to her. 'Is she all right?'

'Oh, she's fine.' She started to hand the baby to me, then changed her mind and offered her to Bebba.

'Here.'

Bebba took her, annoyed at the distraction.

'I gave her some formula,' said Mrs Fitzpatrick. 'She *was* sound asleep till this lad turned up making such a racket.'

The boy coughed, embarrassed to be the centre of attention. There was a pause, and everybody stared at him.

'Well?' asked Bebba.

He stood up straight, jumping a little, like an actor who'd just remembered his lines.

'I've got a telegram for you, sir,' he said.

Peter took it from his hand, turned it over to see both sides and stuffed it in his pocket. The lad gave him something to sign and he hardly hesitated at all before signing Rico's name with a flourish. The lad climbed onto his motorbike, pulled down his goggles and revved his engine.

'Hush your racket!' shouted Mrs Fitzpatrick, as he sped away.

The four of us walked into the house.

'I expect it's important,' she continued. 'You don't send a telegram unless it's important, do you?'

Nobody responded, and I was desperate to fill the silence.

'Thanks for looking after Athena.'

'I hope it's not bad news.'

'Goodnight Mrs Fitzpatrick,' I said.

We filed past her and walked into the flat, closing the door behind.

'It's from Cyprus,' said Peter.

'Here,' Bebba handed me the baby, 'take her. Read it, Peter. Please God, don't tell me he's coming to visit.'

'The old man?' I asked. 'Surely not.'

He locked the door and ripped the envelope open. We stood around as he read aloud, whispering even though it was in Greek.

'*Dear Mr Antoniou, It's with great sorrow that we write to inform you that, yesterday, your father died peacefully in his sleep.*'

He looked up at us and his shoulders sank, as if it was our actual father who'd died.

'Carry on,' said Bebba.

'*Please accept our heartfelt condolences. He was a respected member of the community and will be greatly missed. As the sole beneficiary of his will we require your presence in order to transfer his assets into your name, pending your signature. Please advise us of your arrival date at your earliest convenience, bringing with you your identification papers. Yours, Loizou and Sons (Solicitors)*'

Peter sighed.

'The poor thing,' I said. 'How awful.'

'What are you sad about?' said Bebba. 'You didn't even *know* him.'

'So what?' I put the baby in the pram and sat down. 'He's an old man and he died alone, waiting for his son to come home.'

Peter crumpled the piece of paper and dropped it on the table. 'Well, that's that. No more money from him.'

'That's a terrible thing to say,' I said.

He shrugged. 'But it's true. Though he hasn't sent anything for ages, has he?'

She picked up the ball of paper and opened it again, smoothing it out with the flat of her hand.

'It doesn't say anything else,' he said, as he looked over her shoulder. 'I read it all.' He lit a Woodbine and offered her one, but she refused. 'It was good while it lasted, eh? We certainly strung him along for a bit. How much do you think in total we—?'

'Shut up, Peter.' She read the telegram again, tracing the words with her finger.

'What is it?' I asked. She didn't look up.

'It's over,' said Peter. 'We just have to accept it.'

'No,' she said, looking up. 'We don't.'

I laughed. 'Well, of course we do. He's dead.' I folded my arms, 'Or are you going to magically bring the old man back to life?'

'No,' she said, folding the telegram in half and slipping it into her pocket. 'Not him. But his son, perhaps.'

61

This could work, thought Bebba, as she sat at her dressing table and rubbed cold cream on her face. It would delay her plans, but it would be worth it. She'd miss the liner she'd booked to New York. Her ticket was in her handbag and she was scheduled to leave in two days. But if she was willing to pay a little extra, surely she'd be able to change the date on it? It departed every fortnight after all. She didn't have time now, but would do it when she got back from Cyprus. And on her day of departure, she'd take the key from his wallet as he slept, and pick up the money en route to the docks. Let him keep it for now in case he noticed it was missing.

She remembered the small stash of Cypriot pounds she'd collected from the old man, and that were now sewn into the lining of her bag. Not enough for much, but still, he'd done as requested and sent cash instead of money orders. Soon she'd have everything Rico ever owned.

Gently she used a tissue to wipe her face clean, getting rid of the make-up and being especially careful around her eyes. Her hair was infuriating. It had been impossible to get it styled properly here. The two women she'd visited (one to fix what the other had done) seemed intent on making her look like everyone else. And the colour was all wrong. If she wasn't careful, she'd end up looking like every other brassy blonde.

She wiped away the last vestiges of cream and put the lid on the tub. She'd get back from Cyprus and then worry about that. New York would have excellent hairdressers.

62

As we stood outside Lime Street Station, I watched Peter let go of Bebba's hand and press the heels of his hands over his bloodshot eyes. So, he hadn't slept either? He stretched his arms up high then wide and let out a huge yawn.

'Oh, look Dina,' he said, pointing to the building across the road. 'Do you remember the first time we saw that?'

I glanced up at the large clock, illuminated in the early evening light, and read the familiar slogan next to it: *Guinness Is Good For You*. Gently, I pushed the pram back and forth.

'Oh, yes. The day we arrived here, and all those advertisements were so brightly lit – for a minute I thought we'd made a mistake and were back in Piccadilly.'

'Aaah, Piccadilly.' He smiled. 'Nowhere quite like Soho, is there?'

'I know,' I said. 'By the time we left it really felt like home.'

'More than Cyprus?'

I shrugged. 'Maybe.'

'We did have some good days there, didn't we?' he said.

Yes, I thought. Before her. As though she could hear, Bebba linked her arm through his and tugged him towards her.

'Enough reminiscing,' she said. 'Come on, darling, or we'll be late.'

It was only half-past seven and the train didn't leave for half an hour, but she checked her watch twice as we walked into the station.

Inside, I waited as they collected their tickets from the booking office. The clack of her heels bounced off the cobblestones. I watched them, rocking the pram; from here, you'd never know what they had planned. They looked just like any other couple going on an ordinary journey.

Peter had on his old dark suit with his favourite Rico tie, the red one. She wore her dark coat, and it leached the life from her cheeks, suggesting she was far less remarkable than she actually was.

Last night she'd decided to leave her lovely leopard skin behind, having slung it over a hook on the bedroom door.

'That's my Soho coat,' she'd declared. 'Far too glamorous for where we're going.' And she hummed a tune as she packed a few dresses, a skirt and a blouse into one side of Peter's suitcase.

Now they turned and walked back towards me. Peter waved the tickets in his hand and gave them a quick kiss. I wasn't fooled by the cheery act; his stiff smile told me he was as nervous as I was.

'All present and correct,' he said. 'Straight through to Euston, underground to Victoria and from there we take the train for Calais.'

I was so afraid for him. My throat tightened but I willed myself not to cry. I didn't want her to see my tears.

'How long will it take?' I asked.

'Five days,' said Bebba. 'Through France, Italy and so on. Much better than the boat – you know what that journey's like – weeks.'

'Hey!' Peter gave me a hug. 'Cheer up, look.'

He showed me the date on the return ticket.

'We're back in a fortnight – a week and a day before Christmas. I'll bring you something nice.'

I tried not to blink, but it was no use. A tear fell and he offered me his handkerchief.

She sighed loudly.

'I'm going to get my *Vogue* and some ciggies,' she said. 'I'll let you two say your goodbyes.'

Halfway, she turned and called out, 'But do make it quick, won't you darling? We should board soon.'

I watched as she trotted off with a spring in her step, the cheeriest mourner I'd ever seen.

'Sorry about that,' I said, returning his handkerchief. 'I'm worried for you.'

'I know.' He leaned into the pram. 'Look after your mum, won't you?' She shifted a little and carried on sleeping.

A fist of dread unfurled in my stomach one finger at a time. I knew I couldn't leave it unsaid. I had to make him see before she got back.

'You're making a mistake,' I blurted. 'You won't get away with it.'

He stepped back a little. 'Dina – please. We've been through this. It's fine.'

'No, just listen.' I held onto his jacket now, as my heart drummed faster. 'I know she said the solicitor's from the city and won't know Rico, but what if they have a recent photo of him?'

'Why would they?'

'Or they ask you something you just can't answer? It's not worth the risk.'

'Look, there are no relatives, you heard her.' He gently removed my hands from his lapels, but I kept them on his sleeves. 'Any neighbours won't have seen him for years. It's not even his village we're going to – it's the town twenty miles away. *It's going to be all right.*'

'But the passport – the papers—'

'It's sorted, Dina. It's a once-in-a-lifetime opportunity. This'll set us up. All of us.'

'But you're not listening. This isn't like one of your bets, where if you lose you just scrunch up the slip and throw it away.' I held his sleeves in my fists. 'What if the passport isn't good enough?'

He unpeeled my fingers and pushed my hands off with some force. I was losing him.

'Look.' His voice was stern now and he leaned in so nobody else could see. He slipped his hand inside his pocket. '*Look.*'

He opened the passport. There it was. The face was his even if the name wasn't. According to the words printed on the page, he was officially Andreas Antoniou. He dropped it back in his pocket and flattened down his lapels.

'Would I go all that way to get caught? What do you take me for? The man I used is a professional, he knows what he's doing.'

He gave me a lopsided smile, and although I'd known his face all my life, I didn't recognise him. Something deep in him had shifted and I knew that it was too far gone to click back into place.

I turned to look at the news kiosk. There she stood, magazine under one arm, putting a cigarette in her stupid holder. This was my last chance.

'She can't do it without you,' I said. 'Can't you see she's using you? To get to the money.'

He frowned. 'Shut up. You're being hysterical.'

'Why else would she still be living with us?' There was no time left for niceties.

He took a step back and his face tightened, the way it did when he was about to snap.

'She's been waiting all this time because she wanted more – what was in the suitcase was never enough for her. First she wanted more from Rico's father, and now this inheritance. And you're the only way she can do it. She can't cash the money orders, she can't claim the old man's estate – you're the only way . . .'

'I swear, if you don't shut up . . .'

'And now this reading of the will,' I hissed. 'She's using you and you know it – admit it. And once she has all the money she can get, that's when she'll do it. That's when she'll leave you.'

'For Christ's sake, *gori*!'

'We can go back to the way we were. Before *her*.'

His eyes narrowed as if he was staring at the sun.

'Oh, that's it. You'd like that, wouldn't you?' he asked. 'Do you think I don't know how jealous you are?'

'*What?*'

'Of us, me and her. I have someone and you don't. Someone to love, who really loves me and doesn't walk away at the first sign of trouble.'

I couldn't believe he was saying this to me.

'That's so cruel. After everything that's happened – everything you did. Anyway, I do have someone.' I pointed at the baby.

'What?' He laughed. 'That little bastard?'

My hand flew up to slap his face, but he caught it.

'I should have married you off ages ago,' he said, and threw down my hand in disgust. 'But I was too soft. Too nice. As soon as we got here, I should have passed you on to the first man who'd have you.'

I was shocked into silence.

'You know Dina, you've been nothing but a weight around my bloody neck.'

A soreness blossomed in my chest. I shot a glance at the kiosk and saw that she'd started back.

He followed my gaze.

'Now you want to wreck it for me,' he said. 'For the two of us. Always thinking about yourself. Well, what about me? I've got nothing to lose here, Dina, and everything to gain. I *deserve* this.'

I leaned in close and all the loathing I felt for her and our situation bubbled to the surface. 'Can't you see? She doesn't *love* you. She *needs* you. She'll destroy you and then she'll drop you.'

Bebba was at his side. 'Come on, darling.' He didn't move and she looked between the two of us. 'What? Everything all right?'

'Think about it, Peter. You know it's the truth.'

'What's going on?' she asked.

'Nothing.' He bent down and picked up the case. 'We've said our goodbyes.'

'Peter?' My voice cracked. We couldn't leave it like this.

He leaned towards me, placed his hand on my shoulder, and just as I thought he might say something appeasing or kiss my cheek, he put his lips next to my ear: 'If you don't start showing me some respect, *gori*, I'll kick both you and the kid out when we get back. Then we'll see how you manage by yourself.'

He turned on his heel, took her by the arm and walked away.

63

I took a roundabout route home so I could compose myself. I didn't want Mrs Fitzpatrick seeing me like this. Rubbing at the tears with my coat sleeve, I alternated hands as I pushed the pram through St James's Gardens. My head throbbed and I felt wretched. Peter had chosen her over me again and any fragment of loyalty I still felt for him had vanished with that vicious whisper.

The chrome pram handles felt smooth and steady in my tight grip, and I carried on, trying to take deep breaths and gather myself. I heard the clatter of heels as a couple rushed across my path, bringing me to an abrupt halt. He wore an ink-black dinner suit and she had on a long blue dress.

'We're going to be late!' he said, pulling her along.

'Oh, I can't run in these shoes!'

'Maybe I should carry you?'

He went to grab her, pretending he was about to lift her up, and she squealed in protest. I watched them hurry along in the opposite direction.

Peter had been right: I didn't have anyone's shoulder to lean into, but I did have myself. He'd lost himself months ago. When he'd pushed Rico onto the tracks at St Pancras, he'd tumbled down too.

Athena gave a cry and I looked down at her in the pram. Well, she was still here, and somehow things felt clearer now. Peter had as good as cut me off; after a lifetime of second chances I needed to give up on him too. By the time I got home, the road was deserted, and a weak lamp shone on the front door. Quietly, I let myself in. I couldn't hear the television, which meant that she probably wasn't home. She'd bought the telly for the Coronation and had hardly turned it off since.

Leaving the pram in the hall, I carried the baby upstairs. The flat was in disarray after their frantic packing. Unwashed bowls were heaped on the table, with dried-on remnants of our final meal, a miserable bean soup. Rejected clothes lay everywhere, like bodies dropped from a height. I placed her, sleeping, in the middle of my bed and set about tidying up. First I threw open the window, then piled the dishes next to the sink. I collected a few of Bebba's dresses from the floor and flung them on her bed – I'd be damned if I'd fold them. They could stay there till she got back. As I turned to leave her room, I couldn't help touching her leopard skin that was hanging on the back of the door. I slipped it on, thinking it might feel tight; it was perfect. I looked down at the hem to see how long it was on me, and that's when I noticed a brown envelope on the floor just by the leg of her dressing table.

I picked it up and turned it over, bending it back and forth, then held it up to the light. On the front small, typed capitals read: ELIZABETTA ANTONIOU. The seal had already been broken.

I sat on her bed and slipped my fingers inside the envelope. The colour leaflet showed a beautiful ocean liner at dusk, drenched in the soft yellow of a setting sun. A folded sheet of onionskin paper fell out. It was a receipt. The typed words had bled slightly around the edges:

Single-journey ticket, Brittanic, Liverpool–New York
Tourist Class
Departing Friday 4th December, 1953

In the bottom right-hand corner was the inky kiss of a stamp, with the name of the travel agent in the centre of town, and through the middle the phrase: 'Received with thanks'. Someone had scrawled in a confident flourish: *Enjoy New York!*

So, she'd been planning to leave tomorrow. Only the news about Rico's dad had stopped her. Only the prospect of more money.

You fool, Peter.

I looked again, but she must have taken the ticket. She'd have to spend some of her money after all, to buy another.

'Dina!' I heard Mrs Fitzpatrick trotting up the stairs.

I stuffed everything back in the envelope and into my pocket. She stood on the threshold, her tweed coat still on.

'Oh, heavens!' she said. 'I thought you were her for a minute.'

'Sorry.' I pulled off Bebba's coat and threw it on the bed. 'Did you want something?'

Instead of the usual headscarf she had a shiny row of brown curls framing her face. A tight bud of pink blossomed on each cheek and she looked years younger.

'Could you move the pram, love?'

'Oh, yes. I'll do it now.'

I started down the stairs. Sounds of laughter came from her living room. She must have switched on the television before she'd done anything else.

'I've got some company tonight, and I don't want him tripping over it!' She laughed nervously. Tony must be staying over.

'Your hair looks nice,' I said, as I folded the pram.

'Thank you.' She patted it. 'Did it myself. I'll do yours if you like one day?'

I walked past her to go back upstairs and then stopped.

'Kathleen?'

'Yes, love?'

'Have you ever been to New York?'

'What? Ah, no – I've never been abroad. Though I saw it in that film with Gene Kelly. The sailors. What was it – *On The Town*? Why do you ask?'

I shrugged.

'Oh, nothing. Someone mentioned it the other day and I was thinking how glamorous it seemed.'

She shifted her coat to the other arm.

'A long way to go for glamour,' she said. 'But then again I'd go anywhere if I could.' She looked upstairs. 'They left have they? On their trip?'

I nodded.

'Well, I can always look after the little one, if you ever want a bit of time to yourself. Be sure to let us know if there's anything you need.'

There was a flicker of pity in her eyes, and her kindness stung. She was probably the same age my mother would be now. I'd always told myself that Peter was both mother and father to me, but it had actually been the other way round. As the mean words he'd spoken buzzed inside my head, I started up the four flights with the pram, staring at the steps as I went, each one more blurred than the last.

Damn him. Damn her. I deserved better than this.

64

When I opened my eyes the next morning, the pram was the first thing I saw. A shaft of fragile winter sun lay across its folded hood and trickled onto the lino. I stretched out and remembered that they'd gone.

I'd stayed awake late last night, wondering what to do. My mind had spun through all the possibilities, picking over various scenarios for my future, pulling at the threads to test the practicalities.

As the days went on, I felt lighter, as if the events and lies of the past year had been packed away with the two of them and were now hurtling hundreds of miles across Europe. I decided to abandon my daily drudge of cleaning and explore Liverpool. My new routine was like a balm that soothed my spirits. Each morning, I carried the pram downstairs and opened it in the hall, still in awe of the engineering. I packed it with everything we needed for the day: some cheese and an apple for me, a bottle of formula for her, and my shopping bag. The powdered milk Kathleen had suggested was a godsend and meant I wasn't tied to mealtimes. With everything ready, I laid her on top, and pushed the covers down around her, tucking her dense little body deep and snug.

The fog had trickled through the streets until eventually it lifted, leaving a few days of surprisingly mild weather. When the sun broke through, we'd walk through Wavertree Park and into the botanic gardens. Or I'd gaze in shop windows for much of the day, meandering up Dale Street and London Street, looking at the ladies' hats and shoes.

Rationing had mostly fallen away, and I loved the novelty of staring in the various shop windows, which were now crammed with gifts and draped in paper chains, ready for Christmas. I avoided the department store, Lewis's, even though she was hundreds of miles away. We'd work our way to Great Homer Street, where you could buy practically anything you wanted.

Occasionally, I carried Athena on my front, in a sling, the way I'd seen women carry children in Cyprus. I noticed a few curious looks, but I didn't mind. We caught the half-empty ferry across the Mersey to New Brighton beach, where a handful of people sat, like us, in the warmth of a café and watched as two young men, their trousers rolled up, fooled about in the freezing water. The beach had always made me think of my mother; Father said she'd adored the sea, loved having sand between her toes. I remembered the red-brick public baths on Hornsey Road in London, and how I could barely look at the illuminated woman diving down the side of the building without feeling an ache in my chest. Now, as I watched the boys splashing and laughing, I felt a burst of joy. We wandered through the mostly-shut fairground and the few day-trippers who'd made the journey were in high spirits. The dodgems were still open and tinny music blared out as a group of friends, wrapped in coats and gloves and scarves, raced around, calling out to each other as they passed. Far from finding it all too much, Athena seemed mesmerised by the sounds and colours.

In fact, we both thrived outdoors. With no secrets weighing me down, a wild kind of freedom coursed through me. There was a camaraderie in the company of strangers in cafés and markets, and I realised I'd felt isolated for months.

With a baby strapped to me, other women struck up easy conversations in the post office queue, on the tram, in the market. I felt part of life again. One crisp, sunny day, we went for a walk in Stanley Park. A woman around my age, black curls popping out from under her headscarf, shifted up so I could sit next to her on the bench.

'Girl?' she asked, looking down at Athena asleep in the sling.

I nodded. 'Athena.'

'Aw, she looks so content.'

A brass band struck up the first notes. Athena stirred but kept her eyes shut. A girl aged around four, with a mass of dark curls, started dancing in front of us, running in and out of the swings.

'That's my one,' she smiled. 'Full of beans. Won't sit still.'

'She's gorgeous,' I said. 'She looks so happy.'

The child's thin yellow mac flew out behind her and she stretched her arms wide and spun herself round again and again in the middle of the playground, a perfect tulip.

'She's a kid,' said her mum. 'We were all like that once.'

'I suppose so.'

'Trick is not to let life knock it out of you.'

I watched the little girl. As she whisked around, ecstatic, a breeze caught her mac and blew it high in the air. I was far from beaten. I wanted to find my happiness again, and I wouldn't stop until I did.

65

Bebba's bones rattled in the coffin-shaped bed as the train lumbered through the French countryside. Peter had stayed silent all the way to Dover, smoking, rubbing at his palms, and barely looking at her. Now she hooked her arm over the itchy tartan blanket and glanced across the carriage to where he slept just a foot away.

She'd asked him twice what the matter was, but he'd shaken his head and said nothing. Whatever Dina had said to him in the five minutes they'd been together had burrowed to his core and chewed up his confidence.

There was a rat-a-tat at the door and without waiting, a chubby customs officer, who could hardly have been twenty, slid open the door.

'*Excusez-moi, Messieurs. Vos passeports, s'il-vous plaît.*'

Bebba leaned across and shook Peter's arm. He stirred and sat up suddenly, hair on end, giving her an accusatory look.

'Passports,' she said, and nodded at the young man, who was now looking around the cabin.

Peter grabbed his jacket, slid his hand inside and pulled out a navy-blue passport.

The man took it and gave a bemused look.

'*Mais non, Monsieur. Ce n'est pas vous.*'

'What?' said Peter, 'I . . . I don't understand.'

A finger of icy sweat stroked the back of her neck.

'*Ce n'est pas vous, Monsieur.* This is not you.'

Surely it couldn't end so quickly, before even reaching Cyprus.

'It's him,' she said. Then slowly, so he'd understand: 'It . . . is . . . all . . . okay. It . . . is . . . him. See.' She went to take the passport, but the officer pulled it away.

'No, Madame. It is *you*.' He laughed. 'Much prettier, *non*?' He showed her the picture. 'Your hair is better now.'

'You've given him mine,' she said. 'Where's yours?'

Peter looked stricken.

'Rico, your passport. Is it in your pocket?'

Stupidly, like someone who'd been drugged, he pulled it out and dropped it at the customs officer's feet. They both leaned over to pick it up, but the officer got there first.

'*Merci!*' He glanced at the photo. 'Now this is you, *non*?' he laughed.

'No,' said Peter. 'I mean yes. *Oui*. It is me.'

Both passports were stamped, and the officer left.

Look at him: the fear in his eyes, the way he hunched in the seat, his laboured breath. It was all there for anyone to see. If he ruined it now . . . Her thoughts echoed the clatter of the wheels on the track. *He won't let me down. He can't. He won't let me down. He can't.*

She'd kill him if he did, that much she knew. If he crossed her or changed his mind, she would take him apart, thread by thread.

*   *   *

Bebba's father sat across the table, dressed in his heavy navy suit. His thumb flicked through his white worry beads and they clacked onto each other, one by one. He looked up at her and his eyes were even colder than she remembered.

'*You look better,* Pappa.'

He took a final sip of his kafé skéto *and scowled.*

'*No, I'm worse.' He started the beads again.*

'*But you do look better. Don't you feel better?*'

He shook his head. He turned his cup upside down onto the saucer and waited for the thick coffee sediment to trickle down so he could peer in and read his future.

She leaned across and pulled at his sleeve, to get his attention. 'I'm getting the land back,' she said. 'I've come to get what's ours.'

He looked at her in disbelief and continued to gently shake his head.

'*He took everything we had,*' *she said, her voice angry now.* '*Everything that was mine. Now I'll take everything that's his.*'

She reached across and lifted the overturned cup. For a moment it stuck to the saucer – a good sign. A lucky sign. Then it dropped off and she turned the cup the right way up. The inside was as clean us fresh bone. How could that be?

She grasped his hand, but instead of the rough papery touch she expected, it felt prickly under her skin.

She woke with a start and saw the tartan blanket in her fist.

66

Bebba popped a grilled black olive in her mouth, worked the flesh off it with her tongue and teeth and daintily deposited the stone in the thin paper napkin on the side of her plate. She'd never thought she'd set foot on this godforsaken island again, but here she was back in Cyprus. Get the job done and get back home, she told herself, because this wasn't home any more. It hadn't been for a long while.

She buttered a piece of toasted bread, laid a sliver of *halloumi* on top and ate it with relish. She'd forgotten how good this simple breakfast could be; the fresh saltiness was divine.

'You not eating?' She spoke English. They'd agreed it would be safer.

Peter took another drag of his cigarette and shook his head. 'I'm not hungry.'

It was eight in the morning and the steady December drizzle was running down the café windows. The air inside was humid and he was gently poaching in his shirt. Everything about him – the way he pushed back his hair, dropped his newspaper pages once he'd finished, breathed so heavily at night – all these things that had once meant nothing now were deeply irritating. He'd sign the papers, they'd sell the land and she'd be off.

'I don't feel well,' he said. 'Maybe we should delay it, or cancel. Do it tomorrow.'

'Don't be ridiculous.' She bit into the bread again, chewed

slowly, and only after she swallowed did she continue. 'We've come all this way. You'll be fine.'

He stubbed out his cigarette and put his head in his hands. 'You're not listening. You never do. I *really* don't feel well.'

She pulled her chair next to his, took his arm and held his hand. Then in a calm tone she said, 'Listen to me. I haven't come all this way to lose my nerve now, stumble at the very end.' She squeezed his hand. 'We'll set off in an hour. You'll do what we said, you'll sign, we'll leave, we'll head back. That's it.'

He searched her face as if she were a stranger and his voice was quiet as he spoke: 'You will stay, won't you?'

'What? Why would we stay? We'll go back to England, of course.'

'No, with *me*. When we go back, and sell it all. You will stay?'

She sighed. 'Darling, of *course* I will.' She leaned across, gave him a peck on his cheek and pushed his hair off his forehead. 'Do you honestly think,' she asked, 'I would leave you after all of this?'

The waiter walked over.

'Anything else?' he asked in Greek.

'Yes, my husband would like some toast.'

He nodded and walked away.

She turned to Peter.

'You need to eat something. You'll feel so much better if you do.'

Peter smiled, reassured. 'Thank you. You do look after me.'

He took her hand in his, brought it up to his lips and held it tight as he gave it a long, dry kiss.

67

The droning sounded like a giant lethargic fly. Bebba tipped her head back and stared at the ceiling fan, as the blades whipped the stale air around the room. The room was stuffy and she realised she was taking short shallow breaths and tried to slow down her breathing. More than anything, now was the time for a cool head. She pressed her lips together, thought of what was about to happen and tried to arrange her face in an expression that befitted a grieving daughter-in-law.

Peter fidgeted next to her, his nervousness sparking off him. His chair had uneven legs and he moved it around, trying to adjust it on the warped floorboards.

Just then, an elderly man in a black suit entered the room. There was the shiny mark of an iron on one of the lapels where it had been pressed carelessly.

'Aah . . . *Kyrieh* and *Kyriah* Antoniou?' He put out his hand. 'Mr Papandreou. A pleasure to meet you.'

His tie rested an inch below his collar, which remained unbuttoned. He shook Bebba's hand first then said to Peter, 'My *sillibidíria*. Deepest condolences.'

He sat down and motioned for them to do the same. Then he pulled some papers towards him.

'Your father was a respected man,' he said.

'You knew him?' asked Bebba.

'Well, no. But I heard good things about him. And, what with you being his only child,' he looked at Peter, 'this must be a very sad day for you indeed.'

Peter hadn't said a word.

'Now, let's get down to business.'

Papandreou opened the manila file in front of him and started rifling through the sheets.

'Where is it?' He searched around on his desk, then pressed the intercom.

'*Kyriah* Soria, are you still there?'

'Yes sir,' replied a tinny voice.

'Oh good, I thought you were at lunch. I seem to be missing some of the Antoniou papers.'

'They're here, sir. I'll bring them through.'

Bebba would kill for a ciggie but knew it would be frowned upon, so she clasped her hands in her lap and looked around. It was a soulless, blank room, just a desk, a few chairs and a filing cabinet.

'She knew your father, you know,' said Papandreou, rearranging his file.

'Sorry?' asked Peter.

'My secretary. Mrs Stavrou. She's looking forward to seeing you again.'

Bebba's blood froze.

'You'll recognise her, I'm sure.'

She couldn't look at Peter. She heard the door open and in walked a brisk, sharp-faced woman, still in her coat and with a headscarf on.

'Here you are, sir.' She handed Papandreou the papers.

'Soria, you remember young Andriko,' asked Papandreou. 'Yiacoumi's son?'

The woman held out her hand, but for a few seconds Peter looked at it as if he didn't have a clue what to do. Finally, he stood, and they shook hands.

'I remember you from when you were this high,' she said, putting her hand out to show little Rico's height. 'Always running around. You couldn't keep still.'

A terrible stutter came out of Peter's mouth.

'I doubt you remember me,' said Soria, 'but I was often in your kitchen, waiting for my mother to finish work. She was the old man's cleaner. *Anna?*'

She searched his face expectantly, waiting for a chink of recognition.

'I . . . er . . .'

'Well, it was years ago,' she said, disappointment in her voice. 'Anyway, my deepest sympathies.'

Peter barely nodded, so Bebba got up and shook her hand.

'Thank you,' she said.

Soria gave her a terse smile and walked out.

'So,' said Papandreou. 'Let's get this part over with. Did you bring your papers?'

'Yes,' said Bebba. She took something out of her handbag and passed it to him. He glanced at the passport photo and the ID papers.

'Birth certificate?' he asked.

'I . . . I don't have one,' said Peter.

'He has one, of course,' she said. 'But not on him.'

'Well – this is probably enough . . . I suppose it's at your father's?'

'Sorry?'

'Your birth certificate. Is it at your father's house or did you take it to England?'

Peter gave her a pleading look.

She smiled at him.

'You had it in London, didn't you, darling?' she asked. How could they forget! 'I think we have it,' she said, 'but what with the rush to get back and the distress of it all . . .'

'Yes, yes,' said Papandreou, waving his hand. 'Don't worry. We'll manage without.'

Cypriots: there was always a way around everything.

'So,' he began. He cleared his throat and Peter did the same. 'As you probably know, your father held various plots of land and properties over the years. There were orchards, orange groves and olive trees.' How much? She daren't put a number on it. She wanted to laugh and shout and dance, but used every ounce of energy to keep an interested-but-neutral expression. She stared at his tie to stay focused. 'Then there was also the villa itself, of course, which, in its heyday, was quite something. And the land and assets from your father,' he looked at Bebba, 'that he received on your marriage. That was a nice amount, too.'

Peter coughed. Then coughed again.

'Would you like a glass of water?' asked Papandreou.

There was a jug on the side of the desk and a clean glass upside down next to it. Peter thanked him, poured out some water and drained it. He kept the tumbler in his hand and turned it while he listened.

'So,' continued Papandreou, looking down at the papers and shuffling them. 'That was then.'

He paused, put his index finger above his tie and pulled it down a little. Then he looked up.

She felt a whisper of a shiver.

'I'm afraid it's gone,' he said. 'There's nothing left.' He held his palms out wide, as if waiting to catch something from heaven.

'*What?*' asked Peter.

'I'm afraid so. Well, it's all still there, but your father had considerable debts. He sold most of it off months ago, to pay his creditors.'

A terrible dread dropped through her.

'No,' she said. 'There has to be a mistake. He isn't poor.' Her voice was drum-tight. 'I know him – he's rich. Was rich. He had everything.'

Papandreou created a steeple with his fingers.

'I know that's how it seems, but he'd been in debt for a while,' he said. 'It just grew and grew and, as tends to happen in these cases, if the person ignores it . . . well . . .'

Peter leaned forwards and dropped his head into his hands. The glass rolled onto the floor.

'I'm very sorry,' said Papandreou. 'He used everything as collateral. You obviously had no idea?'

'What about my land?' she asked. 'The land from my father?'

'All of it, Madam.'

'Nothing even for the baby?' she asked, desperation in her voice. She thought she might burst into tears or punch him. 'We have a baby, you know – back in England. Surely there's something for her? From her beloved grandfather?'

'Look, if it's any consolation,' said Papandreou, 'it's not the worst case I've seen. He simply over-extended himself with the new building work. I see from this that he sent money to you in England. Even that was borrowed. He obviously didn't want you to know. God forbid he should have been a gambler or some such – it could have been a lot worse.'

Peter shot up, his face red.

'Worse?' he shouted. 'How could it be *worse?*'

'Sshhh.' Bebba reached out to placate him but he pushed her arm away.

'Why did you send the telegram?' he asked. 'Why bring us all this way, put me through all this . . . this . . . stress. Do you know how ill I've been? I've been sick for days. Can't eat, can't sleep. Sick with the worry of it.'

'Excuse me?' asked Papandreou.

'And now we've come here, and you say there's nothing at the end of it?'

Papandreou got up and came around the desk.

'Please,' he said, touching Peter's arm to try to get him seated again. 'Please calm yourself, Mr Antoniou.'

Peter shrugged him off and slumped back into the chair.

The selfish bastard. So, *he* was disappointed, was he? How did he think *she* felt?

'The reason you're here,' said Papandreou, 'is because we need your signature, to get things moving. And then there's also the matter of . . .' He stopped and seemed uncertain about continuing.

'What?' asked Bebba.

'My fees. And a few small debts that remain unpaid.'

'You have got to be joking!' Peter's face was full of disgust. 'You got me here to pay off his *debts*. A man I didn't even know.'

Her heart beat rapidly a dozen times before she spoke.

'Hardly knew,' she said. 'They weren't that close.'

Papandreou shrugged and walked back to his side of the desk, pulling the papers together.

'Whether you were close or not is neither here nor there, sir. He was your father and therefore you are responsible.' His tone had turned cold. 'You can leave details of where you're staying on my secretary's desk. She'll call you when she gets back from lunch and inform you of the final amount.'

'So, that's it is it?' asked Peter. 'All neatly tied up, eh?'

'Come on,' said Bebba. She had to get him out before he said something stupid. She pulled him up by the arm and tried to steer him to the door. 'Let's go, darling.'

'It won't take long,' said Papandreou. 'You can sign the papers first thing and bring along the amount owed, then be on your way.'

Peter stopped and turned around.

'And what if I don't?' he asked. 'What if I refuse?'

'Pete – Rico, please.'

Papandreou walked to him and straightened up.

'You have to, sir. It's the law. After all, you are his son.'

Peter spat on the floor and walked to the door. 'You people make me sick.'

Bebba picked up her bag and followed him. 'Sorry, he's heartbroken,' she said. 'We both are.'

She was about to shake his hand, by way of a goodbye, but he turned away and walked back to his desk.

68

I sat in Mrs Fitzpatrick's kitchen facing the open fire while she combed out my hair.

'Haven't done anyone as young as you for years now,' she said. 'Before the war I did all sorts, but now I only do friends. Cover your eyes.'

I put my hands up over my brows while she squirted me with a burst of Spray Net.

'There. All done.'

She offered me a large hand-mirror.

'Look at you.'

I stared at the startled reflection. The chin-length wavy bob framed my face perfectly.

'Oh, it's lovely, Kathleen!' I stood and gave her a squeeze, then looked at it again. 'Is that me?'

She laughed.

'I said short would suit you, didn't I?' She started to primp it a little with the steel end of the comb.

I turned my head this way and that.

'I feel different already,' I said. 'Lighter. Let me pay you.'

'Nonsense,' she said, as she tidied her comb and scissors into a large Quality Street tin. 'You need to watch those pennies now, even more than before. Consider it a Christmas gift.' She snapped on the lid. 'Or a goodbye present.'

We'd placed Athena on a checked blanket on the floor, and Kathleen turned now and looked at her.

'I'll miss you both. You'll stay in touch?'

I nodded, but knew I couldn't. Not with things the way they were.

She started to stack the plates.

'And when are *they* back?' She motioned with her head upstairs.

'Day after tomorrow. Seventeeth. But very late. I'm leaving first thing, so I won't see them. And—'

'I know. If they ask, I know nothing. Which is true.'

I'd told her I was going away but couldn't say where, and she hadn't pushed.

'Thank you,' I said.

She leaned down and picked up the baby.

'Now am I still looking after her for a few hours while you go out?'

'If you don't mind.'

'It's a pleasure.' She looked down at Athena's face. 'You know, I stood by once and watched a baby taken from its mother, and I won't do it again.'

I gazed at her, open-mouthed. 'You had a baby?'

She shook her head.

'My sister. God have mercy on her.'

She lifted the hem of her pinny and used it to dab at the corners of her eyes. She took a few moments to compose herself.

'Well, this wee 'un,' she kissed the top of Athena's head, 'this little girl will grow up knowing her mammy. Won't you my darling? Though I can't see why they want her so badly, the way they treat the two of you . . .'

'There's a house,' I said. 'A small place, in Cyprus. Nothing much at all, but Bebba inherits it if she has a child. That's where they are now.'

Half-truths were always better than full-blown lies. I'd learned that from her.

'Ah, money,' she said, passing the baby back into my arms.

Athena started to grizzle, and I rocked her gently.

'Oh! I nearly forgot.' She went to the dresser and pulled a small box from the drawer. 'I got it – here.' She opened the box for me as I jiggled the baby.

A plain gold band. I slipped it on my finger and looked at my hand.

'Thank you.'

'You've got some money left over,' she said, making a fuss of getting her tiny purse out from inside her brassiere where she always stowed it.

'No, please. Keep it.'

Quick as a flash, she pushed it back in. 'Well, only if you're sure.'

69

The world was full of gamblers, losers and thugs, mused Bebba, and she'd met more than her fair share. She glanced across the train carriage through narrowed eyes. They'd hardly spoken for days now and, as they trundled through Italy, Peter shifted and snored as he slept, his hair sticking up against the back of the seat, mouth open catching flies. He'd kept on the same clothes throughout the journey, never even taking off his jacket. She'd had no chance to get to his wallet. He even slept sitting up, not bothering to pull down the bed.

When night-time came, she slipped into her bed but barely slept. During the day she smoked and stared out of the window. As the changing landscape of Italy and then France rolled past the windows, her anger subsided, simmered, then boiled over again. And the further they travelled from Cyprus, the more intensely she tasted the failure. The very thought of the old man wasting that money made her head fill with a bitter fury that slid down the back of her throat and filled her up inside.

But this wouldn't defeat her. Her life would not be dictated by someone else's incompetence. Perhaps Elizabetta was easy to push around, but she'd be damned if Bebba would stand for it.

A snort exploded from Peter's mouth, and he turned his head to one side and continued sleeping. So, she didn't have the inheritance, but then neither did Rico. He was dead and she was very much alive. She stretched her neck a little to one side then the other and rolled her shoulders back, telling herself she was strong enough to shrug off the devastating news.

You could say she'd won in the end. Yes, that was it. She'd won because she was still here. After a moment's consideration, she realised that she was the cleverest person she knew.

It was now the last hour of the journey. As the train crept towards Victoria, she stood, tightened the belt on her coat, and settled down in her seat again. For the first time in days, she picked up her *Vogue*.

She still had the underground journey to Euston, then one final train up to Lime Street. She opened her bag and, without looking inside, placed her hand on the ticket for New York. If she couldn't exchange it for the next crossing, she'd just buy a new one. Money wasn't an issue. And, if her calculations were right, the *Brittanic* set sail again tomorrow evening, so she'd have to move fast. She'd leave the flat in her leopard-skin coat, as if she were just popping to the shops, then she'd go to left luggage and pick up her case en route to the docks. Everything else she would leave behind.

Surely she'd be able to get the key tonight, when they got home? And if not, she'd think of something. She'd rip that locker apart with her bare hands if need be. The suitcase was all that mattered now. All that stood between her and starting over.

She lit a cigarette, placed it in her holder and sucked the life out of it before blowing a long, thin tendril at her reflection in the window. The smoke rose then disappeared. She began to flick through the coming season's fashion, wondering if she needed a new look.

70

A winter breeze whips through Lime Street station, as the woman stands and stares at the left luggage counter just a few feet away. Her short hair is blown one way, then the other, and she raises her hand up to flatten it, wishing she'd thought to wear a headscarf. She mustn't look dishevelled. There's a uniformed attendant behind the counter, yawning extravagantly. She has one opportunity to get this right, just one chance at a new life.

She stands straight, pushes her shoulders back and takes a deep breath. She has to believe in herself now more than ever. She lifts her chin a touch, looks straight ahead and strides towards the counter.

He's an elderly man and, as she gives him her best smile and explains her predicament, the wrinkles on his forehead deepen in concern. She shakes her head a little and confides that she's embarrassed to have done something so foolish. He chews his lip and considers her request. As it happens, yes, he does remember her. It's that coat, he says. Not something you forget. She was here with a man, wasn't she?

Yes, that's was her! And that was her husband! Oh, she's so relieved he remembers. Surely he can help her now? Her husband is away, but if he returns to find out she's lost the key, he'll be livid. The man hesitates. Her eyes fill up, then she touches his arm very lightly. *Please?*

She stands very still while he decides, her heart thumping

so hard she thinks it could burst through her chest. After a few moments, he exhales noisily and asks for her name. Her voice is steady when she speaks. He finds it in the ledger, along with the corresponding locker number, then opens a drawer and pulls out a large bunch of keys.

They go to the locker, he singles out a key and with one twist the door is opened. He hands her the suitcase and asks her to sign the book. With a flourish, she signs a name she never wants to see again.

She thanks him then adds, 'You're a lifesaver, darling,' before she turns and leaves.

The following day, she returns to the station and, as she waits for her train, she notices how beautiful the milky morning light is that pours through the windows. It's chilly, and she pulls together the lapels of her leopard skin till they meet and kiss, glad that she didn't leave the coat behind. By her feet is a suitcase packed with money and a few pieces of clothing – but mostly money because she's taken it all.

She's folded the pram and left it leaning against the wall of the grim flat, and now carries her baby in one arm. The suitcase is hers, the one she came here with; she's emptied that other one, the hateful grey case, and left it on the living room floor, directly in front of the door. It'll be the first thing they see on their return and contains just one item: a card. One side is printed with DC Steele's number and on the other she's scribbled:

If you try to find me, I'll tell him everything.

She's knows they won't look for her. Not with the threat of the gallows hanging over them. She touches her neck and adjusts the exquisite green scarf.

She swaps Athena from one arm to the other and looks at her face. Despite the noise and people, her daughter sleeps on regardless. As the train pulls in, she thinks about the letter that arrived a couple of days ago, and that is now folded in her pocket. She's read it a dozen times but suddenly feels impatient to read it again.

The train screeches to a halt and, baby in one arm, case in hand, she boards. A pinch of excitement tingles in her belly as she walks through and finds her seat. She places the case on the floor with her legs in front of it, and settles back. She looks out at the passengers rushing through the station and soon the carriage doors slam one after the other and the train whistle announces their departure.

From her pocket, she pulls out the note.

Ma très chère Dina,

I was thrilled to get your letter. Yes – of course, my response is YES!

It's a genius idea. Absolutely – 50/50 equal partners all the way. Our very own dress shop, how perfect! I had no idea your poor brother had left you so much. What a wonderful way to honour his memory.

Send me a telegram immediately with the time of your train. I'll meet you at Euston.

We'll make a roaring success of this, just you wait and see. Me, you and little Athena. I'm so looking forward to it.

I cannot wait. And neither can Soho.

With love,

Sylvie

Dina pushes the letter back in her pocket and takes a deep breath that fills her with calm. As the train picks up speed, the wheels clatter against the rails and ring out a tune. It's in perfect time with the voice in her head and it whispers: *you're going home, you're going home, you're going home.*

READING GROUP QUESTIONS

1. 'We're all here for a better life,' says Dina. What do you think she, specifically, wants from London? What about Bebba? And Peter?
2. How do the three main characters – Dina, Bebba and Peter – get others to do what they want? Who is the most honest in the way they operate?
3. Dina assumes her friendship with Bebba is stronger than any friendship between a man and a woman. Do you agree?
4. What's Bebba's view of men? Is it founded in her experience or assumptions?
5. Discuss the theme of identity for all three characters.
6. In the 1950s, the British government invited many commonwealth citizens to live in the UK and take up jobs. How have things changed for immigrants today?
7. Dina spends the early days of their friendship comparing herself with Bebba – are female friendships always based on comparisons? What about rivalry? Is it possible to have friendships without this friction?
8. At the start of her journey, Dina doesn't fit in to London life. At what point does she make the transition?
9. Dina says: 'She smiled at me and, for a second, I caught a flicker of the girl I once knew, the one who threw her leopard skin coat on the floor at jazz clubs and taught me to drink martinis.' Do you think she regrets falling out with Bebba? What has she lost?

AUTHOR'S NOTE

My parents, Elpida and Yiannis Kyriacou, emigrated to London in the 1950s and were the original inspiration for this story. Although this is a work of fiction, their courage, tenacity and innate optimism provided the backdrop to this book. I also interviewed my aunt, Maroulla Avraam, who gave me a memorable account of arriving here as an anxious young woman. The two sisters worked as seamstresses in the same London factories for most of their lives. Along with my sister Kayti and cousin Anna, I was dragged along during the school holidays because there was nowhere else to go. Occasionally I'd be given small tasks to do for pocket money, but most of the time I wrote a dull, uneventful diary, played on the vending machine or complained loudly.

I loved researching this book, and would like to thank the following authors, editors, researchers, photographers and translators:

Here & There: The Greek Cypriot Community in London
Marianna Economou, Paul Halliday

Departures and Arrivals: Turkish Cypriots Who Came to England Between 1934 and 1963, 36 Interviews
Hatice Abdullah, Mark Sinker, Tahsin Ibrahim, Erim Metto, Adrain Wave, Sonay Ozen

An Immigration History of Britain: Multicultural Racism Since 1800
Panikos Panayi

Dr Nicoletta Christodoulou, PhD
Project Coordinator and Principal Investigator Frederick
Research Center Nicosia Cyprus
The Cyprus Oral History and Living Memory Project

Another London: International Photographers Capture City Life 1930–1980
Helen Delaney

Up West: Voices from the Streets of Post-War London
Pip Granger

McDowell's Directory of Twentieth Century Fashion
Colin McDowell

London Fog: The Biography
Christine L. Corton

Soho in the Fifties
Daniel Farson

The Story of Soho: The Windmill Years 1932–1964
Mike Hutton

Recollections of the 1950s
Michael King

The Fifties Mystique
Jessica Mann

Soho in the Fifties and Sixties
Jonathan Fryer

A–Z Atlas and Guide to London and Suburbs (Historical Edition)
Geographers' Map Co Ltd, founded by Phyllis Pearsall

Lost London: An A–Z of Forgotten Landmarks and Lost Traditions
Richard Guard

Liverpool in the 1950s
Robert F. Edwards

The Streets of Liverpool, Volumes 1 and 2
Colin Wilkinson

The Liverpool Echo
www.liverpoolecho.co.uk

Xeni Greek Cypriots in London
Sav Kyriacou, Thasis Papathanasiou

Ethnicity, Class, Gender and Migration: Greek Cypriots in Britain
Floya Anthias

Bloody Foreigners: The Story of Immigration to Britain
Robert Winder

Voices from the Past: An Autobiography of a London Cypriot
Fotis Loizou

Peopling of London: Fifteen Thousand Years of Settlement from Overseas
Nick Merriman

Thank you to the staff of the British Library and the London Metropolitan Archives.

ACKNOWLEDGEMENTS

My first thanks go to Cicely Aspinall, my editor at Hodder & Stoughton, who saw the potential in this story and singled it out during Hachette's Future Bookshelf open submissions. And to Nick Davies, chair of The Future Bookshelf, through which this novel was published. Also to Myrto Kalavrezou and Jasmine Marsh at Hodder.

A huge thank you to Abi Fellows, my agent, for her support and excellent humour, as well as Niki Chang, Arzu Tahsin and Salma Begum at the Good Literary Agency. And of course, to founders Julia Kingsford and Nikesh Shukla.

There were a handful of women who, over the years, not only told me it could be done, but showed me how. Thank you to Erin Kelly, Anna Davis at Curtis Brown Creative, Sally Orson-Jones, Lizzy Kremer, Lisa Evans at the West London Writers' Group, Charlie Haynes at Urban Writers' Retreat, Jane Purcell, Debi Alper at Jericho Writers and Aki Schilz at The Literary Consultancy.

Roisin Clancy helped create Mrs F's Irish phrasing, and Alison and Carlo Lusuardi, and Sylvie Flais made sure I got the French right (any errors are mine, of course).

A huge thanks to my writing group, the Bonnets, Kate Wheeler, Marianne Holmes and Liz Ottosson, for discussing character, plot and fog with me for hours on end.

And to my CBC group of writers for constant cheerleading, with special thanks to friends Caroline Jowett and Alex

Hay for reading early versions. Also, for reading sections at a moment's notice, Alison (again), Claire Ellis, Helen Gent, Julia Kaye and Sat Wilks.

For sharing the whole Cypriot thing alongside me, sister Kaytrina Jons and cousin Anna Kioufi. For being the kind of constant friends that Dina could have really used, Nicole Carmichael, Helen (again), Rosalind Lowe, Angela Martin and Vicky Mayer.

Most of all, thank you to the three very best men I know, Andrew, Ryan and Aaron.